The Prodigy Slave
Book One
Journey to Winter Garden

Londyn Skye

WALDORF PUBLISHING

Published by Waldorf Publishing
2140 Hall Johnson Road
#102-345
Grapevine, Texas 76051
www.WaldorfPublishing.com

The Prodigy Slave
Book One
Journey to Winter Garden

ISBN: 978-1-68419-261-8
Library of Congress Control Number: 2016957005

Reference information for Slave Codes: District of Columbia Slave Code Manual of 1860.

NOV -- 2017

Prologue

Slave:
A human being who is by law deprived of his or her liberty for life and is the property of another.

Slave Code
Article II Section IV
A slave cannot become partially free. The law recognizes only freedom on the one side and slavery on the other. There is no intermediate status. The status of any Negro child's mother is the status of the child. Therefore, a Negro child born of one parent who is a slave and one parent who is free is considered free only if the free parent is the child's mother. All Negro children born of slave mothers shall be slaves during their natural lives, regardless of their father's status.

Nicholas County, Virginia
Slavery Era
January 14, 1845

The shrills of an innocent little girl paralyzed an entire field of slaves, as they watched her mother fighting with the strength of a wild beast to hold on to her during a vicious battle that had kicked up a massive cloud of dust. Somewhere in the middle of the haze, Maya, a slave, held on tightly to her daughter's arms, while her master, Levi Collins, stood at the opposite end yanking at her little legs. They were locked in a tug-of-war, with the little girl nearly being torn apart in the middle. For Maya, the mere thought of life without her daughter inhibited her fear of the punishment she would receive for disobediently fighting, and begging, and pleading with her owner, in heartbreaking cries of pure desperation. Her cries were like the sounds of a woman who was being tortured to death. They were sounds born from the immediate pain of the inevitable loss of her child … the one and *only* child God had ever blessed her with.

Just minutes before their struggle ensued, she had looked up from where she and her daughter worked together gathering laundry into their baskets and saw the way that Levi stalked toward them. The way he walked and the look on his face was a sight she had seen all too often. It was a walk that said he was on a mission, a mission to steal another innocent child away from its mother and father, no different than grabbing a bag of cotton to take into town for profit.

Maya was usually just a bystander in such instances, unable to do anything but watch from a distance in agony, and then help comfort the parents after they had seen their child for the last time. But this day was different. Levi walked toward her and her child now with that familiar menacing look in his eyes. She looked to the right and to the left and saw that she and her daughter were the only ones in his view. At that moment, her heartbeat became erratic, and her tears were instant when she realized that her little girl would be the lone casualty of his mission. After ten years with her daughter safe by her side, she was convinced that Levi would never touch her, that he would never snatch her away and sell her off the way he had with other children on his farm because he was not only her child's master … he was also her father.

Levi had come into the slave quarters the day she had been born, walked over to where she lay sleeping in her mother's arms and reached down to try to pick his daughter up. Remembering what Levi had done to so many other children on his farm, Maya's brand-new motherly instincts caused her to reflexively pull her baby from his reach and nestle her closer to her chest. Despite him being her father, she suddenly feared that it would be the last time she would ever see her baby. That fear, however, quickly subsided when she finally let him hold her and, for a moment, she saw a heartfelt smile dance across his face as soon as he looked at the beautiful newborn girl he had created. "Lily," he called her, the second he laid eyes on her, because she had come into the world out of the womb of a brown-skinned woman so pale and lily white, at first, before settling into a much darker almond-brown complexion months later.

Levi's wife bore him six children, but of the seven he was responsible for producing, the child he had created with Maya was the only little girl. His wife always assumed that he had secretly indulged with his slaves from time to time, like so many other slave owners in the South. But despite her reluctant acceptance of that fact, the realization that Lily was her husband's child made her rife with jealousy, envy, and a deep-seated anger. She simply could not handle the fact that he had granted some other woman the little girl she was desperate to have, and to a lowly slave at that.

To add further insult to her husband's misgivings, of all his children, Lily bore the most resemblance to him. Her skin tone and the texture of her hair may have been a blend of both of her parents, but her father's genes dominated every other one of her features: her eye color, hair color, and facial features were reflections of Levi's. Lily was in nearly every way a darker female version of her father, and it was impossible for his wife to gaze at her and not see her husband's seed staring right back at her.

Levi did his best to keep his distance from Lily after his wife discovered the truth, but despite his distance and the circumstances of her conception, Maya loved her daughter and never gave up the belief that the child they shared would be by her side until the day she passed away. Her belief in that had been so strong because of the sentimental reasons behind the brilliant smile she had seen on Levi's face the day of Lily's birth as he cradled her gently in his arms and whispered her name while gazing at her for the longest time. It was those few simple acts that had convinced Maya that there was an unspoken promise between her and Levi that he would never sell their child away.

It was not until she stood in the middle of a dirt field, fighting with the strength of ten men, that Maya realized that that unspoken promise never really existed. She was forced to accept that it had all been an illusion she had created to give herself a sense of peace and that when it came to a need for money, even Levi's own child had never been off limits. But those realizations did not stop her from fighting mercilessly with Levi to free her little girl from his death grip.

"Noooo!" she continued to cry repeatedly in the cloud of dust that surrounded them, as she attempted to wrestle Lily away from her father. "Pleeease! Dear God, don't let him take my baby away!" she prayed aloud, as tears flowed down her cheeks. "Pleeease don't take my baby away!" she begged Levi, but he was unrelenting. "She's yo' baby too! Don't sell yo' daughta'! Why you doin' this to yo' baby?" she pleaded, in a desperate, last-ditch attempt to make him feel some sense of connection to his child. "Masa' pleeease don't sell our baby!" Then, with the deep searing burn of a lash across her back, Maya was instantly brought to her knees, and it was over.

Unexpectedly, Levi's eldest son had whipped Maya from behind. When she let go and fell, Levi immediately picked Lily up for the first time in years and placed her into the back of his wagon. As he rolled away with his only little girl in tow, she watched through blurry, tear-filled eyes the last gruesome images of her mother, as she lay in a motionless heap on the ground, being brutally beaten into a state of unconscious. Levi's wife, in turn, took twisted pleasure in watching the entire scene play out from the porch with a joyous smirk etched on her face.

Chapter One

Slave Code
Article II Section I

Sundays and holidays are to be strictly observed. No slave shall be permitted to work more than 15 hours per day in summer, and 14 hours in winter, or on any holiday or Sunday, except as a punishment or unless they are paid. All Negroes otherwise found at work on these days shall be confiscated.

Fourteen years later
Fayetteville, Virginia
January 14, 1859

Lily sat quietly at the piano, on this, the fourteenth anniversary of the day she had been stolen from her mother. Although she did not know how to read a calendar, she was certain that this was indeed that fateful day. No different than one's circadian sleep rhythm, Lily's internal body clock set off an alarm to reawaken her misery and anguish on *every* January fourteenth. Today, much like every January fourteenth before it, she had woken up in a cold sweat, gasping for air, after the grisly lingering memories of that life-altering day began haunting her dreams. From then on, those revitalized memories continued to relentlessly invade her mind, making it nearly impossible for her to focus on anything else. Having gone through this torture in the past, though, Lily now knew that playing the piano was the *only* thing that had the power to halt the persistent painful imagery from that nightmarish event.

Preparing to play a song she had composed in memory of her mother, Lily lifted the cover to the piano and sat there a moment, blankly staring at the keys, as the visions continued to roll through her head of the momentous day that had landed her in the place she now considered as her

1

own personal prison. With the curse and blessing of her photographic memory, those horrific images had yet to fade away. She sat there reliving them in her crystal-clear mind, like they had happened just the day before. The precision of her unique memory would never allow her the mental and emotional relief of forgetting every miniscule detail. She recalled the cloud of dirt that surrounded her during her mother's struggle to save her, the desperation and panic in her mother's voice as she begged, the pain in her legs and arms as her parents fought over her, the sound of the whip as it snapped across her mother's back, and the sight of her mother then lying motionless on the ground after her severe beating.

In vivid detail, Lily still remembered being dragged from her father's wagon and being put up on the auction block at The Weekly Negro Auction, then looking down and noticing the red marks on her arms from where her mother had held her tight. Like it was only yesterday, she still recalled the feeling of standing there barefoot and alone on that auction block, with tears pouring from her multicolored eyes, making tracks through the light layer of dirt that covered her almond-tinted cheeks, and how each drop pelted the filthy tattered dress that covered her frail frame, leaving it soaking wet by the time she stepped down. She remembered being incoherent to the pale faces in the crowd, who yelled out bids in hopes of becoming her new owner, while she stared at the man who had placed her up there. Up until that day, she had only known him as "masa' Lee." But after hearing her mother's desperate pleas, Lily had inadvertently learned that the man she stood staring at from an auction block was her very own father. As Lily shivered there alone, she suddenly could not pull her eyes away from Levi, noting the lack of expression on his face as he stared unblinking back at her, waiting for the final bid to come in. When it did, he eagerly took her by the hand and ushered her down the steps to take her to the man who had just purchased her.

"A-are you r-really my father?" Lily cried, begging to know, while looking up at the profile of Levi's face as he dragged her along.

He did not reply.

"A-are y-you?" she sniffled, asking him again after he had lifted her into the back of her new owner's wagon. After securing shackles around her legs, Levi looked up and unexpectedly met a set of eyes that were undoubtedly his, penetrating him with their innocence, as tears careened in steady streams from within them. *"Daddy?"* Lily said in a sorrow-filled whisper. She had spoken the simple word in a solemn tone that pleaded to know why her own father would do this to her. After momentarily holding his daughter's gaze, Levi turned to walk away, holding on to twice the amount of money he had expected, and without so much as a goodbye or even a second look at the beautiful child he had created, nor ever bothering to answer the question that she already knew the answer to.

"Daaaddyyy! Pleeease! Take me back to my maaama! Daaaddyyy! Pleeease!" she erupted, as her new owner began to roll away with her in tow, but Levi continued to ignore her. Just as deep as the anguish of losing her mother was the pain of feeling that her own father viewed her as a useless byproduct of his inappropriate relations, and held less value to him than one of his field mules.

As Lily continued to yell, the carriage came to an abrupt halt. Through the blur of her tears, she never saw the swift hand of her owner as it made its way across her face. "Shut y'ur goddamn mouth, you hear me girl?!" he yelled with his finger in her face, while looming over her as she held her cheek. It was Lily's first interaction with her new master. His brutal introduction quickly set the tone for what was expected of her, and painted a clear picture of the sort of dark world her very own father had so effortlessly cast her into.

Jesse Adams purchased Lily to work alongside his current aging house slave, whom everyone called Auntie. Auntie was a frail, short, dark-skinned woman, who had worked on the plantation with two generations of the Adams family. She walked slightly bent over, grimacing in agony from the pain in her back and knees with every step she took. Years of field and housework had taken its toll on her body, and her multitude of health problems were making it a struggle for her to keep up with the needs of a large family. Jesse and his wife knew that it would not be long before she would need a replacement. Lily was to be that girl.

The Adamses had three sons who all lived at home when Lily first arrived at the farm as a child. Their eldest, Jesse Junior, whom they all called J.R.; Jacob, the middle child; and their youngest, James. A few years after teaching Lily how to run the Adams household, with its three rambunctious boys, Auntie passed away, leaving her to handle the needs of the family alone. It was an overwhelming burden for a thirteen-year-old, but Lily handled the grueling responsibilities with the grace of someone three times her age.

Much to Lily's delight, over her fourteen years with the Adamses, the household duties began to lighten as the family dynamics changed. In that time, J.R. and Jacob had both started their own families and moved into plantations nearby. James, who was the only one of the boys to take after his mother's side of the family in looks and intelligence, had gone away to medical school. Their mother, Elizabeth, passed away suddenly just a few months after Auntie, leaving only their father, Jesse, as the overseer of the farm.

Before her death, Elizabeth Adams was a school teacher who also taught piano to some of the town's children in her home on the weekends. During these piano lessons, Lily would disregard her duties and secretly stand at the top of the stairs, watching as each child attempted to play the compositions that were set before them. Those simple melodies echoing through the house would replay joyously in Lily's extraordinary mind long after the sessions had ended, and soon became a means of mental escape, helping her through her daunting weekly tasks.

Until moving to the Adams farm, Lily had never even seen a piano, but once seeing one, and hearing what it was capable of, she became fascinated at how the simple movement of fingers across the keys could create such beautiful music. Day after day, that notion obsessively drew her to it. She would stare at it and move her fingers in the air near it, pretending to play, since she understood that it was completely off limits to her outside of the daily dusting it required.

One day, though, Lily's fascination and obsession finally took control. Despite knowing she would face severe punishment if she were caught playing the piano, she simply could not stop herself from tinkering on it. After seeing the Adams brood off to school and work, she hesitantly sat down at it. She was reluctant to touch it at first, and got up to look out of all the windows to reassure herself that Elizabeth and the boys had made their way to school and that Jesse had already left the farm to make his daily trip into town for supplies and feed. Once she was certain that nobody would hear her, she sat back down and proceeded to play a classical song that was taught to all of the students. Astonishingly, Lily played the entire song purely from her memory of the mechanics of Mrs. Adams's fingers across the keys and the sounds that accompanied them. She stumbled her way through the first few attempts, but with great determination, she continued until she could play it through with hardly a single note missed along the way. The joy and the smile across her face were immediate, and so too was the addiction to the high she felt afterward.

From that day forward, using that simple copy-cat

method, Lily continued to play every new song she was unintentionally taught from her secret hiding spot at the top of the stairs. However, once she was familiar with the keys and the sounds that each of them made, that initial visual method gave way to replaying by the memory of sound alone, and not long after that, she began creating music on her own. Within only a few months of having taught herself, Lily was playing as flawlessly as a professional who had had years of training, at only the age of ten.

Lily did not even realize the incredible gift she had. All she knew was that it brought her immense joy and that it helped to numb the pain of missing her mother, and to mentally and emotionally escape everything that plagued her in her new environment, at least temporarily. For Lily, the piano had become as necessary as her eyes and her hands. She absolutely had to have it as a part of her life, so much so that playing it became a vital part of her daily household routine: cook breakfast for the family, see them off to their duties, and escape on the piano.

And so, on this fourteen-year anniversary, it was with that obsessive *need* to escape mentally and emotionally that Lily sat at her beloved piano. However, whereas most days she played with the need to drift away from the world around her, this time she needed to escape the haunting last memories of her mother that never failed to torment her on this day. As with *every* February fourteenth, she needed to let her tears flush away her sorrows and to let music help erase the memories of her mother's motionless body and subdue the painful images of her father's cold face as he shackled her in the back of Jesse's wagon.

Attempting to wrestle those yearly demons and temporarily relieve herself of the horrors that always invaded the serene fantasies of her mind, Lily began to play the very first song she had ever composed. Blended within the song was the melody from an old music box that was given to her mother. The new rendition that Lily had created always reminded her of the way that she and her mother used to dance together, just like the tiny couple spinning around inside of the music box as it played. With Lily's new extended version of the old tune, dozens of other wonderful moments she had shared with her mother had time to emerge as she played. The array of cherished memories never failed to trump the yearly nightmarish visions that plagued her.

On this morning, however, unbeknownst to Lily, she had an audience who had walked in just seconds after she began, listening and watching as she flowed through her piece. Her uninvited guest had stood there quietly as she played effortlessly and flawlessly as usual. She never once realized that she was not alone as she swayed to the rhythm of the melody with her eyes closed; she was far too lost inside of the recesses of her mind, reliving the highlights of her brief life with her mother.

After the song and her mother's memories had helped restore peace and serenity to her mind, Lily wiped away the remaining tears on her face. Still none the wiser to the fact that she was not alone, she carefully replaced the lid to the piano keys and got up to continue her household duties.

"My fatha' know you playin' my motha's piano?" A deep, southern, familiar accent startled Lily as she rose from the piano. She was instantly paralyzed with fear, unable to turn and look in the direction of the man whose voice, although deeper than she remembered, she instantly recognized, even though she had not seen him in years. "Answa' me, girl!" he snapped.

"Naw sa' masa' James," she finally responded, her heart racing as she still stared at the piano. After six years away, the Adams youngest son had returned home from school, entering through the back door hoping to surprise his father with his arrival. Instead, he had become Lily's uninvited audience member, catching her in a role she knew full well she was not purchased for. "I beg you not to tell yo' fatha'," she added in a panic-stricken voice, visibly shaking, with fresh tears forming in her eyes. She had seen Jesse Adams's wrath before when other slaves had stepped out of line, and she was not eager to become one of his victims.

"Who taught you to play that way?" James asked her coldly, ignoring her plea.

Lily kept her eyes locked on the piano. "Nobody sa'."

"You 'spect me to believe that? You think I'm some kind 'a fool?"

"Naw sa'!" she answered with urgency.

"Then I'm gonna ask you one more time. Who taught you to play that way?"

Lily finally turned to face James with unshed tears still gleaming in her eyes. "Masa' I tells you the truth, ain't nobody taught me to play." Her eyes spoke of sincerity and fear and forced his better judgment to believe her. "Please don't tell yo' fatha', sa'," she begged, as a tear finally made its way down her cheek.

James nodded his head toward the piano. "Play," he demanded.

"Sa'?"

"I said play." Unsure of what his goal was, Lily sat back down, lifted the key cover, and looked at James as if asking permission with her eyes before touching the keys again. "Go on," he insisted.

Without another moment wasted, Lily played the song she was most familiar with: the simple song she had been unintentionally taught by James's mother fourteen years ago. James instantly recognized it as one that he and his brothers had been forced to play as children. Unlike their mother, however, they were not musically inclined enough to master it. Ironically though, the way Lily played the song made him wonder if even his mother had ever truly mastered it. The slow choppy movements of his mother's hands made her now seem like a beginner in his eyes, compared to the extreme swiftness and agility with which Lily moved her fingers. She was playing the song so smoothly that it was as if the piano was playing itself. She never opened her eyes throughout the entire piece, and never saw as James walked closer to her. He scrutinized her every keystroke as he tried and failed to comprehend what he was seeing and hearing. Watching her as she played and remembering the elegant song just moments before it, he simply could not figure out how such skill was accomplished without her ever having had any lessons.

When Lily finished, she looked up at James as he loomed over her; his face remained cold and unreadable. She was unsure what to say, as was he as he stared down on her sitting at his deceased mother's most prized possession. Judging by the tense, uncomfortable scene in the parlor of the Adams home at that moment, one would never have guessed that this icy coldness in their eyes, and in the atmosphere, that left the room feeling like a brutal winter, had not always existed. There was once an undeniable warmth in the connection between James and Lily when they were younger, a bond that was instantaneous and very profound…

On this exact day, fourteen years prior, James had watched from his upstairs bedroom window as his father took a very young new slave out of the back of his wagon. Something about seeing a child his size shackled in chains tore at him as he stood staring at her from the comfort of his room. He continued to watch this new little girl curiously for a few days after that, secretly peeking his head around corners to catch glimpses of her, peering at her from his window, or from the top of the stairs. Whenever or however he had the chance to quietly watch her, he would.

Soon, what drew young James to watch this new slave began to go beyond the sorrow he felt about seeing a child his age bound in chains. There was something about her that made him look at her in a way he had never looked at any other girl. Without even realizing he was doing it, his eyes would often linger over the almond-brown glaze of her skin tone, the curvature of her little bee-stung lips, and the array of colors swirling in her eyes. He even became curious about what her hair was like underneath the scarf she always wore. He did not understand at that time why he was so captivated by all of the nuances of her unique features, nor why he could not seem to stop the powerful force he felt inside that kept him following her in secret, from place to place, in utter fascination.

One afternoon, that powerful force guided James quietly behind her as she neglected her duties and snuck off into a thickly wooded area near a creek. It was there that his fascination with this new little girl grew to yet another level after watching her talk to a turtle she had found. The day before, he had watched her effortlessly climb into the same tree he was hiding behind, and perch there while picking leaves and dropping them to the ground. And now the fact that she fearlessly held onto a turtle further proved to James that she was nothing like the dainty girls he was used to.

Lily sat down with the turtle on a log near the edge of the water, and lifted him up to her eye level as she spoke. "Don't worry, little fella," she sniffled, "I won't take you away from your mama. I just wanted to play with you for a while. Maybe we can be friends." She suddenly turned her head quickly to the right when she heard leaves rustling nearby. James had stumbled over a tree root as he moved to get a better view, tripping just enough to fall into her line of sight. Lily immediately jumped to her feet in a panic and wiped her tears, thinking for sure she would be in trouble for not minding her duties.

James stood there in silence at first as they stared at one another. "A-are you okay?" he finally managed to stutter, after feeling the embarrassment of being caught.

Although he felt a little foolish standing there, in a way he was glad to be caught, because it was a question he had been wanting to ask Lily for days, after noticing that she always seemed to cry when she was alone.

"I-I'm fine," she stuttered back, still feeling afraid that she was in trouble.

"Sho' don't look like it."

"I-I'm fine," she insisted again while continuing to clear her tears away with her free hand. "Just thinkin' 'bout my mama is all."

"I know," James said, approaching her. "I-I been prayin' real hard every night that you'll get to see her again," he admitted. It was something he had done often after overhearing her on her first night there crying to Auntie about how badly she missed her mother.

Considering what her father had just done to her, Lily did not even know what to say in return after hearing James's touching confession. She just stared at him in silence, stunned that a stranger would do and say something so incredibly kind and deeply moving. Her ability to speak became even more lost when she was suddenly captivated by the innocence of his piercing blue eyes, peeking out from under a mass of dark brown, loose, curly hair. Lily had never looked a white person in the eyes for long, because she knew better, but for reasons she could not understand at that moment, she found it hard to turn away from the beauty of his. She had seen James amongst the family members before, but this was the first time she noticed every detail of his features, how skinny he was, how he stood eye level with her, and his shapely blood-red lips that stood out against his pale skin … but mostly his eyes. They were innocent eyes that somehow made her instantly feel at peace.

"I-I'm James," he suddenly announced, switching the subject swiftly, not even realizing that his words had impacted Lily so deeply just seconds before.

11

"I'm Lily," she replied, still staring as he stepped closer to her.

"What's your turtle's name?" he asked.

Lily was finally able to pull her eyes away from James and looked down, having forgotten she was even holding him. "Don't know. Hadn't even thought to give 'em one."

"I've seen him 'round here before. Maybe we should name him," James suggested.

"Okay, let's think of somethin'."

After instantly feeling a sense of comfort from his presence, and completely forgetting about the possibility of being punished for being there, Lily sat down on a log next to her newfound friend. They sat shoulder to shoulder, feeling just as comfortable together as two people who had known each other from birth.

James reached over, took the turtle from Lily's hands, and gave him a once over. "Maybe Jimmy?"

Lily leaned over and looked at him again. "Nah, he looks like a Willie to me."

"Hmm, yeah, kinda. Or maybe a Wilbur."

"Yeah! I like it!"

"Wilbur it is then!" James said, lifting the turtle in the air before handing him back to Lily. That simple moment instantly ignited an incredible bond between the pair.

After that day, it quickly became a ritual for James to return home from school and secretly help Lily with her housework while talking with her about his day. But *Sunday* was the day he looked forward to the most. It was the only full day of work the slaves were given off, which gave him the entire afternoon to spend with his newfound best friend, after sneaking away from his family while they were distracted by their post-church gatherings.

During the countless Sunday afternoons they spent together, James taught Lily how to skip rocks across the creek and how to swim. They had foot races and fishing contests and competed to see who could collect the most crickets for Wilbur. But by far their favorite pastime was climbing the old oak tree where they had first met. Perched high up on its branches, James would read stories of fantasy adventures that they would then often reenact when they finally climbed down. They were wise enough to keep their time together a secret, and their efforts worked well, allowing their friendship to blossom while they went about creating unforgettable memories that strengthened their bond over six long years.

As they grew older, rock skipping, cricket collecting, and tree climbing turned into long walks and laid back fishing in the shade, while having long deep conversations about all aspects of their lives. Despite all the things they had conversed about, though, Lily never revealed to James her ability to play piano, feeling as though that was the one area of her life she should never speak of. James, however, hid nothing from her up to that point. Lily had become his greatest confidant and the closest person in his life. She was the reason he smiled in the morning and was sad walking to school without her, and the sole reason he ran like mad to get home at the end of the day. He drowned in thoughts of Lily along the way to school, during class, and often dreamed of her at night. James's mind always seemed to be flooded with ideas of what new things he could share with her, and *only* her, and of what new experiences they could have together. In fact, it was on the very last Sunday they ever spent together that he revealed one of the new things he desperately wanted to experience with her. Sitting shoulder to shoulder under the oak tree they once climbed when they were younger, he closed the book he had just finished reading to her and promised that he would teach her to read and write. But just days before her lessons were set to begin came an unexpected moment that caused their innocent six-year-long friendship to begin to crumble.

James had come home from school eager to help Lily get done with her chores as usual. They were both down on

their hands and knees scrubbing the kitchen floor, laughing
hysterically about an incident that happened that day at
school. They were laughing so loudly that they never heard
his father walk into the kitchen. He was in search of a rag
to clean up blood from his arm after injuring himself in the
fields. Instead of finding a rag, he found his son crouched
on the floor like one of his servants. The laughter between
the pair immediately ceased, and they both sprang to their
feet when they finally saw Jesse's boots in front of them,
but just as soon as Lily stood up, she was back on the floor,
holding an eye that was swelling quickly. Jesse's brutal
backslap was his punishment to her for not doing the job
she was supposed to do *alone,* and for having the audacity
to ask his son for help.

Seeing Lily writhing in pain on the floor with her face
swelling and in tears, James became irate. "Why'd you hit
her?!" he screamed, stomping closer to his father, his face
red with anger.

"Who the hell you think you talkin' to, boy?!" Jesse
put a warning finger inches from his son's face. "She
knows goddamn well she ain't to be askin' y'all for no
help!" he yelled, pointing down at her.

"She didn't ask! I wanted to help!" James fired back
fearlessly, as he stared his father down.

"Have you lost y'ur goddamn mind?! What the hell
you helpin' her for?!"

"She's my friend!"

Within two seconds of that raging confession, James
stumbled backward and fell over the kitchen table, bleeding
profusely, after his father landed a heavy blow to his mouth
that split his lower lip.

Jesse realized at that moment that his sixteen-year-old
son had been completely misguided and spoiled over the
years. He had always thought that James's intelligence
would take him to great places in life, so he had not worked
him hard on the plantation. He had not guided him the way

a father should, nor had he taught him about the sort of man he expected him to be, as he had with his other two boys. But that all changed after that day. From then on, Jesse became strict with James, hardly ever letting him out of his sight. He forced his son to work side by side with him in the fields after school overseeing the slaves, teaching him what a master/slave relationship was supposed to be like, and that slaves were never to be considered as friends or family, that they were only property, not people.

When Jesse's life lessons began, Sunday strolls and fishing adventures between James and Lily quickly faded away, along with Lily's chances of learning to read. Long and meaningful conversations about life turned into demeaning demands from her best friend, followed by respectful replies of "yessa'" or "no sa'" from her. For the two years remaining before he went away to medical school, James never spoke another kind word to Lily nor made another memory with her worth cherishing.

…Now, after six straight years of being away, James was once again reunited with his former best friend in his father's parlor, a place they had once dusted together as they laughed and talked about his school day. But, unfortunately, as he stood there with her again, Lily was about to find out very quickly that this was not going to be as joyous as those days once were, and that James had not reverted back to the boy who had befriended her on a log all those years ago. Despite how much Lily had prayed about it over the years, James was *still* the unkind man his father had taught him to be, an unkind man who was prepared to speak to her again in a tone that she had grown to hate in the months before his departure.

Because of James's dark presence looming over her, every note of the song Lily had just played for him reflected the tumultuous months of that dying friendship, yanked in graphic detail from her impeccable memory. The way he used to look at her with such disdain, the way he used to talk to her like she was nothing, the loneliness, the emptiness, the hurt, the sorrow, and every other emotion that accompanied how horribly he began to treat her were suddenly alive again in every vivid memory his presence had awakened. They were ugly memories that, no matter how she tried to empty them into her music over the years, remained locked in her mind in perfect detail. Reliving those moments had brought all its unwanted pain back along with them, but with much more intensity this time around, as James hovered over her at the piano in silence. Lily sat there stiffly, still staring at the piano keys, feeling a sudden chill down her spine under the icy glare of a man whose face she once smiled at seeing. His presence now caused her to feel inferior and drop her gaze immediately to the ground as if it were a punishable sin to look him in the eyes. They were habits that came crashing back the moment he made his presence known, as she sat there with her heart fluttering and her mind racing, waiting for him to speak again.

"You know my fatha' would whip you good if he knew you were touchin' this here piano for anything otha' than dustin', don't ya'?" he finally asked, after staring at her for what seemed like an eternity.

"Yessa'."

"So, you *chose* to defy his rules openly?"

"Masa', it won't eva' happen again. Please, I beg of you not to tell yo' fatha'," she pleaded, as she stood up from the piano bench, suddenly wanting to get as far away from it as possible.

"How long've you been usin' this here piano like it was yo' own property?" James demanded to know.

Lily lowered her head, fearing the consequences of a truthful answer.

"Answa' me!" James snapped, stepping so close that Lily could feel the heat of his breath.

Lily's body stiffened, and she closed her eyes tightly, fearing that James would hit her. When he didn't, she slowly lifted her head to face his cold blue eyes … eyes that she once found great comfort while looking into. "Since a few weeks afta' I's sold her, sa'," she confessed softly, hanging her head low once again.

James's stomach clenched after hearing her confession. He thought that he and Lily had spoken about everything in their lives as children, and he wondered why she had not shared this with him all those years ago. He had never held anything back from her in their six years as best friends, not once, and he was confident that Lily had never kept any secrets from him either, especially not anything of this magnitude. He suddenly felt betrayed and it fueled his anger, which showed in the way he erupted. "Fourteen years!" he shouted.

"Yessa'," she replied, unwilling to look up at his anger-stricken face.

"Did Auntie know?"

"Yessa'."

"Well, it's a good thing she's dead then, isn't it? 'Cause I'd have my fatha' whip both of y'all good for this!"

James knew that the comment about Auntie would hurt Lily more than anything. She had told him when they were children that Auntie was the closest thing she had to a mother since being sold away from hers. She loved Auntie and was devastated over her death. She was appalled over the way her body had been burned and left in the woods for the animals to pick through. She was sickened that anyone would treat her that way after she had spent her whole life working so hard to help raise two generations of the Adams family.

Lily had leaned on James during those days when she never seemed to be able to stop crying over her loss, in much the same way that James had leaned on her after his mother's death. With great passion and sensitivity, they had supported each other through every moment of the unrelenting pain, but now he spoke of Auntie like she was meaningless, knowing his words would be venomous, and not caring that they were. Lily felt a rage boiling inside of her because of it, but she had learned by watching other slaves over the years that emotional outbursts were only rewarded with countless lashes of thick leather, so she quickly calmed herself before she replied. "Please, sa'. I promise you it won't eva' happen again."

"Lily you say that like this is your first time on that piano and you're a child who knows no betta'! Your deceit has dragged on for ova' a decade! This simply *cannot* be ignored!"

Lily erupted in tears, fearing that her back would finally bear the brand of his father's brutal punishments, but James turned and walked to the window, ignoring her tearful reaction. "Sa', if you please…"

"I don't wanna hear your tearful pleas and apologies, Lily!" James interrupted. "Fourteen years of your deception will not go unpunished!" He walked back over to her, crouching down to be sure she was looking him in his eyes. "You're lucky my fatha' didn't catch you sittin' there. You'd be strung up to the whippin' tree by now for disrespectin' my motha's belongin's!" He held his position, staring at her while tears ran from her tightly closed eyes.

After a moment, James finally stood up and marched around the room with his hands gripped around his suspenders. "Way I see it, though, I caught you, so I decide what to do about it. You're my property just as well as my fatha's." He began to walk up the stairs, leaving Lily shaking and crying in the middle of the parlor, but stopped before reaching the top and turned to her. "If you wanna avoid yo'self a whippin' then … Well, let's just say your duties are about to exceed far past fixin' a cup 'a coffee and scrubbin' floors," he said with a devilish grin. "You do what I tell ya' if you wanna keep that pretty little back 'a yours unscathed, ya' hear?"

"Yessa'."

James smirked at her, turned, and walked up the stairs without another word. Lily turned and looked at the piano through tear-filled eyes, and for the first time in fourteen years, instead of feeling joy, she felt sick to her stomach.

Chapter Two

Slave quarters:
An oftentimes rundown or dilapidated village of makeshift lodging or homes for slaves to reside in, located on their owner's plantation.

Slave Code
Article II Section XI
Be it enacted that every master shall provide all slaves, including the sick and the elderly, with a competent diet, yearly health examinations, clothing, and lodging. All such lodging and/or slave quarters are to be searched every two weeks for weapons or stolen goods. Acceptable punishments for these violations include: loss of ears, branding, nose-slitting, and death.

For nearly a week, Lily's fingers had not danced across her beloved piano keys. The only thing left in her life that would comfort her and settle her, the only thing that gave her joy and a reason to smile, had been painfully torn away from her by a man who once would have done anything to take her pain away, a man who now seemed to take pride in ensuring her misery.

Without the comfort of her piano, Lily's mind never seemed to rest. Notes and melodies drifted endlessly through her head with no way to escape and fill the air as they once had, day after day, during her imprisonment on the farm. Letting music flow through her fingertips made her feel free in those moments, but now the music lay trapped in her mind. It was a constant reminder that she too was trapped—like an animal. There was now not one single minute of the day she could escape from that reality.

Since her confrontation with James, the music that floated through Lily's head was angry and filled with sorrow. The notes were infused with the last words he had spoken to her: *Your duties are about to exceed far past fixin' a cup of coffee and scrubbin' floors.* Along with a very dark, brooding melody, that one sentence was currently repeating in Lily's mind as she stood in the kitchen washing dishes, letting the rag continuously circle the plate she was holding. The plate had long since been cleaned, but she continued her incessant wiping while lost in a trance, wondering what it was that James eventually planned to do to her as a punishment. Just the thought of it would nearly make her lose her breath and bring a tightness to her throat that always preceded her tears. She fought to keep it back, though. Her anxiety was overwhelming, but she refused to give James the satisfaction of letting him see or even hear her cry again. She had stomped out the last ember of their friendship long ago, and she wanted him to know that he meant nothing to her anymore. Every piece of her had become numb to him, and she was determined never to let anything he ever did or said affect her in any way.

In the midst of the muddled musical madness in her mind, Lily's dishwashing suddenly became frantic. Out of the blue, she was tossing dishes aside after barely wiping each one. A wave of anger swept through her until she cut her finger with a knife in the water. She could see her blood floating up to the top, but not only was her mind numb, her body was too. She hardly flinched at the pain. And then, as if ending a symphony with a dramatic crescendo, the music in her head suddenly stopped.

"Lord, I want to be with Auntie. I beg of you … Please," she whispered to herself, with her eyes fixed on her hands, which were still gripping the knife and the dirty dish rag. Both of her hands were partially submerged in murky water, a place she knew they should never be *forced* to be. She felt it was a metaphor for her life in some way.

It was the first time Lily had ever wished death for herself. She had not one thing that she could think of that made her life meaningful enough to go on anymore. James had just made sure of that. How a man who was once so charismatic had so drastically and abruptly changed into one capable of such mean-spirited acts, Lily still could not comprehend. Her thoughts of the person James used to be, along with seeing the blood seeping from her superficial cut, suddenly took her back to a fond memory of when the warmth of his heart was still evident and the two of them were still as close as any children could be. They were twelve at the time...

"I bet I'll beat ya' to the creek today," James had teased Lily that day while looking up at her in her usual hiding spot. She had perched herself in their favorite oak tree while waiting for him to join her after church. He would usually climb up to where she sat and talk for a while, but after being beaten by her in foot races to the creek every Sunday prior, he decided to get an unfair head start this time, and he took off running toward the creek before she could even make a move to get down.

"That ain't right, James!" Lily yelled playfully as she began making her way down the tree. "I'll catch you anyway! You run like a turtle with a broken foot!"

James laughed at her comment as he hopped and trotted over the rough terrain toward the creek where he planned to see if he could find Wilbur. With Lily's long legs and blazing speed, he was sure that by the time he got to the creek, she would be right on his coattails. But he reached the edge alone and was greeted by nothing but the sound of the flowing water, the panting of his own breath, and silence in the woods otherwise. He did not hear the familiar sound of leaves crinkling under Lily's bare feet, or the sound of her laughter, and suddenly his heart began to race for reasons other than being tired. James had a unique connection to Lily that he could not explain, even with his level of intelligence. He always instinctively knew when she needed him, and he somehow knew that this was one of those moments.

"Liiilyyy!" he yelled, not caring if anyone heard him. "Liiilyyy!" he cried out again, after he heard no response. He raced back toward the oak tree, calling her name every few feet. In the distance, he could see why his pleas went unanswered. Tears began to flow down his pale cheeks before he reached his destination. He slid on his knees coming to rest near Lily's motionless body.

"Lily!" he said while shaking her. She was face down and still unresponsive. She had cut her leg on a branch in her rush to get out of the tree, and her reaction to the pain had caused her to lose her footing and fall. She had hit her head on the way down and was knocked unconscious, but in James's twelve-year-old mind, her motionless body convinced him that she was dead.

James turned her over to get her face out of the dead leaves. "Lily, wake up! Lily, please get up!" he pleaded, with a sudden burst of tears flowing from his eyes, but she still lay motionless. "Lily, please! Come on get up!" he begged through his tears while continuing to shake her.

"D-d-did I win?" she finally responded softly in confusion. Relief ran through James's entire body. He felt the strength come back to his boyish muscles and the hole in his tiny heart start to fill itself again.

"A-are you okay? I-I'm sorry, I'm so sorry. I-I should 'a helped you outta the tree," he confessed, wiping his tears away.

"Why you cryin' James?" Lily asked, still drowsy and confused by what had just happened.

"Never mind that. Are you hurt?"

"My knee. I think I cut my knee," she replied, grimacing from the pain, as she tried to get up and look.

"No, don't move! Lemme look." James hiked her dress up and saw that Lily's entire knee was covered in blood. He knew he had to remain calm so as not to upset her, but the sight of her deep gash petrified him. His mother was always hysterical about her boys coming home with cuts and scrapes from wrestling around with each other or from working in the fields. She would douse their wounds in rubbing alcohol, scaring them into submission with claims that they would die from infections if they didn't sit still and let her clean the wounds properly. Thinking about his mother's incessant words, the thought of Lily's knee becoming infected played repeatedly in James's young mind. There was no way he was willing to sit and watch his best friend die. "Your knee is bleedin' bad. The cut's real deep," he told Lily, with calmness in his voice after his evaluation. Inside, though, he was ready to erupt into tears again, knowing that he would never be the same without her in his life, especially after having just had the brief experience of seeing her lie there unconscious.

"It'll be okay. Just help me up. I can go down to the creek and wash it," Lily replied.

"No! That wata's filthy! You need some rubbin' alcohol, so it doesn't get infected!"

"Sorry James. You don't have to yell at me."

"Well, it's just that … that … Well, you need to clean it propa', okay? I don't want ya' to, to…"

"To what?"

"Nothin'. Never mind," he said, not wanting to scare her with the possibility of death, while unbuttoning his pure white church shirt.

"What're you doin'?"

"Can you lift your leg at all?"

"Ow! Yeah, but it really hurts."

He slid his good clean shirt underneath her leg, and tied it tight around her knee like a tourniquet.

"You must've gone and lost yo' mind James! Yo' mama gonna whup you good for ruinin' that shirt!"

"Never mind that. I gotta stop the bleedin' and keep it from gettin' dirty. Can you walk at all?"

"I think so." Lily tried to stand up but not only was she dizzy, the pain in her knee was also even worse upon trying to bend it. When she could not stand, James used all his boyish strength to help her sit up against the oak tree she had just fallen out of.

"Will you be okay here by yourself?"

"I s'ppose so, but I don't really wanna be left alone. Not like this."

"I'll be back as fast as I can. I promise I'ma take care of ya', okay?"

"I'm a little scared, James."

"I won't be long. I promise."

"Okay."

James then ran as fast as his youthful legs would carry him out of the heavily wooded area. It was nearly a half-mile journey before his feet hit the plantation grass of his home, but still he kept his pace, running across the fields at blazing speed with his suspenders flapping near his sides during every step. When he made it to the house, he stopped at the back porch and peered through a window to see if anybody would see him come in. He heard laughter and chatter in the kitchen between his mother and a few of her guests. He entered through a rear door and tiptoed up the stairs to find a new shirt, but was startled by his oldest brother, J.R., when he reached the top.

"Where's y'ur shirt?" J.R. asked, looming down on him, chewing an apple.

"Never mind that. Just let me by." James tried to step past his brother, but he blocked his path.

J.R. certainly deserved to be named Jesse Roscoe after their father. Not only did he look exactly like their father, but he was mean and nasty just like him too, especially toward James. "You been tastin' that lil' nigga' girl, ain't ya?"

"What?!" James replied with shock obvious in his tone.

"I saw you," J.R. said, while smacking on his apple. "Last Sunday, you were playin' with that pick-a-ninny." J.R. smirked when a look of guilt took over James's face. "That's right. I's walkin' in the woods and I saw y'all out there in the creek. She the reason you ain't got no shirt on, boy?"

"I don't know what y'ur talkin' about!"

"I don't blame ya' little brotha'." J.R. bent down to within an inch of James's face. "If she was old enough, I'd be tastin' that lil' nigga too," he admitted, with a devilish grin on his face.

With all his twelve-year-old might, James pushed and slammed his brother against the wall. He was not even sure what J.R. meant by "tastin'," but he knew it was something bad, and he absolutely hated hearing him call Lily by such disrespectful names. It immediately enraged him. He held his brother pinned to the wall, staring daggers at him, without so much as one blink, breathing so hard that spit was seeping through the cracks of his clinched teeth.

Despite J.R.'s shock over seeing this angry side of his normally gentle little brother, he refused to show his surprise. He simply stared at James and bit calmly into his apple, as if only a fly had landed on his chest. "I bet Pa would be real eaga' to hear you been tastin' that lil' nigga'."

"You wouldn't!" James spat.

J.R.'s face became hard and serious. He grabbed James by the hair with his free hand. "I suggest you mind me wheneva' I need you to handle my chores, or else the only thing you'll be *tastin'* is Pa's leatha' belt against y'ur skinny little ass, instead 'a that sweet little nigga' friend 'a y'urs. Then you can watch Pa tie 'er up to the whippin' tree and beat 'er good too. She'll be up for sale on the next auction block 'fore y'ur ass stops stingin'." J.R. bit calmly into his apple again. They both heard somebody coming up the stairs and turned in the direction of the noise. James broke free of his brother's clutches and dashed into his room before he could be seen.

J.R. had always been jealous of James. He hated the fact that their father had always gone easy on him with farm work because of his intelligence, and that he always went on and on at family gatherings, bragging about how his youngest boy was going to be a doctor and a fine upstanding man that people would one day look up to. J.R. would seethe inside after never hearing his name mentioned in such conversations, but he was raised to be a man that never complained about hard work, and certainly never to protest the way his father ran his family or any of the things he had to say. Deep inside, though, he always loathed his youngest brother for the comfortable life that was bestowed upon him. But now knowing about James's secret, J.R. felt he finally had the leverage to take the easy life away from his baby brother and to show him what hard work was all about. With J.R. having the upper hand, James felt he had no choice but to obey if he wanted to ensure that Lily—a little girl that had come to mean everything to him—was never abused and remained at the farm and a part of his life.

Right now, ensuring that Lily remained a part of his life meant finding the rubbing alcohol that James was convinced she desperately needed. *Infection, death, infection, death,* were the only thoughts that were on his mind at that moment, more so than his brother's blackmail. Lily's superficial wound was mountainous in his eyes. After finding the solution, a clean rag, and a clean shirt, he carefully made his way out of the house unnoticed and then dashed the half-mile back to where he had left Lily. "Lily, you alright?" he asked, breathing hard.

"I'll be fine, but my leg is still hurtin' somethin' awful."

"This solutions gonna sting, but it's gonna stop it from gettin' infected. Be tough now," James told her as he began

27

to pour it onto the rag. "It'll be alright, I promise. Just squeeze my hand to keep from screamin'." Lily gripped his hand hard as he worked on her leg with the diligence of a doctor. He took great care in cleaning the wound, patching it up neatly, and ensuring her comfort.

Once that was complete, he pulled out something for her to eat and her favorite story from his satchel and read it to her. When he finished, he went down to the creek and brought Wilbur back, since he didn't want her hunting with a sore leg. Between the story he read her and seeing Wilbur, her pain was nearly forgotten.

Lily had been fine to walk for hours, but James would not let her until it was time for them to part ways. He helped her up, and then as if she was a wounded soldier, he walked with his arm around her from tree to tree, out of sight from peering eyes, all the way back to the slave quarters.

Later that night, James woke up in a panic, struggling to catch his breath, after having a nightmare about Lily lying face down in the leaves, the way he had found her after her fall. It took him a moment to realize he was only dreaming, but despite it, worry quickly settled in. He crept downstairs, avoiding every creaky spot he had memorized on the floorboards while on the way down. Too anxious and impatient to grab a coat or shoes, he slipped out of his house barefoot, in just his thin pajamas. The temperature had dropped considerably, but he did not let the crisp air stop him from his mission.

With only the moonlight as his guide, James made his way to the slave quarters, which was more like a barn for animals than a house. Each slave slept in stalls with hay for padding, but with Auntie being the oldest and Lily being the youngest, they shared a room in the back of the quarters, which was the only area with a door and a decent amount of privacy. It was James's first time in the quarters so late at night, and he realized that the chill inside was not much different from the cold air on the outside. He walked past each slave in their stalls, glancing at their thin blankets, which he thought could not possibly be keeping them warm. It was not even winter yet, so he could only imagine the discomfort they endured at night during that season. It made him instantly think of Lily. He hoped that maybe she had been supplied with something more suitable for a child, but upon entering the area where she slept, he saw the harsh reality that his best friend was also vulnerable to the cold Virginia nights. He quietly made his way over to her haystack where she lay breathing lightly, none the wiser to his presence. He looked at her for a long time, studying her rising chest movements carefully, trying to convince himself that she would be okay if he left, that there was nothing to be worried about.

James then looked over at Auntie, who was snoring lightly. He stared at her for the longest time too. Suddenly, at that moment, he felt deep and unbearable sympathy for the lives that these innocent men and women were forced to live. He turned and looked at the haystacks surrounding him with bodies resting on them, and at their thin blankets, and stared up at the holes in the roof that easily let buckets of rain flow through. He could even feel the crisp night air whisping its way through the cracks in the walls. *The animals have better accommodations than they do*, he thought to himself, as tears began to well in his eyes. James had never witnessed but had certainly heard about slaves being brutally whipped. He had heard about the selling of children from their mothers, and he had even watched men and women walk onto the Adams plantation in chains, but it took the simple scene in front of him to break him down into tears about the mistreatment of enslaved human beings, to make him question humanity and why anyone would dare to treat another so poorly.

James felt an overwhelming sense of guilt about going back to lay in the comfort and warmth of his bed after that.

He begrudgingly left the slave quarters and stood outside for a moment and looked up at the stars. With tears rolling down the sides of his face, he silently asked God why He would allow such a thing to happen. Young James had been told all of his life that this was the way things were supposed to be, but his heart rejected such preposterous preaching that night. He was convinced that nobody deserved a life like that … *nobody*.

The next morning, Lily woke up with a strange feeling on her feet. She raised herself up to look and realized that her covers were heavier than usual. She didn't recognize what was resting on top of her until her eyes fully adjusted in the early morning light. She had made his bed enough times to know that it was undoubtedly James's comforter that covered her frail body, and so too were the socks that now warmed her feet. She sat up out of the haystack and nearly smashed the other gift left for her in the middle of the night: a piece of homemade apple pie placed at the side of her makeshift bed. She looked over at Auntie, who was staring back at her with a half-hearted smile.

"You betta' eat up girl 'fo dey catch you wit' that."

Auntie had already eaten the piece of pie left for her and had long since hidden the pair of socks and the comforter that James had laid upon her too. She had caught him on his way out that night, and grabbed his cold little hand as he was adjusting her blanket, which initially startled him.

"You's a fine boy, James. Don't you eva' let the worl' change that, ya' hear?" she told him in a groggy, weak voice, coughing slightly afterward.

James stared at Auntie for a moment as he absorbed her words, then bent down and gave her the warmest hug he could muster before he quietly disappeared out of the quarters.

One year after that night, Auntie was taken away by the Lord, under the comfort of the blanket that James had stolen from his family's guest bed to give to her, and wearing a pair of the warmest socks he had found that night. Up until the day she died, that remained the single kindest act any human being had ever done for her.

Fortunately for Lily, it became the first of many wonderful acts by young James, many of which were unknown to her. James never mentioned to her the threat that J.R. had made, nor did she ever find out about the hell that J.R. had put him through for nearly a year so that their Sunday playdates remained a secret. Barns were cleaned, hay bales stacked, animals were fed, and wood was chopped in Lily's honor, to ensure that she was never sold away, and more importantly, that her back was never scarred by James's father. James took on his brother's duties with pride, never once complaining, knowing that Lily would be safe.

…Lily pulled a hand out of the murky dish water, reached down, and briefly touched the scar on her knee that James had so tenderly taken care of, well over a decade ago, after she had fallen from their old tree. As much as she had grown to hate the man that he had become, the tears trickling down her face were an admission that she truly missed her childhood friend. She missed her mother, she missed Auntie, and she even missed Mrs. Adams too. She treated her decently when Jesse was not around. She figured maybe it was because Mrs. Adams never had any daughters. When Lily began to ache for any of them, she was always able to release her sorrows onto the keys of the piano, but without that, the pain became too overwhelming.

Overcome with grief, Lily raised the kitchen knife from the water and ran her bloody finger down its smooth side. Staring at the blood from her fresh wound trickling down the sharp edges, she realized that the small mass of metal could be a means of escape from a world she no longer wished to be a part of. One swift clean motion and she could be embraced in the arms of Auntie and Mrs. Adams again, and if the Lord had already taken her mother, then she could be in her arms again too. With shaky movements, Lily lifted the blade even higher. It felt cold against the fragile skin of her neck. Her tears stopped and peace overcame her as she began to pray. When her silent prayer was over, the knife fell from her limp hand into the kitchen sink, splashing water onto the counters, and washing away her blood.

With the apron around her waist, Lily began putting pressure on the still bleeding open wound of her finger. She had been startled by the opening of the front door and dropped the knife in a panic. She kept her back turned to the familiar voices that had entered the kitchen behind her while she rushed to collect herself.

"Lily! Ain't you got lunch togetha' yet, girl?" Jesse barked.

"I's workin' on it now, sa'," she answered, doing her best to sound calm.

Jesse wiped the sweat from his brow as he sat down with his youngest son at the kitchen table. "What is it you wanted to speak to me about?" James asked.

"You 'cided where you gonna open you up a medical practice in town yet?"

"No sa', I haven't."

"What's the hold up?" his father asked, sounding irritated. "Don't ya' think y'ur time would be betta' served startin' up a practice of y'ur own here, or at least workin' alongside our old town doctor, 'stead 'a runnin' off for days at a time?" he asked, referring to the fact that James had left town for several days. His absence was somewhat of a relief for Lily. Feeling his presence now behind her sent a chill down her spine.

"Well, I been meanin' to talk to you about that," James replied, clearing his throat. "You see, I decided I'm not necessarily gonna be workin' in this town all the time."

"The hell you mean by that?"

"Well, I decided I'm gonna be a travelin' doctor. I'm plannin' to go from state to state helpin' out as many sick families as I can, 'specially those with children."

There was suddenly a long silence in the room. Even Lily knew not to make a noise.

"Lily, fix me some gin," Jesse ordered, staring coldly at his son.

"Yessa'." She knew from experience that such a request meant that Jesse was not happy about what he had just heard.

"Son, I been tellin' the good folks 'a this town since you was just a young'un that you'd eventually be this town's doctor. People 'round here 'spect me to stand by my word."

"I unda'stand that pa, but afta' doin' some travelin', I realize that not only is our town in need of a good doctor, but so are many otha's. And I think I could be of good use with all the skills I've learned."

"Your gin sa'," Lily said, placing the drink on the table near Jesse. James caught sight of the blood on her apron and locked eyes with her briefly. She dropped her eyes to avoid a prolonged gaze, then turned around quickly to get back to her duties. Jesse never noticed a thing. He picked up his drink just as quickly as Lily had set it down and took a long swallow, as if he was in a rush to prepare his nerves for the attack he was about to have on his son.

"Son, that's mighty noble of ya' to wanna help everybody, but the people in this town are like y'ur family. You can't turn your back on all of 'em."

"I'm not turnin' my back on any of 'em. Just 'cause I'd be travelin' doesn't mean that I wouldn't treat those in need 'round here … when I was in town anyway. But I feel like travelin' is my callin'."

"Son, I've done everything in my powa' to be sure you got y'ur schoolin' paid for, unda' the premise that you was gonna be workin' right here in this town. Way I saw it, you could take ova' and run this farm when I'm dead and gone, and tend to people's needs occasionally when they needed ya'."

"Tend to this farm?! I neva' had any intention on runnin' this place … *Eva'!"* he emphasized. "I neva' made any such agreement with you for payin' my schoolin'."

Lily jumped when she heard Jesse slam his glass down onto the table. "This plantation's been in our family for three generations! Y'ur brotha's done moved on and got married. They got kids and farms 'a their own to take care of, so it ain't nobody left to run this place but *you!*" Lily heard Jesse's chair creek under the pressure of his large body when he leaned forward to get closer to his son's face. "Now this ain't somethin' I'm *askin'* you to do … I'm *tellin'* ya'!" He pointed at James. "Y'ur *gonna* run this goddamn farm! I ain't losin' this place to somebody who ain't none 'a my blood, ya' hear?!"

Lily continued to listen to their exchange in disgust, as she stood with her back to them. Her hatred for the man who had paid to have her imprisoned there grew every time she heard a conversation of that sort. The exchange was a reminder of Jesse's hunger to control *everything*. She hated it, and she hated him.

There was not one thing she did not hate about Jesse Adams. She hated his condescending tone and the way he called her "girl." She hated the way he looked through her and never at her. She hated his walk, his dark yellow teeth, his stench, his wrinkly face, the look of his sunburned dried-up skin, and the sound of his voice. She hated the way his swollen belly protruded over his pants. She hated the disgusting grunting noises he made when he chewed his food while moving his mouth like he had fashioned himself after a cow. She even cooked his food with hate. Her recipes were good, but she knew they could be great, a fact that she would never allow his tongue the honor of knowing. But most of all, she hated that Jesse was the sole reason she had lost her best friend.

Jesse had sculpted his youngest son into what he considered to be a masterpiece of a man. Lily hated that he felt so proud of his accomplishment, like some world-renowned artist. He ingrained in James all the traits that were his own, qualities that made her hate James too. However, she wished she felt differently because she knew that underneath the layers of ugly traits that Jesse had painted onto James, there was a boy who had once risked the belt to leave desserts by her bed late at night, and who escaped Sunday family life to climb trees with her. Underneath there was a boy who once gave her his own blanket to keep her warm, and who looked at her with kind eyes of concern if ever she was hurt or sick. Somewhere inside of the man that James had become, lay a beautiful soul with a heart that was wrapped in pure love and innocence. But Lily knew that so long as Jesse was alive, he would continue to paint and mold his so-called masterpiece, and she would continue to hate him, and his disastrous so-called work of art.

Lily's mind had drifted off so deep into her hatred for Jesse that she had become deaf to a portion of the argument he was having with James. By the time her mind reconnected with reality, Jesse had succeeded in convincing his son to do as he wanted. Lily was not surprised at this outcome. However, she *was* surprised by what she heard next.

"This ain't the dream I envisioned for my life pa, but in this family's honor, I'll bear the burden of inheritin' and runnin' this farm."

"My boy…"

"Only if…" James continued, interrupting the celebration it seemed his father was about to have.

"Only if what?" Jesse replied, with all the joy suddenly gone from his voice.

"Since, I'll be takin' ova' and I'll soon be in charge of all the decisions around here anyway, there's somethin' that I need to do, *immediately*, to see to the stability of this farm."

Jesse's face was cold once again. "And just what the hell is that?"

"This farm is always in need of a way for us to make more money. Not only that, but we also need to ensure that this plantation continues to have its fair share of slaves. I noticed that there ain't any young'un's runnin' 'round the farm these days."

"Get to it, son!" Jesse barked impatiently.

James paused a moment and looked over at Lily, with evil dancing in his eyes. She still worked on their lunch with her back to them. "Well, Lily's young and strong." Lily stopped when she heard her name, but still kept her back turned. "I think she'd produce plenty of strong farm hands to sell and a few for this plantation to keep." James turned back to look his father in the eyes. "So I want you to let me take her to a slave breeder."

Mortified by what she had just heard, the color left Lily's face, and she felt her body grow cold. She had been fortunate up until then. She was a beautiful slave whose body had not been mutilated by fists, chains, or whips. Her femininity had remained pure and unviolated for her entire twenty-four years, which was a miracle considering that abuse in all forms was an inescapable horror for most female slaves, many of them before they even reached puberty. But now, her once best friend wanted to take all of that away and use her body as if she were some meaningless workhorse. The notion made her nauseous. His suggestion was beyond a punishment in Lily's estimation. She suddenly preferred the physical scars from heavy leather lashing into her back over the agony of being ravaged, repeatedly, by some strange human being. She felt she could more easily live with disfigured skin on her back than to live with the mental and emotional anguish of having all of her babies torn from her arms, just as she had been torn from her mother.

Lily remembered Auntie telling her that all seven of her children had been taken away from her. Auntie never got to look into their eyes or touch the soft skin of six of them. She never even knew the gender of any of them up until the last one was born. They had let her hold that baby girl for some unknown reason. She got to smell her, kiss her, touch her, and look into her beautiful brown eyes before they snatched her away too. It was a curse and a blessing for her for the rest of her days.

Auntie began to lose her memory and her connection with the present world in her last few months alive, so much so that she began calling Lily, Sarah. Lily eventually stopped correcting her mistake but decided to ask another slave why she kept calling her by the wrong name. It was then that she heard the story of how Auntie had called her last baby Sarah before they took her away. Lily now feared that she was about to become mentally tortured by the loss of her child in the same way as Auntie, just like so many other slave women, in the name of money and business deals.

"You see fatha', that's what my trip was for: business," James explained. "I met with a gentleman who was willin' to strike a great deal with me for usin' Lily. If you tell me that I can't use her, you can forget about me takin' ova' this farm. If I'm gonna run this place eventually, I want to get some things in orda' startin' *now*," he said, pointing his finger down onto the table and staring just as coldly at his father as his father was at him.

"What the hell was you doin' makin' deals with folks 'fore I even told you 'bout inheritin' this place? Was you plannin' on takin' my property without my knowledge, boy?!"

"No, of course not. I was gonna come to you about it,

but I wasn't sure what you'd say. I know otha' men have offered you breedin' contracts for Lily before, but you've declined because you said you didn't want a pregnant house slave workin' in here, and you weren't willin' to let 'er stay at anotha' farm durin' the duration of her pregnancy. But the man I just spoke to is willin' to pay damn good money for her offspring, and afta' lookin' at your finances, we need the money bad. And it ain't no otha' slave here of baby bearin' age anymore otha' than Lily. Hell, we could even keep a few for ourselves to help populate this damn place. So, I figured since we're at this crossroad, this will ensure that I get what I want … and so do you."

Jesse sat there quietly, staring harshly at his son. He took the last swig of his gin and set it back down without removing his eyes from James. "I don't like you sneakin' 'round, doin' shit behind my back." He hesitated as if the next few words pained him to release. "But you go on and take Lily, and let that travelin' doctor nonsense go to hell!"

"Fine!" James reluctantly replied with an attitude. "But I ain't takin' on all the otha' responsibilities of runnin' this place right away. Afta' I drop Lily off at the breeda's, I'll be headed back up to Ohio University for several months to make some extra money doin' medical research with an old professor of mine. More than likely, I'll stay there until Lily gives birth. I'll be back with 'er afta' that."

"I don't give a shit what you do in the meantime! You just keep y'ur word about runnin' this goddamn farm when I'm dead and gone like I'm tellin' ya'!" Jesse leaned in hard toward his son and gritted his teeth. "Or by God, I'll haunt you from my grave 'til the end of y'ur days." He stood up quickly, stomped out of the kitchen, and slammed the front door. James sat there a moment longer. He said not a word to Lily before walking out himself.

Even after hearing his plans for her, Lily remained true to her promise never to let James see that his words or actions could affect her. She never made a noise, nor did she have a reaction of any kind while he was still there. She stood frozen in silence with her back to her nemesis, but inside, her soul was screaming as if it had just been plunged into the fiery depths of hell. As soon as she heard him exit the front door, like a waterfall into the sea, her tears ran savagely from her eyes down into the filthy dishwater.

Chapter Three

Slave code
Article XI Section I

Slaves have no right to own any kind of property. All that
they acquire, either by their own industry or by the
liberality of others, or by any other means or title,
including their natural born children, shall be the full
property of their masters to do so as they please.

James rode slowly on his horse with his Stetson hat
low and a piece of straw in his mouth. His blue eyes were
fixated on nothing in particular. His thoughts were deep,
removing him from the consciousness of his surroundings
throughout his entire journey into the town's center. He was
headed there to pick up some much needed supplies for his
upcoming trip with Lily. Suddenly, though, his train of
thought was interrupted by the memory of the fresh blood
he had seen on Lily's apron while talking to his father the
day before about breeding her. His heart began to beat
rapidly, just as it had when he first saw the blood there. The
way Lily had quickly turned away when she realized that
he had caught sight of the stains confirmed to him that
there was something deeper than any minor cuts going on
in that kitchen before he had entered. In that moment,
James had to fight his old childhood instinctive urge to
jump from his chair to be sure Lily was okay.

As a boy, James believed that he was born with a
strange, unexplainable intuition in regards to Lily's
emotional and physical needs without her ever having to
whisper a word. But he had since convinced himself that
that was just childish nonsense. His reaction in the kitchen,
however, proved that that intuitive reflex to comfort Lily in
times of need had not faded, even after six years of being
away from her. But James was a man now, ingrained with
his father's teachings, and he knew better than to tend to

the emotional needs of a slave, *especially* in front of his father. James had priorities and responsibilities that he had been taught far superseded the needs and well-being of slaves. Slaves, his father had once told him, were only about business, and nothing more. Remembering the importance of that lesson was instantly sobering and kept him seated at the kitchen table instead of comforting his former friend, despite knowing that she had been emotionally broken before he and his father sat down to talk business.

Even after feeling the strength of his beautiful, unique emotional connection to Lily still very much alive within him during that moment in the kitchen, it was still not enough to stop James from traumatizing her with the threat of being bred. *She deserves this,* James thought to himself as he rode along on his horse. For the fourteen years that Lily had spent playing his mother's piano, he was determined to see to it that her life remained changed forever. His plan drifted through his mind again, calculated and unwavering, and a sinister grin emerged on his face after picturing the moment they would arrive at his chosen destination. He could not wait to drown in a wave of contentment when Lily finally faced the consequences of her actions.

"She deserves this," James reminded himself aloud this time, with the sinister grin still in place. He dug his heels into his horse's side prompting him to pick up the pace. The quicker he could retrieve the supplies on his list, the quicker he could experience the elation of his plan finally coming to fruition.

Before going to the general store, though, James had another important stop to make. He dismounted and tied his horse to a post outside of Dr. Gideon Whitfield's medical practice. He walked over and removed his Stetson hat before entering the good doctor's establishment. "Dr. Whitfield," he called out, after seeing him in the corner of the front office.

Gideon turned toward him after taking a vial from a glass cabinet. "Well, well, well, James Adams. Oh, pardon me," he said, clearing his throat. "I mean, *Doctor* Adams," he emphasized, with a smile on his face, approaching to shake hands. "Good to see you again."

James shook his hand. "No need for that," he smiled. "James is just fine."

"I concur. I think we can certainly dispense with the formalities at this point. Call me Gideon."

"Well then, Gideon, I take it from the smile on your face that your son is doin' much betta'?"

"Well, why don't you see for yourself. He just so happens to be right back here with my wife. She brought him in for a follow-up exam." Gideon guided him to a room in the back where his one-year-old son, Brandon, sat perched in his mother's lap wide-eyed, babbling, and shaking a rattle in his hand, a stark contrast from his condition nearly three weeks prior.

When James had first arrived back in town, he wanted to talk to Dr. Whitfield about the prospect of working with him from time to time in an effort to make some money and to continue gaining medical experience. When he had stopped by his clinic that afternoon, though, he found that it was closed for the day, which was odd for the dedicated small town doctor.

Before riding all the way home to surprise his father with his arrival, James stopped by Gideon's house to see if perhaps he could find him there. After knocking and standing at the front door of his estate for a few minutes, James was finally greeted by the good doctor, but barely recognized him; he had not aged well in the last six years. His wrinkles were much more prominent, he was thinner than James remembered, and so too was his hair, which had lost all its color. Gideon looked nothing like the strapping man who used to give James and his brothers yearly examinations, but the aging doctor looked hale in comparison to his one-year-old son. James had come to talk business, but quickly set that aside when Gideon apologized and explained that his son's serious illness was the reason he was not at his office.

Naturally, James took an interest in the boy's plight and asked what was wrong, hoping his new training could help. Gideon rattled off his child's symptoms with the most forlorn look on his face, realizing that the only son he had been able to conceive might die, and that despite being a doctor, there was not a thing he could do about it. Praying had not worked, and all the skills he had acquired after decades of treating people seemed useless in treating his son's unusual affliction.

After explaining Brandon's ailments, Gideon took James upstairs where his son lay barely moving and unable to open his little eyes, while his mother sat nearby crying and holding his hand. From the list of his symptoms, James already knew that Brandon's condition was grave, but had the doctor not explained a thing, the disheartening sight of the frail little boy would have been more than enough for James to assess that he was knocking on death's door.

All his symptoms, though, reminded James of a little girl he had once come across while working in the field alongside another doctor. He explained to Gideon that he had treated her with an experimental new drug concoction that had saved her life. He then expressed that he would be more than willing to find the necessary ingredients to mix the drug, but warned that there was potential for minor side effects and that it would require the most unpleasant route of entry into his body since Brandon could not hold anything down in his stomach. Under the dire circumstances, Dr. Whitfield was willing to try anything to give his son a fighting chance and therefore allowed James to move forward with treating him.

Before leaving town for his business trip, James had

stopped by and saw that Brandon was slowly improving. Now, with the way the toddler looked, smiling in his mother's arms in the back of Gideon's office, it was obvious that the treatment had been a success.

"Hey, little fella'," James said, approaching him with a smile on his face, happy to see a lively little boy this time around. Brandon smiled at him and reached his arms out, not fearful at all, almost as if he knew that he at least owed James a hug for helping to save his life. James lifted him high into the air, getting a laugh out of him, before settling him on his hip at eye level and tickling his neck. "No more scarin' your ma and pa like that, ya' hear?" he teased, as Brandon giggled.

"Carolyn, darlin'," Gideon said, approaching his young wife. "Unda' the circumstances the otha' day, I don't think I eva' did get to formally introduce you to this young man." Gideon offered a hand to help her stand. "Meet the young man whose fatha's been boastin' 'bout bein' my successor for years now. Him and his brotha's used to keep me so busy as young'uns tendin' to their ailments that, I swear, I can make my way to his farm blindfolded," he laughed. "This here is Dr. James Adams. The man I'm now foreva' indebted to for savin' our boy's life," he said, turning to face James with appreciation in his expression. "James, this is my wife, Carolyn."

"Pleased to officially make your acquaintance, ma'am," James replied, taking her hand delicately into his. Without all the chaos of dealing with Brandon, it was the first time he had really taken a good look at Carolyn up close. She looked to be at least twenty years Gideon's junior.

James had not been home long, but he had already heard the whispers about the unusual couple. Their age difference had caused the conservative small town to shun them when they wed three years prior. Gideon had only lost his first wife a year before that, and so naturally the gossip swirled, especially because of his choice of such a young bride. Gideon and Carolyn did not let it damage their relationship, though, and went on to conceive a son together. The little boy was the first for the good doctor, since his previous wife was unable to bear children.

After the way the town had treated them, the couple had been even more thankful, and rather surprised, at the lengths that James had gone through to help their son. It was with that in mind that Carolyn took James's free hand in both of hers after her husband had introduced them. "I can't tell you how grateful I am to you for helpin' my little boy," she said, running her hand through her son's hair, while he still rested in James's arms.

"And neitha' can I," Gideon added. "I tell you what, son." He placed a hand on James's shoulder. "If eva' you need anything, anything at all, you come and see me, ya' hear? I feel like I owe you the world for what ya' done for my boy, and I don't know how to begin givin' it to ya'." The doctor was nearly in tears as he conveyed the deep gratitude he felt for saving his only heir.

"You have no debts with me, Gideon. Your boy's alive, that's all I could eva' ask for."

"Carolyn, do you mind if I speak to James alone for a moment?"

"Of course not." She took Brandon from James. "I wanted to get home and get him down for a nap, and get dinna' on the table anyway."

"Okay, I'll see ya' lata' then ... Oh, and take this with ya'," Gideon said, handing her the vial of medication he had just retrieved from his cabinet. "Give him two drops of this before you lay him down."

"Will do." Carolyn turned to James. "Bye, Dr. Adams, and thank you again."

"You're very welcome. Take care."

Gideon walked his wife and son out to the carriage, kissed them both, loaded Brandon inside and then helped

Carolyn up. "We'll see ya' back home, Giddy," Carolyn said, smiling down at her husband before she snapped the reins.

Gideon went back into his clinic afterward and quietly watched his beautiful wife from the window for a moment as she departed. "I truly love that woman," he said to James, unexpectedly, when Carolyn was almost out of sight.

James stood there quietly, surprised by his sudden candidness.

"Just wish the rest of this town did," Gideon continued. "People can't seem to accept that I married her … for *obvious* reasons," he added with a lighthearted laugh, certain that James had noticed their age difference. "I get that we don't fit this town's mold of the ideal married couple, but I don't feel we deserve to be shunned because of it," he expressed. Gideon felt a rare comfort speaking to James about the matter since he had been willing to help his family despite the ugly things the townspeople had to say about them. "If everyone just ignored us, fine," he continued, "but it kills me that people 'round here have treated Carolyn so poorly because of it. She's so kind, such a truly gentle soul. She doesn't deserve to be mistreated," he said, sounding a bit sad, still staring out of the window even after Carolyn was long out of view.

"They've treated both of us poorly, really," Gideon continued. "I haven't let it botha' me on a personal level, but it does hurt that my business has suffered for it. Hell, if it wasn't for the fact that folks truly needed my services from time to time, I doubt they'd come to me at all anymore. They only seem to call on me now when it's an extreme emergency. Can't hardly get folks to come in for routine examinations anymore."

"Sorry to hear that, Doc, but I reckon you can't expect much else from small town, small-minded folks. They don't know any betta'."

"I agree," Gideon replied. He finally turned from the window and looked at James oddly. He had often used that same phrase in his head to help himself cope with the town's behavior. "Look, I'm sorry to dump all of my troubles on you. I'm just explainin' 'cause it's part of the reason I wanted to talk to you. You see, despite how harsh everyone in this town has been on me, I'd neva' walk away from helpin' any of 'em when they need it, not unless I's certain I'd be passin' 'em along to the right set of hands to take good care of 'em." He looked down at both of James's hands. "And I just saw a pair of hands that worked a miracle on my boy. I could use those hands around here James," he said, waving his finger at him. "And so could this town. That's why I's kind 'a hopin' there's some truth to what y'ur fatha's been sayin' all these years, 'cause I sure could use the help takin' care 'a folks 'round here, 'specially from a man who's quite obviously a masta' at savin' lives. And hell, maybe a fresh face is what it'll take to get folks rollin' back through these doors."

"Well, ironically, that's actually what I'd originally come to discuss with you the otha' day when your boy was sick," James replied. "I wanted the opportunity to work with ya' from time to time, to get some more experience."

"Actually, I's hopin' for more than just your occasional help. I ain't gettin' any younga', as I'm sure is plain to see," Gideon said smiling. "I'd really love to turn this place ova' to you in due time. I'm sure folks 'round here wouldn't object … 'specially the ladies," he mentioned with a laugh. He had heard all the whispers around town from all the giddy young girls that were gossiping about his return.

"Well, I didn't originally plan on settlin' here in Fayetteville."

"I don't blame you," Gideon snickered.

"My hope was to be a travelin' doctor, and I's just wantin' to work with you before I set out on the road."

"I see," Gideon replied, looking rather disappointed. "That's certainly a noble unda'takin'."

"Thanks, but if my fatha' has it his way, that may not happen, so right now I'm still tryna weigh my options. None-the-less, I'm honored that you'd trust me to take ova' for ya'."

"Well, you let me know if you eva' change y'ur mind. Eitha' way it goes, I'd be glad to have ya' here. Hell, far as I'm concerned, you can start now if you'd like."

"Well, unfortunately, right now I've got some much needed business to take care of out of town that's come up unexpectedly, so I'll have to postpone all of this for a while. But I'll certainly keep your offa' in mind for the future."

"You do that. Anytime you're ready, son. I'm here to help ya' in any way I can. You can count on that."

"Thank you, Doc. I'll rememba' that. I certainly do appreciate it."

"No, son … Thank *you*. I won't eva' forget what ya' done for my family."

James simply nodded his approval, shook Gideon's hand, and headed out the door toward the town store.

Dr. Gideon Whitfield's words about the women in Fayetteville could not have been more accurate. James Adams's return was undoubtedly the most popular gossip topic amongst many of them, especially after some had heard about him helping Brandon. In just a matter of days back at home, James had become the talk of the town, and by far the county's most desired man.

There had always been something unexplainable about James Adams that gave women a sudden case of moral amnesia. As James crossed the road, it was clear that several young ladies had suddenly come down with a case of the immoral affliction by the way they stared at him with naughty visuals erupting in their minds. It was an odd phenomenon considering that the presence of all the other

Adams men triggered the flight response in most women. The fact that J.R. and Jacob had managed a bride was a miracle. James was certainly fortunate to be an identical copy of his maternal grandfather. Much like his grandfather, he never failed to catch the wandering eyes of his female peers in his youth. With the way all estrogen-driven eyes were currently fixated in James's direction as he walked to the general store, it was blatantly evident that his ability to attract them had not changed ... but his body certainly had. During his six-year hiatus, James had gone from an adorable teenager to a strapping, well-built, virile man. Even through his coat, it was easy to see that his once slender teenage body was now wrapped in a layer of chiseled muscles. His shoulders were broader, he had grown to an unusually tall six-foot-two inches, and the fresh shadow of a dark beard now covered his once smooth baby face. He had cut his hair short as a teen, but it had since grown back into a mane of dark, loose curls, that lay on the back of his neck and covered most of his forehead, contrasting with his blue eyes, causing them to stand out even more than they already did. Giving in to one of his anxiety-driven ticks, James ran his hand through his thick mane of hair as he walked mindlessly across the dirt road to Albert's General Store. He was lost in thought about the journey he was about to take with Lily, completely oblivious to the eyes that were glued on him ... especially the eyes of one Mary Jo Parker.

Mary Jo, or MJ, as James had started to call her in his youth, was the only young lady that his father had approved of out of the frenzy of women who swarmed him during his teen years. Jesse wanted only the classiest woman as a wife for the son he was certain would go on to greater things in life. But Jesse's approval of the beautiful, strawberry-blonde gem was mainly because he knew that a union between the two would be a great benefit to his bank account.

Mary Jo's father, Joseph Parker, was by far the wealthiest man in Fayetteville. He had cotton and tobacco contracts with the Adams family long before James and Mary Jo were even born. So, in Jesse's greedy mind, the merging of the two families would mean a definite increase in social and financial status, and would be his ticket to the security of riches for generations to come. For that reason alone, Jesse was all but shoving James into Mary Jo's face every chance he got, hoping for a natural connection between them before resorting to more forceful tactics. Even from infancy, he had laid his youngest son in the crib with Mary Jo during her visits to the farm, wanting to build a bond between the pair long before they could even walk. However, Jesse's plan failed miserably. The more time James was forced to play with MJ through the years, the more he disliked her.

As he got older, James recognized that the average man would probably consider Mary Jo pretty by traditional standards, but she was simply not his cup of tea. She was way too frilly for his taste, and she talked about things that rarely interested him, speaking in a high-pitched southern belle voice that was as pleasant to his ears as screeching nails on a chalkboard. He also could not stand her snotty attitude and felt that her ways were far too snobby and contrived. On top of those *wonderful* attributes, he was not physically attracted to Mary Jo's beady green eyes, red hair, fake smile, skinny shapeless frame, or her ghostly complexion. To him, she was far paler than the average white person, so much so that he often jokingly wondered if she naturally repelled sunlight, or if her daddy had dipped her in porcelain to preserve his pasty little "pumpkin," as he would call her. That term of endearment further annoyed James; he felt that title should be reserved for little girls who were sweet, not ones he considered thoroughly irritating.

Even Mary Jo's name bothered James; he hated that

her father had arrogantly named a little girl after himself. It got under his skin enough that he began calling her, MJ. He hoped that it would irritate her just as much as she irritated him, but unbeknownst to James, Mary Jo thought it was sweet, and that he had given her that nickname because she was special in his eyes. Not only was she clueless as to the truth behind the name change, but she was also *completely* clueless as to James's true feelings about her altogether.

Mary Jo's misconceptions had everything to do with the fact that, despite how utterly annoyed James was by her, he had always been kind to her, never once revealing the slightest hint of the depth of his distaste. In fact, it was quite the opposite. He went above and beyond to be sweet to her to please his father, understanding full well that it was important for business. Deep down, though, MJ meant nothing to him. He secretly loathed every minute of catering to her needs while she was at the farm. After he had befriended Lily, however, she helped turn Mary Jo's visits into a source of humor.

Whenever Mary Jo visited, Lily was notorious for peeking her head around corners and making "silly" or "kissy" faces at James that only he could see over MJ's shoulder. James would fight hard to keep a straight face, but Lily would not stop until he burst into laughter. And it never failed to be poorly timed laughter that seemed mysterious and bizarre to MJ, which made it all that much more hilarious to Lily as she listened to James struggle to come up with ridiculous excuses for his unexplained outbursts. And their fun did not end there. Long after Mary Jo would leave for the evening, she continued to be a source of comedy for the duo. The mischievous pair would then joke about how James had become so good at playing the role of someone who gave a damn about anything Mary Jo had to say. They would sometimes even role play things that had happened that evening, giggling nonstop for hours about it afterward. Little did they know, though, that for Joseph Parker's little girl, it was no laughing matter.

While the secret best friends continued laughing at MJ's expense, Mary Jo was lying in her bed daydreaming about what her wedding day with James would one day be like. While Lily had James in stitches imitating MJ's frilly little walk, Mary Jo was picturing the children she would one day have with him. While James had Lily howling with laughter, after listening to him impersonate MJ's high-pitched voice, Mary Jo was thinking about how sweet James had been to her while she was there.

James was simply making the best of the miserable position his father had put him in. He did not realize that the kindness he was forcing himself to show MJ was creating a monster, a monster that had developed serious feelings for him, a monster that wanted him in every way possible, a monster named Mary Jo Parker, who would do and say anything to acquire James Adams at anyone or anything's expense. For Mary Jo—a ridiculously spoiled, self-entitled, daddy's girl who rarely heard the word "no"— it was not a question of *if* she would have James, it was only a question of *when*. And as MJ stood outside of Albert's General Store watching James walk across the road, she was about to attempt to have that question answered.

When Mary Jo heard that James was back in Fayetteville, she had been on the prowl like a lioness ever since, always coming up with some excuse to go into town, dressed up, made-up, and hair perfectly done, hoping to "accidentally" bump into him. Unbelievably, all of her efforts were about to pay off. While she blended in amongst a group of her friends, her eyes coasted up and down the only man she had been dying to sink her claws into for years. Mary Jo had lain in wait for long enough, and now she was finally about to seize the moment to pounce on her prey.

"James? James Adams? Is that you?" she asked from behind him as he collected a few things off the store shelf and put them into a wicker basket.

James was still lost deep in thought and did not hear a thing. He did not come out of his trance until Mary Jo tapped on his shoulder. Startled, he turned around and was greeted by the last face he had hoped to see in town.

"James Adams! What a surprise to see you! I had no idea you were back in town," Mary Jo lied.

"*MJ?*" he replied, with surprise in his tone, after noticing how overdressed she seemed for a leisurely trip to the store.

"Why yes, it's me." Her bright tomato-red, lipstick-stained lips stretched into a wide smile. "You haven't forgotten me, I see."

"Of course not." *But I've certainly tried.*

"One would think so. I sent you several letta's while you were away at university."

"You did?" James replied, trying to sound surprised. "I neva' received any letta's," he lied.

"I declare … You mean you neva' got a single one?" she whined.

"No, not a one. I certainly would've written you back had that been the case," James fibbed once again. He had read the first few lines of two of MJ's letters, tossed them aside, and never bothered to open the ones that followed before throwing them away. They were meaningless to him.

"All that effort for nothin'. I put all my heart into those letta's."

"I'm so sorry, MJ. I have no idea what could've happened to 'em. Maybe you just used the wrong address."

"But I got the address directly from your fatha'."

"Well, all I can say is that I neva' received 'em."

"I s'ppose there ain't nothin' we can do 'bout it now, can we?" she asked rhetorically, forcing the fake grin that James hated so much.

53

"I guess not." There was an awkward silence before James resumed picking up items off of the shelf. All the while, he was hoping Mary Jo would disappear, like the ghost she reminded him of, but much to his dismay she found something else to speak about.

"Speakin' of your daddy, he's invited my fatha' and me to anotha' dinna' at your home soon."

"Is that so?"

"That's right! This comin' Saturday, I believe," she announced excitedly.

"Well, I'll be travelin' for a while, so it looks like it just might be the three of ya'. Or maybe my brotha's might show up and keep ya' company."

"It's been six long years, James!" she exclaimed, momentarily exposing her snotty attitude before calming herself back down and trying to sound sensual. "I's certainly lookin' forward to seein' you there, and hearin' all about your time away at school, or perhaps reminiscin' about all the good times we used to have togetha' when we's young," she smiled, while touching him delicately on the shoulder.

What good times? "I wish I could, but this is a trip that I absolutely have to take, MJ. I'm sorry, but there's no gettin' out of it. It was good seein' ya' again though," he said, infusing a lie into the last part of his statement. James turned around and resumed his shopping, hoping Mary Jo would get the point and leave him be, but the porcelain-colored princess was nowhere near finished trying to seduce the man she had missed for years.

"Well, how about you and I celebrate your return before you depart? Just the two of us? I could make you a great home-cooked meal. I'm sure you could use that afta' bein' gone so long. And my cookin' is far betta' than that house slave of yours, Leela…"

"Lily!" James quickly corrected her.

"Whateva'." MJ dismissed his correction with a wave

of her hand. "It's much betta' than hers. So, what do ya' say? I can make your favorite ... fried chicken and mashed potatoes."

That was not James's favorite. He suddenly felt a headache coming on, the kind with the strength to bring even the toughest man to his knees. "Listen, maybe some otha' time MJ. I have a lot I need to take care of before my trip."

"Maybe when you get back then," she insisted.

"That'd be nice. I look forward to it," he lied just to please her, in hopes he would no longer have to listen to the sound of a voice that was giving him a migraine.

Another broad smile stretched across Mary Jo's pale face. As giddy as she suddenly felt at the prospect of spending an evening alone with James, one would have assumed he had just proposed to her. "I can't wait to see you when you return then. It'll be an amazin' evenin'." She looked at James with hunger in her eyes. "I promise you won't regret it," she said in a seductive tone, as she glided her finger down his arm.

It took every bit of James's strength not to groan aloud. He let out a frustrated breath instead. "Bye, MJ," he uttered coldly, dismissing the hungry look in her colorless face and the lust in her headache-inducing voice, knowing that he had zero intentions of spending one minute alone with her.

James stopped at two other shops before loading up the satchels on his horse and eagerly riding out of the town square. He had only been back a short time, but already some of the people in town were making him wish that he had never returned. He had tired quickly of all the long-winded conversations, of being questioned, and passively propositioned by multiple women that he had no interest in. He wanted to be polite as they welcomed him back to Fayetteville and asked him questions about his time away at school, but he was feeling oddly angry about the way that most of them had treated Gideon and his young wife, despite all the years he had spent selflessly serving the community. It didn't help that Mary Jo had his temples throbbing in unforgiving pain.

James remembered that he had always felt as if he did not fit in, in Fayetteville. His brief interactions since his return reminded him why. As he rode hard and fast out of the town square, he found himself already looking forward to escaping the place that had brought him so much misery as a boy. More than anything, he was eager to avoid dealing with MJ and the vomit-inducing migraine she was sure to bring him again at his father's business meeting.

James galloped back onto the farm and headed for the stalls to feed and water his horse, and to begin preparing his wagon for his journey, but his attention was drawn to another matter that suddenly became urgent to him. In the distance, Henry, the oldest and by far the biggest, strongest slave on the plantation, was away from his duties in the field. James looked at his pocket watch and realized it was time for one of the two meals the slaves received daily. But Henry was not eating. He was having a leisurely conversation with another slave who James felt had no business being over there. They were tucked away behind the barn looking for a little privacy while they talked, but James could see them easily from where he stood.

"You've been lookin' so down the last few days, Lily. You ain't been smilin' that pretty smile like usual. That ain't like you," Henry confronted her in his deep baritone voice.

"Ain't got much to smile 'bout no mo'," Lily confessed, looking down at the empty clothes basket perched on her hip.

"What's wrong?"

"I'm gonna be leavin' here soon, Henry. That's why I wanted to come and say goodbye to you," she told him, placing her free hand warmly on his arm. "You've always been so kind to me."

"Jesse ain't sellin' ya', is he?" he asked, with great concern.

"Truth be told, I wish that was the case."

"I don't unda'stand. Don't tell me you's runnin' away."

"No, masa' James decided he's gonna take me to a breeda'."

"My God Lily, I'm so sorry," Henry replied, placing a comforting hand on her shoulder.

"It's okay, I…"

"LILY!" James interjected. He had heard and certainly seen enough. The pair jumped back with fear dancing in their eyes. "Looks to me like you done finished hangin' them clothes on the line, so you wanna explain to me why you're still out here 'steada tendin' to your duties in the house?" he barked at her, all the while staring Henry down without blinking.

"Sorry Masa' James."

"Don't be sorry. Just get back to mindin' your work. And you too Henry, if ya' know what's good for ya'," he threatened, still staring intensely at him.

"Yessa'," Henry nodded.

Lily walked away hastily with anger in each step. She could feel the heat of James's eyes on her back as she made her way up the plantation house steps. She busied herself in the kitchen, hoping that he would go on about his business and have nothing further to say about her conduct. Much to her chagrin, he leaned up against the frame of the kitchen door with his arms folded, letting his silence speak first.

"My fatha' informed me that you were pure, which is what I told the man who plans to breed you. From the looks of you and Henry, I'd say you done went and made a liar outta me."

Lily was appalled to hear him say such a thing and did not understand why that was important or any of his business. As much as she wanted to put him in his place about minding his own business, she kept her wits about her. "May I ask why that makes a difference … *masa'*?" She could not help but add the latter word with a hint of an attitude.

"I can't present them with a slave that's already pregnant, Lily!"

Lily kept her eyes on the vegetables she was chopping and did not immediately react to the sudden anger in James's voice. She was calm and purposely delayed her response, which allowed more time for the visions of Henry having his way with her to replay graphically, over and over, in James's mind. "No need to worry, sa'," she finally answered, never looking up from the vegetables in front of her. "I ain't made a liar outta you."

James felt his heartbeat return to a normal pace and calmness return to his demeanor, but his brief visions of Henry lying on top of Lily had surprisingly destroyed his appetite for the rest of the evening.

"We're leavin' tomorrow at sunrise," he mustered up the strength to say while trying to force the images in his mind to subside. He retrieved a satchel from the parlor and tossed it onto the kitchen table. "Fill this with food and whateva' belongin's you have. Be sure it's enough for about two days of travel."

"Yessa'."

James then turned and headed to his room to gather his belongings, but could not make it there without turning to stop and watch Lily from a distance for a moment. He knew she had to have overheard what was to come in only a few short days, yet he never once saw fear in her eyes, nor ever saw her shed a tear, nor have the slightest reaction whatsoever. He was amazed at her strength and courage but wondered if those attributes would fade in the face of reality, as he finally turned and trotted up the stairs.

After James had left, Lily did as she was told and gathered canned goods, fruits, vegetables, and bread for their journey, then went into the slave quarters to gather what little she had. There were no fancy shoes, nor shoes at all for that matter. There were no beautiful dresses or even ugly ones to change into; no pretty hats, expensive jewelry, or any other frilly things fit for a lovely lady. One scarf and an extra apron were all that lay next to her makeshift bed. She stuffed the extra scarf into the satchel, and her packing was complete.

Lily then walked over to the secret storage spot in her rundown room that still housed the two pairs of socks and blankets that James had so kindly brought to her and Auntie on that cold night over a decade ago. She pulled out Auntie's blanket and hugged it tight. It still had her scent on it. As Lily inhaled, she began to think about all seven of Auntie's little babies and how they had been stolen from her, including baby Sarah. It made her wonder if she would ever get to see the faces of any of her own children, or know their genders, or be the one to name them. She wondered if maybe it was best to have them snatched away so that there was no chance to form a connection to them at all, no chance to be tortured by the memories of their names, their scent, the softness of their skin, and their petite faces as they lay snuggled in her arms. Either way, she realized, she was about to leave the Adams farm with a filthy scarf, and return with nothing but the same. Soon Auntie's blanket was covered in the moisture of her tears. The torture had already begun.

Chapter Four

Slave Code
Article III Section II

Slaves are forbidden from leaving their owner's property, unless accompanied by a white person, or carrying a license or letter showing he has authority from his master. If any be without either, they shall be considered as a runaway, and to suffer such penalties provided against runaways.

Lily sat in the back of James's covered wagon surrounded by various bags and blankets with her knees drawn up to her chest, watching her "prison" get further and further out of sight in the morning sunlight. It was the farthest she had been off the Adams plantation since her life sentence there began. While confined there for fourteen years, all Lily had known was the same miserable routine of waking up daily to serve a man that she often wished she would find in his bed no longer breathing. Escaping her prison warden for a while was bitter sweet. She was happy to be relieved of the irritating sound of Jesse barking orders at her all through the day but sickened by what that would shortly be replaced with.

Despite where she was headed, Lily was somehow trying to enjoy the two days of freedom she was being allotted on her ride into hell with her ex-best friend at the reins. She prayed that James would not utter a word to her during their travels. She wanted to get lost in her own thoughts and pretend that she was on a journey to see her mother again for the first time since being tortuously dragged away from her. The thoughts of her mother only sustained Lily for a little while before the tears began to fall, collecting on her blood-stained dress. Every clip-clap of the horses' hooves reminded her that she was closer to the humiliation of being violated by some man she did not know, and closer to experiencing the loss of a child the way her mother and Auntie had. It was for those reasons that she lay with her head on her knees, crying silently, and begging God for infertility.

Lily turned and peeked through the cover on the wagon, staring at James in disgust. His face was emotionless, much like his father's usually was unless he was upset about something. It had been years since she had seen James smile. She missed that smile and the tender man who once lived behind it. She once believed that James would have fought tooth and nail to save her from the sickening things that were about to occur. Now, though, he was a man who was cold and callous enough to be the one throwing her to the wolves.

After staring at James momentarily, Lily began to reminisce about her old friendship with him, just as she had many times since his return. She found that every time a negative thought of him crossed her mind, it was preceded by a fond memory of them together. This made the pain of his disdain for her run even deeper. Lily became angry with herself for not being able to let go of the past. She constantly had to remind herself that the James she knew as a girl was dead. Despite feeling that way, though, the fond memories were far too strong and full of happiness to let dissolve. They played on in her mind along with her piano music, soothing her just as her beautiful melodies had the power to do. This time, she recalled an occasion one summer when they were sixteen…

James and his brothers had been sent away for a short while to visit their aunt and uncle in a neighboring town this particular summer. He and his brothers were only gone for about two or three weeks during their summer breaks, but every time James left, Lily remembered feeling like each day dragged on like months. She was always unsure when he was due to return, which made the heartache of him being away even more intolerable. Aside from her mother and Auntie, James was the only person whose absence weighed heavy on her heart at bedtime. For reasons she did not fully understand yet, the heaviness was much worse this particular summer, which was painfully clear in her music. By the third day of James's absence, Lily's loneliness presented itself in the form of a beautifully composed piano piece. She played no other song during his three-week absence; it was the comfort that she needed to sustain herself while James was away.

Late one evening, after Lily had already been sent to the slave quarters, she heard a team of horses arriving onto the plantation, and then the unmistakable sound of a voice in the distance that brought a smile to her face, and the comfort to drift into sleep with lightness in her heart again. She awakened the next morning to find a gift that had been placed at her bedside in the late night hours. From what it was, she knew instantly to be at the old oak tree near the creek to see her friend again after three long miserable weeks.

Lily's smile was as full as a harvest moon as she sat on a blanket at the base of the oak tree with her gift in hand, watching James dash from tree to tree on his way out to find her, with a smile on his face that was equally as grand as hers. This time, Lily had not the willpower to just sit idly and wait for him to join her. She stood and walked toward him as he approached. James slowed his pace as he got closer, taking time to absorb the sight of a young woman who had completely taken over his thoughts while he was away, a young woman he had only been able to see and be near in his dreams for three weeks, a young woman that he missed beyond his capacity to express with words. Their smiles faded when they were within feet of one another. There were no words exchanged, just an intense gaze that they held for a moment … and then a hug. It was a hug that dissolved any need for James to express how much he desperately missed her. The length, the strength, and the warmth of his embrace conveyed those words for him. He hugged her in a way that said, *please forgive me for leaving you here so long alone.* It showed that their misery was mutual and made Lily wish that James would hold her like that for a lifetime.

When James finally released her, Lily thanked him kindly for the gift that he had placed at her bedside: a book that she eagerly waited to hear. She handed it to him, and they sat shoulder to shoulder under their childhood tree as he began to read a story that would become by far her favorite of all the ones he had ever read to her. When the story was over, Lily was in tears from a mixture of emotions: happiness from the return of her friend and the ending of a magnificent story, and sadness, she expressed to James, over the fact that she could never read that story to herself. It was her tears that day that eventually brought forth the promise that he would change that fact forever. James wanted nothing more than his gift to be the first book Lily was ever able to read herself.

… After losing herself in that memory in the back of the wagon, Lily's emotions from that day were fresh again. During all the years that James was away, she had been able to repress and numb herself to all of the feelings and memories associated with him. Now that he was back, though, she found that it was all starting to resurface again. It was crushing her to accept that those beautiful memories, and that wonderful man, were all in her past and that their new relationship would never be anything close to what it once was, no matter how hard she reminisced or wished for it to be different.

Despite the onslaught of joyous childhood memories resurfacing, Lily quietly accepted the lack of interaction on the entire first day of her journey with James. On the way to their destination, they had simple conversations about food and water and breaks to relieve themselves, but both seemed reluctant to say anything beyond that. Lily even chose to eat her food inside the covered wagon instead of taking the opportunity to sit in the warmth of the sunlight near her nemesis. She wanted to avoid looking at James for any unnecessary amount of time; the sight of him destroyed her appetite. It did not seem to make much difference to James either. They both seemed content with the distance, the silence, and suffocating in a cloud of emotional negativity, three things that would have been inconceivable between them eight years prior.

After a long sleep through a rather mild winter night, the pair proceeded on in the second day of their journey, much like the first … in silence. Aside from a brief break for snacks, they rode steadily for a few hours until the sun was high in the clear blue sky. The beautiful conditions brought an unseasonable warmth for a winter day. It made a body of running creek water, down the banks of a small hill, look inviting to James. Lily suddenly overheard him calling the horses to a halt. "Lily, we're breakin' here."

"Yessa'," she replied, even though she wanted to ask why they were stopping so soon. They had just eaten and relieved themselves not long before. She did not dare to step out of line by questioning him, but instead got out and found a place to relieve herself again. It was more of a way to separate herself from James than a necessity to go. When she came back, he was dropping bags onto the ground from the back of the wagon. She walked around the back to help him, but then quickly turned away when she realized that he was shirtless.

"Lily," James called out to her back.

"Yessa'," she said, stopping with her back to him.

"Take this satchel."

Lily turned back around but felt uneasy with where to place her eyes as James handed it to her. "Is there some food in here needs cookin'?" she asked, being sure to keep her eyes glued to the satchel.

"Naw, there's soap, and towels, and some otha' things for you. You can use that creek ova' yonda' to clean up. Quicka' you get cleaned up, quicka' we can carry on."

"Yessa'."

Lily walked a long way down the stream and set the satchel on a large rock once she felt she was in a place that gave her plenty of privacy from the potential of prying eyes. She opened the bag in search of the soap and towels, but sitting on top of the supplies she was searching for were new undergarments, a neatly folded dress, and a scarf that matched it. Thinking that her eyes were deceiving her, she pulled the dress out, laid it on top of the rock, and stared at it in confusion. It was definitely not an evening gown or even a dinner dress. She was not even certain if it was brand new, but that did not matter to her, she was just happy that it was free of holes and tattered ends, like the one she had on. She held it up to her body and saw that it even looked to be a perfect fit, unlike her old one. It was basic but beautiful in her eyes, so beautiful that she almost refused to believe that it could possibly be for her.

James was in the distance tending to his own bathing needs. He wanted to respect Lily's privacy and kept his back to her for as long as he could, but his desire to glance in her direction was much stronger than he had anticipated. Discreetly, out of the corner of his eye, he caught sight of her holding her new dress up to her body. The dress was among the many things he had picked up on his trip into town when he had run into Mary Jo. He wanted Lily to represent his father's farm well and figured that a new dress, free from bloodstains, filth, and holes, would be beneficial to their representation … at least that's what he told himself. After leaving Albert's General Store, James had gone into a clothing shop and found a woman that looked to be Lily's height and shape, and asked what size she wore. He hoped that he had made an accurate assessment. He now stood in the creek, secretly peering at Lily, waiting impatiently to see.

Lily, however, had reluctantly put the new dress down. She was unsure why James would get her a new one but figured there was definitely some personal motive behind it. Although she appreciated it, she knew not to assume that James *wanted* to do something special for her. Never-the-less, just as any woman would be, she was excited to have a beautiful new piece of clothing, especially after having worn the same tattered garment for so long.

Before disrobing, Lily leaned over and touched the creek water with her hand. Despite the slight chill, she decided to go for a brief swim since she was rarely ever afforded such an opportunity. Not wanting to put her private areas on display, she swam in her old dress. The chill touched her bones as she entered, but it did not deter her at all. Floating in the water reminded her of when James had taught her to swim. On such a warm beautiful day, she suddenly found herself not wanting to rush the opportunity to enjoy the cool water against her skin while reliving that happier time in her life with James. She reverted to her childlike ways for a spell and began to swim around in the creek like she was ten again, not even caring if her lack of urgency made James angry. She was already more than halfway to her punishment anyway, and figured there was nothing worse he could ever do to her.

From the moment he had turned toward Lily, James had yet to take his eyes off of her. He had mindlessly washed himself as he observed her backstroking in the water, but anger over her leisurely swim and lack of haste was not his reaction at all. He too was instantly taken back to his youth. He simply watched her and reminisced. As a boy, he admired how Lily was able to go from a disciplined, hard-working young woman, to a young woman with childlike playful ways and youthful silliness. Gazing at her now, he realized that she had not changed, nor did the fact that he still appreciated those simple traits.

After swimming for a short while, Lily finally decided to get to the business of cleaning herself. She moved toward the shallow end of the creek to get her footing, and then unbuttoned her old dress. She slid it down off of her body, unknowingly revealing her bare back to James's waiting eyes. Feeling a false sense of security, she walked toward the shore to lay her garments down and retrieve the soap and towels. Little by little, her body emerged from the water, revealing the length of her long legs and the roundness of her buttocks. All the while, from a great distance, James stood watching her in a trance, not even bothering to hide the fact that he was doing so. Not much detail could be seen from where he stood, but still his eyes followed her every movement back down into the water as she began to lather herself.

James's own bathing and dressing needs instantly became irrelevant to him as he watched Lily. He knew where he stood with her as her master, but he was still a man, and the knowledge of his status was not enough to stop the onslaught of desire he suddenly felt, nor the envy he felt toward Lily's hands as she ran them slowly over her body. More nights than he could count in his youth, he had dealt with the embarrassment of waking up with the front of his pajama pants covered in the results of his dreams about her. His body began to react to the vision of her now just as it had then. No matter how cold their relationship currently was, it simply could not stop those fires from raging within him again, while watching a woman whose beautiful features he had always considered as a work of art.

"Hey there!" a voice called out from behind James that seemed to rain down from the heavens. His mind was so distracted by Lily that he had not heard the sound of a horse approaching behind him. He turned to find a sheriff glaring down at him, clearly unhappy about him using the creek as a bathtub. Luckily, James had just put on a pair of trousers that hid the truth about what was on his mind. "This here is private property," the sheriff explained.

"Sorry Sheriff, it didn't look like it belonged to anybody."

"Well, I'm here to tell ya' that it belongs to the Blacksmith family, so I suggest you load up y'ur wagon and be on y'ur way if you don't want no trouble." Lily was so far down in the creek that she did not hear any of what was going on. She was still diligently bathing herself when the sheriff caught sight of her movement in the distance. "She with you?" he asked James.

"Yessa', she is."

"She a nigga'? I can't hardly tell from here."

James felt the heat in his blood start to rise upon hearing his question. He could not stand that word. Although it was typical slang for most, he felt it was degrading. "She's a *Negro,* yes," he said, through gritted teeth.

"She y'ur slave?"

"Yessa'."

"You carryin' her papers?"

"Yessa'."

"Get dressed and let me see 'em."

James put on a shirt, retrieved the paperwork, and then handed it over.

The sheriff took a moment to read the documents. "Well, you and y'ur lil' monkey need to move it along, 'fore I arrest the both of ya'," he said, after handing the forms back over to James.

"LILY!" James called out. She turned around abruptly, embarrassed to find not one, but two pairs of eyes centered on her. "COME NOW! WE HAVE TO MOVE ALONG!"

"YESSA'!" she yelled back, feeling the heat of embarrassment crawling all over her. She frantically retrieved her belongings while trying to keep her body as covered as possible. James tried to distract the unwelcomed visitor with unnecessary conversation, in an effort to pull his eyes away from her. Slave or not, Negro, Caucasian, or otherwise, he knew men would be men, and he did not like the idea of the sheriff using Lily in his fantasies the way he looked to be doing.

After Lily had dressed and walked back to the wagon, the sheriff continued to watch as they gathered their belongings and loaded everything up, pretending as if he did not trust that they would move along as he had advised them to do. But Lily knew better. For the first time in her life, she felt the disgust of a man she did not want conveying his desires for her with his eyes. She had not experienced such things on the farm. Although Jesse was in every way an evil man, he would have never allowed such violations to take place with his most valuable slave, so slithering eyes from a repulsive man was certainly not something she was used to. It made the hair stand up on the back of her neck.

Lily was not the only one seething inside as the visual assault took place. James had tried hard to turn it off over the years, but the urge to protect Lily began to swell within him again. He had to dig deep to find the strength to keep his anger from spilling over into a physical assault that would certainly have landed him in jail. Just as Lily fought with herself to let the memories of their past subside, James too found himself constantly fighting to be the man his father had taught him to be in her presence, and free himself from the desire to protect her more than a typical master would. But as the sheriff sat on his prancing horse, raping Lily with his eyes, Jesse's teachings had become nearly impossible to obey. James was so irritated that his eyes squinted into hate-filled slants, and his face turned a deep shade of red, but the anger he exuded did not deter the sheriff.

"What you got worth showin' me unda' that dress,

nigga'?" the sheriff suddenly asked Lily, continuing to stare at her with his mouth open.

"Nothin' that ain't gonna cost you your fuckin' eyesight!" James barked, jumping in front of Lily to block the sheriff from glaring at her any longer. Lily remained hidden behind him, feeling appreciative of his maneuver, but stunned by the fact that he would bother to come to her defense.

"Don't you threaten me, you uppity white boy!" the sheriff bit back.

"That ain't a threat!" James snarled.

The sheriff purposely spit near James's foot. "Y'all move it along 'fore I arrest the both of ya'."

When the officer finally left, James and Lily both continued on their journey, in the silence that they had become accustomed to. Lily realized as they rode away, that the dirty old man was only the first of many who would soon look at her as an object to be used in a sexual way, be it for pleasure or financial gain. The tears began again, christening her new, perfectly fitted dress, as she tried unsuccessfully to swallow that painful reality. James, too, had a difficult time accepting what had just happened, as well as his uncontrollable reaction to it. It took him hours to settle himself and put his focus back on the benefits of their journey. When he reminded himself of things to come, it was instantly calming for him. A smile even danced for a moment across his face, and he prompted his horses to pick up the pace.

* * * *

Athens, Ohio

James tried to reach his destination by nightfall, but darkness had long since settled in by the time he finally pulled through the steel gates of Werthington Estate with Lily in tow. In the distance, William Werthington, an average-sized, older, white, British man, with a goatee and a full head of graying hair, emerged from the front door of the sprawling, white, plantation-style mansion. He stood there between two tall columns, in a plain gray suit with a red bow tie, smoking a pipe on the porch steps, waiting for James to walk over and greet him. Their arrival had been greatly anticipated, but he had expected them much earlier in the day.

"Well now, I was starting to think maybe you'd changed your mind, or decided to take her elsewhere," William told James, in his proper British accent as he approached the mansion steps while extending his hand for him to shake.

"I'm a man of my word. I wouldn't dream of backin' out on such a thing," James replied, firmly gripping the older man's hand. "I'm so sorry we're late. I had to make a few more stops along the way than anticipated."

"No need for an apology. I'm just glad you made it here safely."

"Listen, Mr. Werthington…"

"William. Please call me William."

"William, if ya' don't mind, I know you wanted to get things started when we got here, but it's been a ratha' exhaustin' day, and…"

"Say no more. I wouldn't dare let her jump right into things at this ungodly hour."

"Thank you kindly, sa'. I think we could both use a little rest."

"After two days on the road, I can certainly understand that. By the way, where is this … umm, Lily, I believe you said her name is?"

"She's in the back of the wagon, more than likely asleep."

Lily had overheard every word of their conversation. Her body did not crave sleep, it craved death. Despite hearing that this William character had no intention of turning her into a breeding animal that night, she still sat

71

with her knees drawn up to her chest, quivering, rocking side to side, and praying for God to make her heart stop beating right where she sat.

Lily had thought that by the time she arrived, she would have come to terms with her fate, and would have gathered the strength to face the physical, emotional, and sexual abuse that was about to take place. But as soon as the wagon halted in the plantation yard, all she could seem to dwell on was Sarah, the only baby Auntie ever got to name. That one name lingering in Auntie's demented mind during her final days of life was proof to Lily that despite how strong all slave women seemed to be after having suffered through situations of that nature, it was only a facade. She now felt that the pain and heartache she was about to endure would be like an incurable disease that ravaged her soul until the day she drew her last breath. That knowledge trampled Lily like wild horses, paralyzing her where she sat. She did not have the power to speak, to scream, or even to run. She just sat there like a weakened, helpless flower waiting to be destroyed by an oncoming thunderstorm.

"Lily!" James called out to her, but crickets and croaking frogs were the only sounds in the air. "Lily!" he called to her again, but still, not a single movement was made. "Just like I thought, she's probably asleep," he turned to William to say, feeling a little embarrassed that Lily had yet to emerge.

"It's quite alright. Take your time waking her and gathering your things. I'm going to go on in and see to it that Anna Mae's got your room ready. She's already made dinner and put it away, but I'll have her warm it up and set it out again for the both of you."

"That's mighty kind of ya'. We'll be in shortly."

James knew that Lily was awake, but he did not want to reveal that to William. He was glad that he had gone back into the house before retrieving her. Something told him that he may not be prepared for what he was about to come face to face with in the wagon. And he was right. Lily still had not the strength to move from her upright fetal position. Her body shook uncontrollably, and her eyes glistened with moisture, but when she heard footsteps approaching the back of the wagon, she prayed quietly, "Dear God, give me strength."

"Lily," James said, as she came into his view.

She did not answer. Instead, she gathered their bags and placed them on the end of the wagon for him to collect. It gave her time to let her emotions and nervousness subside. She was still determined not to give James the satisfaction of admiring her tears.

James stood there momentarily as the bags piled up. He did not know what to make of what he was seeing. It looked to him like Lily was eager to move forward with his plans, which was the last thing he would have ever expected from her. Then again, he remembered that her strength was one of the things that captivated him as a young boy. He felt that he should have known better than to have expected anything less of her. In that moment, for that very reason, he suddenly felt like a fool.

"Lily, I've been callin' your name."

"Yessa', I's sleep 'til just a moment ago," she lied.

"Well, I can handle all the bags lata'. Mr. Werthington is eaga' to meet you," he told her, offering her his hand to help her down.

"Yessa'," she replied coldly. She had cleared her eyes before she presented them to him. She was thankful for the darkness, as it helped to hide any remnants of her sadness, but she still had to fight to gain control of the shakiness in her voice and in her hands.

James let Lily lead the way up the mansion steps, and as any southern gentleman would do, he held the door open for her to enter. As she walked in, her eyes glided over the foyer with its grand dual staircase, and then down the long hallway in front of her that seemed to go on forever. She instantly felt sorry for the house slave who had the unbelievable task of maintaining such an enormous home. It could have easily fit Jesse's house within it four times over with plenty of room to spare.

A dark-skinned man with a black suit suddenly approached and greeted the pair in the foyer. "Evenin'," he nodded with a smile. "Mr. Werthington is right this way," he informed them as he began guiding them toward the dining room.

James and Lily followed behind him in silence. Despite her predicament, Lily could not help but be fascinated by the beautiful art, sculptures, flowers, and furniture spread throughout the house. From his home alone, she knew that the owner was not a man who dabbled strictly in the sale of tobacco or cotton, but that he must have many other entrepreneurial endeavors as well.

Lily entered the dining room, which was just as grand as the rest of the house in her opinion. On top of the massive dining table sat silver cutlery, china for sixteen, and a spread of food fit for a Thanksgiving feast. At the head of the table, William sat in his red bow tie, still smoking his pipe, waiting patiently for his guests to join him. When he saw Lily, he smiled, laid his pipe down, and stood as she approached. "You must be the Lily that I've heard so much about," he said, taking one of her hands into both of his ever so gently.

"Yessa'."

"I'm William Werthington. So very pleased to meet you. I hope the journey wasn't too rough for you."

"No sa'. I feel mighty fine, thank you," she said shyly, noticing he spoke with an accent that she did not recognize, although, she knew it certainly was not American. It made him seem extremely intelligent to her, and so too did the glasses that he wore perched halfway down his nose.

"I know you must be hungry, so please feel free to eat

whatever you like. I wasn't sure what the both of you preferred, so I asked Anna Mae to prepare a variety of different items. I hope you find something to your liking."

"Thank you kindly, sa'." Lily had grown to feel over the years that kindness of any sort by rich white people was usually selfishly motivated. She thought maybe it was important to William that his breeding slaves had access to as much food as they wanted. Seeing that he was obviously a man who loved the finer things in life, she had no doubt that money and greed dominated his every decision, even a simple one like offering a slave an endless amount of food. So despite his kindness, she felt uneasy with not playing the role of a servant. "Should I fix y'all a plate first before I eat," she asked, motioning to pick up William's plate.

"Nonsense," he quickly replied, grabbing her hand gently to stop her from taking his dinnerware. "You're a guest here. Besides, I'm plenty capable of fixing my own plate, if you can't tell," he said with a laugh, patting his barely protruding belly. "Believe it or not, this body of mine used to be made out of stone." He laughed at himself again. "Seems that old age has chiseled away at that."

James gave a faint smile and a nod of appreciation in William's direction for his genuine effort to make Lily feel comfortable. He knew she felt out of place, nervous, and scared, despite what her demeanor showed, so he was glad that William was attempting to make her feel welcome. Lily, on the other hand, still believed that the jokes and the kindness were all an act. She only pretended to be amused and gave a weak smile in return for his efforts.

"My apologies, sa'. I'll leave you to make your own plate then," Lily replied, feeling a little embarrassed.

"No apologies required, my dear. It's quite alright," William smiled, as Lily picked up her own plate and began to scan the array of food on the table. When she stepped away, William turned his attention to James. "So James, are you willing to divulge the secret of how were you able to talk your father into this whole transaction?" he asked, as Lily found a few items to add to her plate. "From all that you've explained to me about him, I'm surprised that he was okay with this little *arrangement* we've got."

"Well, truth be told, I don't think he was okay with it at all. But he's 'spectin me to take ova' the farm soon, so I told him that if that was the case, then I wanted to start makin' some of the decisions 'round there, the way I see fit. 'Specially matta's relatin' to the slaves."

Lily cringed on the inside after hearing him boast about his new duties.

"Ahh, very clever! It's certainly true that there comes a time when a father has to start trusting his son to take over his legacy."

"That's exactly the point I's tryna make to him. But I guess it's a little hard for a man to let go of the reins sometimes, no matta' how much he might trust his own son."

"A statement I'm sure you'll fully understand when you become a father yourself one day."

"Yessa', I'm sure that's true. I'll just have to take your word for it, for now, I guess."

"Well, in any case, I guess it's really not important how you got Lily here, is it? She's here, that's all that matters."

"I reckon it is."

Lily was already thoroughly annoyed by their manly small talk and did her best to tune them out as she decided what to eat out of the massive spread of food.

"I must admit, I've been looking forward to this since the day you came and talked to me about her," William continued. "One doesn't get many opportunities like this in their lifetime with a young lady such as Lily," he said, smiling at her, as she gathered the last of the food she wanted onto her plate.

Hearing what William just said, and seeing the way that he smiled at her afterward, made Lily feel sick to her stomach. She thought that it would be another one of his slaves that would impregnate her, but now she wondered if William was going to do the honors himself, if he would truly be sick enough to pleasure himself and then callously reap the financial benefits of one of his own children, just as her father had done. Just the thought of it made her loathe him even more.

Lily suddenly looked at James with a face that exuded her disdain for him. She could not believe that he had the audacity to make her sit and eat across from a man who looked forward to being her rapist. She had confided in James long ago about what her father had done, yet here he was now turning her over to a man with equally perverted morals. She waited for James to turn to her, and when he did, she did not blink, hoping that her eyes conveyed her unforgiving anger for what he was doing to her.

"Sa', is it a place where us servants s'pposed to eat they food?" Lily asked William, while still looking at James, not fearful of his reaction or any accompanying punishment for her misbehavior.

"Now you just sit right down and eat your meal with us. You aren't on the Adams farm anymore. I know that may be a strange adjustment, but I won't have you thinking that servant nonsense while you're here," William replied with lightness and kind reassurance in his voice.

Lily was hoping that he would have sent her away to avoid being in a room with two men who disgusted her. She instead sat amongst them as the pair chattered on for at least half an hour about topics that did not interest her in the least. They were both completely unaware of how she was seething inside while she picked at her food, ingesting just enough to sustain her life. She did not remember tasting any of it. It was yet another symptom of her melancholy state of mind. Nothing gave her pleasure, joy, or happiness anymore; even breathing seemed like an insurmountable chore. She found herself wishing to find a means of escape from the dining room, from William's plantation … from her own life.

After sensing James's lack of remorse for bringing her there, Lily felt her spirit crumbling into a million little pieces. He seemed so coldly content for William to steal her innocence, to emotionally and physically wound her. She detested herself for believing that this very same man had once loved her. Despite the fact that there had never been any verbal admission by James about such a thing, she thought she had felt his love at one point in her life. But the fact that he had actually kept his word about her punishment, and had literally dragged her there to face the greatest tragedy of her life, made Lily realize that what she once thought was love was nothing more than an illusion.

"Well, it's awfully late," William said, putting his pipe down after his long-winded conversation with James. "And as you know, we've got business to take care of come early morning," he said, looking in Lily's direction with a smile. She wanted to vomit at the sight of him looking so joyous over something that was about to devastate her in the worst way.

"William," James said, standing up and reaching his hand out for him to shake. "You've been more than kind to allow us to rest a while this evenin'. And I thank ya' for this fine dinna'. Again, my apologies for the late arrival."

"Not a problem at all. Life doesn't always go as planned, now does it? Better late than never," he smiled again. "Come, come, let me show you to your rooms."

Lily followed behind the both of them with her head hanging low. Absorbing the beauty of the massive mansion no longer interested her. She knew there was no point in it; she was sure that after James was comfortable in his room, all she would see from then on was the dilapidated walls of the slave quarters anyway.

"You'll be here tonight, James," William told him, after opening a set of double doors on the first floor at the end of a long hallway. The bedroom looked more like a miniature home than a guest bedroom. "Anything you need, you can call after Ben, the gentleman you met earlier at the door. He'll be glad to get you anything you need."

"Mighty kind of you, sa'," James replied, looking around at the beautiful room in awe, just as Lily would have if the heaviness of her sorrows had not been weighing down her heart and her head.

"Ben will also be waking you for breakfast, bright and early," William explained.

James nodded his head. "I'd appreciate that."

"Rest well until then."

"I certainly will. Thanks and goodnight."

"Goodnight," William replied just before he closed the doors.

Lily stood with her hands clasped together in the middle of the hallway, now completely alone with the man she was convinced she would have her first *unwelcomed* intimate experience with. She did everything she could to remain calm as he walked toward her. She continued looking down at the floor as if she would somehow find a route down there to make her escape. She searched her mind for what to do: cry, scream, claw, scratch, run, vomit. Suddenly, though, the only thing Lily finally found was the strength to accept her fate.

Unexpectedly, William gently took Lily by the arm. She jumped slightly and let out a startled gasp. "I'm so sorry. I didn't mean to frighten you," he exclaimed, close enough for the sweet scent of his tobacco breath to overwhelm her sense of smell. Unable to conjure up a coherent reply in her racing mind, Lily simply stared at him in return. He held his hand out in front of him. "Right this way, my dear," he said, before releasing her.

Lily fell into step behind William as he led the way. For once in her life, she could not wait until she reached the slave quarters. She was eager to get as far away from him as possible. He guided her down the hallway back toward the front door and turned to go up the stairwell. He began marching his way up but then heard the front door open behind him when he was halfway up. He turned around looking perplexed. "Lily? Where in the devil are you going?"

"Out to the quarta's, sa'."

"The quarters?" he asked, looking confused.

"Yessa', the slave quarta's."

William laughed, making Lily feel embarrassed about her assumption. "Well, my lady," he began, as he marched back down the stairs toward her. "As I told you at dinner, you are *not* on the Adams farm anymore," he reiterated, as he reached around her to shut the massive front door. "There will be no fixing food, nor serving it, nor cleaning, nor washing and…" he explained, grabbing both of her shoulders and looking at her in a way that she was uncertain how to interpret. "I most certainly will *not* have you sleeping outdoors." He extended his arm in the direction of the stairs. "Your room is right this way."

Lily did not like the feel of his hands on her. Even through her dress, his touch repulsed her. The way his eyes danced over her face disgusted her. The pipe odor that lingered in his pores made her nauseous. The fact that she had to sleep anywhere in the vicinity of the man she believed to be a twisted sexual predator, who would soon be forcing himself on her, made her long for her haystack in the run-down accommodations of the Adams farm. She would have slept in a horse's stall, with no covers, near piles of manure, over being a guest in William's home if she were given the choice.

As William guided her up the stairs, Lily saw Ben out of the corner of her eye, glancing at her with a look of empathy. Her humiliation ran even deeper, knowing that even the house slaves knew what was shortly to become of her. Her legs fought with her every step of the way as they ascended the stairs, but against her mind and her body's will, she was soon standing helpless at the top of the grand foyer, mere feet away from the room where she was sure her life was about to change.

She walked meekly behind William to the end of another long hallway that led to the east wing and yet another set of double doors. He pushed them open and revealed what Lily reasoned could not possibly be a guest bedroom, but rather William's personal master suite. There was a canopy bed with lavish bedding décor, sitting on top of a stage-like platform in the middle of the room, accessed by two steps. To the left of it was a fireplace with a reading sofa in front of it, and to the right were bookcases with leather-bound classics and a writing table nearby. The curtains on the windows touched the ceiling, and trailed all the way down to the floor, sprawling out like the train of a wedding dress. It was a room designed for a king, or in Lily's mind, the owner of the home.

Being offered an actual bed of any kind would normally have caused Lily to be overcome with joy, but under the current circumstances, she simply fought to keep her food down. She thought that she at least had the evening to herself before having to succumb to the evils of a man she wanted nothing to do with.

"This will be where you'll stay for the evening," William expressed with joy on his face, walking to the center of the room and seeming to burst with pride. "Come, come," he said excitedly, in his British accent, waving Lily over. "This room possesses some of my most treasured family heirlooms. My father and I built this desk together when I was just a boy. One of my most fond memories with him. And these books," he explained, grabbing one off of the shelf. "They were all books that my father would read to us after dinner every night." He paused as he thumbed through the one he was holding. "Oh, and over here," William continued, guiding her up the two small steps to the bed. "My mother hand stitched this quilt herself," he told her, as he glided his hand over the folded treasure at the end of the bed. "She was a master seamstress," he said, pausing and staring into nothing as he remembered his mother for a moment.

With all that Lily was surrounded by, it confirmed to her that the room most certainly had to be William's. She offered no response or reaction to the excitement of his nostalgia. She was too busy emptying herself of any feelings and emotions, numbing herself in preparation for what she believed was coming next. Standing so close to the bed with William just inches away, her heart began to beat wildly against her chest.

William suddenly reached an arm out and gently touched Lily on the shoulder. Feeling her skin crawl underneath his hand, she flinched slightly. She closed her eyes, and her mind reflexively began to drift away into a parallel world to protect her fragile emotions. Suddenly, she felt him no more. William's scent was gone, and she was all alone in the room, so her mind told her.

"Well, Ben has set your belongings in the chair over there," William said with a smile, removing his arm from Lily's shoulder. "If you need anything further, just let him know. He'll be glad to assist you. Get plenty of rest this evening m'lady, you'll certainly need it for tomorrow."

Lily lifted her head and opened her eyes only to see William walking away, turning to shut the double doors behind him, but not before bidding her goodnight. To her welcomed relief, it seemed as though he was keeping his word about allowing her to rest for the evening after her journey there. Shortly after his departure, Lily heard another door shut down the hallway, startling her. Although she was alone, she was reluctant to move from the spot she was standing in. She let only her eyes parade around the enormous candlelit room, looking at every corner as if someone might creep out of the shadows and attack her.

But all she noticed after a long while was the silence. She did not hear crickets chirping or the frogs croaking. She did not hear the rustling of hay, as the other slaves tossed and turned to find comfort. If any owls were hooting, she did not hear them either, nor did she hear the growling of her empty stomach.

Lily finally let go of enough fear to step out of the spot she was standing in. She walked slowly to the window and held her hand up to it, then ran her hand along the wall. Not one crack, not a single breeze she felt. There was no way for the cold night wind to access her tender skin. She looked up at every inch of the ceiling and saw that even the rain had no way of seeking out her face as she slept. She stopped in front of the crackling fireplace and saw that she even had an alternative means of warmth, a luxury she had not had since living with her mother. She then walked back up the two steps on the platform and ran her hand over the king-sized bed, adorned with William's mother's bed linens. Lily had never in her life known the comforts of a mattress on her back, nor the softness of a pillow underneath her head … and she did not want to know. She wanted none of it, not at the price she had to pay. She would just as soon take back the croaking of the frogs, the chirping of the crickets, the hooting of the owls, the cold of the night air, the rain on her face, and laying on a pile of prickly cow's food while listening to the growling of her empty stomach, if it meant never having to give away her body and her beloved baby to a rapist.

Lily lay down next to the massive bed on the floor, balled herself up like a lonely infant, and cried herself to sleep.

Chapter Five

Slave Code
Article X Section III

If it shall so happen at any time that any Negro shall strike a white person, even in self-defense, it shall be lawful upon proof made thereof before any justice of the peace for such justice to cause for one of the offending Negro's ears to be cropped for the first offense; the second offense shall result in capital punishment.

A single ray of sunlight had yet to peek along the ridge of the eastern sky. The nocturnal creatures of the night had yet to crawl back into hiding. Even the morning melody of the birds had yet to be heard. But there, Lily lay asleep, still curled up next to the bed, uncovered on the hardwood floor, with a cold hand slithering its way up her thigh. The chill jarred her from her sleep, and she instinctively recoiled to get away, bumping her head hard on the edge of the nightstand nearby.

"Don't touch meee!" she screamed, with her head throbbing, scurrying to get away while slapping fiercely at the hand that had found its way under her dress.

"Shhh, this doesn't have to be a struggle," her invader told her, pulling her close and whispering that sentiment in her ear in a tone that was heavy with lust. "Just let it happen," he continued. The scent of his tobacco and his familiar British accent easily gave his identity away.

"Get away from meee!" Lily screamed again, despite his warning.

William grabbed both of her legs in a death grip. "I said be quiet! This is what you came here for. You might as well enjoy it," he reminded her, with his face buried in her neck, inhaling her scent, despite her struggle to free herself.

"Why?!" she begged to know. "Why you doin' this to me?! Let me be!" She then reached out in the darkness,

84

grabbing for anything she could. She gripped and tugged William's hair with one hand, and knocked his spectacles off of his face with the other. In her fit of defensive fury, Lily unintentionally dug her finger deep into his eye, instantly sending him into a rage.

"Damn you, nigga!" William yelled, slapping her hard in the face, bringing her painfully into submission. "I let you stay here in my home, and you dare to disrespect me!" He scooped her body up and threw it onto the bed. Lily continued to kick and claw, scooting back until her movement was impeded by the headboard. With no place to go, William was finally able to grab and steady her legs, planting his knees firmly on top of her thighs, catching her new dress underneath. He ripped it clean down the middle to gain access to what he wanted, then grabbed both of her wrists in one hand to cease all of her movements. All Lily had left was her voice and the tears that now rolled in streams down the sides of her face and into her ears.

"Jaaames! Help meee! Jaaames! Pleeease! God! Anybody, Pleeease! Help meee!"

"Shut your goddamn mouth!" William yelled, slapping her hard again. This time drawing blood from her lip.

"Lily!" she heard as she thrashed and thrashed, still fighting to save herself from the invasion. "Lily!" she heard once again. "Lily!"

"Get away from meee!"

"Lily! Wake up!" Ben called out to her, as she lay thrashing on the floor, screaming in her sleep, acting out her dream. "Wake up, Lily!"

"Get away from meee!" she cried out again before waking up and opening her eyes, feeling totally confused as to where she was or who was talking to her. She finally caught sight of Ben looming over her and retreated backward until she bumped into the nightstand. She looked around the room with her mind racing, her chest heaving, and sweat pouring from her face. It took her a moment to collect herself and realize she was trying to escape from nothing more than a nightmare. She shamefully looked up to meet Ben's eyes. He looked just as terrified and confused as she was.

"You alright? Sh-should I get Mr. Adams?" Ben asked.

"No! No, please don't ... Please, I..." Lily struggled to find her words, after feeling horribly embarrassed.

Ben was not entirely sure how to react himself. He just stared at her, hesitant to touch her, fearful that he would only make things worse. "I-I just come to tell you that breakfast is on da' table."

"Th-thank you," Lily replied, still scrunched up against the nightstand like a scared little mouse.

Ben began to walk away but then turned around before grabbing the door knob. "You sho' you alright?" he asked with compassion in his voice.

Lily lied and nodded her head only to get him to leave. She wanted to feel alright. She wanted to feel something good for once. She wanted to feel hunger, thirst, or any other normal human function to sustain her life, anything but the chronic emotional pain that pierced her body through and through and destroyed her desire to be alive.

After Ben had shut the door, Lily continued sitting quietly against the nightstand with her legs drawn up to her chest, and her face buried firmly on her knees. She closed her eyes and drowned out all other thoughts, and memories, and sounds, and listened solely to the music she heard in her head. The mood changes in the melody took her from laughter, to love, to a feeling of floating through the heavens and back, to start the myriad of welcomed emotions all over again. She opened her eyes suddenly, though, and raised her head slowly, realizing that the music she was hearing was not her mental composition, but instead, was a beautiful melody that was penetrating her bedroom walls and had pleasantly invaded her ears.

Lily had not heard another pianist since Mrs. Adams's

death, but her music paled in comparison to what she was hearing beyond the bedroom doors. What she was absorbing instantly ceased all of her pain, dried her tears, and temporarily erased the memory of her nightmare. It was, to her, the kind of music that healed, the way hers tended to do for her. The music gave her the motivation to stand and walk toward the double doors. She opened them quietly and let the sound rise and take over her room. Without any conscious effort, she had moved from the bedroom to the top of the stairs, standing there briefly to listen. Then, like a moth to a flame, she descended the staircase, drawn toward the sound.

With the music still guiding her, Lily soon found herself standing near the entrance of an enormous library. Every wall was made of shelves, on which there was not one inch of space that did not house a book or decoration of some sort. A sparkling crystal chandelier hung from the ceiling directly over the centerpiece of the room: a magnificent mahogany grand piano. It sat with its lid raised, allowing the deep tones to erupt into the room in a way that Lily's ears were unaccustomed to hearing with the old upright piano back on the farm. When the song ended with a few soft strokes of the lower register keys, Lily was torn between wanting to applaud and wanting to cry, after being soothed by the beauty of the melody.

"It's considered rude to lurk in doorways where I come from," a voice called out from behind the piano, startling Lily. From where she stood, peering around the corner of the door frame, the raised lid was blocking the view between her and the pianist, so she did not know how he could have known she was standing there.

"I'm sorry, sa'," she replied sheepishly, stepping into the frame of the door.

"Beautiful piece, don't you think?" he asked, sounding proud.

"Yessa'. Incredibly beautiful."

"Come, come. I'll play you another."

Lily walked slowly toward the voice, with hesitancy in every step, holding her head low like an animal chastised for its misdeeds. She had done nothing wrong, but naturally exuded a sense of inferiority in the presence of white men. She made her way around the open lid of the grand piano, and William's face came into view. He looked up at her through green eyes that were wrapped in wrinkly skin, with his spectacles riding low on his long pointy nose as usual. She stopped and stood next to the piano in silence, with her hands clasped in front of her. At that moment, William began to play again and right away he took Lily to another frame of mind. His music, and the way he played it, had a way of embracing her, like she was a child in the warmth and comfort of her mother's arms once again. She listened with her eyes closed, trying not to cry, absorbing every note, locking it all away in her memory, with the hope that one day she would have the honor of soothing herself all over again with the precious melody.

"Did you enjoy that one as well?" William asked, with a smile on his face when he completed the song.

"Very much, sa'. It was beautiful. Very soothin'."

"Please, dear lady," he begged of her, using phrasing from his British roots. "No more of this 'sir' nonsense. Please call me William. It would make me feel like much less of an old man," he said, wrinkling his nose playfully at her.

"Yessa'. Sorry, I mean, Mr. William … William," she stumbled, feeling the heat rise in her body from embarrassment.

"Much better," he smiled. "Well now, I've graced you with a song. It's your turn, wouldn't you agree?" he insisted, with a cheerfulness exuding from his tone. He got up from the bench and offered it to Lily with a hand gesture.

James's words, and his level of anger, after he had

found her at his mother's piano came flooding into the forefront of Lily's mind. Playing the piano was the sole reason she was about to face a punishment more damaging than being strung up and whipped, in her opinion. That fact made the thought of touching the keys terrifying for Lily, and she began to panic. "I-I don't know nothin' 'bout playin' no piano, sa'," she lied, taking a few steps backward, staring intensely at the keys, as if they were wild wolves ready to pounce on her.

"He knows," a voice said from behind, startling Lily. She turned around to find James standing there with both hands in his pockets, leaning against the frame of the doorway.

"Sa'?"

"He knows you can play. I told him. No need to lie. Go on and play if he wants you to." As James often did, he read Lily's mind and knew that she needed to hear more, "You won't be punished for it, Lily." They held each other's gaze, and after a few moments she knew she could trust that he was telling the truth.

Lily then turned to face William, and he motioned once again for her to sit on the bench, allowing her access to yet another of his prized possessions. "Play anything you'd like, my dear."

Lily walked hesitantly toward him, looking at every inch of the piano in disbelief. She had not known they could be built like works of art. She sat down gracefully and looked at every key, familiarizing herself before lifting her hands. She knew exactly what she wanted to play, but she looked at William again, seeking approval from him with her eyes before she began.

"Go on, m'lady. It's quite alright," William reassured her.

Lily's eyes met James's as well, and they held each other's gaze again before he finally nodded his head in reassurance. After a moment, she turned her attention back to the piano, inhaled deeply, and closed her eyes. With lightness and agility in her fingers, she began tickling her way across the keys. For Lily, everything in the room faded away. The books, the shelves, and the chandelier all disappeared. William and James were no longer present. Her fears and anxieties melted away with just the lightest touch of the ivory. Like any addict who had fueled herself with her chemical of choice, she was on a high, in a place mentally where pain could not touch her, where heartache did not exist, where sorrow could not penetrate her, where tears were only from happiness, a place where nothing existed except the piano and the memory of the notes that guided her fingers gracefully along the keys.

The particular song Lily chose immediately motivated James to leave his stance against the door frame. He began walking toward her as she played, circling around the far end of the piano without taking his eyes off of her. After he had approached, he and William both began scrutinizing her every keystroke and watching the way the beautiful inner workings of her mind were written into the expressions on her face. William's eyes became transfixed on the way her hands glided effortlessly across the keys without ever missing a single note, despite the fact that her eyes were closed for most of the song. It seemed to him as though she was reading the notes as they appeared in her subconscious. He was equally impressed with her theatrics: the way her hands crossed one over the other, mimicking someone who had been taught to perform in front of an audience for years.

When Lily completed the song, William slowly removed his spectacles, as if he blamed them for deceiving his eyes. He stared at her in stone-cold silence. For once he was speechless. He then turned to look at James, who reluctantly pulled his eyes away from Lily to return William's glare for a moment.

"That sounded a lot like the song I heard you playin'

just before I walked in here," James said to William with a perplexed look on his face, referring to the song that had coaxed Lily from her room earlier.

"That's because it *was* the exact same song," William replied, with shock evident in his tone, as he turned to look at Lily again. "Every note played flawlessly." Although it was indeed the song he had played, William was astounded by the lightning speed of Lily's fingers and the fluidity with which she had just played it back, especially considering that it was her first attempt. He felt as though her choice to add speed had enhanced the beauty of the song.

"I-it was so pretty and so soothing. I just had to hear it again," Lily explained shyly.

"B-but how on earth are you able to accomplish such a thing?" William asked, truly baffled. "Is this some sort of game the two of you are playing?!" He turned to look at James again. "Y-you must have found the musical pieces I had laying around here and given them to her before your journey!" he accused, searching his puzzled mind for the answers to what he felt was an impossibility. "How else could she have just done that?!"

James felt slightly offended by the accusation but understood his skepticism. He, too, was shocked by the fact that Lily was capable of retaining music of that complexity so quickly and replaying it with such accuracy. "William, I completely unda'stand your doubts, but I assure you I've done nothin' of the sort. I honestly had no idea she was capable of doin' that eitha'," he admitted, turning and fixing his eyes on Lily, as a wave of questions swept through his mind. It was another revelation about her that bothered him deep inside.

"With all due respect, William," Lily interjected. "I couldn't read my own name if my life depended on it, let alone read any music."

The room was silent, but James swore he could hear Lily's words echoing over and over again. He turned his eyes away from her, suddenly feeling overwhelmed with guilt and shame because of the truth in her statement. He would rather have taken a knife to the stomach than to hear her say it again; it would have been far less painful.

After seeing the sincerity in Lily's face, William felt foolish for doubting her. "Lily, I'm so sorry. I shouldn't have made such an accusation. It's just that I've never witnessed such a thing in all of my life," he explained, with the truth in his statement still written all over his face.

"It's alright. I unda'stand."

"Please, I must know how you've learned to play so magnificently. Somebody must have instructed you."

"No sa'. Bein' a slave, ain't nobody willin' to teach me anything."

Her words penetrated James once again. Such a simple conversation was affecting him in a way he had not anticipated. He propped his hand against the piano to steady himself, feeling like he had been punched in the stomach again.

"Not even the basics?" William questioned.

"No, sa'," she answered. "I tell you no lie."

"Beyond your level of skill, your ability to retain is simply remarkable. I must know how you've come to accomplish this."

Reluctantly, Lily began speaking, feeling unsure of how much of her story she should tell. "Well, when I's just a little girl, James's motha'…" she paused, and looked over at James, uncertain if she should continue. He simply nodded, reading her mind once again. "Sh-she used to teach children to play piano. I used to hide at the top of the stairs and watch her, and memorize the way her fingers moved across the keys wheneva' she played, and…" she froze, feeling her fears surfacing again.

"Go on," William urged her.

"Well wheneva' I's alone, I'd play back the songs I remembered her teachin', by mimickin' the movement of her fingers. But afta' a while I didn't have to hide and see the way she played. It got to the point where I could memorize just by listenin', and then play back the notes I heard runnin' through my head."

"So, Mrs. Adams never actually gave you any personal lessons?"

"No sa'. I just push the keys that match the sound in my head," Lily clarified, touching her temple lightly.

"May I?" William asked, motioning his hand toward the piano bench.

Lily scooted over and allowed him to sit next to her.

"Close your eyes," William told her. He immediately felt her apprehension. "Only for a moment," he reassured her. When she finally relaxed and closed her eyes, he played three random notes simultaneously. "Can you play the notes I've just played?" Without opening her eyes, Lily reached up and quickly repeated the three notes. William proceeded again to play four notes, then five, and then used both hands to play six, and more at one time. Without ever looking, Lily played back every chord flawlessly.

James watched Lily in awe, just as he had many times throughout his life. He remembered thinking as a boy that she was always so great at everything she had ever done, but he knew that what he was currently witnessing her do was light years beyond great. He realized that she was born with a very special gift that left her with extraordinary capabilities. The look on William's face further confirmed that he was justified in his beliefs. The combination of it all left James thoroughly convinced that Lily—a woman who had the misfortune of being born as a slave—was truly the prodigal genius he believed her to be.

When William was finished running through dozens of various musical chords with Lily, he turned to look at her like he had found the most priceless treasure. "It is quite rare that anyone has the ability to hear a series of notes and play them back perfectly as you just did, m'lady. In the world of music, it is known as having perfect pitch. After all my years of training, I am unable to accomplish this. I've come to realize that you're either born with this ability, or you're not. It simply cannot be taught, and it most certainly cannot be learned." There was a sudden softness in William's voice as he continued. "I don't think you realize just how unique and precious a gift this is that God has blessed you with, or how special you truly are." He took Lily's hand in his. "Please, believe me when I tell you that you are truly one-of-a-kind."

Lily raised her head slowly to meet William's bright green eyes and saw nothing but sincerity in them as they gazed upon her. She had forgotten what it felt like to receive genuine words of kindness, and almost did not remember how to respond. "Th-Thank you kindly, Mr. William," she said shyly.

"I would certainly love to hear you play some more if you don't mind."

"No, sa', I don't mind at all."

Like two children who shared a favorite toy, Lily and William continued playing on through the morning, one song after another. Each of them showed the other their favorite compositions, and at times easily played songs together in harmony. William was instantly mystified by her. Of all the people he had known with years of fine piano instruction, he had never seen one who had achieved the level of professionalism he was witnessing in Lily. He felt honored to be sitting beside a young woman whose hands and prodigal mind he was convinced had been touched by God Himself.

James had sat down and was watching the pair quietly from the corner, wondering how Lily was able to hide that side of her from him through the years. He wondered what he had done to make her feel as if she could not trust him with such an unbelievable secret. It stung him deeply as he watched her play and kept him from fully enjoying the symphonic sounds erupting in the room. He even began feeling a twinge of irrational jealousy after noticing that William and Lily seemed to have a profound connection with one another rather quickly.

"Excuse me for interruptin', but lunch is ready," Ben announced from the doorway.

"My goodness, is it lunchtime already? Why, we've been here all morning," William said, pulling out his pocket watch and glancing at the time. "You must be starving by now," he said, patting Lily's hand gently. "You go and have your fill. James and I need to head into town to handle some much-needed business, but you are more than welcome to continue playing whenever you'd like."

After being touched by William's music and his kind words, for the first time in days, Lily felt a slight return of her appetite. She was initially floating on the clouds after being temporarily allowed to play her beloved instrument again. However, as she walked toward the door, she caught a glimpse of James in the corner, and she suddenly wondered the nature of the "business" that he needed to handle in town with William. It quickly reminded her that soon she would be forced to face her inevitable punishment. With that thought, Lily instantly fell from her high back into the hell of reality. Suddenly, the little desire she had for food vanished, along with her desire to continue playing.

Chapter Six

Manumission:
The act of a slave owner freeing his slaves.

Slave Code
Article IV Section III
*Masters, when twenty-five years old, shall have the power
to manumit their slaves, either by testamentary
dispositions, deed of manumission, or by their last will and
testament.*

Even though William had offered it, for three whole
days, Lily found that she still had no interest in playing his
piano. There was something that sickened her about the
way that he and James would traipse off together after
breakfast each morning, claiming that they needed to
handle some "business" in town. After hearing that, Lily
simply could not bring herself to play, nor be in the same
room with either of them anymore. "Business," she
assumed, had everything to do with what James had
originally dragged her there for. In Lily's mind, there
seemed to be no other explanation for the two to be
conspiring together. With her belief in that so strong, Lily
began to have a paralyzing fear that they would eventually
take her along with them after their negotiations, and drop
her off in some foreign place, leaving her there to do the
sort of "business" they were expecting from her, with some
man she had never met.

The notion of what Lily would soon face brought on an
anxiety that was far too overwhelming for her to overcome.
Despite the fact that William and James were gone from
sunup until late night, Lily craved solitude. She remained
hidden in her room, politely declining requests for meals by
claiming she was not feeling well. Having quickly plunged
into a state of immobilizing depression, that claim was not

far from the truth. The emotional and mental pain of her despair was indeed taking a toll on her health. Even her free reign to play the piano was not enough to alleviate the aching of her soul. There was not a song worth playing, or one she felt she could ever compose, that would soothe even the thought of losing her child. Death, she still felt, was her only solution.

The constant desire to end her life trumped most of Lily's other thoughts as she lay on the cold hardwood floor next to her bed, hour after hour, for the three days she had been in William's home. The thought of it even kept her from sleeping. On the few occasions she was able to sleep, sickening nightmares, similar to the one she had had about William, would force her awake, robbing her of the chance to escape her emotional pain for a while. To make matters worse, neither James nor William had bothered to explain anything to her about when or with whom she would be forced to fulfill her dreaded duties. That left Lily to fill in the missing details with the horrors she had cultivated in her imagination.

Along with the awful images rolling around in her head, Lily had a question, but, ironically, it had nothing to do with breeding. There was something about William and the whole situation she had been cast into with him that did not make any sense to her. During their brief interaction playing the piano together, Lily had noticed a vibrant enthusiasm in William that was unlike any other man she had ever met. He seemed to enjoy life and being in the presence of people, and most certainly took great pleasure in music. Lily also noted that William lacked the coldness, harshness, and mean spirit she had seen in other slave owners. But what stayed with Lily more than anything were the words that William had graced her with after discovering her gift of perfect pitch. The memory of how genuine his words were penetrated the darkness she had hopelessly sunk into, filling it with a brief spark of light. It was not only William's words, though, but also the manner with which he had spoken them, with softness and sincerity, while gently holding her hand, and looking at her with such tenderness.

But despite William's kind nature and the fact that he had given her access to his piano, a beautiful bedroom, and more food than she could ever possibly eat, Lily still loathed him. Simply for the fact that he owned slaves, she considered him an enemy. She, therefore, remained guarded, always assuming that his gentle words and kind acts were to earn her trust so that he could more easily manipulate her into whatever it was he would eventually want from her. Being so keenly aware of that—along with the memory of the injustices that occurred in her past after trusting a white man—Lily kept an emotional and physical distance from him. But *still*, a nagging question about William dangled loosely in her mind because of that unforgettable moment between them at the piano. That ever-present question became even more prevalent when, after three days of lying immobilized on the floor, Lily finally found the strength to get up, walk over to the window, draw back the curtains, and look out onto the massive spread of plantation land that surrounded William's enormous mansion. It was Lily's curiosity about what she saw out of the window that finally drew her from the room on the afternoon of her third day there.

Long after William and James had left for the morning, Lily quietly tiptoed downstairs and ventured outside. She stepped out from under the shadow of the porch onto the grass and squinted her eyes as the sunlight hit her face for the first time in days. She appreciated the feel of the warmth on her skin as she then walked from one end of William's land to the other. While absorbing all of the sights surrounding her, Lily began to realize that perhaps all of her fears, nightmares, and worries were unwarranted. At the same time, however, it left her feeling even more perplexed about her situation and about who this William Werthington really was. The culmination of what she had witnessed after her leisurely stroll and of her unwavering curiosity, finally gave Lily the confidence to get answers to all of the things she had been truly puzzled by. However, she had no desire whatsoever to seek clarity from James. She had an intuition, though, that she could trust two people in particular, to give her insight without worrying about the potential consequences her questions may have carried if she were to ask James.

Anna Mae and Ben, the elderly Negro couple who took care of the home, were in the kitchen working on their long to-do list to prepare for William's upcoming fundraising gala, which was only a few weeks away. It was an event that William's wife, Emma, had begun years prior. It started small but then grew into a massive annual event that welcomed some of the town's most prominent well-to-do citizens. Emma had put her heart and soul into perfecting it and very much looked forward to every year. Despite his wife's death, William continued the gala in her honor.

Anna Mae and Ben were diligently working on party decorations for Emma's gala, but both turned toward the kitchen door and froze after Lily suddenly entered. She had just returned from her stroll in the yard and now stood there meekly looking at the both of them. The elderly couple was happily surprised to Lily; it was the first time she had willingly left her room. They had both become concerned about her well-being after the nightmare Ben had witnessed her having. Since then, Anna Mae had knocked on Lily's door a few times every day to ask her if she wanted to eat. Noting the sadness in Lily's eyes as she politely declined, Anna Mae would set the meal on the nightstand anyway and tell her to at least try to eat a little, then pat her gently on the arm and leave Lily to her solitude. Lily always noticed Anna Mae's concern, and she very much appreciated the couple's compassion and their efforts to make her feel comfortable. In fact, it was because of their warmth that Lily approached them in the kitchen after her much-needed walk around the plantation, trusting that perhaps they could give her the clarity she was hoping for.

The question that Lily finally found the heart to ask them brought the party preparations to a standstill. The couple soon found themselves seated together at the dining room table as they told Lily a story that brought a blend of painful, yet happy, memories of a moment in time that changed their lives forever. Even Ben could not hold back a few stray tears while recalling what had happened to them so long ago.

When the story was over, Lily stood up and glanced out the window as she heard William and James approaching in their carriage. "I knew a man as kind as that once," Lily told the couple while staring directly at James, comparing him to a certain man in their story. Lily was sure to wipe away her tears before James entered the house. He stormed through the kitchen door, looking extremely frustrated, and breezed by her without so much as a hello or a glance in her direction. His actions did not faze Lily, though; her skin had become impenetrable to the coldness her former friend emitted.

Later that same evening, Anna Mae was making her way up to Lily's room to see if she was hungry but was surprised that she was already heading down the stairs. Feeling motivated by what she had seen on the plantation and by the story she had been told earlier in the day, Lily decided to join William and James for dinner on the porch instead of hiding away in her room. Both men ceased their conversation after she quietly stepped outside and stood there looking quite nervous.

"Oh, well good evening, m'lady!" William smiled, surprised to see her. "Please make an old man happy and tell me that you'll be gracing us with your presence at dinner this evening."

"I's very much hopin' to, Mr. William."

"Delightful!" William stood and pulled out her chair. Anna Mae smiled from the doorway and went to retrieve a plate of food for her, while Lily walked meekly toward the seat he had pulled out. She sat down and placed a cloth napkin in her lap, feeling hesitant to lift her eyes up after doing so.

"Please forgive my absence throughout the past few days," William began, as Anna Mae sat a plate of fried chicken, green beans, and mashed potatoes in front of Lily. "I'm afraid I haven't been much of a host since you've come here, but I hope that Anna Mae and Ben have been gracious substitutes."

"No need to ask forgiveness. I know y'all are busy. And, yes, Ms. Anna Mae and Mr. Ben done been more than kind to me."

"That's wonderful to hear," William replied, smiling at her. "So tell me, have you taken the opportunity to play again since…"

"William, could I see you for a moment?" Anna Mae interrupted while standing in the doorway, with a tone in her voice that made the matter seem urgent.

"Certainly," he replied, removing his napkin from his lap and excusing himself from the table.

Lily was now left to sit alone, face-to-face with James. She had felt extreme discomfort sitting there before William left, but with his absence, the discomfort grew to another level. As awkward and anxious as Lily suddenly felt, though, she wanted to seize the opportunity to speak to James alone.

Lily twirled her spoon around in her mashed potatoes, before clearing her throat and finding the courage to speak. "I-I, umm, been meanin' to tell you, thank you."

"For what?" James asked flatly, still shoveling food in his mouth.

"For the unda'garments and the new dress. They's real

101

nice."

"I figured it was due time for new ones, that's all," he responded matter-of-factly.

"Whateva' the reason, I thank you."

James suddenly stopped eating. "You're welcome," he replied after a moment, as if it was one of the most difficult things he ever had to say.

It had been years since the two of them had had a civil conversation. The tension between them was so thick in the air it was almost visible. James returned to his meal when a few awkward moments had passed without a word, but Lily could not continue to hold on to what she truly wanted to say. "I had a real long talk with Anna Mae and Ben this afta'noon while you and William was out," she began, as she watched James continue to eat. He still did not bother to look up from his plate. She continued to speak, though, despite the fact that he seemed not to be paying attention. "They say they used to live down in Georgia a long time ago. They was workin' togetha' on the same plantation there with their two children. Of course they didn't like the idea of bein' slaves, but they was just glad they was all togetha' as a family and all. But then Anna Mae told me that afta' several years the owna' of the plantation decided he was gonna sell some of his slaves. Anna Mae, Ben, and they two children was among the ones he planned to do away with. She say he needed the money any way he could get it, even if it meant splittin' up families." Lily's voice suddenly began to quiver. "So he took 'em all down to the Negro auction and…" She stopped for a moment and looked at her wrists as they lay in her lap, remembering the red marks that her mother had left there from holding on to her so tightly the day her father dragged her away to be sold.

James finally stopped eating, laid his fork down slowly, and stared at Lily in a way that let her know she finally had his undivided attention. She looked up from her wrists when she felt a sudden change in his disposition and met a pair of eyes that were still stunningly beautiful to her. It reminded her of the first time they had come face-to-face in the woods as children. She had forgotten how easily she could get lost while looking into them. The look in James's eyes rattled her confidence to continue speaking, but also brought her a sense of comfort all at the same time, just as they had all those years ago as she stood staring into them near the creek.

Lily had to force herself to look away. She cleared her throat and cautiously continued. "H-he dragged 'em all down to the Negro auction. When they got there, Anna Mae said she was cryin' like she ain't neva' cried before in all her life. She was holdin' on to Ben and her children so tight, she had to be whipped one good time just to let 'em all go."

The expression on James's face, upon hearing of Anna Mae's whipping, did not escape Lily's notice. He suddenly let his eyes wander away from her face and down to the table. She always read his subtle gestures well and was surprised that it seemed painful for him to hear such a thing, but Lily did not let it stop her from continuing the story. She had to free her mind no matter how uncomfortable James might feel hearing what she had to say.

"She say Ben was the first one their owna' marched up onto the auction block. Back then they called 'em Big Ben. He was strong and worth quite a bit of money, and there was hands flyin' up in the air everywhere tryna get bids in to buy 'em 'fore he could even get all the way up the auction block steps. Once they was well into the biddin', Anna Mae say she noticed it was one man in the crowd who was raisin' the bids by a hundred dolla's every time someone tried to outbid him. One-by-one, folks was quickly droppin' out of the auction, and all their eyes drifted toward him when they realized that he just wasn't gonna quit 'til he got what he wanted … And they were right. When there was only one man left to challenge him, he raised the bid by five hundred dolla's and it was ova'. He had purchased Big Ben for twice the amount most slaves his size was goin' for, but despite all the money he'd just spent, he still wasn't finished. He stood out in that hot Georgia sun that day and didn't stop biddin' 'til he got himself three more slaves. And when he did, he loaded 'em all up in his carriage, and brought 'em all back to his home … *Right here* on this very plantation."

James still just sat there watching Lily closely, without saying a word, entranced by the compassion in her voice as she spoke.

"*William,*" Lily finally revealed. "He was ridin' through that town in his carriage right before that auction started and seen Anna Mae holdin' on to her family, cryin' like the devil was rippin' her soul apart. He pulled ova' and bid every dolla' he could to buy her, Ben, and they two children. And just as soon as they set foot on this here plantation, he signed they papers and set 'em all free. Every one of 'em," she whispered. "They's free as birds," she said, looking out into the trees, wondering what that kind of freedom must feel like.

"William told 'em all they could stay here in his home for as long as they liked until they got on their feet. In return for his hospitality, Ben and Anna Mae decided to take on the responsibility of cleanin' and cookin' all the meals and helpin' with his children. Eventually, they all became so close that William didn't want any of 'em to leave. His wife especially begged them to stay because her two boys had become so close to their children, and she sho' appreciated them keepin' her company in this big ol' house wheneva' William was travelin'. And in all these years, Ben say William and his wife ain't neva' treated 'em like anythang less than they own kin folk. Both of 'em swear William got a heart bigga' than the moon itself."

Lily paused for a moment and briefly looked out onto the plantation fields. "Masa' James, I's walkin' out on those fields today, and I realized that the very man you claim to bring me here to breed for don't have one row of cotton or tobacco in his fields, no slave quarta's, and not one slave eitha'. So afta' seein' how empty these fields were, I just couldn't help but ask Ben and Anna Mae who this William fella was and where all his slaves were. They both laughed and said I'd neva' see a single solitary slave roamin' around within these gates. Anna Mae said William neva' believed enslavin' folks was right. In fact, she said he worked for years with some anti-slavery society ova' in London, and even raised money to help fund their fight to abolish slavery. He was standin' there proudly side by side with memba's of parliament when they signed the Slavery Abolition Act into law in 1833. Ben said a big part of the reason William came to the United States in the first place was to help in the fight against slavery here. He was even heavily active in the anti-slavery movement with some group here called the Republican Party until his wife passed away.

"So afta' hearin' those incredible stories, it just didn't make much sense to me why you'd bring me to a man like him to be bred … not until Ben and Anna Mae told me one otha' thing about William." Lily looked directly at James. "They say he ain't just some rich farmer that happens to know how to play a piano. They claim he's a man that done been all ova' the world playin' piano in symphonies since he was just six years old, and that he became one of the most well-known composa's and musical conducta's in all of the United States and even ova' in Europe. Ben say he eventually became a music teacha' at the university you attended, and that he was even willin' to teach both of they children … two *Negro* children," she emphasized, "how to read and write, but most importantly … how to play *piano*."

James continued to stare at Lily for a moment in silence before slightly nodding his head. "I know, Lily," he finally replied in a faint voice, sounding as if he was ashamed to admit that he had withheld the knowledge of the inspirational story.

A glimmer of tears began to form in Lily's eyes after James's admission. "They also told me that we's here in, Ohio … a *free* state. Is that true?"

James nodded again. "It is," he replied sheepishly.

Lily's eyes drifted down to her hands for a moment as she searched for the courage to ask the question she finally wanted to have answered. "James," she said softly, fighting to keep her tears from falling, "You ain't eva' really had any intention on breedin' me at all…" There was suddenly an immense amount of hope written into her facial expressions when she finally glanced back up at him. "Did you?" she whispered.

"James!" William interrupted from the mansion door.

"Yessa'," he said, without turning his attention away from the beautiful woman in front of him.

"Could we borrow you for a moment?"

"Yessa'," he replied again while watching the tears that he knew Lily was fighting hard to keep from escaping. He kept his eyes on her for a moment longer before rising and leaving the table without ever saying another word. But he didn't have to. The expression on his face had answered all of Lily's questions with crystal clarity. She had seen that expression often, once upon a time, during years that included some of the happiest Sundays of her life. Based on that expression alone, Lily now knew for a fact that her friend was still in there somewhere and that he had undoubtedly revealed himself to her in a major way for the first time in many, many years.

While everyone was inside, Lily tiptoed past the kitchen where they had all congregated trying to fix something, and she stopped in William's library to stare at his grand piano. She never even knew such a beautiful version of the instrument existed, let alone that she would ever have the luxury of playing it. In her eyes, everything about it far exceeded the definition of grand. She walked around it and ran her hand along the artistically carved lines that were engraved on the side of it, then stepped back to absorb the entire beauty of the masterfully crafted piece. In that moment, the desire to play again began raging inside of her. She held off for the time being, though, and went upstairs, wanting to be alone with her thoughts for a while. She entered the room that William had so generously allowed her to stay in, but this time, everything looked different to her. Everywhere she turned, the colors seemed so much brighter, she noticed the patterns in the curtains, and every detail of the décor. The scent in the air was inviting, and there even seemed to be a warmth there she had never sensed before.

Lily walked over to the window, drew back the curtains, and watched the last piece of the sun hanging in the sky. It was one of the most beautiful sunsets she had seen in years. She closed her eyes while it warmed her body, and let the images of James's face at dinner appear in her mind. Standing at that window with him in her thoughts, Lily began to breathe again for the first time in weeks, without feeling as if she had to force herself to take every breath.

After every inch of the sun had faded away into the horizon, Lily lit an oil lamp and then walked over to a bookshelf and glanced over the array of William's books. She selected a rather large novel and opened it to a random page, only to be overwhelmed by a sea of meaningless letters staring back at her. She suddenly wished there was an oak tree with a blanket spread out at its base, and a familiar face seated next to her who could decipher the words to her as passionately as he once did.

Lily then glanced up from the book, and the bed she

had refused to lie in was in her line of view. Like the open arms of a mother, it suddenly seemed welcoming to her. As she walked over to it, she looked down at the cold, uncomfortable area of the hardwood floor where she had lain for three days and recalled the disturbing nightmare she had had about William. She suddenly felt guilty for dreaming such a horrible thing about a man whose heart she now believed should be replicated and placed in the chest of every human being.

William's mother, Lily finally noticed, was certainly the master seamstress he had boasted about. The patterns of the quilt she had made were unlike any other Lily had ever seen. She now understood why William cherished them so much. Lily placed the book on the nightstand and reached down to feel the bedding. She suddenly could no longer resist the need to let her body experience the softness and comfort of linens that felt like they were made by a woman who wanted her children to feel wrapped in love as they slept. She lay down slowly onto the mattress and let the plush covers melt around her body. The feeling was so foreign to her, but it only took a moment for her body to admit that it never wanted to go back to hardwood floors or haystacks ever again. Nestled in the comfort of a real bed for the first time in her life, Lily drifted off quickly into a deep sleep. She fell into her slumber without her face surrounded by a puddle of her own tears, because she knew now that, despite the evil shell Jesse Adams had sculpted around his son, deep inside of James there still beat a heart filled with compassion.

Lily rested peacefully that night, but the same could not be said for James. He lay in his bed tossing and turning, awakened by a recurring nightmare that he had become all too familiar with over the last eight years of his life. The nightmare was triggered by a gruesome memory that had been seared into his subconscious at the tender age of sixteen, in the late-night hours of the very same day his father had found him helping Lily scrub the kitchen floor. The torturous memory was created after he was forced that night to witness an incident that took less than ten minutes to imprint itself, seemingly forever, on his impressionable young mind. The grisly details left visuals in his head that would make him sick to the point of regurgitation every night in the first few months that followed the horrific event. It ended up being an event that drastically changed who James was as a man, along with every decision he would ultimately make in his life moving forward.

James had since gained control of his stomach during the nightly episodes despite the memory eclipsing his mind whenever he closed his eyes at bedtime, but the nightmares, night sweats, and sleeplessness persisted on a regular basis, for nearly eight years. He had adjusted to the nights of five hours of sleep, or six if he was lucky, but upon returning home again after so many years away, the night terrors had only become worse, reeking even more havoc on his ability to get proper rest.

Since arriving at William's home, whenever the gruesome nightmare awakened him, James was immediately drawn to one particular place: the outside of Lily's bedroom door. He would stand there for a few minutes fighting the intense desire to turn the knob and enter. For three nights, his rationale had won the battle, stopping him from doing something he might regret. But after sitting alone with Lily on the porch, absorbing the sound of her voice and the beauty of her soft features, his intense desire to see her finally laid to rest what little willpower he had left to stay on the opposite side of the border in between them.

James unlatched the door and walked in as quietly as a church mouse, unprepared with an excuse if Lily happened to be awake. He simply did not care. There was so much he had wanted to say to her at dinner anyway, but silence, he believed, was his only sane option for the time being. If he said what he truly wanted to say, he had no doubt that the sprinkle of tears glistening in her eyes would have turned into a downpour. But the way he felt, upon entering her room, he knew he would continue to abandon all rationale and tell Lily the perils that were at war in his mind … things that he had kept to himself for years.

James's eyes adjusted to the darkness and he walked over to find Lily curled up, sleeping peacefully, with not one blanket on top of her to keep her warm. He reached down to the end of the bed, pulled the folded quilt up slowly, and placed it gently over her body. He refrained from what he instinctively wanted to do next, but just the visual of himself pressing his lips against Lily's soft skin was enough to awaken another part of his body. He took a deep breath, regained control of himself, and reluctantly sat down in a chair near the bed and watched her sleep. It was a ritual he had started as a teenager when the night terrors began to strike. Much like this night, Lily was completely unaware that James was so comforted by her presence while watching her chest rise and fall, as she lay there in those vulnerable moments. Such a simple tradition reassured him that she was still alive and safe, which, ultimately, subdued the horrific recurring nightmare that contradicted those facts.

On this clear night, with the curtains still drawn back, the moonlight hit Lily's face in such a way that James was able to cherish all of her angelic features for the few minutes that he sat watching over her, before slipping away into the dark of the night to return to his own bed. As soon as he lay back down, it was evident that, as always, his secret ritual still remained the one and only sleep remedy that gave him the peace of mind he needed to fall pleasantly and quickly back into a deep sleep of his own.

Chapter Seven

Slave Code
Article III Section VIII
It is a felony for any person who shall transport, secretly carry, or send away out of any state, any slave belonging to an inhabitant within it, such offenses are punishable by jail time and costs to be adjudged by the justices of the provincial court.

Lily's assumptions were accurate, and so was her intuition about William Werthington. Questioning Anna Mae and Ben about who William really was had indeed led her to the truth about where James had taken her and why. Just hearing Lily play two songs on his mother's piano was all it had taken to convince James that she was far greater than the average pianist. Those two songs had James wide awake nearly all night in the hours after discovering Lily's gift. He lay there staring at the ceiling for the longest time, mystified about how beautifully she had played.
Eventually, he began to pray. He prayed until he fell asleep. Hours later, James was jarred from his sleep. He quickly sat up, feeling convinced that God had just sent the answer to his prayers in the form of a dream. That dream drove him to immediately get out of bed and set out before dawn, headed to Ohio in search of William Werthington.

James made the two-day trek to Ohio despite having no idea where, or even if, he would be able to find the highly regarded composer. He had not heard anything about William since learning that he had retired from Ohio University years earlier. James, therefore, prayed during his journey that his close friend and fraternity brother, Harrison Mitchell, might be able to help with his search.

Harrison and James had become friends after being assigned as roommates in the dormitories at Ohio University. Harrison was a tall, sandy-blonde haired, hazel-eyed rowing champion with a thin muscular frame, chiseled jaw, an infectious, broad smile and a brilliant mind to boot. He was easily the pick of the male litter on campus before James arrived a year later and subsequently demoted him to the runt. Despite being dethroned, Harrison took it in stride and quickly became great friends with James. The extraordinarily handsome pair were rarely seen without one another on the yard and at get-togethers. Despite Harrison's slight demotion, he and James were still *both* extremely popular on campus with the ladies. And they both *definitely* took full advantage of the benefits of their magnetic aesthetics as often as any sane virile man would. At gatherings, Harrison's smooth-talking ways won him plenty of women, but James's quiet mystique easily tilted the female scale in his direction. James's natural introversion unwittingly caused dozens of women to attempt to prevail as the first to unlock the mystery of his mind and his heart. Despite the selfish, cold-hearted way in which James tended to deal with women and the long list of broken hearts he left in his wake, the gossip about his intoxicating intimate prowess still kept his female counterparts eager to win his affections. Harrison gladly capitalized on James's cold-hearted ways. He was more than happy to "comfort" the leftover heartbroken women that James swatted off like flies after they had all failed at penetrating the rock-solid walls of his heart.

After graduating, Harrison put his smooth-talking ways, his quick wit, and his fast-thinking mind to work as an attorney in his hometown of Athens. Knowing that Harrison had worked and resided in the city of their alma mater his whole life, James figured that his old roommate would likely know of William Werthington's whereabouts. Fortunately, James's assumptions were correct. When Harrison was just a boy, his family had been to several of the Fourth of July celebrations and Spring Extravaganzas that William held annually at his home, so he was easily able to give James directions to William's estate.

It seemed an odd request for James to be searching for William, but Harrison never once questioned James's motive for seeking the retired musician. The fact that Harrison never wanted to pry personal information out of James was a rare trait amongst small town people. It was something that James always appreciated about him. Harrison never wasted time trying to decode who James was as a person, nor did he ever divulge stories about their weekend party adventures and create unnecessary gossip in school. Harrison was always much more concerned with just having a good time with his longtime friend. He was trustworthy and loyal, and treated James like more of a brother than J.R. and Jacob had. It was another one of the reasons that James had come to his fraternity brother first when he returned to Athens in search of William. With Harrison's proven level of loyalty, James never once doubted that his search would remain a secret, without ever needing to tell Harrison it needed to be.

After catching up with Harrison over a brief lunch at Buck's Tavern, James began making his way to William Werthington's estate. Despite venturing there unannounced, he was fearlessly prepared to ask the world-renowned musical genius for an astronomical favor. James prayed all the way there that his words alone would be enough to move William to help, the way that Lily's music had moved him to ride two days in search of a man he had never formally met. James's two-horse team pulled him down a long tree-lined, decorated dirt trail that eventually led to two large, partially opened steel gates with the words "Werthington Estates" sculpted into them. Inside of the gate, William's expansive, white plantation-style mansion sat perched in the middle of fields of endless, perfectly manicured green grass, with shrubbery, trees, flowers, fountains, and sculptures strewn about. The entire visual looked to James like the grounds of a king's palace.

On his two-day journey there, James had gone over what he wanted to say to William a million times in his head, but as he climbed down from his wagon, a sudden bout of nervousness threatened to destroy his ability even to speak. He stood there a moment and looked up at William's beautiful home in utter amazement. It was a sobering reminder that he was about to speak to a man of great means, wealth, and power, and that he needed to present himself as a man on that level, who possessed the utmost confidence. After reminding himself of the reason he was there, and the impact it could potentially have, pulling himself together suddenly became easy.

James dusted himself off, adjusted his attire, removed his Stetson hat, and fixed his hair before proceeding up the steps to knock on the artfully carved double doors.

"May I help you?" Ben asked when he finally answered.

"Yes. My name is James Adams. I's hopin' I might speak with William Werthington. Is this his residence?"

"Yes, it is. Is he 'spectin' you?"

"No, but the matta' is very urgent. I've traveled two days in hopes that I could speak with him about somethin' very important."

Ben invited him into the foyer. "Wait here a moment?"

"Certainly." James blew out a breath after Ben walked away, and immediately began pacing to calm the nerves he felt beginning to brew again.

Ben walked into William's study, where he sat reading his mail and smoking a pipe. "There's a young man at the door here to see ya'."

"Who is he?" William asked, looking over the top of his spectacles.

"I believe he said his name is James Adams."

"Adams, Adams, Adams," William whispered to himself, trying to recall anyone he knew by that last name. "Doesn't ring a bell. I don't think I know anyone by that name."

"Me neitha', but he says the matta' is urgent."

"Oh, how so?"

"I don't know, but he claims to have traveled two days to get here in hopes to speak to you."

"Two days?"

"That's what he claims."

"Interesting." That alone was enough to spark William's curiosity. "Stranger or not, I don't think I have the heart to turn someone down who's that eager to speak to me. Send him in," he said, as he snuffed out his pipe and laid it down.

Ben returned to the foyer and startled James, who was still pacing incessantly in an attempt to calm himself down. "Right this way Mr. Adams."

"Thank you." James followed Ben, but only half paying attention to where he was being led after the interior of the home made him eager to absorb the elegance of it all. It looked to him more like a museum full of fine arts and decorative antiques than a place where someone actually lived. His eyes roamed everywhere in wonderment, much like Lily's had when he brought her there days later.

"Right this way," Ben beckoned again, as he opened the double doors to William's study. "James Adams this is William Werthington." William stood, walked toward James, and shook his hand. Ben exited and closed the doors behind him.

"Hello, Mr. Werthington. Forgive me for showing up here unannounced. I thank you for seein' me despite it."

"Not a problem at all."

"I'm truly pleased to meet you."

"Pleased to meet you as well, Mr. Adams. Can I offer you something to eat or to drink? I believe Anna Mae's made chicken and dumplings, the best in the world!" he smiled.

William's smile and generosity calmed James at once.

"Thank you kindly, but I've already eaten."

"Have it your way, but I promise, your taste buds will never forgive you," he joked while motioning his hand to offer James the chair in front of his desk. James laughed lightly and sat down at the same time as William.

"It truly is an honor to finally meet you," James began.

William smiled in appreciation. "Well, thank you."

"I've heard a great deal about you ova' the years, about your music of course, among many otha' things."

"Among *other* things?"

"Yessa', actually, in all honesty, somethin' I once heard about you is part of the reason for my visit."

"Really? And exactly which *something* might you be referring to?" William replied with questioning eyes, wondering if he might suddenly need to be on the defensive.

"Well, to be quite honest, rumors."

"Ahh, *rumors*! Of course. I shouldn't have expected anything less with the way this town loves to jabber on about other people's lives," he said, waving his hand in the air dismissively. "But now, if I might be quite honest with *you,* Mr. Adams. If you have truly traveled two days to speak to me, as Ben has just informed me, then I have to believe that this conversation will eventually lead to something much more important than any silly rumors." He leaned back, placed his elbows on the chair, and touched the tips of his fingers together in front of him, suddenly looking at James very seriously over the top of his spectacles.

"Yessa', *far* more important, I assure you of that," James responded quickly. "But I can also assure you that there really won't be a need to carry on with this conversation if there's no truth in the whispa's I've heard about you at school and around this town."

"And just which *whispers* might you be talking about Mr. Adams?"

"Well, I've gotten different details dependin' on who was tellin' the story, but at the core of it was always the fact that you once helped a slave family out of an awful situation."

William's curiosity was piqued after noticing the term that James used to describe their circumstances. "An *awful* situation?"

"Yessa'."

"And you say there's no need to carry on with the conversation if the story is *not* true?"

"Yessa'."

"So, you're saying that you'd actually prefer that it *was* true?" William asked, looking perplexed. He was intrigued by what this young man might want but wanted to be absolutely clear about his stance on the matter.

"Yessa', more than you know."

Because of his word choice, and the sentiment in his voice, William felt in his gut that James did not want to believe the story was true so that he could inflict harm on him, like many others had threatened to do in the past. He felt that James wanted it to be true for the purpose of something good, but still, he was a man that William did not know, and so he proceeded with caution. "Young man, why don't you explain to me the nature of your visit, then maybe I'll decide if you're worthy of hearing about my personal life."

James leaned forward and put his elbows on his knees, clasped his hands tightly in front of him, and let out a long breath before he began. "Well, sir, six years ago, I left home and went to school at Ohio University, where you once worked, to begin my training to be a medical doctor. I'd dreamt of bein' a doctor since I's just a boy. It was somethin' I wanted more than anything in my life. So when I arrived there, I was dedicated, and focused, and ready to get through with my studies as quickly as I could. I doubled up on courses and even took courses ova' the summa', but for me, that still wasn't enough. So durin' winta' breaks and afta' my graduation, I started workin' alongside anotha' doctor, who took me unda' his wing. I worked with him because it was important to me, not just to train to be an average doctor, but to be one who was *great*, and I was certain that this particula' man could guide me there. He was brilliant and one hell of a mentor. I watched him like a hawk wheneva' I's with him, tryna absorb every bit of knowledge I could. Any and everything he was willin' to show me, I clung to it. I locked it all away while I had the chance to work alongside a man that seemed to me to be a true mastermind. In fact, he was so impressed with my eaga'ness to learn that afta' I completed my degree he took me on a mission trip with him. We traveled togetha' from city to city helpin' folks. We treated all kinda folks, no matta' who they were, or what their status was. We helped 'em all. I saw things and learned things that a classroom could neva' have taught me or prepared me for. It was truly one of the greatest experiences of my life. From then on, I knew that's what I wanted to do. I wanted to travel, and take care of folks from all ova' the country the way we did for all those months.

"That doctor was undoubtedly the inspiration behind me wantin' to take my skill on the road. And afta' everything I experienced with him, you'd probably think that he was also the one who inspired me to work so hard to be *great*. But oddly, I can't give him the credit for that." James paused a moment and looked William in the eyes. "Because that honor belongs to *you,* Mr. Werthington."

William was taken aback by James's unexpected words. He was inwardly affected but kept a straight face as he continued his story.

"Because of you, I aspired not only to be a great *doctor* … but to be a great *man,*" James confessed. "I wanted to be the sort of man who was as charismatic as I had heard you were through all of those rumors. I know most folks were outraged by the fact that you'd supposedly helped a family of slaves. But for *me*..." James tapped his fingers on his chest. "It touched me deep." He shook his head, thinking back to the first time he had heard about William as a freshman. "It changed my life to finally know that there was a man like you that existed. It did wonda's for me just to *hear* that there was a person fearless enough to help otha's in need, no matta' who they were, and fearless enough to be his own man regardless of the rules of society. What that did for me, Mr. Werthington, I honestly don't have the words to adequately express. But I *can* say that in the six years since I heard your story, it's neva' once left my soul, not for one minute ... And I swear it neva' will."

William still sat there quietly, completely gripped by the candidness of this unfamiliar man's confession, noting the sincerity in his voice and eyes as he spoke.

"Mr. Werthington, that story was truly an inspiration to me, and if it's true, the way I've always believed it was, then I know I've come to the right person."

"Come to the right person for what?"

"Ya' see, afta' six years of avoidin' goin' back home, I just recently..."

"*Avoiding*?" William interrupted, suddenly feeling very curious. "A man only says that when he's running from something."

James noticed how William analyzed his every word, and realized that perhaps he needed to be more cautious about what he chose to say. "Yes, well, it's just that..." He froze and closed his eyes for a moment. "The person I had to be..." He stopped again as a rush of unwelcomed memories suddenly flooded his mind. "I ... I just couldn't," he said faintly, lowering his head momentarily like a shamed puppy.

William simply nodded his head and prodded no further, after seeing in James's face that he was deeply troubled by whatever had stopped him from returning home.

"But afta' six years of bein' away, I had to force myself to return," James continued. "I knew I needed to go back before I went off to live my life on the road. Of course I had to see my fatha' and brotha's again, but more importantly, I knew I's gonna need some help while I's on the road and … well, I had someone in mind there that I wanted to take along with me."

William smiled faintly, realizing by James's slight hesitation that this "someone" had to have been a woman.

"But when I finally got home last week, everything changed," James further explained. "All the plans I had for myself and for headin' out on the road … *everything*. It all changed. Afta' what I witnessed that day, suddenly the dream I had for travelin' the country didn't seem so important to me anymore." He stared emptily at a bare area of William's desk as the memory resurfaced. "Not nearly as important as what I saw when I walked through the door that afta'noon."

"After you'd been dreaming for so long to be a traveling doctor, what could possibly make you have such a drastic change of heart so quickly?" William asked.

"The woman that I's hopin' to take along with me, she … she has a *gift*, Mr. Werthington. A gift that could take her fartha' in life than I could eva' take her in the back of my dusty wagon, draggin' her from place to place while I take care of folks. She has a gift to play the piano unlike anyone I've eva' seen," he said with conviction and an intense look in his eyes. "Her abilities are so incredible that I feel she's worthy of me puttin' my dreams on hold for a while. What she can do is so astonishing that it's guided me to travel for two days to find a man I ain't neva' met before, a man whose story that I've been prayin' every minute of the way here was actually true. Because I'm hopin', with the strength of almighty God, that you'd be willin' to help this woman too, the way you did with that family all them years ago."

William leaned back slowly in his chair after being bowled over by the compassion of James's words. Everything about James was truly riveting to him: the fact that he had traveled a great distance to seek him out, the desperation in his voice, the desperate look on his face, and his compelling story. Something so extraordinary was the last thing he had expected to hear on such an ordinary day. "I am certainly moved by your passion, Mr. Adams, but I still don't understand why whether or not the rumors are true would have anything to do with this."

James felt his heart start to race. He paused a moment, looked down at his hands again, squeezed his hat tight, and blew out a breath, knowing that his next few words could potentially be a turning point in William's decision. "The young lady who was playin' that piano…" He hesitated. "She's … she's a slave on my fatha's farm, Mr. Werthington," he finally confessed, embarrassed that he had to admit that a human being would ever be labeled as such a thing. With hesitancy, James looked up and met William's solemn green eyes, not knowing what to expect of him next.

William sat quietly for a moment, staring back at James while contemplating his surprising admission. He suddenly stood and went to look out of the window. "And what exactly would you be hoping I could do for her?" he finally asked.

James heard no hostility in William's voice or agitation over the fact that he would dare to ask for help with a Negro woman. Instead, it was a calmly stated question that showed interest and the sort of compassion that he was hoping for. The soft, simple reply settled the speed of James's racing heart since it seemed to confirmed that the story that had seeped its way into his soul so many years ago was true. It left James able to respond to his question feeling an overwhelming since of relief. "Well, I'm well aware of your level of musical talent, and the kind of power and respect you have in the field of music. So first, I's hopin' you'd be willin' to hear her play, and if you felt she needed any fine tunin' then perhaps you could help her with that. But more importantly, if you think she's worthy of it, I's hopin' you'd use your influence to help me get her some work somewhere 'round here. Ohio's a free state, and I'm sure she could earn a good wage here. I don't know, maybe she could teach children to play, or perform in small venues somewhere, or perhaps even work with an orchestra. Anything along those lines that'll give her the financial means to take care of herself."

"I haven't touched a piano, or any other instrument for that matter, in over two years," William replied, still staring out the window at his wife's heavily flowered gravesite in the distance. "Haven't taught anyone, nor worked in that field, in just as long either."

"I know this is askin' a lot, Mr. Werthington, but you're my only hope at this point. I really believe if you just give her a chance, just listen and watch the way she plays," James said, closing his eyes for a moment to remember how Lily's music had affected him that day. "Then maybe you'll think she's worth the trouble the way I do."

William turned from the window to face James with his arms folded. "And you coming here to ask all of this is something that she's asked you to do for her?"

"No sa', she has no idea I'm here."

"Hmph. Certainly lends credibility to how strongly you feel about this."

"Truthfully, Mr. Werthington, I don't think my words can do any justice to how strongly I feel about this."

"Trust me, if you were listening with my ears, I don't think you'd be saying that," William replied, staring down at James, still fascinated by the whole ordeal, and by the man who sat before him. "Have you any idea how long she's been playing?"

"Fourteen years." James shook his head in disbelief. "Claims she taught herself."

William smiled. "Really?" he replied, thinking about himself as a boy and how he had done the same.

"Yessa'."

"And you'd truly be willing to put your medical career on hold for a while just to help her?"

James finally got up and stood with William near the window. "Afta' hearin' her play, Mr. Werthington, my medical career can go straight to hell for the time bein'. The sorta healin' I can do as a doctor pales in comparison to what she's capable of. She may not have eva' had one minute of trainin', but I swear 'fore God she could heal a man's soul the way she plays that piano. I ain't neva' seen or heard anything like it before in all my life." He never once blinked or turned away from William as he spoke. "And so, yes. If puttin' my career on hold for a while is what it takes to help her pursue this, then you're damn right I would."

Again, William was astounded by his passion. "Young man, I don't think I've witnessed a grander act of altruism since my wife was alive," he said, continuing to stare at James, almost as if to convince himself that he was not a figment of his imagination. "What is this young lady's name?"

"Lily."

The name instantly reminded William of something else about his wife. "Well, you bring your Lily to me, and I promise that no matter what the situation, I'll do everything in my power to help her."

"You're certain?"

"You have my word."

"I can't thank you enough, Mr. Werthington!" James exclaimed, with a great amount of relief in his voice, vigorously shaking William's hand. "I can't tell you what this means to me!"

"I think the fact that you're even here says more than enough about what this means to you."

"If only I could make my fatha' see that." James's excitement waned a bit thinking of how Jesse would be, by far, the toughest obstacle on his path to helping Lily. "Which reminds me, I'll have to send you word by letta' to let you know of our arrival because knowin' my fatha', it might take me some time to convince him to let Lily go for a while."

"May I ask why that might be?"

"My fatha' doesn't know that she can play, nor does he know about what I'm askin' of you here today, and he doesn't take the matta' of his property lightly. You'd swear he paid a million dolla's for every slave on that plantation and five million for Lily. So long as he's alive, he'd neva' let her set one foot off of that farm."

"And so just how were you planning to convince him to let you take her on the road with you when you went on your medical journey?"

"Just like how I plan to get her here … by any means necessary."

Loving James's tenacity, William smiled, nodded, and gave his shoulder a squeeze, as they began walking toward the front door. "Are you sure I can't offer you something to eat? You could have dinner and stay the night if you'd like and have breakfast in the morning before your departure. I know you have a rather long journey ahead of you. It might be best to go about it on a full stomach and well rested," William offered, as they walked down the long corridor to the entrance.

"Thank you, but I'm eaga' to get back on the road."

"Well, at least wait here and let me have Anna Mae prepare you a bowlful of her chicken and dumplings to take along with you," he smiled. "You'll thank me for it later!"

"I'd appreciate that." James waited by the door until

William returned with more than enough food to last him on his journey. "Thank you for your hospitality, Mr. Werthington. You're incredibly kind. And again, I thank you in advance for your willingness to help Lily."

"You're quite welcome, but I almost feel as though I should be thanking you. I find myself very much looking forward to meeting this lovely young lady you speak of." They shook hands again after they stepped out onto the porch. "It was truly a pleasure to meet you, Mr. Adams."

"The pleasure was all mine. I look forward to seein' you again soon." James walked away and was about to proceed down the porch steps but then stopped. "Oh, and one otha' thing. Please don't mention anything to Lily about what we're tryna accomplish when she gets here. I don't know how any of this is gonna work out, and I don't wanna get her hopes up for now. I'd just prefer to speak to her about things when I feel the time is right."

"As you wish. But a little optimism will take us far, don't you think?"

"I am optimistic, but also realistic. I know this won't be easy."

"Agreed."

"Good day, Mr. Werthington." With that, James put his Stetson hat back on and trotted down the porch steps.

"Mr. Adams," William called out when he reached the bottom of the stairs. "Are you certain that it was *just* your need for an assistant that prompted you to want to take Lily along with you on the road?" he asked unexpectedly.

James said not a word. There was nothing but the sound of the chirping birds and silence otherwise. His eyes drifted momentarily to the grass and then back up at William with a sudden innocence present in them.

"Forget I asked," William said, after the look on James's face answered his question with more clarity than he felt his words ever could. It was an answer William presumed may have had a lot to do with why James had avoided his own home for six long years. "Have a safe journey home, Mr. Adams."

James tipped his hat, climbed into his wagon, and went on his way.

William stood on the porch watching James ride off of his property. "Something tells me that it was far more than a rumor that inspired you to be a great man for all these years, Mr. Adams," William whispered to himself. "Something so powerful that I doubt you ever really needed to hear a story like mine at all."

That one-hour meeting with a man he had never met before had greatly impacted William that day. In William's estimation, James's words did not seem to be driven by his brain's superficial ability to form coherent sentences, but rather by something much more profound and complex. The entire conversation had William eagerly anticipating the arrival of the woman who had motivated a complete stranger to bare his soul.

When James set out on his voyage back to Ohio with Lily, he was not ignorant about the risk that his actions may potentially carry by asking prominent white men an astronomical favor for a Negro. Despite the fact that Ohio was a free state, and that he would have William's assistance, James was still well aware that that did not automatically mean everyone would be accepting of Lily. But those facts never once fazed him. James felt the strong presence of a divine force that worked through him. It was a voice that did not seem to know the definition of silence. Even in his sleep, it continued to tell him that Lily's existence had a purpose far beyond that of being a slave. Through her very fingertips, James felt that Lily had the potential to help subdue the ill-fated morals and the hatred that had severed society. That voice told him that Lily simply had to be heard and that the reward would greatly supersede any and all risks. And after hearing just one piano session with Lily, not only did William understand why James had been so passionate in his plea for assistance, but he too was willing to face the risks that he knew would come along with helping her to achieve success.

Feeling even more motivated by seeing Lily's talent with his own eyes, William stayed true to his word. He had set out with James, feeling cautiously optimistic, traveling to different towns, carrying out the "business" that Lily was unnecessarily concerned over. William was spending all day speaking with old acquaintances who were music directors to see if any of them had an interest in using Lily as a pianist in their orchestras. With no luck there, he and James resorted to asking owners of taverns and pubs to see if perhaps they would like to use Lily as an entertainer. However, all of them declined, many in the cruelest way, upon hearing of her color.

Three days into their search—around the same point in time Lily had finally gathered the strength to venture out of her room—the duo was pressing on in her honor. They were exhausted from traveling countless miles and talking to at least a dozen people with grim results. Despite that, they rode along still filled with optimism, and eventually found themselves in a very familiar place. At the very moment that Lily had stepped out of the front door of William's home into the sunlight for the first time in days, the hopeful pair stepped through the front doors of the very building that William had retired from two years prior. It was also the very place that James had hidden himself away for six years of his life during his quest to become a doctor. They were there to speak to Richard Wells, who had once been part of William's orchestra for decades when he was touring. William considered him as a close friend. He had even personally recommended Richard to be his successor when he retired from Ohio University. Because of that recommendation, Richard now held the title of music director there. William figured that of all the people he knew, Richard would undoubtedly be willing to help. As they walked through the corridors of the building on the way to the music department, William explained his relationship with Richard to James, which gave both of them a boost in their confidence that perhaps this was the gold they were searching for. William was so confident, in fact, that he cursed himself for having not started their search with Richard.

William and James approached the orchestra room and could hear the starting and stopping of a classical arrangement. They peered through the door while waiting impatiently for the class to end, and could see Richard standing at the podium, lecturing the brass section on how to improve the portion of the piece they were working on. The sight of the podium, the classroom, the sound of the instruments, and even the scent in the hallway all brought back fond memories for William. It casted him into a trance of sorts. Moments later, he was suddenly shaken back to the present when the students began to file out of the classroom, filling the hallways with their chatter. When the last student left, William made his way into his old music room with James by his side.

"You have them playing that piece in the wrong key, you know?" William began, startling Richard, who was scribbling notes on his music sheet. "Sounds dreadful, I tell you," he teased.

"William Werthington! You bloody bastard!" Richard erupted in an accent similar to William's. "So good to see you!" he said as they shook hands.

"Good to see you again too, old friend. This here is a friend of mine, Dr. James Adams. James, this is Richard Wells."

"Pleased to meet you, Mr. Wells," James responded while shaking his hand.

"Likewise, Dr. Adams." Richard turned his attention back to William after releasing James's hand. "Well now, I was certain I wouldn't be seeing you again until the fundraising gala for the music department at your home in a few weeks. Seems the only time of year I can catch a glimpse of the elusive William Werthington. Lord knows, it's not often that you emerge from that palace of yours anymore these days," he joked. "So, to what do I owe the honor of your visit?" he asked as they all filed into his office and shut the door.

"A favor actually."

"The great and powerful William Werthington in need of a favor? Say it isn't so," Richard replied sarcastically after he took a seat at his desk. "After all you've done to get me here, I'd be glad to do what I can for you."

"That's encouraging to hear."

"Oh, come now, how could you expect to hear anything less? Just name it, and I'll do all I can to help."

"Well, I have a friend who's in need of work."

"Let me guess, his name is James?" They all laughed at his sarcasm.

"No, Lily, actually."

"Ooohh, a lady." Richard raised a single eyebrow. "Now I'm really eager to assist," he joked again.

"Yes, she's a pianist … one hell of a pianist actually. I admit without a doubt that she's far better than anyone I've ever heard … myself included."

Richard folded his arms and raised his eyebrow again, but this time in disbelief. "Really?" he asked with seriousness finally evident in his tone.

"Yes, it's true. And you know that I'd never admit to such a thing lightly."

"Oh, trust me, I know," he replied, feeling genuinely shocked by his admission.

"She has perfect pitch, Richard."

Richard sat up straight in his seat with a curious look on his face. "You're certain?"

"I've witnessed it with my very own eyes. Tested her

myself."

"That's truly a rare gift … a gift that some claim is just an old wives' tale."

"Well, I can assure you this is no wives' tale. Not in my whole life did I ever think I'd meet someone of her caliber, especially with the few years I have left. Hell, even if I lived another five lifetimes, I don't think I'd ever be fortunate enough to meet another like her. I'm telling you, Richard, she's truly one in a million."

"In all the years I've known you, William, I have never recalled you carrying on so passionately about someone in this manner."

"I can't seem to help it. It's just that, what I saw…" He thought back to the few hours he had spent playing with Lily. "Richard, it was incredible. Not only her gift of perfect pitch, but the indescribable precision of her memory made me question my own sanity. It was a feat I didn't even know humans were capable of. She absorbed and replayed an entire song after I played it only once." He held a finger up. "One damn time!" he expressed, still in disbelief over the matter.

Richard quietly turned his head to James with an inquisitive look on his face, seeking confirmation about a story that seemed like an impossibility. James simply nodded in affirmation.

William ignored Richard's doubt-filled glance and carried on talking about Lily. "Her theatrics, and the speed and agility with which she was able to play it back, it was all just…" He shook his head. "Absolutely astonishing." William stared blankly at Richard as he continued to think of her. "The most incredible part of all is that every element of what Lily can do is simply God-given talent. She's never once had a lesson. Everything she knows, every instinct, everything she can do, she learned on her own."

Richard sat there a moment with a look of pure shock on his face while trying to wrap his head around this mysterious young lady's capabilities. "Good heavens. I've only heard rumors of such people before now. I was beginning to think that no one like that really existed, much less that I would ever be offered the opportunity to actually meet someone like that in person."

"Well, meeting her will change you in some way. I can promise you that."

James nodded his head in agreement.

"Hearing you speak of another musician with this kind of passion, I'm forced to believe you. I find myself suddenly wishing that you would have brought her along with you today. I'm now more eager to assist than ever, so that I have the honor of becoming acquainted with this young lady as soon as humanly possible. So tell me, how exactly can I help you where she's concerned?" Richard asked.

"Well, I know sometimes the students are seeking tutoring and mentoring for their music, and so I thought perhaps Lily could be of assistance here in your department as a tutor."

"That's all?"

"Yes."

"Well, as I'm sure you already know, we can always use extra tutors for the students, so, of course, that wouldn't be a problem at all."

"That's wonderful!" William exclaimed, turning to look at James, who nodded his head again in agreement.

"But if that's all you want, then there's something I just don't understand."

"And what's that?"

"Well, you've come here claiming that this young woman is a far greater pianist than yourself, going on and on about all of these incredible gifts she's been born with, but yet you want to reduce her to a simple music tutor? Doesn't make any sense to me."

William's excitement waned upon remembering that he

had yet to mention the most important element of the favor he needed to be fulfilled. "Well, we were hoping that this would only be a temporary way for her to earn some money until we can find her some permanent work with an orchestra, because, trust me, she is certainly worthy of it. She is truly brilliant, undoubtedly every definition of a genius as I've explained, but…"

"But what?"

William looked over at James, suddenly understanding how embarrassing it was for him to have to admit to what he was about to say. "She … She was once a slave," he confessed, lying about the fact that she technically still was.

Richard stared at William in silence for a moment and then began to laugh uncontrollably. James and William could both feel their optimism start to melt away as Richard continued to snicker. "Y-you're joking, right?" he asked after his laughter subsided.

"Of course I'm not joking!" William fired back with his lips pursed, suddenly feeling very irritated with Richard's behavior.

"You know, rumor has it that you retired because you had lost a marble or two upstairs," he replied, swirling his finger around his ear. "I didn't very well believe it until now, though," he laughed again.

"Enough of the jokes! Are you going to allow her to work here or not?!"

"Oh come on, William! You didn't really expect that I'd allow a Negro to work with my students, did you?" he asked, finally sounding serious.

"And why not?"

"William, how is some former slave, who has no formal education, supposed to tutor anyone?"

"I could train her myself how to go about it. She's brilliant. Absorbs everything like a sponge."

"A *sponge!* Now there's something I would gladly give her, because I'm certain that the only thing a former slave would ever be able to *absorb* is the water off of the floors around here. I simply refuse to believe that a Negro has the capacity to learn things of such complexity."

"Are you really that dense?! I just told you that she's a gifted, brilliant pianist, who possesses skills you and I could only ever dream of!"

"Well, even in the rare circumstance that she does have the capacity to learn enough to teach, which I doubt very seriously, I don't think my students would be very receptive or welcoming to a person of her *hue*. She'd be nothing but a disruption in my classroom!"

"Come now, Richard. Eventually, they won't give a damn about her complexion once you show them that you've accepted her. It's not always about *what* you know, or *who* you are, or what *credentials* you have, it's about who you know that has the greater influence. You of all people should know that!"

Richard slammed his hands on the desk and rose from his seat. "Don't you dare throw that in my face! I don't give a damn who you are, or what you've done for me!" He pointed at William. "You have most certainly come to the wrong place if you are expecting any *influence* from *me* to help with a lowly Negro! You truly *have* lost your marbles if you think I'd be willing to defame the legacy I'm trying to build here by disgracing the walls of this place by doing such a thing!"

James tensed and took a step forward, but William grabbed him by the arm before he could make another move. "Don't trouble yourself over him, James. I'm sure he'll soon be regretting his moronic words and his foolish actions much like everyone else we've spoken to before now," he said, staring his *former* friend down. "Let's go."

"Yes, do as you're told," Richard replied, dismissively waving his hand at James. "Saves me the trouble of throwing you out."

James clenched his jaws tight to keep from verbally

erupting, and clenched his fists even tighter to keep from reaching over and snatching Richard from behind the desk. With William still gripping him tight around the arm, they both turned and stormed angrily from Richard's office without another word.

Unfortunately, the way that meeting had ended was something that William and James had quickly become accustomed to in the three days they had ventured together. Infuriating rounds of ridicule, sarcasm, and laughter seemed to be a recurring theme with everyone they had crossed paths with. In every instance, it revealed the nastiness and ignorance of people William had once considered as dear friends. The annoying, predictable cycle left both men feeling utterly frustrated as they left their old university.

While their meeting with Richard had plunged them, yet again, into a temporary darkness, Lily had been slowly rising from her internal abyss toward the light after walking the grounds of William's estate, still unaware of all that James and William were enduring for her. As both men made their way back home in silence, Lily had just made her way into the kitchen and was already seated listening to Anna Mae and Ben tell the emotional tale about the day William had set them free. And as their story had ended with tears of joy for the three of them, James and William had also ended their journey back to the estate.

After riding in silence the entire way, William halted the carriage on the estate grounds, eager to share a suggestion that had been on his mind. "James, perhaps I can find Lily some other sort of work in the meantime while…"

"What?!" James snapped, instantly offended by the notion. "Are you givin' up already?!"

"No, I was just…"

"It sure as hell sounds like it to me!"

"I just thought that maybe while we searched, she

could earn some money…"

"Doin' what sort of work, huh?!" James threw his hands up. "Workin' as a seamstress?! Cookin' somebody's goddamn meals?! Takin' care of somebody else's children?!" His face was red with anger. "Don't you get it?! I don't want Lily doin' the sort of work that reminds her of…"

"Being a slave," William finished calmly, completely unfazed by his companion's sudden outburst. He quickly understood why James was so upset and felt that he was right. Lily deserved far better than that.

After listening to Anna Mae and Ben's emotional story, Lily had gone to the kitchen window and watched as James climbed down from the carriage right after his outburst. She stared at him as he marched toward the house, thinking about how much William's story had reminded her of James during his teen years. For eight years, she assumed that that compassionate young man no longer existed, but after the revelations of that day, Lily was beginning to realize that perhaps her assumptions had been wrong. At that moment, though, James had stormed into the house with an attitude, breezing by her coldly without a word and slammed his bedroom door moments later. His actions allowed the doubt about the man James *really* was to linger in Lily's mind just a while longer, before she confronted him on the porch later that evening with the true details of William's rumored story.

Just before Lily had joined them on the porch at dinner, William felt the need to make amends with James for their misunderstanding. He genuinely felt sorry for sounding defeated in the carriage earlier in the day. "James, I'm sorry about what I suggested earlier. I was only trying to help, but I completely understand why you were so upset," he told him, as soon as they sat down together. "I assure you, though, that I haven't given up."

"No, I'm the one who needs to apologize. You're doin'

so much for Lily, and I acted like a complete ass."

"Actually, you're acting like a man who cares a great deal about someone. Maybe more than he's willing to admit outwardly." Much like the moment William questioned him about Lily before leaving his home the first time, James did not verbally respond, but his eyes spoke for him yet again. And just like that last time, William let him off the hook and changed the subject. "Anyhow, I just want you to know that I stand united with you and your dream for Lily."

"I know, William. And despite what my temper may have made you think, I truly do appreciate it."

"Actually, your temper only further helps me understand how important this is to you."

"It really is."

"It is to me too, which is why I wanted to speak to you about a potential idea."

"Idea?"

"Yes, a plan that I think might help to move things along for Lily, if all else fails."

"I'm willin' to do whateva' it takes. I'm listenin'."

Before William could begin to explain, however, he ceased the conversation with a smile when he caught sight of Lily emerging from the front door to willingly join them for dinner for the first time since being dragged there. Although the conversation halted at that moment, in the days to come, as they continued to search together, William laid out his back-up plan to James. From then on, they both methodically began to put all of its elements into action.

Chapter Eight

Stripes:
A forceful stroke on bare skin from a whip, rod, or cane that oftentimes leads to stripe-like scarring.

Slave Code
Article II Section X
Persons willingly entertaining slaves, unlawfully absenting, or permitting them to be about their houses or plantations for one hour or longer shall forfeit one hundred pounds of tobacco for each hour or pay a monetary penalty equal to the cost of the aforementioned goods. Free Negroes so offending shall be whipped; not to exceed thirty-nine stripes.

Saturday
February 12, 1859
Ohio University Music Department
Fundraising Gala

Lily kept her head down staring at the piano keys. She was afraid to look up and face all of the eyes that were pasted on her as she sat at the grand piano *alone* in the midst of a sea of guests that had collected in William's library during his annual fundraising gala. The sound of meaningless chatter, the shuffling of footsteps, and the clinking of wine glasses had long since ceased after watching her performance. No one was quite sure how they were supposed to respond after her last note rippled through the air. The other festivities were easily forgettable compared to the brief show that Lily had just put on, but because of who she was, complete silence was the only reaction.

"They say ol' William been trainin' nigga's here for years!" Tucker McCormick shouted, cutting into the silence with a very demeaning tone in his voice. "Looks like he done taught himself anotha' monkey!" he added, with slurred speech from his drunken state. Tucker was never one to bite his tongue, especially if it meant he had the opportunity to degrade another human being. He slapped his hand to his knee and gave a hearty laugh after rudely reminding everyone of the rumors that had circulated for years in their town. But no one other than Tucker found his joke amusing, especially James, who suddenly appeared in his face out of nowhere.

"Mind your fuckin' mouth!" James snapped, in a tone that seemed to instantly sober the heckling drunk.

Lily finally raised her head from the piano keys after hearing James snap at Tucker. She was shocked that James had bothered to come to her defense when the deputy disrespected her near the creek on her journey to William's home, but she was even more stunned this time around, considering that James had done so in front of a large crowd. After witnessing how fiercely protective he had suddenly become, Lily continued to stare at James with a warmth running through her. But he never noticed her eyes on him or her expression of gratitude; he was still too busy trying to stare a hole into Tucker's face.

James's bold reaction made it obvious that Tucker was not the only one who had had too much to drink that night. James had certainly had his fill. Not only was he tipsy, he was aggravated by something that he had witnessed prior to Lily's performance. It left him ready and eager to pounce on anybody who crossed him, a fact that Tucker realized after spitting out his nasty words.

James had tried, but he could not seem to depart from the uproar of emotions that began in the earlier part of the day with the arrival of Anna Mae and Ben's two children, Isabel and Elijah, who had both returned to help with William's fundraiser. Their oldest, Elijah, had taken immediate notice of Lily and had not ventured far from her side from the moment he laid eyes on her.

James was there when Elijah first got a glimpse of Lily in the kitchen. He saw the way that Elijah's eyes lit up and slowly careened up and down the length of her body the moment he spotted her. Elijah then introduced himself to her and let his hand linger in hers for the longest time while shaking it, causing James to feel an irrational urge to pry him off of her. His strong desire to intervene grew as he continued to watch the way Elijah smiled at Lily and did not seem to blink while engrossed in conversation with her. But what James hated more than anything was the double take that he saw Lily give to Elijah when he first entered the kitchen. Lily had instinctively turned toward the sound of a deep, unfamiliar voice and found a man equal to James in size and height, flashing a smile at her with brilliant white teeth that stood out against his chocolate brown skin. Lily quickly turned back a second time and noticed Elijah's sculpted body covered by gray trousers, a white long-sleeved shirt, and black suspenders that clung to his muscular frame. His ensemble was topped off by a single-brimmed gray cloth hat, slightly tilted to one side, covering his tightly cropped Afro. Elijah was so well put together that even James had to admit to himself that he was worthy of Lily's second glance. But capturing a glimpse of the beautiful smile that accompanied Lily's glance was the beginning of the deterioration of James's night. After realizing her mutual attraction to Elijah, James suddenly found it difficult to focus on the importance of the plan that he and William had laid out for the evening.

After his disastrous meeting with Richard, William concluded that his words alone would never be enough to find Lily work as a musician. He realized that her abilities had to speak for her. William felt that his fundraising gala would be the perfect opportunity to give Lily a chance to showcase her talent and prove that she was worthy of working as an entertainer. As part of William's scheme, he was sure to invite everyone to the fundraiser who was affiliated with an orchestra, pub, or tavern, including the ones who were unwilling to hire Lily. Despite the ugly ending to their meeting, Richard Wells was also among the attendees since the money being generated was specifically for the Ohio University music department. In attendance as well was Tucker McCormick, a tavern owner who had stood amongst the many guests in the library rudely letting words fly uninhibited from his intoxicated mouth.

To ensure that their plan continued to run smoothly, William had worked feverishly during the party, talking to all of the prospects who could potentially be of help to Lily. James was supposed to be doing the same, but instead, he was standing in the corner of the room drinking one glass of whiskey after another, watching Elijah interact with Lily throughout the night. While he was scrutinizing the pair, several women had taken notice of James in his tailored suit with his freshly groomed face and his neatly sculpted hair. The design of his expensive attire accentuated his physique in a way that instantly turned the heads of every lady who breezed by him, many of whom stopped to introduce themselves in hopes of winning his affections. But for James, they were just an endless stream of blank faces who could barely win his attention, let alone his affections. He was way too focused on Elijah stealing every moment he could to whisper in Lily's ear, which James noticed never failed to make her laugh or smile. And with every laugh that Elijah evoked and every smile he put on Lily's face, the heat in James's veins went up another degree.

As meaningless as the women at Ohio University were to James, jealousy was a foreign concept to him. He had never once had to emotionally fight with such a thing. But on this night, watching Lily smile at Elijah's playfulness, jealousy had run him over like a freight train. After six years of being away from Lily, James thought that he would be able to continue to suppress any emotions he had for her, but he realized how wrong he was the very instant he saw her beautiful face sitting there at his mother's piano. Since then, he kept trying to convince himself that being with Lily would never be right, that she was not the woman for him, and that he could never give her all that a woman deserved. Excuse after excuse he tried to create, but his body, his heart, his soul, and even his dreams always contradicted the lies he tried to force himself to believe. Deep down he knew they were nothing more than the ignorant beliefs of people like his father, who could never see past one's color or status in life.

James saw so much more in Lily than just a colored slave girl, so much so that all other women had been invisible to him through the years, including the ones he had slept with. Every single one of those women were never anything more to James than a means of satisfying his natural urges, or were alcohol-driven attempts at forgetting about Lily which, ironically, caused quite the opposite effect. Had any of those competitive college women succeeded in unlocking the secrets of James's mind, they would have been disappointed to discover that his thoughts were dominated by Lily, especially while in the throes of passion with them. Fantasizing that he was buried deep between Lily's thighs while sleeping with other women had been the key element in James achieving a gossip worthy sexual prowess. Lily was also the sole reason James was so coldly dismissive to women after he had used them. He never failed to feel as though he had betrayed Lily after coming out of his fantasy trance, opening his eyes, and facing the fact that it was not her that he had just made love to. The weight of that guilt left him regretting every single sexual encounter he had ever had.

Unlike those college women, Lily was far more to James than just a warm body he desired to be one with. It was through Lily that James first learned that judging someone from their appearance was foolish and that there could be more to a person than what the eyes could see, a fact further proven after witnessing her prodigal abilities. Lily taught him about the inner and outer strengths of a woman, about perseverance, the true meaning of beauty, the definition of a best friend, and about how laughter could lift a heavy heart. Many nights, James even had vivid dreams after leaving Lily's bedside that convinced him that she was the *only* woman capable of defining to him the true meaning of passion and lovemaking.

With all of his true feelings having quickly resurfaced, it was crushing James to endure the sight of Elijah making his interest in Lily known, very loud and excruciatingly clear. Since he was a teen, James was thoroughly convinced that no other man would ever hold Lily as sacred to his soul as him, yet there Elijah stood trying to prove that notion wrong. The sight of it drove James to drink like a madman who was trying to extinguish the jealousy-fueled fire raging within him. While watching Elijah try to win the affections of a woman that was extraordinarily precious to him, sweat was quickly accumulating on James's brow. Minute by minute, his appetite began to decrease. Second by second, his irritation began to rise along with the alcohol in his veins. James longed to be the one whispering in Lily's ear in place of Elijah, evoking laughter and putting a smile on her face, something he had failed to do for her in years. Graphic visions of Elijah and Lily entangled together began erupting in his inebriated mind, tying his stomach into knots, causing his heart to beat a song of pain. Imagining just the small possibility that Lily could end up lying in Elijah's arms at the end of the night had James ready to dive headfirst over the edge of insanity.

James suddenly threw the last bit of whiskey in his glass straight to the back of his throat, ignoring the fire that erupted in his chest shortly thereafter. He slammed his cup down on the table beside him and began weaving his way through the crowd toward the corner that Elijah and Lily stood speaking to each other. He passed by several ladies who hoped that they were the reason he seemed so desperate to make his way through the maze of people, but each would end up watching the backside of his tailored suit in disappointment after he brushed by their unmemorable faces.

"It's time!" William exclaimed with excitement, placing a firm hand on James's shoulder, suddenly stopping him in his tracks. Fate had intervened on his march into battle and grabbed him just as he was about to put his foot over the edge of insanity.

"What?!" James erupted, staring at the hand on his shoulder that had the audacity to impede his onslaught.

"It's time!" William announced again with delight, oblivious to James's frustration.

"Time?!" James replied, still sounding very irritated and confused. "Time for what?!"

"Our plan," William reminded him, still ignoring James's odd behavior.

"Oh, umm, yeah … Yeah, of course," James said, finally gathering his emotions to make sense out of what William was talking about. "You found someone to play an original song then?"

"Yes, yes," William whispered. "Richard, of all people. I didn't much enjoy having to speak to him again after our whole debacle in his office, but he has a new composition that I talked him into playing, which didn't take much. I still know the old bastard well. A few glasses of Scotch and he's always ready to be the center of attention. Bring Lily along quickly. This will be our opportunity."

"Will do. Try to stall a moment until we get there." James definitely welcomed any excuse to get Lily away from Elijah. Fortunately, the brief interaction with William had allowed James's mind and body time to cool down a few degrees to retrieve Lily without resorting to the drunken brawl that likely would have ensued.

"Lily, William would like to see you in the library," James said while staring at Elijah in a way that neutralized the smile on his face.

"Yessa'," she said, sitting her service tray down.

James gently took her arm and guided her through the crowd, glancing over his shoulder at Elijah with a look of disgust on his face. They arrived together in the library just in time for the mini concert Richard was about to bestow upon the awaiting guests. The song Richard planned to play began the sequence of events that would soon have Lily parked at the piano bench, bringing the room to silence, and prompting Tucker McCormick to make his rude drunken statement.

Despite the numerous glasses of Scotch that William had happily drowned him with, Richard was able to play his new piano piece quite skillfully, and there was a round of applause upon its completion. William then stepped forward to say a few words to his delighted guests. All his years of playing center stage gave him a certain confidence in his demeanor and a special tone in his voice whenever he addressed a crowd. "For those of you who don't already know, this fine composer and dear friend of mine is Richard Wells. He is the director of the music department at Ohio University. It is a department that my lovely wife began raising money for many years ago with this very event while I was the director there. Emma began the fundraising efforts because, unfortunately, music is one of a few departments that receives very little money throughout the fiscal year. So your donations here tonight will help to ensure that music will always be a part of Ohio University's curriculum. Every dime will be greatly appreciated by the school, by Richard, and of course, by all of the wonderful students, whose lives your money will directly impact."

The audience gave a brief applause in response.

"Speaking of Richard and all of the students he has so

brilliantly trained," William continued, waving his arm toward all of them. "If you find yourself in the mood for fine music and you've never been to one of the many shows they put on throughout the year, I highly suggest it. Richard has just given a small sample of one of the incredible pieces you might have the luxury of hearing while in attendance."

William looked over at James, who stood silently next to Lily laughing to himself about how skilled his counterpart was at boosting Richard's ego and saying whatever was necessary for their plan to run smoothly, despite their fallout. James then gave a nod in William's direction signaling that he and Lily had been present for Richard's entire song.

"The song Richard just played was quite splendid, wouldn't you all agree?" William asked.

The room gave another round of applause. "Simply beautiful," an older lady from the crowd professed.

William sat down at the piano after Richard stood and gave a bow. "Yes, simply beautiful indeed," William concurred. "Such a magnificent piece is certainly worthy of another listen, don't you think?" William then attempted to play a few chords, but abruptly stopped after just a few notes. "Ahh, old age has done a little damage to an old man's memory," he laughed at himself.

"I'd be glad to play it again," Richard replied. He was still slightly inebriated and eager to be the center of attention once more.

"Ahh, no need," William replied, dismissing him with a wave of his hand. "I have a very special guest here tonight, and I'd much rather hear her rendition of your beautiful piece, if you don't mind." He gave Richard no time to object to the request. "Lily, come, come. Would you be kind enough to grace our ears with Richard's delightful song again this evening?"

All eyes immediately went into the direction of the

woman whose name and face nobody recognized. Lily's eyes surveyed the crowd as muffled murmurs began to emerge after they realized who William was talking about. Lily hesitated to answer. At all other gatherings, she had always been as insignificant and transparent as the very wine glasses she was expected to keep filled. She had always felt that every man of William's status had not even considered her as human, much less as a *special guest*, especially at such an esteemed event.

James stood shoulder to shoulder with Lily in the tightly packed room and could feel her body start to tremble as a bout of nervousness began ricocheting through her. Without her needing to say a word, James gave her the reassurance she was looking for. He gently caressed her back and leaned in close to her ear. "It'll be alright, Lily. You can do this." She turned to look at him, and he could see the fear in her eyes. "I believe in you," James whispered, stroking the side of her arm softly and then parting the crowd with his arm so that she could step through.

"Come, come, Lily," William urged her again, smiling at her as she began to weave through the crowd toward him. He stood up and extended his hand to her to guide her the rest of the way to the piano. "Everyone this is…"

"Is this the Negro girl you told me about?" Richard asked, rudely interrupting.

William did not like him referring to her as a *girl*. The way it rolled off of his tongue sounded demeaning in his ears. "Yes, this is Lily, the *young lady* I spoke to you about."

"Oh, come on, William! You don't really expect *her* to replay this piece, do you?" Richard fired back with disgust, waving his hand dismissively at Lily with a sneer on his face.

"Well, yes and no," William answered.

"What in the devil is that supposed to mean? Either she

will or she won't," Richard scoffed, in his snotty proper dialect. Despite their longtime friendship, William was always annoyed by the arrogance in his tone.

"Well, I don't think that's anything I can explain." William turned to look at Lily and gestured with his hand toward the piano bench, inviting her to sit down. "Lily, the floor is yours," he said, wanting her to explain exactly what he meant to Richard, in a way that his words could not.

Lily sat down slowly while letting her eyes drift across the sea of faces staring back at her. She thought that she would never be able to focus on such an insurmountable task while sitting in the center of the room alone, feeling like a sheep surrounded by lions. But she suddenly found a pair of striking blue eyes in the crowd tenderly staring back at her. For a moment, Lily did not want to turn away from James. The way he gazed at her gave her a sense of peace and comfort that suddenly made her feel like he was the only person in the room she was about to play for. *I believe in you*, she could hear him saying again in her mind as she looked at him. His words had resonated deep within her, more than he probably realized.

James nodded his head at Lily as another small gesture of his support and finally broke her trance. With that, Lily closed her eyes and began. From the very first strike of the piano keys, the submissive mannerisms and body language typical of a slave faded far away from Lily, giving way instead to the gentle dances of a woman who had just been freed. From soft swaying through the delicate portions of the melodies, to aggressive pounding of the keys that erupted from the core of her body, it seemed that Lily had transformed herself into another person as she played. The fact that she rarely opened her eyes, coupled with the constant change of expressions on her face, gave the impression that she had transported herself mentally into another world. The world she looked lost in seemed far more beautiful than the one she found herself trapped in with Richard currently looking at her with envy and disgust as she replicated his song in her own special way. William snickered at the look on Richard's face then turned and smiled proudly at Lily, just as James was currently doing. In fact, James had never once taken his eyes off of her, much like the rest of the room.

The precision of Lily's memory was uncanny, as always. But what made her level of skill even more remarkable were the runs she sometimes blended into some of the songs she replayed, like she decided to do with Richard's complicated piece. She changed certain moments in the music that made the more bland verses come to life. Instinctively, she infused those dull parts with an array of beautiful notes that began connecting with the emotions of everyone in William's library, consequently hypnotizing them all. By manipulating Richard's song in her own way, Lily was belting out sounds that were uncommon to classical music of the era and foreign to everyone there who had the honor of hearing her distinctive style. She was showing not only her ability to mimic but the level of her spontaneous creativity and brilliance. It was that particular authenticity that gave clarity to Richard's question in a way that William felt his words could not. It was also the sole quality that William had hoped Lily would share with all of the men who had denied her the chance to work for them in the weeks before.

William proved to everyone how easily Lily could replay a piece she had never heard, but he also knew that she was not just restricted to copying the play of others. It had become William's morning ritual to play piano with Lily for hours over the previous few weeks. In that time, he had learned that dozens of songs were alive in Lily's genius mind. Each song had a name and was born from a wide array of her life experiences, from the sweet memory of her little turtle, to the simple light and airy emotions she felt when listening to birds sing, to deep and heartfelt arrangements inspired by the trauma of past pains. William was well aware of that side of Lily's talent, but wanted to bring that to light later when he felt it was more necessary. For now, he wanted to win over his former friends and colleagues with her innate ability to memorize, improvise, and manipulate the most difficult arrangements in a matter of seconds, as if it were child's play. However, he would be forced to wait and see in the days that followed whether or not her crowd-silencing, flawless performance had done just that.

Chapter Nine

Slave Code
Article V Section II

Any free Negro intermarrying with any white person shall become a slave for life, and any white man or woman intermarrying with any Negro shall become a servant for seven years, to be disposed of at the discretion of the court.

William sat in his den with his hands clasped together on top of his desk. He was as still as a stone statue, staring blankly across the room at nothing in particular. His frustrations were rampant on his mind and had put him into a hypnotic trance of sorts. He had not even gotten up the energy to play alongside Lily this particular morning, which was something they had both come to look forward to on a daily basis.

"William, you alright?" James asked, after stepping into his den unannounced. The fact that he just woke up was apparent by his scratchy voice and his disheveled hair. He had not been awakened early by the sound of piano music as he had in the previous weeks. "I saw Lily in the kitchen a moment ago, but she said she hadn't seen you this mornin'."

William was still silent and continued staring blankly at nothing. By his lack of reaction, James wondered if he had even heard a word he had said. Out of the blue, William finally spoke, but it was like he was talking to an imaginary person in the room. "Why does it matter so much to people?" he asked, still not bothering to look in James's vicinity.

James was confused for a moment but then realized that William was not replying to his question. It was suddenly obvious that he was troubled by something. "Why does what matta'?"

"*Who* we are? I just don't understand it. Why does it

150

matter so much to people?" William finally blinked for the first time since James entered the room. He then turned to look at him with puzzled eyes, like he hoped that he really did hold the answer to his question.

"Sa', I'm sorry, but I'm not followin' you," James replied, trying to make his half-asleep mind comprehend where he was going with the statement.

William got up from his chair and walked over to a wall that had a portrait of his deceased wife hanging on it. When he looked at her, images of his wedding day began erupting in his mind. He suddenly closed his eyes to see it more vividly, hoping to feel like he was reliving the day all over again. He opened his eyes when the imagery faded and said with great reluctance, "Let's face it, James, nobody is going to be bold enough to pay to see a Negro woman perform." William still did not dare to remove his eyes from his beautiful wife's picture. "It doesn't matter how phenomenal she is, all people will ever care about is *who* Lily is."

William's natural jubilant outlook was undoubtedly absent. It was the first time that James had ever heard defeat in his voice, and he suddenly became afraid that William was truly on the verge of giving up for good this time. Giving in so easily was something he never would have expected from a man like William, but at the same time, James understood where his doubts were coming from. It had been well over a week, and not one single guest from the fundraiser had bothered to offer Lily a chance to breathe life into their venues the way William knew she could. Despite her talent, it seemed that nobody would be able to see past who she was ... a lowly enslaved Negro.

"But..." William began.

"But what?" James replied.

"There is something in me that just won't allow me to give up," William confessed, with his eyes still transfixed on his wife. His words were something James understood all too well. That same unexplainable *something* had been swirling inside of him since the moment he found out that Lily could play. "Since the bigger concern for people is about *who* they are paying to see perform, I do have another idea," William continued. It was then that James finally felt himself awaken fully. William may have sounded down, but James appreciated that his willpower to help Lily succeed was still thriving. "Talk to Lily about something for me, will you?"

"Sure, of course. Anything."

William asked James to close the door and then proceeded to explain what he had in mind.

* * * *

Not long after his conversation with James, William stood at the tomb of his beloved wife, Emma. He had buried her on his estate next to her cherished garden, wanting her to always be surrounded by the beauty of the flowers that she was so passionate about growing and caring for. But more importantly, he wanted her there so that she would never be too far away from him. When she was alive, Emma had truly been William's best friend and most loyal confidant. They told each other everything, never holding back about even the smallest details, or the darkest of secrets. Even after her death, confiding in his wife was a ritual that William refused to part ways with. Every Sunday, he would venture out to her gravesite and take a seat on a stone bench near her tombstone and talk aloud to her about all of the things on his mind. This particular Sunday, his frustrations about finding Lily suitable work was the topic he chose to share. He told Emma that he was angry about how the hue of Lily's skin superseded her talent in the eyes of so many. He admitted very readily that Lily was far superior to him on the piano, and that he feared she would never be as well received by an audience as he once was, simply because of something as superficial as her God-given color.

The fact that William was one-of-a-kind in a world that judged heavily on complexion and status was the dominant trait that Emma found the most endearing and admirable about him. When she first met him, Emma began noticing how charismatic William was toward people from all walks of life, including Negroes. Talking with him as often as she did, she soon came to learn about William's part in abolishing slavery in his home country as well as his efforts in fighting against the institution in the United States. Emma immediately gained a deep respect for William for being the sort of man who was brave enough to stand up and speak out against such a popular belief. Once Emma learned that William's beliefs were similar to her own, it became a rock solid foundation between the pair that strengthened their already profound connection, sparked an inseparable friendship, and ignited a blissful romance that led to marriage and the birth of their two sons.

But after forty years of marriage, Emma became seriously ill. It was then that William retired from his job at Ohio University. He wanted to spend every day by his wife's side, trying all that he could to get her well. But his unrelenting efforts were in vain. For two years, he watched as a bizarre illness slowly withered the love of his life away into only a shell of a person. But day after day, William was there to tend to her every need and talk with her about the highlights of their life. Despite him sharing such beautiful stories, the memories of the life they had built together faded away from Emma's mind completely, along with the mental and emotional burdens of the dark secrets in her life that she had openly shared with William throughout the years. It was a painful thing for him to witness and even harder for him to accept. But, at the very moment that Emma drew her last breath, William was there holding her hand, tearfully telling her how much he loved her, and thanking her for all the years of joy she had brought into his life.

Even after two years, the death of his beloved wife was still just as fresh to William as the day that she had passed away. It caused him to lose his zest for life and destroyed his desire to write, play, and even listen to music. It was the sole reason why William was so reluctant to assist when James first approached him for help. It was not until he heard the passion with which James spoke about Lily that William quickly changed his mind. It reminded him of the passion that he always exuded whenever he talked about Emma. That factor alone convinced him that he had to summon the mental and emotional strength somehow, to assist a young lady who sparked such emotion from a man.

The morning after Lily's arrival was William's very first day back on the piano since his wife's passing. At the time, he felt like he had to push himself to strike every key, but it was not long after working with Lily that he found that deep, dark hole between music and his desire for it starting to fill itself. As the hole began to fill, William was suddenly overcome by the feeling that everything that had happened in his life was for a much grander reason. He began to believe that his musical ability, his job at Ohio University, and especially his marriage to a woman who deeply opposed slavery, had all finally led him to his ultimate purpose: dedicating the last years of his life to helping present one of God's precious gifts to the world. If Lily so chose, William was suddenly willing to risk all that he had, including his life, to do just that.

In many ways, William felt that helping Lily would be a way to honor his wife and her strong opposition to slavery. He truly believed that it would be people like Lily that could lead the misguided to see that the Negro people were worthy of far more than a life of oppression, that it would be people like her that would slowly drive the world to be a place where no other human would have to deny their ancestry, or be ashamed to be proud of who they were, the way his wife had always dreamed it should be for *everyone*. William was not foolish enough to think that Lily would single-handedly put an end to hatred, slavery, or racism, but he certainly believed, much like James, that people were not handed special gifts from God without purpose. He believed that Lily was simply one of many special human beings that God would send in His good name to assist in mending a broken society. Simply put, William was convinced that Lily and her unique gifts were invaluable to the world. So, despite the current frustrations that he was sharing with his beautiful wife, there was not an ounce of him that thought to give up. In William's mind, doing so would be parallel to giving up on God's request for his help.

It was all of those matters that William sat speaking to his wife about on this Sunday, helping him to feel as close to her as he did when she was alive. Whether happy or sad, or thoughts of how much he missed her, William released it all to help ease his mind. And ease him it did, but more so because of how strongly he always felt the presence of Emma's spirit sitting right there beside him on his little stone bench under the shade of a massive oak tree, not far from her beautiful garden. William would easily sit there with her for hours and even then find it hard to part ways with her. It was only when he absolutely had to leave that he would find the strength to do so, but never before placing a handful of fresh, pure white lilies—Emma's favorite flower—in a marble vase near her headstone. The coincidence of the name of his wife's favorite flower was yet another sign, in William's mind, that helping *Lily* was truly a part of his destiny. After arranging the bouquet neatly, William kissed his hand and touched it to his wife's tombstone. "I love you, Em," he whispered as his tears dripped down into the grass.

* * * *

"I hate to break it to ya', but you won't find Wilbur

155

anywhere out here," James said, picking up a rock and skipping it across the lake on William's plantation as Lily stood staring out into it. He had walked up behind her quietly after watching her stand there alone from his window for a short while. He had not startled her, though; she had sensed his presence long before he said a word.

"Ol' Wilbur. World's fattest turtle," Lily replied, with a slow smile creeping onto her face.

"What did you expect? You gave that turtle more crickets in a day than he could eat in a lifetime," James reminded her.

"I can't help that I's always betta' at catchin' crickets than you," she said with a sly smile. James laughed at the truth in her words and at the same time realized how much he truly missed that playful side of her. "You still had a small hand in fattenin' him up too, ya' know … *Very* small, I might add," she teased.

"Guilty as charged, your honor." They both gave a light laugh.

In the previous weeks, some of James's silence toward Lily had certainly been his effort to keep the secret about the true mission of their journey, but the majority of it had to do with him feeling overwhelmed with where to begin again with her after so many rocky years between them. He could easily sense Lily's discomfort whenever she was in his presence which gave him even more anxiety about what he could possibly say that would ease the tension between them. So he was glad that William had requested for him to speak to her. It finally gave him a substantial reason to force himself to approach her. So far it seemed that he had chosen the right topic to start with. He was happy to see how receptive Lily was to his initial comment about Wilbur and even happier to know that he, for once, had given her a reason to smile. To see her smile and hear her laughter was something that uplifted James, but unfortunately, it would not last for long. There was an immediate awkward silence between them after their shared memory. Lily turned her eyes back toward the water and folded her arms across her chest. The smile faded from her face, and she was serious all over again. Her body language told James that she had put the brick back into place that he had just taken down from the protective emotional wall she had built around herself. He did not like how quickly she had undone his work.

"May sound strange, but I sho' do miss my ol' friend," Lily suddenly said, continuing to stare out into the water.

James slid both of his hands into his pockets the way he always did when he felt uneasy. He was silent for a moment while he stared at the profile of Lily's face. "Me too," he admitted, knowing full well they were no longer speaking about their old turtle. James did not like the silence or the look on Lily's face. He wanted to see her smile again and continue being comforted by her laughter and her voice, the sound of it was something he had not let fade away from his memory while he was away at school. He missed it dearly. He knew he had to think of something quickly before Lily shut him out altogether again. "This is the second time I've seen you standin' here at the lake this week. Where's your mind run off to when you're out here all by yourself?" he asked, turning to stare out into the lake along with her.

Lily was surprised that James actually had an interest in her thoughts. It caught her a little off guard and made her hesitant to speak at first. She bought a little time for herself by wandering over and plucking a leaf off of a nearby tree. "You'd just laugh if I told ya'," she finally thought to say.

"Try me."

Again, Lily hesitated a moment. "Well, wheneva' I'm tryna let my mind escape from my troubles, I always daydream about what it'd be like to…" She stopped, suddenly feeling that maybe her intimate thoughts were not something she should share, especially with James.

"To what? Please, go on."

"I-I ain't neva' said these things out loud before. Don't know how foolish it might sound."

"Your innermost thoughts and secrets are safe with me."

"Promise you won't laugh?"

"You have my word, Miss Lily."

There was something endearing about the way James added "Miss" to her name. She liked it. Lily looked over at him a moment, hesitated again, but decided she would trust him with her thoughts on this occasion. "Well, I daydream about what it'd be like to walk into town wearin' one of them real pretty summa' dresses, totin' me a purse. Nothin' fancy, ya' know, just be nice to have one to carry my things," she said, nervously fiddling with the leaf in her hand. "Anyway, I walks into one of the stores to buy me some groceries, and some of the town's white folks are in there, and they actually smile at me when I walk past 'em. Some of 'em even stop and talk to me 'bout things goin' on in they lives and such. Even the clerk asks me how I been doin' when I get to the counta' and hand him my money. We chat for a moment, then he smiles and wishes me well. He even tells me to come back soon when he gets done givin' me my change.

"I walk outside in the fresh air afta'wards and start makin' my way back home. I look up and it ain't a cloud in the sky. It ain't too hot and it ain't too cold, so I decide to take my time walkin'. All the way home, I'm passin' one white person afta' anotha', but they don't run off and find the sheriff, they don't ask to see my papers, they don't sic no dogs on me or look around to see if my masta' is nearby keepin' watch ova' me. They simply wave, or smile, or ask, 'how do you do?' like it ain't nothin' to see a Negro woman walkin' down the road in a summa' dress, totin' a purse, and an arm full of groceries.

"Then I finally get back to my house. It ain't a big

house … but it's *home*. I get my groceries out and start fixin' dinna'. By the time I get finished I…" she paused feeling a little embarrassed to continue.

"Go on. Then what?" James asked, truly eager to hear what was hidden in her thoughts.

Lily nervously fiddled with the leaf in her hand again. "Then I hear my husband comin' up to the house on his horse," she continued, smiling sheepishly. "I walks on outside and wait for 'em on the porch. He gets off his horse, walks up the steps, and hugs and kisses me like he ain't seen me in years, even though he only been off workin' for a few hours." Her smile broadened like she could feel his arms around her. "I pour him some lemonade that I just made fresh, and then he sits on the porch swing with me, wraps his arm around me, pulls me in close, and asks me 'bout my day. I tell 'em how I been into town, and 'bout all the folks I seen and talked to, and how nice everybody was to me. We sit there talkin' and laughin' 'til we see our children runnin' home in the distance. We stand up and watch 'em racin' each otha' down the dirt path. But they ain't runnin' away from no dogs, or no evil men chasin' 'em, or worried 'bout a sheriff gettin' 'em … 'cause the day I brought 'em into the world they was free. Me and my children … we *free*. They don't know nothin' about chains, and auction blocks, o-or worryin' 'bout bein' sold away from they family, or runnin' for they lives. They's just runnin' home from the schoolhouse as fast as they little legs'll carry 'em, 'cause they miss they mama and daddy … And that's the *only* worry they eva' known in they little lives."

James was totally silent when she finished. There was nothing but the sound of the leaves in the surrounding trees rustling in the wind for what felt like an eternity to Lily.

"Foolish thinkin', ain't it?" Lily asked, feeling uncomfortable with the silence.

James could not look at her for fear that the tears that

her story had stirred in him might actually fall. "Not in the least, Lily … Not in the least." As always, after listening to Lily, James found himself viewing the world from a different perspective, just as he had so many times in the past. It gave him such insight, not only into her mind, but into the mind of a slave and how something so simple could mean so much to them. James's tears had begun to surface knowing that the pretty dress, the simple purse, and even the home were things he could easily pay to give Lily, but a Negro walking down a road free of chains and being welcomed by *every* white person with a smile or a 'how do you do?' had a price tag labeled "IMPOSSIBLE!" It bothered James deeply to know that it was a luxury he could never afford to give her. Not only that, but he knew that her freedom rested in the hands of a man who would surely die first before allowing her to have such a thing.

Despite the reality of how sad the story was, James still admired the simplicity of Lily's dreams, and that she was a woman who was never impressed by extravagance. She had not daydreamed of a faraway vacation, a trip to a stage play, or even imagined a lavish home. She simply wanted to go to a store alone in town and be greeted with kindness and return to her simple home to prepare an intimate meal for the family she loved.

Although he could not empathize with Lily about how grand it would be to walk to a store, James certainly understood and shared the part of her dream about having a family to come home to. In his daydreams, Lily was the *only* woman he had ever imagined as his wife and the mother of the children he desperately wanted with her. Quite often, he had envisioned their little ones with dark curly hair, their mother's lovely skin tone and her beautiful sparkling eyes. His daydream lived on despite learning that not only did his father forbid such unions, but so too did the laws. So while listening to Lily's story, James could not help but wonder the identity of the man who had the honor of calling himself her husband and the father of her children. The thoughts were starting to weigh him down. He wanted to change the subject and think no more about the complexities that stood as an enormous wall between himself and a woman who unknowingly owned all of his soul, a woman that he had no regrets about giving it to either, despite what his father and any unjust laws had to say about it.

James cleared his throat before speaking again to be sure that Lily did not hear any emotional breaks in his voice. "The piano. I assume you escape there too in times that you're feelin' down?" he asked her, in an attempt to steer the conversation in another direction.

Lily nodded her head. "I don't know what I'd've done without it all these years. All my tears, my worries, my fears, and my pain, I lock 'em all up in songs to help ease my troubled mind. Just don't know what I'd've done without it," she answered, her voice trailing off as she dug deep in her mind for what the alternatives may have been.

"I don't know how you do it. Don't matta' how much time my mama spent trainin' me on that thing, I ain't neva' see that piano of hers as nothin' more than a pine box with ivory keys. It ain't neva' make any sense to me. None whatsoeva'."

"So many things in the world don't make no sense to me. Don't make no sense how I can be a human who thinks, talks, senses, feels, and even loves just like everybody else, but just 'cause I's born in a darker wrapper than white folks, I'm treated like an animal. Long as I live, I'll neva' unda'stand that. The only thing in my whole life that's eva' made complete sense to me is the piano. It ain't nothin' I can explain." Lily shrugged her shoulders. "Somehow it just does."

Again, Lily had infused James's mind with a different point of view. He had never even considered that a slave would think of themselves on the level of an animal. At times, he found it too difficult to hear of such things, especially after the way he had treated Lily before departing for college. He was not yet ready to face all that he had done, so he was sure to continue steering the conversation into safer territory. "So, how did it feel? The otha' night, I mean, playin' in front of all those people?"

"I love playin' the piano and all, and I usually feel so at peace, but that night I ain't neva' felt so terrified in all my life with all them people lookin' at me. There wasn't nothin' peaceful about it. Thought my heart was gonna beat clean outta my chest. But then…" she paused, remembering what James had said to her before she sat down to play. "Somehow I found the strength to get through it. But when it was all ova' and wasn't nobody clappin' like they was for that Richard fella', I-I didn't really know what to think. But even if nobody else cared for it, I's proud of myself 'cause I knew I put all my heart into it," she admitted, once again remembering the four words that James had whispered to her that ignited such motivation.

"Well, I'm quite certain the reason they didn't react had nothin' to do with you playin' badly. I think they just couldn't make any sense of it Lily. I know I couldn't at first and neitha' could William. Hell, I think most folks would have to live four lifetimes 'fore they eva' meet somebody again who's capable of what you do. So, I don't think you can blame everybody for bein' in a state of shock. Personally, I think everybody was amazed by you, but they just didn't know how to show it, or maybe they were just flat out afraid to."

"I guess that makes sense."

James bent down and picked up a rock. "That audience may have been hesitant, but there's certainly one person who ain't afraid to tell me how he feels about you," he said, skipping the rock across the lake.

"Who's that?"

"William. He's mighty fond of you, ya' know? You're

all he eva' talks about. He goes on and on for hours about you sometimes."

Lily smiled. She had grown close to William rather quickly during their morning piano sessions. "I really like Mr. William too. He's been awfully kind to me. I bet all his students at that fancy school really loved him too. You just can't help but love a man like him."

Hearing how Lily felt about William, James turned toward her, finally feeling ready to ask what William had sent him there for. "Lily, I need to ask you somethin'," he said, suddenly sounding very serious.

The way he was looking at her suddenly made Lily nervous. "Okay."

"You rememba' Anna Mae and Ben tellin' you about William bein' an orchestra conducta' and composa', and about how he's performed all ova' the United States?"

"Of course."

"Well, William told me today that, for the first time in years, he's wantin' to put on anotha' concert. He misses bein' onstage a lot, and well…" James paused a moment to be sure that the next thing he was about to say came out the way he wanted. "Well, he was wonderin' how you'd feel about lettin' him use your music for his show? He said he'd write all of the accompaniment for the rest of the orchestra and conduct the show, but he wants every song that's played to stem from your personal collection."

Lily's astonishment was apparent by the look on her face. She was stunned that a man of William's status would consider, even for a moment, using her material. "He wants to use *my* music?" she asked in disbelief.

"He sure does. He thinks many of the arrangements he's already heard you play are phenomenal. He's confident that everyone else would say so too. So what do ya' think?"

"I think I…" Lily's bewilderment caused her words to get lost in her mind. "I think I find that nearly impossible to believe."

"Believe it. He asked me to ask you just this mornin'."

"B-but I don't know how to write the music I hear in my mind. I only know how to play it," she replied, feeling a bit embarrassed about that fact. She sheepishly turned to stare out at the water again, wondering how she would ever pull off such a feat.

"Well, you wouldn't have to worry about that."

"I wouldn't?"

"No," James assured her.

"Well, why not?"

James walked in front of Lily and blocked her view of the lake to be sure it was he who held her attention. "Because it's *you* that he wants to play the piano durin' the entire show."

Lily's heart immediately began to pound mercilessly against her chest, pumping adrenaline into every corner of her body, flooding her with fear and anxiety, especially because of her experience from the previous night. "*Me*? H-how would I eva' be able to do that? Wouldn't nobody eva' let somebody like me play in a…"

"Don't you worry about that, eitha'," James interrupted, already knowing exactly what she was thinking. "William has a way."

"But how? Th-this wouldn't just be some gala in the middle of William's library. I mean, th-this would surely be a huge audience, right? In an elaborate theata'? I-I just, I don't unda'stand how it would eva' be possible," she rambled, trying to spit out every question that had overtaken her mind all at once. "Is he certain this is what he'd want to do?"

"I unda'stand that you probably have a million questions, but the only thing you need to worry yourself about for now is whetha' or not you're willin' to be there by his side, and nothin' more."

Lily's mind continued racing, and her eyes were darting nervously from place to place as if she would somehow find the answers lying in front of her. "I-I just don't know. M-maybe he should get someone else. I…"

"Lily, wait, please just listen to me a moment," James interrupted, wanting to stop her before she could continue to talk herself out of it. He then took her gently by the shoulders to help calm her. "Lily, please look at me." He proceeded to talk again when she finally relaxed enough to look at him. "William couldn't possibly conceive of anotha' person he'd ratha' have the honor of sharin' the stage with," he explained. "Because it was *you* who inspired him to perform again."

Lily did not respond at first, but her face certainly expressed how moved she was by his statement. She slowly pulled away from his grasp and turned toward the lake again, feeling the sudden need to be comforted by the glistening waters, just as she always had been as a child.

"Trust me," James continued, as he walked up behind her. "If you say yes to this, it would mean the world to William."

"Forgive me if I'm outta place for sayin' this, but I know the fact that you brought me here to meet William, and everything else that's been happenin', ain't all been some kind 'a coincidence. I just … I don't unda'stand … W-why you doin' this for me?" she asked softly, a little fearful of his answer.

James stepped in front of her, blocked her view of the lake again and waited for her to look at him. Lily was slow in doing so, but when she did, he answered with the most sincere tone in his voice. "'Cause I've been inspired by you too, Lily. Have been since the day I heard you playin' my mama's piano," he admitted. "The way you play and seein' all that you're capable of without eva' havin' had help from anyone … It's truly remarkable."

Feeling moved yet again by his words, Lily closed her eyes and said nothing in return. She just wanted to hear it echoing again in her mind.

"Listen, I know all of this may seem surreal, and maybe you're a little afraid. I can unda'stand that," James continued. "So whetha' you decide to play with William or not is completely up to you of course, but…"

"But what?" Lily asked eagerly.

James moved even closer to her. "I'd give everything I have to see you up there on that stage with William. You're amazin' Lily. And if you decide this is what you wanna do, come hell or high water, I'll be damned if I eva' miss a minute."

After having lost her belief in James's ability to say anything kind to her, Lily was suspended in disbelief listening to him now. She stood there speechless, assuming that she was bound to wake up at any moment, that the things she was hearing were only possible in her dreams.

"But ultimately, it's all up to you," James continued.

"I thank you kindly for your words, I really do. It means more to me than you'll eva' know," Lily finally managed to say, staring at James as if the man she knew him to be years ago had finally reappeared before her very eyes. "But this is all so unexpected, and I really don't know what to say."

"I see," James replied, with a twinge of disappointment evident in his tone. "I completely unda'stand your reservations, but will you at least take the time to think about it a while before you make a permanent decision, and then let us know?"

"Yes. I promise I will."

"Take your time, okay?"

"Okay."

Despite his overwhelming desire to stay and spend the rest of the day by Lily's side talking and rebuilding the broken bridge between them, James figured it would be best to give her time to think things through alone. So reluctantly, he turned and forced himself to walk away, leaving Lily to contemplate the outcome of her future for the first time in her life.

As James walked away, the thoughts that ran through Lily's mind were of how up until a few weeks ago no one except Auntie had ever heard her play. For Lily, music had been a simple thing that brought her comfort, joy, and a means of escape, but here her music was now being praised by one of the world's finest composers with the chance to be unburied from the secret world of her mind and heard by thousands. Lily had never once given thought to the idea of that level of vulnerability, nor considered the impact, or how it might make her feel. Contemplating it all had momentarily ceased her ability to give even the simplest reply until one thing came rushing back to her mind.

"James," she called out before he had gotten too far.

He stopped immediately and turned around. "Yes?"

Lily took a moment before she spoke again. "Do you really believe in me?" she finally asked, staring nervously at the little leaf she still held in her hand.

James walked back over and stood in front of her once again, but this time placed his hand underneath her chin and gently raised her head so that he could look her in the eyes. "With all my heart," he assured her without the slightest hesitation or ever taking his eyes off of her.

That was all Lily needed to hear.

Chapter Ten

Slave Code
Article II Section XII

Any person convicted of assisting a slave by advice, donation, transportation, loan, or otherwise in any way cause them to be deprived from their master, shall pay damages to said master to be adjudged by the justices of the provincial court or shall spend up to one year in jail.

William had been certain after his wife's death that he would never again return to playing the piano, let alone the stage. But in this special instance, he felt as though his return was necessary in order to serve a very prodigious purpose. If people were not motivated to come and see a Negro woman play, who ironically surpassed his capabilities, then his belief was that perhaps they would flock to see William Werthington's grand return to the stage. William was not the arrogant type, but after decades of being regarded as one of the world's greatest classical musicians, he knew that his name alone held lots of power. During his years on the circuit, William had never played to anything less than packed theaters, which often had to add shows just to accommodate the demands to see him. He was such a well-respected and appreciated composer that his sheet music remained in high demand, even after his retirement. His music was a main staple in many schools and was played a world over by other professional orchestras. Knowing those facts, William wanted to take advantage of who he was and what his name stood for, in hopes of convincing people to see a show that in actuality belonged to an indentured woman.

But the idea of using William's good name to attract an audience was irrelevant considering that there were still a few problems that he and James needed to resolve. During his discussion with James in his den, William realized the grave mistake he was making where Lily was concerned. He and James both had this magnificent dream for her to succeed onstage, but had failed to ask her if she even had an interest in pursuing such a thing. They believed so much in what they wanted for her that they never took into consideration her personal life goals and desires. They had foolishly ignored the importance of her well-being altogether. James and William both agreed that putting Lily on the spot at the gala without her permission was wrong. They both also concurred that forcing her to play piano in a show was no different than them playing her master and continuing to make her submit herself to them as their slave, which, ironically, was the role that James had literally gone out of his way to remove her from.

In an attempt to atone for what he felt was about to be an unforgivable mistake, it had been William's first order of business to find out what Lily's desires were and if she would allow *him* the honor of sharing the stage with *her*. He wanted the decision to be hers alone and not something she ever felt forced into doing. If Lily had no interest in performing, then William would accept that with much understanding, yet still be proud to announce to anyone that he knew a woman of her brilliance. But if she wanted it to be so, then it was *he* who was ready to submit himself to *her.* With that knowledge, James had set out to speak to Lily as she stood alone at the lake about the prospect of using her music and performing along with William. With the news James delivered to him later that evening, William was pleased to hear that he would indeed have the honor of helping Lily carry her musical dreams to any corner of the world she wished them carried. He silently pledged that to her for as long as there was still strength in his legs and air in his lungs.

The second problem William faced, though, was that he had no orchestra to play the accompaniment portions of the show. So he set out to resolve that matter by returning to Ohio University. This time, however, it was not Richard he wished to speak with. William had only retired a few years prior, so he was certain that many of the students he had worked with remained at the school. He went in search of his best musicians, keeping in mind that most students often struggled financially throughout the school year. William found twelve of his old students who would cover all that he needed for the percussion, brass, and string portions of the music. But he knew he needed to be extremely persuasive to get them to agree. Using food as an ally, he bought them all lunch and began to explain to them his plight as they ate. All was received well by the hungry brood until William mentioned Lily. When he heard their predicted reluctance, he then mentioned the substantial amount of money he was willing to pay them for their assistance. For the band of broke students, suddenly, reluctance was no longer an issue. After they all had agreed to proceed, William insisted that they whisper nothing about the show to anyone. He gave them each a small down payment to ensure their silence and their participation and assured them that they would receive the rest of their money upon completion of the show.

With the issues of ensuring Lily's willingness to participate and finding her an orchestra resolved, the only matter that now remained for William was securing a suitable venue for all of them to perform in. But he was confident that the solution to that problem would soon be arriving to his home.

Chapter Eleven

Slave Code
Section V Article XII

Be it enacted that slaves and free Negroes are exempt from the right to dispense medication. Selling, preparing, and/or administering medicine shall result in a public whipping, not to exceed twenty stripes.

James stormed into the kitchen frantically opening and slamming kitchen drawers and counters without saying a word. Lily stopped preparing lunch and looked at him like he had lost his mind. "What on God's green earth is wrong with you?"

"Nothin'," James spat. He had his hand balled up in a fist clutching it to his chest.

Lily could easily see blood dripping from his palm and onto his shirt. "Lemme see." She stopped him, turned his hand over, and gasped. "That sho' don't look like *nothin'* to me! You done just about tore your hand off!" she said, after seeing the massive open wound he had accidentally sustained while handling a sharp piece of wood.

"It's not that bad!" James retaliated, trying to convince himself of that.

"Sit yo'self down!" Lily commanded, shoving him into a chair.

James was calm while Lily searched for some first aid products, but then lost his wits again when he saw what she put on the table. "I don't need that!" he objected, nearly falling out of his seat. He was referring to a bottle of the same solution that he had used on Lily's knee after she had fallen from their old tree as a kid. James had always hated the sting and the burn that lasted long after it was applied.

"I do believe it was *you* who once insisted that this was necessary to keep from gettin' infections," Lily reminded him as she shook the bottle up. James blew out a breath of

171

frustration after knowing he had no argument against her. "You always were like a scared little cat when it came to this stuff. Your mama would find you halfway up a tree by the time she caught you to put it on."

"Well, I's just a kid then," he said, yanking his hand away when Lily tried to grab it.

She rolled her eyes. "Mm-hmm, I can see how much things have changed," she said sarcastically, trying to stop his hand from moving.

"Well, I ain't up a tree," James pointed out, trying desperately to defend his cowardice.

"Not *yet* anyway," Lily smirked, finally grabbing a firm enough hold on him to use a pair of tweezers to pull out the large shards of wood that were still lodged in his hand.

"Ow!" James kept grunting as each piece came out.

"What in the world y'all doin' out there anyway?" Lily asked, referring to all the men she had seen hammering away at the wagonload of wood James had brought onto the plantation earlier in the morning.

"William hasn't told you yet?"

"Naw, he ain't said a word. We've been workin' nonstop on my music pieces."

"Well ... OW!" James yelled and flinched again. "Let's just say, I hope it's sturdy enough for your piano."

Lily suddenly stopped tending to his hand and looked up at James with an expression on her face that he had a hard time translating. "You mean, y'all buildin' a stage?"

"We are."

Since James had come to her at the lake asking if she was interested in playing, Lily wondered what theater was ever going to let her be a part of a show along with someone as prominent as William. She now had her answer. "William wants the show to be here?" she asked.

"Right here on this very plantation," James replied.

Lily let go of his hand, stood up, and stared out of the

window. "Won't no otha' place be willin' to let me play, will they?" she asked, suddenly feeling like more of a burden than anything else. "He has to do it this way 'cause of me." She momentarily hung her head. "Don't he?"

"Lily," James said, trying to get her attention, but she still continued to look out of the window. "Lily, look at me, please." She finally turned to him, but he could tell by her expression that she did not feel good at all about all that William was having to go through on the count of her. "William *wants* to do this," he emphasized. "And don't you look at it any otha' way, ya' hear?"

"He's right," William said, appearing in the kitchen doorway, startling both of them. He approached Lily and held both of her hands in his. "And I'd have them build ten stages if that's what it took to have the honor of playing alongside you."

"William," Lily whispered appreciatively. It was the only word she could seem to find after being touched by his words. The rest of her reply was in a single tear trickling down her face.

"But not eleven stages, though!" William suddenly interjected into the silence with a silly tone in his British accent. He waved a single finger in the air. "No, no, I'm afraid you aren't worth building that many!" he joked, as he so often did with her. He instantly turned her tears into a burst of laughter the way he had hoped. His joke was actually more of an effort to silence his own tears, but when Lily suddenly hugged him tight, those tears nearly threatened to fall.

William pulled back from Lily's hug, smiled, and wiped away her remaining tears. "I don't need you to worry yourself over these trivial matters. I need only for you to bring your heart onto the stage that this young man is building for you," he said, glancing over at James, winking, and then turning his attention back to her. "Okay, my dear?"

Lily nodded her head. William then cleared the rest of her tears and left her and James alone again. When he was gone, Lily turned again to stare out the window in amazement at all the men busy hammering away and carrying wood. She truly had no words to describe how she was feeling over what William was doing for her and for the fact that James had brought her there in the first place. She was so overwhelmed, she did not know where to begin in thanking them for gifts and opportunities she felt she could never match in return. Her music was all she had to give. She only hoped that within every note she played they would hear the depths of her immeasurable gratitude for the kindness they were bestowing upon her.

While Lily was pasted to the window watching the others work, James took the opportunity to weasel his way out of having his hand further tended to, in hopes he could avoid the solution he detested so much. "I guess if we're gonna finish on time, I need to get back out there," he said, as he tried to slide out of his seat.

Lily grabbed his hand without even looking before he escaped. "Wait! I ain't nowhere near finished with you yet," she said with a firm grip on him as she sat back down. She grabbed the solution, dabbed it on the wound, and was surprised at how relatively calm James was in the process. She was even more shocked that he did not once flinch as she stitched the wound closed.

Calmness had quickly come over James when his attention drifted from his injury to Lily while she diligently worked to clean and mend his hand. Lost in a world of lovely thoughts about her, his pain was suddenly irrelevant. Lily looked up when she was finished and met his unblinking eyes. He did not try to look away or make an excuse for the way he was gazing at her. There was an intensity in the way he stared that ignited all of her nerve endings within seconds of noticing him, a force so intense that she could only hold a return gaze for a few seconds before she felt the need to escape it. She jumped up abruptly and began digging around in a kitchen drawer to help ease the way she was feeling inside.

"Umm, m-maybe you should use these," she said, after finding a pair of gloves for James to use. She hoped that by the time she turned around, he had freed her from his sight, but Lily turned to find that she was still his visual prisoner. The way he gazed at her raised the heat within her another degree. She walked slowly back toward him, finally gathering the courage to watch his eyes fearlessly in return.

James stood as Lily approached. Still gazing intensely at her, he reached for the gloves with one hand, but at the same time used his other to gently hold her wrist while he took them. "Thank you," he said, still holding on to her and never letting his eyes waver from her face. After a moment, he reluctantly let her hand go and proceeded to head back out to the field.

With his eyes off of her, Lily suddenly felt like she could breathe again. "James," she called out, just before he walked out of the door. He turned to her and enjoyed finding that he was still trapped in her sights. "Be careful," she told him after a moment.

"I will," he replied. He stared at her a moment longer before proceeding back out to the area of the field where he would soon have the chance to be entranced by her beauty yet again, but instead, while she was perched high above an audience, seated behind a grand piano, on a stage that he took great pride in building her.

With the construction of the stage underway, the third and final problem on William's list had been resolved. If nobody would have Lily in their venues, then William simply wanted to build her one. He and James had worked together to design a beautiful outdoor amphitheater with the acoustic structure necessary for the music of an orchestra in mind. It would all be situated on the wide-open land of William's sprawling estate lands. The wood, the labor, the seats, the décor, the paint, and any other costs incurred were coming directly from William's very own pocket. Fortunately, the price tag for the project would do little to dent the enormity of his wealth. To the average person, it would have been an expensive undertaking, especially considering that William did not plan to charge a fee, at first, to any of the patrons who attended. Being able to help a woman of Lily's caliber with the creation of a show that was all her own was payment enough for William Werthington.

Chapter Twelve

Slave Code
Article I Section VI

*Be it enacted, that any person whatsoever, who shall
hereafter teach or cause any slave or slaves to be taught to
read or write, or shall use or employ any slave as a scribe,
in any manner of writing whatsoever, shall for every such
offense, forfeit the sum of one hundred pounds, current
money.*

March 1859

The preparations for the fundraising gala paled in
comparison to the efforts needed to prepare for Lily's
upcoming musical spectacular which was set to be held at
the very end of William's Spring Extravaganza. The event
was once another of Emma's favorite traditions. She used
to invite families from all over Athens, disguising the party
as the welcoming of spring weather and the coming of
Easter. In actuality, it was her clever way of forcing people
from all walks of life to mix and mingle with one another.
It was Emma's lifelong passion to break down the invisible
social barriers in between class and race, and she felt there
was no better way to do that than by luring a variety of
colored faces to her spring affair with music, food, and fine
wine. She especially hoped to influence the impressionable
minds and hearts of children, slyly attempting to change the
future by teaching the next generation social acceptance
and tolerance of all people through play and games.

After Emma's death, however, William could not bear
to continue the tradition without her. But with a very
specific purpose in mind, William decided to revive the
highly anticipated event. There were now exactly three
weeks left before that beautiful celebration was to resume.
Normally, that would have been plenty of time to for

William and his pseudo family to prepare, but with the added element of Lily's show everyone was putting in overtime to meet the deadline. For weeks, everyone assisting knew nothing but long work hours, brief dinners, and very little sleep. The resulting exhaustion was evident on everyone's faces by the end of each day, but knowing the amazing feat they were trying to accomplish not a single person complained about the intense labor.

Typically, William was responsible for collecting wine, food, and setting up games, but this year Anna Mae and Ben took over his tedious to-do list since nearly all of William's time was dedicated to working with Lily. After having Lily choose eight songs from her mental archives to use in the performance, William taught her to read and write music. He also showed her each instrument that required accompanying musical pieces and taught her the basics of playing each. Lily quickly absorbed the knowledge William provided with ease, far surpassing what he expected of someone after just a few weeks of teaching or even years for that matter. In fact, Lily's musical instincts were unlike any other William had ever known, including himself. All aspects of music came as naturally to Lily as a baby's ability to eat and sleep, further proving to William that music was clearly what she was born to do.

William and Lily had initially collaborated to create the background sounds that would enhance Lily's piano melodies, but soon William was afforded the luxury of relaxing and reveling in her accomplishments from afar. In a short amount of time, Lily had learned enough to write the majority of the accompanying pieces on her own with no effort whatsoever. She was thriving and soaring under William's wings, not only because of the clarity and precision of his instruction but also because of the way he caressed her spirit with kind words and fatherly affections. With him by her side, her brilliance was shining bright.

James did not know much about music and could not

offer Lily any assistance in that area of her life, but he took a great deal of pride in contributing to her grand cause by creating a masterpiece in the middle of William's fields with his very hands. Even the serious injury Lily had stitched did not stop him from working himself to the bone until his body was nearly ready to give out at the end of every evening. He wanted to ensure that Lily's amphitheater was ready on time and done with artistic perfection.

Unbeknownst to James, the diligence of his efforts did not go unnoticed. Lily happened to glance out of the window one afternoon while pouring herself some lemonade. What she saw stole her attention to the point that she overfilled her glass. The mesmerizing visual kept her coming back to that window every afternoon since. Lily was drawn to the kitchen window for one thing only, or rather, one *man* only. Every day, she hypnotically gazed at James as he worked without a shirt in the hottest parts of the day. She was amazed to see with such detail that nothing more remained of his boyish body. His chiseled stomach, chest muscles, and well-defined arms were a sight she struggled to pull her eyes away from. Since the day she had taken notice, she had been creating new excuses during her rehearsal time with William to escape for short periods of time to watch James work. Some days it was laundry, other days it was food or extended bathroom breaks. Lily was simply using any reason she could think of to delight her eyes with the sight of such a ruggedly handsome man.

Today, Lily's lie to William was that she needed a break because she was thirsty. As far as William knew, she had gone into the kitchen to pour herself some water, but instead of filling a glass, she was filling her eyes with the view on the other side of the window, where James and another man were carrying a large piece of plywood.

"Now I see why you were so thirsty," William teased, startling her, after he had quietly peered over her shoulder and saw what had her pasted to the window in a wide-eyed trance.

"Williaaam!" Lily smiled sheepishly. She buried her face in her hands and covered up her cheeks which had turned fire-red with embarrassment. William put his arm around her, she laid her head on his shoulder, and they let out their laughter together.

James heard William and Lily from the kitchen after having stepped inside for a drink, just moments after they had returned to the library. He walked around the corner to see why the two were giggling like school children, but they had returned to the song they were working on by the time he peeked in on them. For James, just hearing Lily's laughter, versus the tears he had seen when he saw her at his mother's piano, had made his journey to find William so worth it. To see the smile on her face when she played alongside William and to hear the joy in her voice each time she spoke about the choices they had made for the show, made every blistering hot day in the sun, every splinter, and every aching muscle James suffered through to build her stage, worth it as well. It was a reminder of why his work in the field was so important and gave him the continued motivation and strength to work from sunup to sundown. James was willing to do anything to see to it that this happy side of Lily never vanished again. And watching the way that William interacted with her, he had no doubt that he, too, would indeed give the same toward that cause.

"Thank you, William," James whispered softly still peeking around the corner as Lily played with her smile firmly in place and her uplifting laughter filling the room. James's words of gratitude were for the way that William treated Lily more like his daughter than just an ordinary friend. For allowing Lily to experience that sort of special affection for the first time in her life, James felt forever in William's debt.

Ironically, though, the fatherly love and affection that

William hopelessly showered Lily with had assisted in creating a problem. Between that and the fact that she was living in a bubble of isolation, surrounded by people whose eyes did not seem to see in color, Lily quickly began to have a false sense of reality about how she might be perceived during the show. But she would soon be placed into a situation that would, just as quickly, readjust her perspective.

The student orchestra had worked separately on the pieces that Lily had written for the past few weeks, but they had just arrived at William's home for their first rehearsal together. Lily had greeted them all at the door with enthusiasm, but the student's reception was nowhere near as warm. They chose not to shake her hand nor even give their names after she introduced herself. They left her standing in the foyer feeling foolish, quickly reminding her of how people from the outside world truly viewed her.

While waiting for William to return home from running an errand, Lily and the students all gathered in the library. They all sat quietly surrounding Lily at the piano like she was their prey. To Lily, their eyes felt like cold shards of ice burrowing holes into her skin, making the climate in the room feel like winter in the midst of the warm spring weather. However, the moment that William finally arrived, his presence instantly cured their nasty attitudes, like a sergeant walking into the barracks of his misbehaving soldiers. From then on, they all worked cooperatively for an hour or so, but when William was called away briefly for a second time, the frigid winter conditions returned.

"Alright everybody," Lily commanded. "While William's out, let's just go over bar two on the third page right quick."

"We don't take no goddamn orda's from nigga's," Austin said while twirling his timpani baton.

Lily just turned and stared at the arrogant

percussionist. She had already accepted that none of the student orchestra liked her, but she was hoping that they would all just continue to do as they had been paid to do— in silence—rather than dealing with hearing the things that were on their minds. She already had enough on her plate to deal with and was not in the mood to take on anymore.

Despite the fact that Lily did not react to Austin's initial verbal attack, he kept on with his rude remarks while leaning in a relaxed, cocky fashion against his timpani. "I rememba' you from the fundraisin' gala, sittin' in here mimicin' Mr. Well's music like the little monkey you are."

Lily looked Austin up and down and scoffed. In her opinion, there was something about him that reeked of the need to feel superior over someone … *anyone.* But Lily felt just as equal in her need to let Austin know that that *someone* would not be her, not now … not *ever.* She made a decision right then and there that she would not tolerate any disrespect from him, or anyone else in their group, without defending herself, despite the consequences that may arise.

"That was reeeal original." Lily squinted her eyes at Austin. "I bet you proud 'a yo'self for that one, ain't ya'? Go on and give yo'self a pat on the back and when you're done … turn to page three," she replied, allowing a brief flash of the strong woman she truly was on the inside to peek through the crack in the cloak of meekness she had been forced to cover herself in over the years.

Lily's words roused Austin from his cocky stance against the timpani. He stood tall with his chest out, ready to fire back. "Just 'cause y'ur workin' with someone like William, you think you can talk to a white man any kind 'a way now, do ya'?!"

Lily refused to respond, but he was relentless.

"How is it y'ur payin' him to teach ya' anyway, huh? You know you ain't got no goddamn money. So go on and tell us." He looked Lily up and down and stepped closer.

"Just how many times did you have to get down on y'ur knees and wrap those nigga' lips around William's cock to earn y'ur way?" he smirked.

Lily lowered her eyelids, rose from the piano bench, and fearlessly took two steps toward him too. "Far fewer times than it's taken you to run through this song without messin' it up for everybody," she said with her lips pursed and pure ice radiating in her tone. Everybody in the room began to snicker at how slyly she had exposed the truth about him being their weakest link. He was the main reason they had been stuck rehearsing the same song for the last hour instead of moving on to another.

Lily's response wiped the smirk clean off Austin's face. "What the hell are all 'a y'all laughin' at?!" he fired at his band mates. His face was red, and his hands suddenly gripped tight around his batons. He and Lily stared each other down until William and James entered seconds later and instantly restored civility to the situation. William seemed oblivious to the climate in the room, but James immediately sensed something was off.

It had become James's routine to spend his lunch break in the library watching Lily and William rehearse together, but with the presence of the orchestra, he noticed that the atmosphere in the room was not how he usually found it. Sweat began to bead on his forehead when James noticed that Lily's laughter no longer enveloped the room and that the smile he looked forward to seeing was missing. Even the way Lily played her music told him immediately that something was wrong. When James read the expression on her face, his stomach clenched, and he set his plate aside, suddenly no longer interested in his meal. After continuing to watch for a while, the sick feeling in his stomach began to fester over the drastic change in Lily's demeanor, until he could no longer handle sitting idly by. "Lily!?" he suddenly erupted, when he had reached his boiling point. Everyone in the room stopped the music and turned in his direction. "Can I see you for a minute?"

"Yessa'," she replied.

James cringed every time Lily referred to him as "sir," but even more so when she said it in front of others. For the moment, he did not correct her use of the word. He was too busy staring at the way she briefly locked eyes with Austin before she headed out into the hallway. Though brief as it was, their exchange spoke volumes to James. He glared at the troublemaking percussionist with questioning eyes as he held the door open for Lily and then stepped out into the hallway with her.

"Lily, what is it?" James asked her after closing the double doors behind her.

"What do you mean?"

"Somethin's botherin' you. I ain't seen you like this in days. Now, tell me what the hell's goin' on in there."

"I don't know what you're talkin' about." She folded her arms up and looked away as she told her lie. "Ain't nothin' botherin' me." Her body language and the way she turned away confessed to James that she was not forthcoming. Even before her silent confession, though, James was convinced that it was the percussionist who had upset her. But he was only partially right. It had not been Austin's words that directly affected her. Lily suddenly had the realization that Austin's thoughts would be a reflection of the sea of people she was soon to sit centerstage in front of. Austin's words and actions had quickly forced her to remember that not everybody would be as open and welcoming as William had been. The whole ordeal made her realize that she somehow had to strengthen herself emotionally to prepare for the judgment and ridicule that were sure to go hand in hand with such a huge undertaking. The negative effect of that emotional preparation was written all over her face and was very easily read by James as he sat in the library stewing over the matter. It was even more obvious to him now while standing only feet away from her.

"I don't believe you," James admitted, staring at Lily intensely.

"I'm tellin' you the truth. I'm fine!"

"Are you sure? Because it doesn't look that way to me."

Lily thought for a moment to tell him her troubles, but with all that he and William had already done for her, she did not wish to burden them with small things. She was, however, taken aback by how concerned James was over her emotional state. "I'm just tired is all. We've been workin' awful long hours to prepare."

"*Tired?* You're certain that's all it is?"

"Yessa'." She looked up at James and then quickly looked away again. "I-I'm certain."

James wanted to know what it was that Austin had done. He was ready to set him straight and anyone else, if need be. But Lily still refused to tell him and he did not want to press her any further for fear of upsetting her even more. "Well, listen, if you feel you need a break, don't be afraid to speak up, okay?"

"Yessa'. Thank you. I promise I will."

"Good."

"Well, everyone is waitin' for me, so I betta' get on back."

James nodded his head, and she proceeded to walk past him.

"And Lily," he called, as she grabbed the handle of the library door. She stopped and turned around. "*James* ... Please, I'd really like it if you'd only call me James from now on. No more 'a this 'sa' nonsense. It's not necessary, okay?" Although she had dropped the "master" and "sir" from time to time when they were not around other people, he wanted to be sure it became a permanent ritual.

"Okay, I'll rememba' that." She tried to force herself to smile in appreciation of another one of his wonderful gestures, despite how she was feeling on the inside at that moment.

After making a mental note of another act of James's kindness, Lily's focus returned to the fact that she had to walk back into the library to finish dealing with the wolves that she had allowed to destroy her mood. When she returned, though, she felt an even greater tension in the room than before. Everyone, including William, stopped talking and stared at her. She lingered in the doorway, afraid to ask what she had just walked in on. She somehow knew from the lack of warmth in William's expression that something was seriously wrong. James walked up behind her just in time for both of them to hear the end of the heated conversation that had just taken place while they were absent.

"Figure it out, William! Or we walk!" Austin left William with those final words before he and the others began packing their instruments to leave for the day, two hours before rehearsals were due to end. For the few minutes that she had stepped away, Lily's arch nemesis had finally found the position of superiority he was seeking. Austin had led the charge that caused every member of the orchestra to stomp out of the library, cutting their eyes at James and Lily on their way out as they stood on either side of the double doors.

"DAMN!" William yelled, slamming his hand on his grand piano, causing Lily to jump.

"What the hell just happened in here?!" James asked as soon as everyone had filed out.

William had taken his spectacles off and was rubbing his eyes in an effort to soothe himself. "Lily, do you mind if I speak to James alone a moment?" he asked, trying to sound like his usual gentle self, but she could easily hear the anger in his voice.

"Please, if you don't mind, I wanna know what's goin' on."

"Please, I really don't want to trouble you with such trite things."

"I don't mean to ova'step my boundaries, but judgin' from what I just seen, it doesn't seem trite at all. Please, I'm just as much a part 'a this as the both 'a you and I'd really like to know." She wanted to begin the process of strengthening herself to the things that were soon to come her way and figured this would be the place to start.

William realized that Lily was right and that it was probably not wise to always try to shelter her from the harshness of reality. So in honoring her wishes, he began to explain a more subtle and respectful version of how he had been blindsided by Austin with news that threatened to put an end to their chances of opening the show during the Spring Extravaganza as scheduled or perhaps even at all.

"Well, let me apologize to you, Lily, before I even begin. It's so hard for me to say these things in front of you, but just know that they don't remotely reflect any of my beliefs."

"Of course, I know betta' than that."

William looked at Lily again with solemn eyes and sighed, embarrassed to reiterate what was said in her absence. He had to turn away from her before reluctantly proceeding. "Well, if you must know, the students admitted to me that finally being here in the reality of this situation has opened their eyes to what they may be getting themselves into. They said they had not carefully considered all the risks that they were taking by performing with a Negro woman. They don't feel that any amount of money is worth bringing embarrassment or shame to themselves or their families by playing background to someone who was once enslaved. They told me that I needed to find a way for them to remain anonymous during the performance or that they would take the money I've already given them, yet not bother to fulfill the rest of their agreement." William spoke the whole time staring down at his desk. He was just far too embarrassed to look Lily in the eyes.

Lily stood across the room expressionless and numb as she listened to all that had transpired in the short time she was away in the hallway. She tried to ignore it, but the feeling of being a burden began to weigh heavily on her again.

"I know Lily is capable of incredible things, but a symphony is not only about the music," William continued as he began pacing about the room. "It's about the artistry of the instruments and performers dancing and swaying in unison! Taking that away destroys the visual appeal of the show. Proceeding without such a thing would be highly unusual. The stage will seem empty and lifeless without it," he professed, sounding utterly aggravated. "Not only that, but we've advertised this as an entire symphony. It's what patrons will be expecting to see."

"You paid those little pieces of shit! They agreed to this! They can't back out now!" James spat, unable to sit still either. His anger was on a whole different level than William's.

"The reality is that they can do whatever they want. Unfortunately, I never had them sign any formal contracts. I trusted that a verbal agreement and an upfront payment would be enough to secure their participation."

"We've been advertisin' for weeks and invitin' people from all ova' to see this! We can't possibly push this back to find a whole new group of people now! What the hell do they expect us to do?!"

"They've asked for us to redesign the stage and possibly create some sort of barrier or simply add a curtain for them to sit behind. Of course, it can be done, but again, a symphony loses its elegance without their visual participation."

William and James continued to bicker about what to do. James had yet to lower his voice as he spoke of forcing the students to do as they agreed. William, in turn, paced back and forth in frustration, trying not to let the feeling of defeat settle upon him. But the one who should be more upset than either of them stared quietly out the window at the lake in the distance with a longing to be near it. Lily wanted to stand on its shores and drift into a fantasy land or think back to happy childhood memories, the way the sparkling water always had the ability to do.

"Please, just let 'em be." Lily's soft and fragile voice penetrated into James and William's angry banter and brought a sudden peace to the atmosphere in the room. They both ceased their conversation and turned to find Lily with her back to them, still gazing out the window. She did not want to argue with the students, force them, or fight with them as James was suggesting. Pushing against one's will was something she was painfully familiar with. She wished it on no one, including those who held unnecessary ill will against her. "If that's the way the students want it, then so be it. But please … Please, just let 'em be," she continued softly. "Besides, I think I have a way to give 'em what they want and still have the kind 'a show you're talkin' about, William."

William walked over to her, gently turned her around to face him, and then held both of her hands in his. "You need only speak it, and I will see it done."

"But with only three weeks left, I just don't know if we could eva' make it happen."

"Lily, I *will* see it done."

With his insistence, Lily proceeded to explain what she knew would give the student orchestra the anonymity they had requested, and what she hoped would give the audience a show that would truly be unforgettable.

* * * *

"Beautiful day isn't it?" James said, walking up beside Lily, holding two fishing rods.

"Sho' is." Lily had finally made her way out to her

favorite spot on the lake. She was in dire need of a way to mentally escape after the earlier rehearsal disaster.

"I'd love to do me some fishin' right about now, but seein' as how it's been pointed out to me that I ain't so good at catchin' bait, I sure could use me some help from an ol' pro," James teased.

"I don't see the point. I could dig you up a whole bucket full of worms, but you couldn't catch a fish if it jumped in your lap," Lily smiled.

The origin of her joke flashed instantly in James's mind. As kids, he and Lily had set out together one Sunday in his tiny fishing boat at the same creek where Wilbur lived. Out of the blue, James was startled by a fish that leaped out of the water into his lap. Frightened, he jumped up and started dancing around to get away from it. He lost his balance and fell out of the boat with his arms flailing everywhere, screaming like a little girl. The sight of it had Lily bent over howling with laughter for minutes afterward.

"Guess I'll neva' live that one down, will I?" James laughed after recalling the embarrassing moment.

"Nope, 'fraid not ... nor the fact that I's always a much betta' fisher-*woman* than you," Lily reminded him.

"Now, that part seems to have slipped my memory. You'll have to prove it to me. I've got two poles here." James held them up. "And there's a boat ova' yonda'," he pointed out, motioning his head in the direction of a little rowboat that was tied to a small dock.

Lily looked in the direction of the boat, thought about it a moment, but then declined. "Naw, that's alright, you can go on without me."

James felt his heart sink a little. He had no desire to fish without her. "Come on, now. It'll get your mind off of things for a while. Besides," he said, rubbing his temples like he was attempting to conjure up a memory. "I really just can't rememba' you bein' all that great of a fisherman."

"Fisher-*woman!*"

"Oh, excuse me! I stand corrected. Well, I'm gonna need you to jog my memory on how great of a fisher-*woman* you truly are, 'cause I have an awfully hard time believin' that." The Lily James knew as a boy never backed down from challenges. He figured he would try the old tactic on her and see how well it worked nearly ten years later. By the look on her face, though, he figured there was no way she would take him up on the offer.

"Well…" she started.

"Well, what?"

"Well, you'll have to make it worth my while."

"Oh." He raised an eyebrow. "How so?"

"If I catch more fish than you, then Anna Mae and I get to watch you cook dinna' for the rest of us tonight."

"Well, what do I get if I win?"

"The simple honor of finally havin' caught more fish than me for the first time in your life!" she answered, snatching one of the poles and giving him a smile dripping with playful arrogance.

"Alright, you got yourself a bet," he smiled in return. "But it doesn't count 'til we shake on it."

Lily reluctantly extended her hand. James took it gently into his, barely shaking it all, concerning himself more with the softness and warmth of her skin. Lily was not oblivious to the way his facial expression changed when he touched her. It was subtle, but she read it well. "Now, it's official," she said, creating an excuse to take her hand out of his and settle the rapid beating she suddenly felt in her chest after the way he had just looked at her.

James gestured his hand toward the boat and allowed her to walk ahead of him. Shortly thereafter, he rowed them out into the middle of the lake. Lily let her eyes roam everywhere else except for on James. She could feel him looking at her, but she did not want to reciprocate. When they reached the deepest part of the water, James continued to watch her bait her hook with worms and cast her line out

191

as if she had done it just the day before, and not years. While gazing at her, James was thinking about the fact that Lily only allowed him short glimpses of her old self before quietly slipping back behind her carefully crafted wall and shutting him out. Even while they were just feet apart, she sat staring at her fishing line, having yet to say another word since their interaction on the shore. "What's on your mind, Lily?" James asked unexpectedly, in hopes that she would give him another glimpse of her old self for a while.

It had been so many years since James had concerned himself with anything in regards to Lily's emotional state. Over the last few weeks, she realized that it was a lot more challenging to adjust to his kindness than she had anticipated. After everything that had happened between them in the past, she kept telling herself that it made more sense to keep her private thoughts as just that. But there was something about the way James spoke to her lately, in such a gentle tone, that was slowly making her want to open up to him just as she had in her youth. Lily often wondered, though, if she would regret unlocking the entrance to her protective wall and allowing him in, even if only for short periods of time. Despite her fears, she let him in yet again but proceeded with great caution. "Well, I been wantin' to tell you how sorry I am about rehearsals today. I…"

"No! No! No!" James replied, cutting her off and startling her.

"What?!" Lily jumped, thinking it had something to do with his fishing line. "What is it?"

"You don't owe anyone any apologies, ya' hear?! If anything, those little rats should be apologizin' to you! I don't appreciate the little stunt they pulled today! And I'll tell you right here, and right now, if any one of them personally gives you a problem, you let me know," he demanded, after remembering the cold glance between her and Austin. "Alright?!"

Lily just stared at him a moment, surprised at his instant high level of hostility, and again noting the fact that he seemed genuinely concerned for her well-being.

"Alright?" James insisted again.

"Alright," Lily finally replied. "I'll rememba' that. But I hope maybe we can get the changes done on time and everything will be fine," she said calmly, attempting to settle James down.

"Me too, but it neva' should've come to this. They…"

"They what?"

"Neva' mind," he said, running his hands through his hair and blowing out a breath to help calm himself down. "Listen, we're not s'pposed to be thinkin' or talkin' about anything like that while we're out here, don't you rememba'?"

"Rememba' what?" Lily asked, looking confused.

"Surely you rememba'," he said, with calmness finally having returned to his voice. He took a second to reflect before diving back into a moment of nostalgia. "It was the summa' right afta' Auntie passed away and my parents were about to send me and my brotha's away for a couple of weeks to stay with my uncle and cousins for a while." He continued talking as he baited his fishing line. "Rememba' we were both feelin' mighty down about everything? So that Sunday, we decided we's gonna do a little fishin' before I was due to leave. But before we left the shore, we promised each otha' that wheneva' we was floatin' out in the middle of the wata', just like we are now, that we'd always pretend like we's in anotha' world, in a world where no troubles could touch us, where we talked about nothin' but happy things." He turned to look at the profile of Lily's face. "Don't tell me you've forgotten?"

Lily turned and finally reciprocated his glare, suddenly feeling warmed by the fact that he had recalled something that meant so much to her at the time. "How could I eva' forget somethin' like that?" she smiled, feeling comforted by the memory. "I guess I'm just surprised that you haven't forgotten eitha'."

"You ain't the only one here with an amazin'' memory," James boasted, sticking his chest out, pretending to be arrogant.

Lily tried not to smile at his playfulness, but she could not help herself.

"Ya' know, speakin' of my cousins, that reminds me," James said, finally casting out his fishing line.

"Reminds you of what?"

"I neva' did get around to thankin' you way back then," he said, as they both turned to focus on their fishing lines in the distance.

"Thankin' me for what?"

"Back when my uncle had sent my cousins to stay with us for a change, I rememba' us boys decided we's gon' try to make a tent usin' some of my mama's dresses. Wasn't too bright of an idea, but we was just a bunch of dumb little boys."

"I can't argue with that," Lily teased.

"Wasn't long 'fore we ended up rippin' a hole in two of her favorite dresses, not to mention all the dirt stains we'd gotten all over 'em. I rememba' I tried to hide 'em thinkin' maybe she wouldn't find 'em. But the oddest thing happened…"

"And what might that be?"

"Three days lata', mama was dressed for church in one of the dresses we tore up. I saw her walkin' toward me in that thang, and I swore she was comin' to grab me by my scrawny little neck, but she walked right on past me with her dress flowin' in pristine condition. She must 'a thought I's half outta my mind the way I circled 'round her two or three times lookin' for that big ol' hole that I swore I'd put in the backside of that dress. But magically…" He waved his hand in the air. "It was nowhere to be found, nor were the stains," James recounted, in a hypnotic voice.

"Ya' don't say!" Lily replied sarcastically.

"Can you believe that?" he smiled, sounding just as sarcastic.

"Simply amazin'!" she smiled back. "But, I'll let you in on a little secret." Lily looked around as if somebody was going to hear her. She then leaned in close to James. "You don't have me to thank for that."

"No, well who else could it've been? I know good 'n well my brotha's and my daddy can't sew worth nothin'."

"Shh, this is a well-kept secret amongst all us slaves." She looked around once more and whispered, "It was The Sewin' Fairies who fixed your mama's dresses."

"The who?!"

"Shh! Keep your voice down!" she insisted, looking around again. "The Sewin' Fairies."

"The *who*?!"

"You mean you ain't neva' heard 'a them?"

James just kept looking at Lily like she had lost her mind.

"I just don't know what we'd do without The Sewin' Fairies. See, they float around at night searchin' for clothes that dumb little boys done tore up tryna build tents … tents that actually look more like flags blowin' in the wind," she sarcastically pointed out. "Then when they spot 'em all balled up in the back of the closet … where any blind man can find 'em," she teased again, "they swoop down outta the sky, wash 'em up, sprinkle a little mendin' dust on 'em to make 'em good as new, and hang 'em back on the rack 'fore anybody eva' notices a thang."

This time around, floating out in their fantasy world of happiness, drifting far away from the reality of their troubles, it was James who sat in the fishing boat laughing uncontrollably at Lily.

"I can't believe you's laughin' at The Sewin' Fairies afta' they saved your little scrawny behind all them years ago. You should be 'shamed 'a yo'self," she joked, fighting to hold back her laughter until she finally lost it too. She began laughing along with him like they were two silly twelve-year-old children all over again.

When they regained their composure, James was quiet for a moment while he reflected on the flash of many memories from his youth that were the most precious to him. In every single one of them, he realized that Lily was always there by his side. "Thank you, Lily," he said to her out of the blue, in a very serious yet appreciative tone.

"I already told you it wasn't me," she kidded again.

"No, I really mean it … Thank you," he said turning toward her.

Lily looked at him with inquisitive eyes.

"For helpin' to give me a childhood full of unforgettable memories," he continued.

Lily could feel her cheeks flushing red as he stared at her in a way that conveyed his sincerity. "Thank you too, James."

"For what?"

"For givin' me a childhood at all."

Chapter Thirteen

Slave Code
Article VIII Section XI
No slave is permitted to work for pay, or to keep horses; or to own or wagon, or carriage; or to buy or wear clothes finer than "Negro cloth."

Saturday
April 15, 1859
Annual Spring Extravaganza
and
"The Return Of William Werthington"

William had never known what it meant to be nervous or anxious about a performance … until this very moment. Not being able to foretell the future had his stomach in knots, his heart racing, and sweat threatening to seep through his clothing. The stage was normally like his second home. But now, sitting at the piano in front of a lawn full of people about to strike the keys to begin a show that would undoubtedly be epic in the most magnificent of ways—or in the most disastrous—had William experiencing a feeling that had always been foreign to him. He prayed silently before he began that the end result of the nights events would be worth crying tears of joy and not tears of heartbreak. But it was not himself that he sent that prayer for. He wanted the night to be spectacular … for Lily. Anything less than that would have devastated him.

Even in the hours before he took his seat at the piano, it was apparent that William wanted nothing but the best for Lily. Not wanting nerves to affect her leading up to the show, William expressed to James that Lily would more than likely benefit by having her mind and body far away from the night's approaching events. He explained that drowning one's thoughts in every detail of the show just

197

hours before could be detrimental to the outcome. After that advice, Lily had been awakened that morning by Anna Mae and her daughter, Isabel, standing over her bed, greeting her with smiles and a warm breakfast. "Wake up, sunshine," Anna Mae said to Lily as Isabel drew back the curtains, letting in the beautiful spring sunlight.

"What time is it?" Lily asked, rubbing her pasty eyes.

"A little after nine o'clock. You's the only one still asleep in the whole house."

"Nine o'clock!" she screamed, throwing the covers off of herself in a panic. She was usually wide awake helping Anna Mae prepare breakfast for everyone long before then. "Why didn't anyone wake me?" She scurried to get out of bed.

"Whoa, whoa, lay down chil'! Just relax," Anna Mae said, stopping her. "Everything's fine. We all wanted you to rest before your big performance tonight. We figured it'd do ya' good to let you sleep in for a change."

"Oh, thank you," Lily yawned. "I didn't fall asleep 'til well afta' midnight," she admitted.

"No worries baby. 'Sides, we here to pampa' you and help you relax a lil' before tonight anyway," she smiled. "We don't want you liftin' a finga' 'til then."

"*Pampa'* me?"

"That's right!" Isabel smiled. "And you can start with breakfast in bed."

"Breakfast? Sittin' in bed?"

"Yeah, ain't you eva' had breakfast in bed?" she asked bewildered. Anna Mae nudged her spoiled daughter. She had led a privileged life thanks to William. She was only six at the time that he had bought them at auction and hardly remembered much of what being a slave was like. "Me and Elijah used to make mama and daddy breakfast in bed nearly every Sunday," she continued, despite her mother trying to get her to be quiet. Isabel was in her twenties, but often still acted much like a mindless teenager, despite her sweet disposition and good intentions.

"Naw, ain't nobody eva' served me nothin', 'specially not while in a *bed,*" Lily laughed, finding the thought of such a thing amusing.

"Well, there's a first time for everything!" Isabel squealed, sounding like an excited school girl. She then handed Lily a tray filled with eggs, biscuits, bacon, fruit, oatmeal, and a glass of freshly squeezed orange juice.

"Thank you," Lily smiled. "This is mighty kind of you ladies to go outta y'all's way like this." She then began to eat her breakfast. She was appreciative of Anna Mae and Isabel's efforts, but still could not help feeling a bit strange about someone bringing her food and eating it in a bed. The oddities continued, though. Breakfast was only the beginning of Anna Mae and Isabel's efforts to treat Lily like a pampered princess. While she finished eating, Anna Mae stepped out of the room for a moment. Isabel then sat on the edge of the bed and chattered on and on about all the latest gossip that had gone on in her life since the last she had seen Lily at William's gala. When they first met there, they had an instant sisterly connection. Isabel talked so much that Lily could hardly get a word in edgewise back then and the same held true this time around. Lily did not mind it, though. She was always thoroughly entertained by Isabel's stories and found her bizarre unfiltered comments amusing. She loved the ignorant bliss that Isabel's mind seemed to wallow in and thought it was cute how she always went on and on talking about Elijah, her parents, or her latest beau.

"Maaama! Is it ready yet?" Isabel suddenly screamed while slap in the middle of a story. She then sporadically jumped up out of bed like a hyper two-year-old and peeked her head out of the door.

"Is what ready?" Lily asked her.

"Your bath wata', silly," Isabel replied like the answer was obvious.

"Bath wata'?"

"Don't tell me you ain't neva' had one 'a them eitha'?" she asked, putting both of her fists on her hips, not realizing how offensive she was being as usual.

"Naw, it ain't that. I've had plenty since I been here in William's house. Truth to be told, I done had more here than in my whole life." Lily rubbed her arm, feeling the dramatic change in her skin's softness in the previous weeks. "It's just that I ain't neva' had nobody draw up the wata' for me."

"Oh, you'll love it! Mama always used to make my baths when I's just a girl. She adds in a little honey and milk and some of the finest fragrances. And she always knows how to make the temperature just right! Now come on and get them clothes off," she said, in her high-pitched tone, while pulling Lily's arm to get her out of bed.

Lily followed along with Isabel's wishes. She went down the hall to soak in the warmth of the bubble-filled bath water while Isabel and Anna Mae washed her hair. She found it hard to sit still and let them do all of the work, though. It was normally she who was in such a position, so it was difficult for her to make the adjustment.

"I didn't know you was hidin' all this hair unda' yo' scarf. Sho' wish my hair was this long and soft," Isabel confessed. "Me and mama gonna have a fine time fixin' it up."

"Y'all gonna do my hair too?"

"Nails, make-up, and all!" Isabel told her.

"Y'all bein' so kind to me. I-I really can't thank ya' enough. I wouldn't know what in the world to do without the both of ya'. I ain't neva' wore make-up in all my life," Lily laughed. "Come to think of it, I ain't neva' really done my hair eitha'."

"Well believe me, when we's finished with you, Elijah gon' be sorry he couldn't be here to see you again tonight," Isabel blurted. Her mother nudged her again. "What

Mama!? It's true! Elijah told me how pretty he thinks she is."

"Hush up girl! Quit tellin' business that ain't yours to be told."

"Yes, Mama."

"It's okay, Ms. Anna Mae, the feelin's mutual. I must admit, you and Mr. Ben make fine lookin' children. Isabel's so beautiful." Isabel smiled at the compliment. "And Elijah is awfully handsome."

"Well, thank you baby, but Isabel still needs to learn how to hold her tongue sometimes."

Isabel was not saying something that Lily did not already assume about Elijah. The simple tone of his deep voice when he spoke to her, and the way his dark eyes would linger on her, clearly conveyed how attracted he was to her. The attraction was mutual. Lily found Elijah's chocolate-colored smooth skin, his tall muscular frame, and his smile difficult to turn away from. But oddly, Isabel's mention of her brother suddenly made Lily curious about what a certain someone else would think of her with make-up and a new hair style. Lily let her mind drift away as she leaned back with her eyes closed in the enormous garden tub, washing herself slowly with a loofah. Suddenly forgetting that there were two other people there with her, she began pretending that her hands belonged to the man whose face and shirtless body she saw in vivid detail behind her lowered eyelids.

Lily then began reflecting on the weeks since her and James had fished together. From that day forward, the awkwardness they once felt around each other faded away and there began to be an increasing comfort and ease in their interactions. More and more, they found themselves wanting to speak to each other when the small windows of opportunity would arise. The topics were always light and silly and were an escape that each of them needed in the midst of their daunting tasks. Each time, though, it seemed they were always called back to their duties sooner than either of them wanted. Every conversation was always left lingering, leaving both of them eagerly awaiting the next time they could exchange a few words. Little by little, the wall Lily had erected to keep James from trampling on her emotions was starting to crumble. However, she still remembered to proceed with great caution while allowing him into the security of her protective bubble.

Lily was so absorbed in her thoughts and at ease in the warm water that she did not want to get out when Anna Mae and Isabel finished her hair. With reluctance, she emerged from the wonders of her soothing bath and wandered back into her room with them and locked the door. When she completely dried herself off, Anna Mae gave her a bottle filled with a homemade lotion that she had been making for decades. She swore every woman needed to use her secret formula if they were going to keep their skin looking youthful and feeling soft. Anna Mae's supple skin proved that her theory must be true. She looked nowhere near her actual age. Again, as Lily applied her new lotion, she found that she could not help but imagine that it was a set of strong hands gliding down the length of her legs, across her abdomen, up her arms, and into a light massage of her shoulders. She literally had to shake herself from the image to stop her body from reacting to the mere fantasy of it all.

"Naw, baby, you keep that," Anna Mae told Lily after she suddenly tried to thrust the bottle back toward her. She felt as though she needed to get rid of it in order to put an end to the erotic visions in her head. "That's my gift to you in celebration of your first show."

"Thank you, Ms. Anna Mae," Lily replied, sounding truly appreciative. When Anna Mae stepped away, Lily looked at the bottle in her hand again and smiled while imagining its many pleasurable uses.

Isabel stepped up beside Lily and snapped her out of

her trance. "Now yo' skin gon' be nice and soft unda'neath yo' new dress!"

"New dress?" Lily replied, sounding surprised.

"Yeah! You didn't think we's gon' let you wanda' up on that stage wearin' this ol' rag, did ya'?" Isabel asked, holding up the dress she wore daily. Anna Mae rolled her eyes wondering where she had gone wrong with her absentminded daughter. She was convinced that her mindlessness was a trait she had inherited from Ben's side of the family. Still oblivious to her insulting comment, Isabel wandered happily over to the closet and pulled out the dress she was so excited to show Lily. Knowing the laws about the sort of generic fabric that slaves were limited to wearing, Lily assumed that her new dress would not be too far different from the one James had given her on the journey to Ohio. What Isabel revealed, though, completely obliterated her expectations.

Lily gasped. "Oh my," she said, unable to take her eyes off of the beautiful gown in front of her. She stepped closer to it and reached out to feel the sort of fabric a slave would normally never be allowed to wear. "This can't possibly be mine."

"Well, sho' it is!" Isabel assured her. "You like it, don't ya'?"

"*Like* it? Like isn't the word," Lily replied, with awe obvious in her tone. "It's the most gorgeous dress I've eva' laid my eyes on!" Isabel handed it to her. Lily took it and walked over to the mirror and placed it in front of herself, trying to imagine what it would look like when it was finally on her body. She got just as excited and giddy as Isabel at the prospect of being allowed the honor of wearing such a beautiful piece of clothing. "Oh, I love it!" She turned and hugged Isabel. "Thank you both so much!"

"Don't thank us."

"No, well, who else then?"

"James!" Isabel said excitedly. Anna Mae just shook

her head again at her silly daughter. She was not supposed to tell her about the hand that James had in any of their affairs that morning.

"James?" Lily asked curiously.

"Yeah!" Isabel confirmed. "He say he knows red's yo' favorite color. He brought us the fabric and asked if we could fix you up a real nice dress. He gave us a catalog filled with all kind 'a pictures of fancy dresses in it, so we could pick the one we liked best! He sho' do want you to look pretty!"

In fact, all of the morning's events were requests that had come from James. Even if William had not told him about the powers of relaxation, James planned to bombard Lily with an array of pleasantries to help ease any lingering fears or worries leading up to her performance. William's words of wisdom simply confirmed that it was a wonderful idea. However, James knew nothing about primping and styling a woman. For that, he had called on Anna Mae and Isabel to meet the call of duty, feeling that women would be more suited to handle all of Lily's personal needs. After mother and daughter happily obliged, James gave them money and a list of things that Lily might like. He then swore them to secrecy about the hand he had in their arrangement. He wanted it to seem like a genuine gesture from Anna Mae and Isabel, rather than making Lily feel as if it was just another chore he had added to their to-do list. After sworn silence from both ladies, James handed them the insurmountable task of distracting Lily's mind from the night's coming events.

"That dress is gonna look even more beautiful when we get it on ya'," Anna Mae told Lily after joining her and Isabel in front of the mirror. "Go ahead and try it on, so I can see if I'm needin' to take it in an inch or two."

While Anna Mae worked on fine-tuning her dress, Isabel started working on styling Lily's hair. In the process, Lily asked to hear stories of what it was like living with

William for all the years that they had. Anna Mae took the opportunity to inundate her with embarrassing and funny tales of her children, especially stories that had to do with Isabel as a way to retaliate for all of her unintended rude comments. In between stories, wild outbursts of laughter, and working on the fine details of Lily's makeover, Isabel would sneak food and wine in from the kitchen to help further relax them all. The scene was less like the preparation for a major show and more like that of a mother enjoying the simple pleasures of having two daughters. It was exactly the sort of escape that James was hoping Isabel and Anna Mae would provide for Lily.

For James, however, the morning had been a far cry from relaxing baths, pampering, and pleasantries. From the moment he woke up, he had been going full steam to finish off every last minute detail for the show. With a little over an hour left before the show was set to begin, he finally had a chance to shave, cut his hair, take a much-needed bath and get into his new suit, in preparation for the few minutes that he would be onstage. When he was finished, James glanced out of the window and watched Ben and some hired helpers guiding anxious audience members from their carriages to their seats. Parades of people in flowing dresses, fancy hats, and expensive attire began settling into place, filling the freshly finished amphitheater fast. James stood there for a moment to admire his work of art, but before long his nerves began to toy with him again. He had already been incapable of eating, and despite how tired he was after weeks of labor, he had gotten very little sleep the night before. His worries had nothing to do with his own well-being, but with that of Lily's. He had not seen her all day, which left him worrying obsessively over the state of mind she might be in. After making a few minor adjustments to his hair and his attire, he planned to finally head to her room, hoping to learn that she was doing much better than he was at that moment.

As James was leaving his room, William had just come in from backstage to retrieve something from his desk. He took the free moment away from the madness to collect himself. He paced nervously in his den, stopping to look out of the window every so often at the crowd that steadily gathered. For the three weeks since the debacle with his students, William had been highly stressed while expending all his efforts to make the necessary changes to bring Lily's show idea to life. It had taken twelve to fourteen-hour days without a single wasted minute of time, and damn near an act of God, to turn something that was once going to be relatively simple into something that was now going to be extremely elaborate. Where Lily was concerned, William was not surprised at her level of creativity and innovation, but he was surprised, however, that they had pulled off her extravagant idea in as little time as they had. With everything completed on schedule, William's stress and worry had now shifted to the unpredictability of the audience and their reaction to what they were about to see.

As William was pacing in his den, he heard footsteps coming down the hallway. He peeked his head out and startled James who was in a hurry to see Lily. "H-how is Lily? Is she alright?" William asked, talking fast and fidgeting with his glasses. "I haven't bothered to go up and see her. I'm a nervous wreck, and I was afraid I would just end up stressing her."

James was surprised at William's demeanor. He was usually calm and collected, but that was not the case in this instance. "I tried to go up and see her earlier, but Anna Mae caught me in the hall and shooed me off. She assured me Lily was fine, though. I'm headed back up there again now. I'm sure Lily's dressed by now."

"Perfect. It's less than an hour before showtime. She'll need to warm up a bit," William explained, rubbing his sweaty palms together. "Everything from the list I gave you this morning is prepared and ready, correct?"

"Yes, William, everything is in place." James noticed the jittery sound in William's voice and the way he was continuously smoothing his hands over his clothes, and looking everywhere but at him. "Listen, are you gonna be alright?"

"I just … I just hope I've done enough."

James realized that William was beyond being just a nervous wreck. He was in a state of panic. James pulled him into the den and shut the door, hoping to say a few words to him in private to help calm his nerves. "You hope you've done enough?" James reiterated. "My God, William, the only thing you've yet to do for Lily is snatch the moon down from the sky so she can have a betta' look. You've done so much for her that I don't even know where to begin thankin' you for all of this. When I brought her to you, I certainly didn't expect it to escalate to all of this."

"Be honest with me, though, James. Do you think Lily's truly ready for this? O-or do you think we've pushed her too hard?"

"I assure you, William, Lily's more than ready for this. I have no doubt about that. This show is all she eva' talks about now. Besides, I've known Lily nearly all my life, and she's, honest to God, the strongest woman I know. So no matta' what her demeanor may show, I know that when the moment comes for her to show her strength, she will." James really believed that despite how worried he was feeling on the inside as well.

"I just want this to be perfect for her, James … I really do," William said, walking over to stare out of the window again at the artistically crafted amphitheater sitting in his yard.

"If there's anybody in this world who knows that already, William, it's definitely me. It's one of the many reasons I appreciate you as much as I do." James walked up behind William and put his hand on his shoulder as a gesture of his sincerity. They were both silent afterward while they continued to stare out into the fields at the grand open-air amphitheater.

"The amphitheater, James. It's just marvelous. Even better than I imagined it would be. For all your labor, I truly thank you."

James simply nodded his head and took in his compliment with silent gratitude and pride.

"Well, I'm headed backstage to be sure everyone is ready and in place," William said, sounding much calmer. "I assume you're headed to fetch Lily now."

"Yes, we'll be there shortly."

After William departed from the den, James immediately refocused on the only person whose company he had wanted throughout the day. He ascended the stairs two at a time, feeling like a child anticipating the opening of a birthday gift. He was anxious and eager to see the fruits of Anna Mae and Isabel's labor, but most importantly, he was hoping to find that Lily was doing fine emotionally. He checked his hair and straightened his bow tie in the mirror at the top of the stairs before he proceeded to knock gently on her bedroom door. Isabel opened it slightly and peeked her head out.

"Hey, Isabel. You ladies decent?"

"Yeah, come on in," she smiled, stepping aside and opening the door all the way. "Mama's just about finished."

Lily sat at a vanity table in the corner with her back to James while Anna Mae finished making a few adjustments to her hair. James turned in Lily's direction, and his eyes immediately became fixated on the length of her hair and the way it fell in long spiral curls down her back. It never dawned on him that he had never even seen her before without her hair wrapped neatly in a scarf or bonnet. Underneath Lily's hair, he could see a few of the silky white drawstrings that held her brand-new handmade dress firmly in place. Suddenly, the anticipation of seeing her began to pump adrenaline heavily throughout James's body.

Anna Mae stepped back and smiled at all of her hard work. "All finished!" she said, with a look of pride on her face.

Lily took a moment to look at herself in the mirror, turning her head from side to side and touching her hair. She found it hard to believe it was her own reflection she was looking at. She then stood up and looked at herself from head to toe in the floor-length mirror nearby. Once she absorbed the fact that it was indeed her own reflection, Lily smiled and held back the urge to cry. Nervously, she then turned around for Isabel and James to finally see her for the first time ever with her hair neatly styled, in make-up, and adorned in her beautiful, floor-length, red Victorian dress. The exquisite flowing gown hugged Lily's waist tight and hung like the shape of a small bell from her hips on down. It highlighted the sultry curves of her body that were typically hidden underneath her usual plain attire. Aside from a few wispy bangs hanging neatly across her forehead, the top portion of Lily's hair was pulled back out of her face and styled decoratively on top while the rest of it fell in perfect spirals around her shoulders and down her back. She wore eye shadow that matched her dress and thick black mascara that accentuated each one of her long, dark eyelashes. A light application of foundation gave her face a soft glow and Anna Mae added just a hint of shiny color to her lips that easily brought attention to the sensuality of their illustrious shape.

James drank in the sight before him. Lily's lips, her lines, her curves, her hair, the sparkle in her eyes, all of her accentuated beauty overloaded his mind and temporarily rendered him speechless. The mass amounts of adrenaline coursing through his body had genuinely taken its toll on him. He began sweating, his mouth had gone dry, and his mind remained blank. Lily had always been beautiful to James, but at that moment, her beauty had reduced him to a nervous schoolboy with a crush. He just stood there unable to take his eyes off of her, struggling to find words that were worthy of expressing how phenomenal she looked in his eyes.

Lily smoothed her hands down the sides of her dress, her nerves having escalated as well. She was suddenly questioning her transformation because of the way James was looking at her, but yet, not saying a word. "I-I ain't neva' had my hair done before," she said nervously, not knowing what else to say to fill the silence.

"My God, Lily." James's eyes careened up and down her entire body. "You. Are … *Stunning*," he told her, after finally remembering how to string a few words together. "Absolutely stunning." James had yet to move, or even blink, for fear of interrupting his view. Isabel gave a girlish giggle, but he did not even hear her. To James, nothing else in the room existed except for Lily, who finally gave a smile of relief after his compliment.

"I certainly agree with that," Anna Mae said, smiling and stepping up beside Lily.

James's body certainly agreed too. Having forgotten that there were two others in the room, it had instinctively reacted to what he was seeing. He cleared his throat, looked around, and suddenly remembered that there was a need to gather his composure before he embarrassed himself any further.

"Come on here, Isabel. Let's you and me go on down to our seats," Anna Mae suggested, wanting to give James and Lily a moment alone.

"Okay, mama."

"I just know you's gon' be incredible tonight," Anna Mae told Lily as she gave her a hug.

"Thank you for everything today, Ms. Anna Mae, and you too, Isabel."

"No problem," Isabel replied from the doorway. "And good luck tonight!"

"Thanks, Isabel."

"I'm glad to help suga'," Anna Mae told her. "Now, you go on up there and show them folks how piano playin' is really done, ya' hear?"

"Yes ma'am," Lily answered with a smile.

Anna Mae kissed her on the cheek, and she and Isabel departed from the room, finally leaving Lily and James alone. Lily watched the door close and then turned to look at James, who still had yet to remove his eyes from her. They stood there quietly for a second, staring at one another. While they were both dressed as elegantly as ever before, they both found it hard to turn away, especially in the absence of other people.

Lily suddenly smiled nervously when she began to feel self-conscious. When she did, James's demeanor quickly changed, like he had finally snapped out of a trance. He stepped closer to Lily, wanting to be nearer to the intoxicating scent he smelled on her. "You really do look beautiful tonight, Lily," he could not help but tell her again with a low and soothing tone in his voice, while still helplessly absorbing every inch of her.

"Thank you, James. That's awful sweet of you," she said shyly, beginning to blush a little. "Y-you look wonderful too." She had certainly noticed how his rugged features of the past few weeks had been traded for a fresh, clean-cut look. Whether dressed in fine linens or shirtless, clean-shaven or with facial hair, Lily was finding that she was always impressed by James's strapping good looks in all cases.

"So umm, how are you holdin' up?" James finally asked her, in a desperate attempt to turn off a certain part of his body. "Much betta' than last night, I hope," he added, referring to an unintended encounter they had the previous night …

After several weeks of draining work in the fields, James had gone a lengthy amount of time without being awakened by the ghastly reoccurring nightmare that had become an unfortunate part of his life. His streak, however, had ended the night before. As usual, he found himself wandering into Lily's room to check on her. He had walked in quietly, not planning to stay long. After a few minutes, he opened the door to leave until he heard Lily's voice call out to him in the darkness. "Please don't leave," she had said.

James stopped and turned around with his heart pounding, feeling the heat of embarrassment spreading throughout his body. "I-I'm sorry, I was just…"

"Please stay," Lily requested again.

"A-are you sure?"

"Yes, please. I can't sleep, and I really don't wanna be alone."

Without contemplating it any further, James happily fulfilled Lily's request. He closed the door back softly and pulled a nearby armchair closer to her bed before sitting down. "Bein' wide awake this time 'a night doesn't seem like you at all. You usually sleep like a baby … I-I assume," he added, not wanting her to know that he had visited her while sleeping on multiple occasions.

Lily sat up and lit the oil lamp on the nightstand. "I know, but … It's just…" She sighed. "I know it may sound childish, but I'm a little scared."

"Scared of what?"

"Tomorrow night," she replied.

"The show?"

"Yeah."

"Well, from what I've seen, you and William have prepared well. So why the fears?"

"It's not that at all. I feel like we're well-prepared despite all the last-minute changes."

"Then what's botherin' ya'?"

Lily leaned back against the headboard and drew her knees up to her chest. "It's just that … Well, all my life most people ain't neva' bothered to look at me for more than two seconds. It seems like most folks don't even really see *me*. It's like they's lookin' right through me or somethin'. I dunno, it's hard to explain, but it's almost like I don't even exist to most of 'em."

After all James had put Lily through, he somehow hoped that she had not grown to feel that he viewed her that way as well, but figured she would certainly be justified if she did.

"But tomorrow," Lily continued. "A whole audience full of people gon' finally *see* me. Not the servant that most folks look right through. They gon' see, *Lily* ... And that scares the hell outta me."

After many years of repressing it, James's instinct to comfort Lily finally resurfaced. He suddenly took her hand into his without any hesitation. "Lily," he began. She looked down at his hand covering hers as he continued. "Anybody who doesn't love who you are afta' they come to know you is a damn fool. Let those who choose not to love you wallow in their stupidity and neva' worry yourself ova' their foolishness. You need only to sit at that piano and pour your heart out onto those keys just the way you always do. You shouldn't concern yourself with anything more than that, ya' hear?"

James's words immediately struck a chord in Lily and calmed her racing thoughts. She said nothing in return at first, though. She simply sat quietly for a moment, enjoying the feel of her hand in his. His words and the simple gesture had quickly evaporated all of her reservations and suddenly fueled her desire to share her current intimate thoughts. "More nights than I can rememba', I've dreamt of you sittin' quietly at my bedside." She finally looked over at James. "In those dreams, your presence always brought me so much comfort..." Lily suddenly paused and closed her eyes when she felt him begin to caress her hand. "But even more so in reality."

James was astounded by Lily's confession, but it also made him wonder if her dreams were not really the place she had seen him. He thought perhaps this was not the first night she had caught him there at her bedside. That possibility initially made him feel a hint of embarrassment, but knowing that it was a comfort to her quickly settled him.

"Will you stay with me a while?" Lily asked. "Jus' 'til I fall asleep."

"Of course. I'll stay here as long as you need me to." He took her covers and lifted them up with his free hand. "Come on, lay back down. You need your rest."

Lily slid under the covers, arranging herself in a way that she did not have to let go of James's hand. "Thank you, James," she said yawning, her body already giving in to sleep.

"You're welcome." When Lily closed her eyes, James blew out the oil lamp and stayed there holding her hand until it grew limp and he was certain that she had drifted off into a deep sleep.

… Lily was truly appreciative that James was willing to stay by her side for as long as he did. And now, as she stood in the middle of her room alone with him, she wanted to be sure that she expressed that sentiment. "Thank you for stayin' with me last night. I thought I's gon' be up 'til mornin', but your kind words put me so at peace. I slept well and I owe that to you."

So did I, James thought to himself, suddenly feeling that *he* was the one who should be thanking *her* for all the nights of peaceful sleep, but he kept it to himself for the time being. "Anytime, Lily … Anytime," he replied, holding back the desire to touch her face.

"Well, I betta' get down to the amphitheata'," Lily said, trying to find a way to get James to stop looking at her in that certain way that always ignited her insides. "I'm sure William's probably worried to death about startin' on time."

"Oh, yeah, of course," James replied, shaking himself from his fantasies and remembering there was a show to do. "Shall we?" he asked, extending his arm. Lily smiled and gladly slid her arm around the crook of his elbow.

James felt a sense of pride having a woman of Lily's caliber on his arm. He walked in a way that exuded that fact as he began to guide her out of the room like an upstanding gentleman. Lily, too, walked tall and confidently on his arm down the grand staircase, suddenly feeling like a princess on the arm of a prince as they made their descent. James stole glances at her while she walked alongside him. He did not see or feel an ounce of nervousness in her at all, which consequently relaxed him. To James, Lily seemed like a completely different woman than the one he had spoken to the night before, who lay awake well after midnight drenched in her fears. He hoped that fact could be attributed to her growing confidence as well as the pleasantries of her day.

Before heading backstage, Lily stopped first in the library so that she could warm up on the piano for a few minutes. James watched on, unexpectedly becoming emotional while thinking about what Lily was about to accomplish in front of a crowd full of people. When her warm-up drills were complete, James offered a hand to help her stand. He smiled at her as she rose from her seat, still thoroughly entranced by her beauty. He then continued guiding her like a gentleman out of the house and through a long makeshift tent that lead from the porch to the backstage area of the amphitheater. When they made it to the staging area, they both stopped and watched as William ushered everyone to their positions and gave last minute instructions.

James turned to Lily. "You ready for this?"

She truly felt calm and collected, especially while he

stood there beside her. She took a deep breath. "Ready as I'll eva' be, I s'ppose."

In the chaos of trying to get everyone in place, William turned and caught sight of Lily and immediately froze. Wondering what it was that stole his attention, one-by-one, everyone he had been talking to began to turn in Lily's direction as well. Even Austin, the scheming student percussionist who had berated her during rehearsals, did a double take when he saw her. When all eyes were finally on Lily, complete silence came over the room.

William instantly abandoned everything he was doing and made his way toward Lily with a slow smile creeping onto his face. His eyes began to mist with the reflection of her beauty dancing in them. When he reached her, he took both of her hands with his smile so wide his kind green eyes had nearly squinted shut. "My darling, you are truly a vision."

Lily's cheeks flushed red. "Thank you, William." She smiled and gave him a warm embrace.

Like everyone in the room—including Austin—James still struggled to take his eyes off of Lily while they embraced. He wanted to be sure that every detail of the night, especially her beauty, stayed locked away in his memory forever. When William finally released her, James then took Lily by the hand, wanting to say a few words before he departed. "I can hardly wait to see you up there. You're gonna be amazin' tonight. I really do believe that Lily," he said, finding it hard to fend off his desire to kiss her, even as everyone watched. "Good luck."

"Thank you," she replied, giving him a beautiful broad smile filled with sincerity and appreciation.

"Come now James, time is of the essence," William interrupted. "I promise you're leaving her in good hands."

"I have no doubt about that," James replied, placing a firm hand on William's shoulder. "Good luck to you too."

"Thank you. Now get going, my boy. We have only

moments to spare." With that, James headed toward the stage, checking first to be sure that all the other performers had already settled into their positions.

After he left, William once again turned his attention back to Lily. He raised one of her hands and kissed the back of it. "I have all the confidence in the world that you will be stellar tonight," he told her, caressing her with uplifting words as he so often did.

"Thank you, William." The smile had yet to fade from Lily's face. It was a symbol of how wonderful she was feeling, inside and out. All of the rare opportunities that William and James had blessed Lily with in the past few weeks suddenly brought forth another surge of unadulterated joy within her. *This*, however, was an opportunity unlike any other. Her two leading men had given her a chance to do something that no other Negro, slave or not, had ever been afforded the luxury of doing. Lily felt humbled and honored by that fact, and she wanted to perform in a way that proved she was worthy of setting such a monumental precedent. But more than anything, she wanted every note on this epic eve to convey to James and William that all of their efforts were not in vain. "I promise you that I'm gonna give it my all tonight, William. But no matta' how tonight ends, I just want you to know how truly grateful I am to you for all of this." Her voice cracked as her emotions began to rise. "I don't think there are words to describe how much this all means to me."

"No worries, my dear." William moved his hands to the sides of Lily's face. "Sometimes words are not necessary to convey one's sentiments. Trust that I have felt the sincerity of your gratefulness and the depths of what this means to you long before you ever whispered of it. And tonight, I know this audience will feel it too." Lily gave him a final hug and fought the urge to cry again, not wanting to ruin the make-up that Anna Mae and Isabel had worked nearly an hour to put in place. "Now then," William said, pulling back to look at Lily once more. "Are you ready to begin your journey?" he asked, extending his elbow.

Lily interlocked her elbow with his. "With all that you've instilled in me, I'd say I'm more than ready for anything." Arm in arm, they made their way to take their places onstage.

* * * *

The remaining sliver of the sun cast an orange glow on the horizon just behind the massive audience awaiting "The Return of William Werthington." With the sun in perfect position, James knew it was now the precise moment to make his way out in front of the packed amphitheater. Many women, old and young, sat up tall in their seats when he finally stood at the forefront of the stage with the remainder of sunlight bouncing off of him at all the right angles. Their colorfully decorated hand fans began to pick up speed as thoughts about him began to dance in their minds, thoughts that those with husbands would certainly deem as inappropriate. When the chatter and fidgeting stopped, and James had everyone's attention, he began the show with the brief and simple introduction that William had requested. "Ladies and Gentleman, afta' ova' ten years away from the stage, I give you the world-renowned..." He waved his arm to the right. "William Werthington." James then abruptly took his seat in the front row. He had not yet seen the finalized version of their show, wanting to be just as surprised by it as the rest of the audience.

Walking with the confidence of a polished professional, William made his way on stage. The very moment he was visible, the entire audience stood and applauded to show their appreciation of his much anticipated return. William stopped and stood just in front of his grand piano and took in the applause with gratitude. He then bowed, tossed his short gray coattails out behind him, and sat down on the piano bench. It was at this very moment that William's nerves hit him full force and he said his brief prayer for Lily. After begging God to shower her with a wealth of blessings, he gracefully struck the keys to officially begin the show. Everyone instantly recognized the well-known tune he began to play and roared into another round of applause. William could feel that he was already starting to draw them in the way that he needed to. Lily recommended the clever song choice to start the show, figuring it would instantly remind people of why William and his music had become such a worldwide sensation. He was playing a solo piece that he had originally composed as a boy before he had learned to incorporate the harmonies of accompanying instruments. It was by far Lily's favorite song to hear him play and still remained a popular tune that was performed by no other the way William was capable. After sixty years of playing this particular number, his fingers automatically danced in a beautiful elegant cadence. Although on this occasion, unlike in times past, William intentionally paced the song slowly, wanting the ending to coincide with the exact moment that the sun dropped completely out of the sky.

The very minute the sun sank below the horizon, William's melody suddenly transitioned into one that was just as dark as the night sky had quickly become. A large red curtain then began to sweep slowly from the left side of the stage. By the time it passed William completely, he and his piano were gone. The audience gasped when the tall tiki torches that glowed at the end of each row of seats faded away along with him, engulfing everyone in pure darkness. They were left only able to hear the extreme musical mood change that continued to be played by the seemingly invisible William.

When the night sky became even more prevalent, the deep acoustic sounds of the cello began accompanying William's sullen melody, followed shortly thereafter by the soft tap of the timpani. The violins, French horns, oboes, and all other woodwinds softly joined in, cuing the percussion to begin a long drawn-out ascent of power and intensity. In the midst of the timpani's rising reverberation, a sudden flash of light appeared and faded away onstage in the background. It appeared like lightning with the powerful sound of the percussion as its rumbling thunder. With every other beat, the sudden flash of light illuminated again and faded away just as quickly, revealing a sheer, white, satin sheath that hung like an enormous curtain from the top of the raptors clear down to the floor. It stretched from one end of the stage to the other just behind where William's piano once stood.

As the brooding piano music continued and the power of the timpani was nearing its peak, another flash appeared, but this time the dark silhouette of a man holding a sword high above his head was cast onto the thin, curtain-like sheath. Before being drowned by darkness, the audience reacted audibly again to the sudden appearance of the shadowed knight. As the booming bass sounds of the percussion continued, the light appeared briefly again and unveiled the silhouette of a woman on a makeshift mountain, clinging tight to a child. When the light faded out again, the mysterious music began to gather speed. Together with the intensity of the rolling timpani, the entire orchestra roared into a sensational climax, meeting the exact moment that an explosive burst of flames erupted on both sides of the stage. At that moment, the white sheath simultaneously lit up in full brilliance, revealing the dark shadow of a fire-breathing dragon standing between the damsel on the mountain and the armored man with his sword and shield.

With a constant beam of light now shining behind the dragon, the princess, and the knight, their large dreamlike images were all now etched in permanence onto the sheer sheath. A mighty duel then commenced between the dragon and the knight. After the very first shadowy fireball erupted, William began pounding away at the keys, unleashing sinister sounds that coincided with the movements of the dragon. As soon as the knight took his first swing, voracious chords of music from a second piano became intertwined with the movements of the knight while he jousted to take down the looming dragon. Hidden behind the scenes, Lily had watched and waited patiently for her cue to begin a musical duel with her very own mentor. While the shadows were locked in war, Lily and William were in a musical fight of their own, even playfully exchanging mean glares with one another as they battled each other with their menacing melodies.

Lily's playfulness proved that she was confident, relaxed, and completely lost in the moment the way she needed to be. Her calm demeanor was attributed to the warmth of James's words from the night before still caressing her soul. James, on the other hand, was anything but calm. His excitement was at immeasurable levels. The moment he heard Lily join in the battling duet, his face lit up just as bright as the light in front of him. He, along with the rest of the audience, watched the elegant dance between blade and flame in awe, completely enraptured by every note that Lily had composed. There was a discharge of flames on either side of the stage that even had everyone physically reacting every time the dragon hurled balls of shadowed fire across the sheath toward the heroic knight's shield. Having never seen imagery of the sort, everyone was fighting the urge to even blink, not wanting to miss a microsecond of the poetic silhouette movements of the armored man and the beast he was wielding his sword to strike down.

While riding on a confident high, Lily continued delicately trotting across the keys, playing musically in sync with her knight. Not long into the battle, William's melody began to chop, slow, and fade, along with the life of the wounded dragon his fingers were representing. When the dragon began to falter, the knight hurled his sword end over end in its direction, but before it reached the creature, the light and all music ceased, leaving the audience surrounded by silence and darkness all at once. After a few moments of suspense, muted sound, and blindness, the timpani rolled into ascension, joined shortly thereafter by the entire orchestra just as the bright and beautiful light source returned. At the peak of the orchestra's crescendo, a magnificent display of fireworks was set off into the sky in celebration of the heroic knight, whose larger-than-life shadow now stood with the slain dragon lying near his feet. He then pulled his sword from inside the beast and raised it in victory, invoking massive cheers from the delighted spectators. Fireworks continued to rain colorful sparkles into the star-filled night sky, in time with tickling piano notes that were equally as beautiful as the silhouette of the knight embracing his rescued family.

When the fireworks trickled away, and the applause finally settled, every member of the symphony returned to play for the next song, except for William. With the slaying of the dragon, he had playfully placed his hand over his heart and pretended to pass away along with the beast, causing Lily to giggle. William then got up from his piano bench, smiled, and bowed toward Lily with pride. Lily smiled back as he waved his hand toward her, symbolizing that he was now passing the piano reins solely to her for the remainder of the show. After playing just two songs, William returned to his role as the orchestra's conductor, feeling as though he had fulfilled his obligation to give the audience what they had initially come to see.

After proudly taking the reins William had handed her, Lily began the next music-infused, dreamlike story. The melody Lily played for this occasion was light and uplifting, and was once again intertwined with the movements and emotions of all the shadowed characters. It began with the prince and his child after they had returned home to their castle. The prince left his armor and savage side behind and let loose his softer, gentler side. His shadow tossed his young daughter into the air, read stories to her, and would sit with her at the piano to teach her songs. Each time the little girl sat at the piano with her father, the stage would fade into darkness and light up again to reveal the prince sitting next to an older child. The little girl grew and grew until the lights faded in for a final time with the prince's daughter now sitting alone at the piano surrounded by a symphony of violins, cellos, and soft harps while her father watched on from afar. For the first time in the show, it was Lily who sat in front of the projection of the light with her dreamlike silhouette cast out to the audience onto the sheer sheath that protected her identity. She was portraying the prince's adult child while the student orchestra swayed eloquently as shadowed figures by her side. The crowd, none the wiser to who she was, applauded in grand fashion when she softly completed the piece and the light slowly faded away.

Lily looked over at William when that song was over. He gazed back and gave a proud smile, but she did not hold his gaze for long for fear that she would cry. Lily had not told William, but the shadowed story about the knight, as well as that particular song, had been inspired by simply knowing him. Lily wished that she had been rescued by William along with Anna Mae and her children, and she readily admitted to herself that she was envious. Many times, she had fantasized about William nurturing her until adulthood, passing his fatherly love, guidance, and knowledge down to her. The imagery of the prince with his child was the fairytale version of the way she had always imagined it would be while she stood alone at William's lake some days letting her imagination run free.

For a little over an hour, seven more glorious songs Lily and the student orchestra played in conjunction with actors and dancers in front of the light projector, portraying stories with their silhouette shadows on the specially designed material that spanned across the stage. The stories ranged from silly satires to simple dances to very deep and emotional. But most importantly, as requested, not once was there a single face of the orchestra or other participant revealed to the crowd, that is … until the very last song.

Before the final song was to begin, William made his way to the forefront of the stage to the applause of the awaiting audience. "Have you all enjoyed tonight's show thus far?" he asked, once everyone had settled.

Everyone applauded once again in affirmation of his question.

When all was quiet, William took a deep breath and a few unnecessary steps forward to calm himself before stopping and clasping his hands together behind him. "Well, I must confess, I cannot take all the credit for tonight's incredible showing," he admitted. The very second he made his confession, his paranoia raced to a new high and sweat began to quickly accumulate on his brow. He then nervously cleared his throat before he continued. "You see, I had the honor of collaborating with a rather extraordinary young lady, who at the age of ten years old, despite incredible odds, taught herself to play the piano. In fact, most everything you have seen and heard tonight has come from the creativity and imagination of her ingenious mind. And so it is not I alone that you owe your appreciation of this evening's entertainment." People in the audience began to turn and look at each other with questioning eyes, but William was not detoured. He took another deep breath and proceeded. "So ladies and gentlemen, I would like to proudly present to you the true mastermind behind tonight's mystifying show." With the wave of his arm, the stage was overcome by darkness. When William disappeared once more, the white sheath illuminated, displaying the first of a series of sentences upon it as a solo piece from the piano began to play softly.

I lost my mother 14 years and 4 months ago…

The sentence faded away and another illuminated. Every line thereafter continued in that fashion:

But she did not pass away

Nor did she abandon me

In front of her very eyes

I was stolen from her

That particular line truly heightened everyone's curiosity about the mysterious person behind the music. Some were visibly confused, turning to look at one another while they waited for what would be presented next after the stage emerged again from blackness.

All that I have left of her now

Is the distant memory of her face

And this very song that I play

A song that keeps her alive in my mind

Along with the belief that one day

I know I WILL see her again…

When the words concluded, the stage remained enveloped in darkness until Lily's solo climaxed and transitioned into a melody of anguish. It was then that ballet dancers took to the stage behind the screen with graceful, poetic movements in front of the light. Their silhouettes appeared to float from place to place as they began the final dream story with the ugly scene of a child being pulled away from her mother. The mother's distress was apparent as her child was being carried away kicking and screaming and reaching out for her mother, who was held in place by two large men. Their movements, of course, were silent, but the desperation in their body language and the pain in the music spoke loudly for them.

In the scene that followed, the young girl was perched on an auction block as shadows danced violently around her in unison. They circled her like lions around their prey, throwing their hands up in rhythm with the melody. From high to low, Lily's music sank into a dismal plethora of notes that mirrored the confused mind of the child, who stood as prey to the animalistic men surrounding her. Much like the young girl, every note seemed to be crying, while the sullen sound of the strings added to the heaviness of her ordeal. With the conclusion of their predatory dance, all the greedy men, except one, hung their heads low and rhythmically took slow steps away from the auction block. The one man remaining crept slowly in sync with the beat toward the vulnerable child, proudly displaying chains high above his head. When he reached her, all music and lighting ceased.

When next the little girl's silhouette appeared, she knelt alone, scrubbing a floor in a tattered dress, her arms sweeping side to side to the softness of nothing but violins. The piano then began to tiptoe in to join them, along with a little boy who quietly appeared behind the little girl, curiously watching her from afar. He quickly disappeared when the little girl felt his presence and turned to see who was there. She stood slowly and gallivanted across the stage alone with her dress flowing behind her, being just as playful as any child would, but then stopped to tinker with a piano. She then danced and twirled around it with ballet-style pirouettes and leaps as she neglected her duties until colliding unexpectedly with the evil man who once held the chains. He angrily waved his finger in her face, and she hung her head in shame, dropped back to her knees, and continued scrubbing and swaying in time with the soft violins as the light faded out.

When the screen brightened again and represented a new day, the young girl in her tattered garments rose from a stack of hay. In sneaky fashion, she proceeded to leave her resting place, escaping to an outdoor place that only a child could see as a world of wonderment. As the little girl carried on in her wooded playland, the music suddenly began to float as beautifully as the butterflies and birds that surrounded her. She then picked up a turtle and twirled him around, but she would soon learn that she was not alone. The little boy, who had curiously watched her earlier, peered at her now from behind a tree and was forced to reveal himself when he tripped and fell from behind it. The music momentarily ceased as the young boy and girl stared at one another. In dramatic fashion, they slowly approached each other, their footsteps represented by the light touch of the highest key on the piano. When they reached one another, together, they held the turtle high in the air, and the entire symphony crescendoed once again. With happy and uplifting notes as their guide, the two children sat their turtle down and suddenly danced playfully in unison, chasing the butterflies and the birds above them. The ease of their beautiful bond brought an instant smile to every audience member's face.

With each new day that passed, the two young children continued their adventures together, fishing, climbing trees, and reading books together. Their friendship was acted out through elegant artistic dances, making it clear that the strength of their relationship continued to grow along with the size of their dreamlike images. The entire visual reflected the passing of years, all while Lily and the orchestra captured the emotion of their journey through her carefully crafted ensemble.

By now, many in the audience had already surmised that this last shadowed story was about a slave. A few, who had attended William's gala thought perhaps it was the same young lady they had seen play there. But that did not seem to matter to anyone. Only seeing the shadow of a child, with no true color or identity,—who was trying desperately to find a way to cope with the turbulence of losing her mother—began to resonate deep with everyone. The music and stunning visuals had quickly moved many of them to feel that no child, Negro or Caucasian, deserved such a fate. For that reason, not a single solitary soul in the audience dared to object, complain, or pull their eyes away as the story continued to unfold of the friendship between a young white man and a young lady, who was undeniably a *slave*. As the twosome danced fluently together across the flowing satin sheet, everyone still sat in awe watching the beauty of their innocent movements flourish into those filled with deep emotion. But just as the audience began to feel the intensity of the pair's connection, the graceful dance between them was interrupted by the appearance of the villain who once held the chains. He danced onto the stage in a manner all his own, to notes now filled with anger. Suddenly, the two dear friends no longer danced as one and slowly began to drift apart. Closer and closer, the young man pranced toward the villain, gradually adopting his soldier-like moves and dancing in step with him instead. He then quickly disappeared from view, leaving the young lady to dance in solitude to the now weeping melody of Lily's piano until the light melted away.

When the light illuminated again, the story began to show the passing of years. The young lady's age and loneliness were reflected by the sorrow in the music and the slow emptiness of her movements. Pirouettes around her beloved piano, birds, butterflies, books, and all other parts of her previous adventures, including the boy she had danced so beautifully with, now only appeared as part of her dreams. Every night as she slept, they all appeared as elusive illusions near where she lay, bringing temporary joy back to her life and into the beautiful piano music that accompanied them. Sadly, though, the aging woman would awaken each morning to the misery of finding that she was still alone and left to the monotony of scrubbing her floors, year after painful year.

As the emotional music continued, the light soon revealed the silhouette of the once youthful girl as an old woman, hunched over, clenching tight to a walking cane, unable to move as gracefully as she once had. With Lily's symphonic music guiding her, the old slave lady hobbled over to the piano that she once drifted around as a child and touched it gently. She then painstakingly made her way out to visit the tree that she once climbed with her friend. She looked up at it and let the precious memories it held prance in her mind. Afterward, she crept back to the haystack that had been her lifelong resting place. She slowly sat down and laid her walking cane next to her. From a hidden compartment, she then pulled out the book that her old friend had once shared with her during happier years. She opened it and ran her fingers slowly down the page before lying back and placing the book upon her chest. On this night, when she finally drifted off to sleep, her dream was unlike all the others in the previous nights that had passed, and so too was the sorrow in the music that Lily's orchestra now played. This time, there were no mystical visions of butterflies fluttering randomly from place to place, and there were no birds to chase. Her dreams did not show her the tree that she once loved to climb or the face of her dear friend. Instead, drifting high above where her motionless body lay, she was graced with the image of someone she had not seen since her childhood.

The soft hymns of a choir suddenly joined in with the

harps, other strings, and the piano of Lily's orchestra. When
the harmony began, an apparition adorned in a flowing
robe, floating above the old lady's bed, suddenly spread its
wings far and wide. The girl who had spent her life
enslaved had lay for the last time on her makeshift hay bed.
Her shadowy soul began to rise from her lifeless body
toward her angelic mother as she awaited her daughter in
the sky with her wings lovingly outstretched, ready to
finally set her only child free. As her soul rose toward her
angelic mother in the sky, so too did Lily along with the
grand piano she sat playing. She rose slowly into the view
of the crowd from the pit beneath the stage that William
had been lowered into during his act of illusion.
Throughout her ascent, Lily felt her heart in her throat and
her nerves beginning to attack her, but despite it, she kept
the ultimate composure. Fully prepared for the risk and the
potential backlash, she reached the top of the stage playing
stoically in front of everyone, figuratively naked, with no
sheets, no curtains, nothing to hide her true identity, putting
an end to the mystery of the show's actual creator. As soon
as Lily was in full view, the harmonies from the choir
deepened and radiated out into the field. At that very
moment, the angelic mother, floating high above everyone,
wrapped her wings warmly around her daughter's spirit,
embracing her for the first time since she was stolen away
from her as a child.

It could be visibly seen in the faces of all who were
watching that the power of the heavenly scene, blended
with the intensity of the music, had completely captivated
them all. Before the orchestra and the choir delivered the
last of the emotional notes, every member of the audience
was on its feet, and a standing ovation began. Enthralled by
the touching story and the heartwarming music that
coincided, ladies started dabbing dainty cloth towelettes to
their eyes while the men next to them did their best to hide
the effects of a truly grand finale.

After the last of the piano melody rippled out into the night air, with great poise, Lily stood up in her beautifully designed handmade red gown to the overwhelming applause of the audience. She stood there silently a moment and absorbed their warmth with profound and abiding gratitude. With the way her piano was situated onstage, William was the first person she saw when she stood up. He was in the wings beaming at her with pride as he applauded with the rest of the crowd. Her first emotional instinct was to walk over and hug him, but he prompted her to walk forward, wanting the celebratory moment to be hers and hers alone. Lily nodded her head toward him and bravely took her first steps toward the audience. With every step that she took, the sound of the reception grew louder, and William's strength to hold back his tears grew weaker.

As Lily continued moving forward in her beautiful gown, she looked to her right and caught a glimpse of the student orchestra hidden on the other side of the stage. Ironically, they were a group that she owed a portion of this unforgettable moment too. Aside from their musical accompaniment, it was their malicious act of cruelty and attempt to diminish the quality of her show that catapulted her creativity to new heights. That very day, Lily had explained to William her desire to create a show that somehow depicted the shadowed imagery in her mind when her songs were born, and that she wanted to combine it with his love for pyrotechnics. William spared no expense and had completely exhausted himself to ensure that every element of her wishes would be fulfilled exactly how she had envisioned. To do so, he turned to the technology of gas light projectors, which had been in its infancy during his days as a performer. He remembered how the machines had drastically changed the power to control the intensity and operation of light in theaters. He took something that had simply been used to illuminate the halls and walls of theaters and used it to breathe life into Lily's ingenious ideas in a way that had never been done before. At the same time, Lily's idea ultimately gave all the other performers the anonymity they had requested.

With the simple control of the light, Lily was able to visually share her happiness, pain, sorrow, and all of the memories from her life that ignited such passion in her music, through silhouettes. As a result, her color, her race, and her status became irrelevant in the span of the hour and a half that she presented her art. She had simply become a human being, who had grasped the heart of every person watching her visions come to life as elegant shadows. She had uplifted and inspired them all and had unexpectedly brought many of them to tears. Lily had become extremely vulnerable, embracing her audience with open arms while allowing them inside the brilliance of her mind. And now, they all stood on their feet embracing her warmly in return.

No one, however, was touched by the evening's performance more so than James Adams, whose happy childhood years with Lily had just played out in front of him in such a magnificent manner. It left him emotionally riveted. James recognized the final song as a modified version of the one Lily had played upon his return home from school. He had heard Lily explain to William that the images in the show would be reflections of her thoughts as she created her music. He now understood the reason for her tears while she played that particular song that day. Not knowing entirely what to expect from the show, James had sat amongst the audience watching the moment that he had abandoned Lily come to life. And as painful as it was, he was then forced to see the loneliness she had suffered through in the years afterward. The misery he had caused her was the reason he could not stop the tidal wave that rolled out of his eyes during the final moments of the finale. At the same time, though, he recognized the brilliance of Lily's performance as well as the overall visual show. He, therefore, allowed that to overshadow what he was feeling, wanting to celebrate Lily as she undoubtedly deserved, instead of dwelling on the upheaval of emotions that had migrated into every corner of his body.

Feeling as if she was living in the most surreal dream, Lily had slowly made her way to the forefront of the handcrafted amphitheater stage as everyone continued to applaud. Only joyful and tear-filled faces greeted her as she stood there, proving the sincerity of their reception. But more important to her than all of the pomp and circumstance was a particular face that she was eager to find in the crowd. She looked sporadically from place to place out into the sea of people, and in the very center of the front row, she finally spotted the man who had inspired many of the portions of her show. As soon as she laid eyes on James, Lily's smile illuminated to full brilliance and so too did his. With that, the tears that she had held back during the show finally overflowed down her cheeks.

After a few minutes, William finally made his way out from behind the scenes. When he reached Lily, he took her hand in his and kissed it. With his other hand over his heart, he then took a graceful bow toward her. As Lily's tears continued to flow, together, her and William turned and bowed in unison to the delight of their grateful audience.

Chapter Fourteen

Slave Code
Article II Section VIII

It is required that any runaway slave, committed to the custody of any respective Sheriff, be advertised in a public newspaper, making particular their whereabouts, description of clothing, and any bodily marks of such runaway.

Saturday
June 4, 1859

The immense success of Lily's first show was undeniable, but despite that fact, there was no critical acclaim printed in any headlines to commemorate that precedent-setting evening. Even in the free state of Ohio, newspapers were still not willing to take the risk of writing any story about a Negro unless they were wanted by the law or being listed as a runaway. Since Lily, fortunately, did not fall into either of those categories, there was not a single word printed about her grand achievement during William's annual Spring Gala. But, amazingly, that did not stop the news about her show from spreading by word of mouth with the ferocity of a wildfire and with a speed that nobody could have ever predicted.

The disclosure of Lily's identity after her first flawless performance did absolutely nothing to stop the onslaught of pleas for her to perform more shows. Lily was absolutely floored by people's wishes to see her again, and she was more than happy to fulfill their requests. To meet the demands, she began putting on shows every Thursday, Friday, Saturday, and Sunday night for nearly two months following the Spring Gala. She could have easily done shows seven days a week and never once have had an empty seat in the amphitheater. Whites amongst blacks, the rich amongst the poor, the young and the old were flocking in droves to see a blend of shadowed artistry and music that they knew full well was composed and choreographed by a Negro. Many were even traveling from places far off to witness what had been deemed as *The Dream Symphony*.

Since the first week of *The Dream Symphony* was free, seats were filled in the amphitheater two or three hours before showtime. After the first week, William began to charge a fee to get in, but even then the demands to see the show continued to climb quickly. In fact, even after all the amphitheater seats were sold out, people still insisted on paying to get through the gates. Spectators were happily willing to spill out onto the plantation grass and sit on blankets to satisfy their curiosity about a show that had stirred up a great amount of gossip and controversy. Most covered up their curiosity by proclaiming that they were only attending in order to protest or object to William's antics, but, in the end, they would simply leave with a true understanding of the passion and enthusiasm of those who had already fallen in love with the exhilarating spectacle.

A month after the shows began, William held a party after a Friday night show to fulfill the desires of those who had requested to meet Lily. For once at a gathering, Lily was not dressed in attire that prompted demands from the hungry or the thirsty, nor was she expected just to linger in the shadows. Instead, Lily stood as the center of attention in William's drawing room, wearing yet another one of Anna Mae's elegantly designed gowns, as streams of people approached to ask questions and shower her with an array of compliments. All the while, James was by her side with his pistol visible on his hip, leery of everyone and watching carefully for anyone who might dare to make any violent advances.

Much to James's dismay, though, his position of authority by Lily's side also accomplished the goal of always appearing as her true and rightful owner. The way the laws were written, he knew that even in a free state Lily could be hauled off to jail without the appropriate paperwork or her master nearby keeping watch over her. James, therefore, played his role well. Protecting Lily had become his number one priority. The constant terror of what may happen to her if he stepped out of character was far more strenuous on him than even building the very stage she performed on.

James even wanted to protect Lily from the stream of hate letters and threats that had made their way into William's mailbox and even onto his front porch. After reading the barbaric details written in the first batch, James questioned whether or not he should let Lily proceed with further shows, but the delight on her face and the excitement that she exuded after her performances always answered that question for him. He simply could not bear the thought of bringing rain and hail to the warmth of the sun that had been shining on Lily in the weeks since her show began. In fact, James was so adamant about letting Lily float in an ignorant bliss that he and William embellished the truth as to their reasons for suddenly hiring a security team. Lily was naturally curious as to the need for the barrage of men she had seen standing at the front gates with rifles and those on horseback with six-shooters keeping watch over the plantation and the crowds at her show. James explained to her that they were just for precaution. He was simply not willing to share with her the real, unspeakably cruel reasons why it was a necessity to have the men standing guard twenty-four hours a day.

William had hired the sort of men that he knew always worked best for security detail: half-crazy and willing to do anything for money. Most importantly, they were the sort of men whose loyalties genuinely lay with those they worked for. Up to that point, William's choices had been worth it. The first few weeks on the job, the team of unkempt bandits had yet to allow any gruesome threats come to fruition. The amount of money that William was paying the loyal band of misfits was an excellent incentive to assure that things remained that way. But even without the hefty paycheck, the filthy bandits were just naturally the sort of guys that would have loved nothing more than to blow a man's head off of his shoulders simply for the pleasure of doing it. The proof of that was evident on this particular Saturday afternoon when a man they did not recognize approached the entrance to William's estate. The bandits had not been made aware of any scheduled visitors for the day, so the unfamiliar face was greeted by the barrel of four pistols, held by two scraggly men with a multitude of missing teeth, who were in desperate need of bathing. They asked the unwelcomed visitor to state his business. When he claimed to be an old friend of William's, he was escorted to the front door like a criminal being marched to his chambers with a cocked six-shooter not far from his head.

Tucker McCormick was the man in question. He was hardly someone that William considered as a friend, especially after his rude drunken comments about Lily at his annual fundraising gala. Although William was not fond of him, he had gone to speak with Tucker during the period when he and James were searching for work for Lily. They had hoped Tucker would hire Lily as an entertainer at "McCormick's," which was a tavern that Tucker owned. McCormick's started out as a pristine bar and restaurant with a sizable theater in the back that was once bustling with business. In its prime, it was considered as a fine establishment and a popular place to be for late night entertainment, drinks, and food. Tucker's successful business had initially earned him lots of respect as a prominent man in the community. However, he lost that title when his wife divorced him and took their children as a result of his numerous bold and much talked about affairs with his employees and his clientele.

After the loss of Tucker's family *and* his many

mistresses, he took to heavily drinking his own supply of liquor. The more he drank, the less he seemed to care about the success of his business. McCormick's slowly began to lack theatrical bartenders, outstanding service from beautiful, curvaceous women, cleanliness, and the exciting entertainment it was once known for. After all of the unique nuances of the fancy establishment began to fade away, so too did the willingness of patrons to spend their money there. It left the once thriving bar barely hanging on by a thread and propped the door wide open for a pub called "Buck's Tavern" to become the centerpiece of the town for food, fine wine, and spirits. As a final blow to Tucker's ego, his losses also gave everyone in Athens good reason to label him as an alcoholic, a laughing stock, an entrepreneurial failure, and the town's ultimate outcast.

The town's lack of empathy and the constant snickering behind Tucker's back turned him into a man who was bitter, cold, and liable to bite the heads off of anybody who whispered anything he did not like. But despite the way the town treated him, Tucker continued to hang around at gatherings, always slithering his way into social events without an invitation—especially William's massive parties—just to torment people with his presence for betraying him and his establishment during a rough time in his life. But most had simply come to expect his foolish antics. They either ignored the nastiness Tucker often exuded or resorted to using his attendance as a source of humor.

Despite the town's distaste for Tucker, William and James had approached him months earlier with the angle that Lily might have the ability to breathe life back into his dying business. But despite the dire situation of McCormick's and the financial ruin he was facing, Tucker still refused to let an extremely talented Negro set foot on his stage. But now here Tucker stood, quaking in his beat-up dress shoes with a pistol at his head, suddenly wishing to speak to *William* about something. Tucker had actually hoped to talk to him during *The Dream Symphony* post-show party a few weeks earlier, but the constant presence of James with a pistol on his hip made him quickly change his mind. He still recalled the way that James had snapped at him during the fundraising gala for calling Lily a monkey. But now, after seeing James at a store in town, Tucker decided to take advantage of the opportunity and finally drop by—uninvited as usual—to speak to William in private, hoping for a rather calm interaction in the absence of James. It was a cowardly maneuver that everyone in town who knew Tucker would have expected.

"Excuse me, William," Ben interrupted, just as William was dipping his pen into ink for a letter he was preparing. "Tucker McCormick is here to see you."

William looked at Ben over the top of his spectacles, laid his pen down, and leaned back in his chair. He immediately thought back to the nasty way in which Tucker had turned him and James down when they asked him to help Lily. With that on his mind, William could not help but wonder why the town reject would now have the audacity to show up at his home again, unannounced at that. "What for?" he replied to Ben.

"He didn't say."

"Well, let him in I suppose," William said, even though his first instinct was to have the bandits put him out of his misery. He was actually kind of curious about what Tucker had to say. William figured he would at least give the old babbling drunk a brief opportunity to state his business, hoping that somewhere in the midst of what he had to say it would include an apology for the nasty things he had said to Lily during the fundraising gala.

After William gave the okay, Tucker was handed off to Ben by Samuel, the mustiest and filthiest goofball on the security bandit team. Samuel had patiently watched over his prisoner on the porch, never once pulling his gun away from Tucker's skull. He had stood there with his pistol cocked and a smile on his toothless face, feeling giddy about the opportunity to take Tucker out if need be. While Tucker waited with the bloodthirsty bandit, he had sweated profusely through two layers of clothing. When Ben returned for him, he scurried into the house like a wet, hungry kitten, eager to get away from the man who would have been more than happy to rid him of his brain and then receive a bonus check for doing so.

"G-good a-afternoon," Tucker managed to stutter after Ben lead him into William's den.

William looked up at Tucker from his paperwork and almost laughed at the frazzled look on his face and his ridiculous attire. He had slicked his stringy hair back and was wearing an old suit that he had tried desperately to make look new and fresh again, which looked even worse now with his sweat stains soaking clear through the underside of his sleeves. "To what do I owe the *pleasure* of your visit?" William asked sarcastically, sounding very monotone.

After being so rattled by the pistol-packing patrolman, Tucker had forgotten his whole pitch and nervously bypassed any small talk that would have helped ease him into the conversation. The fact that he was slightly inebriated did not help matters much either. "Uh, umm, the whole town's abuzz 'bout y'ur, Lily." He was trying his best to mask his deep country accent and his drunken slur, in an attempt to sound proper and professional, but to no avail.

Lily? William thought to himself. *What happened to calling her a monkey?*

"I-it ain't a tavern or shop I been in where I don't hear her name mentioned," Tucker continued.

William took his glasses off and rubbed his eyes, already feeling annoyed by the fact that he had started out the conversation with town gossip. "I can't say as though I blame them."

"Me neitha'. A lady friend of mine begged and begged me to go to that there dream story show a few weeks back. Said she just had to see what all the fuss was about."

"You have no friends, Tucker," William interjected, easily sensing his filthy lies. And he was right. The only thing that had convinced Tucker to go to the show was greed. He was curious to see what profitable opportunity he had mistakenly passed on. "What are you here for? I have work to do." William picked up his pen again and proceeded to start writing.

"Well, ain't no doubt about the fact that this Lily girl can play the hell out of a piano…"

"Something I remember trying in vain to express to you months ago, but I recall being quickly dismissed by you … rather rudely, I might add," William pointed out. All the while he continued drafting his document, giving Tucker a clear sign that whatever he had to say from there on out was not of importance to him.

"Dismissed? Come on, ol' pal," Tucker replied, throwing in the endearment as if they truly went way back as old friends. "Now, I don't recall bein' dismissive at all. Matta' fact, I planned to speak to ya' the day before y'ur fundraisin' gala 'bout the opportunity for that Lily girl to play in my tavern's theater. I-I simply needed a day 'r two to think things ova' before givin' ya' a firm answa' to y'ur request."

"Firm answer?! *'I'd ratha' shoot my own eyes out 'fore I watch a Negro perform on my stage!'* sounded like an awfully firm answer to me!" William said, mocking Tucker in his best southern accent.

"W-well, i-it was only the sort 'a answa' that *any* wise businessman would 'a given while contemplatin' the considerable risk he'd be takin' by entertainin' that kind 'a request."

"I've heard more subtle remarks from white

supremacists," William mumbled under his breath. Tucker had been there less than two minutes, but William's patience had already run out. He realized that he should have expected nothing but lies and nonsense from a man like him. He cursed himself for thinking that he would ever even consider offering an apology to anyone, let alone Lily.

"Let's just be realistic, William," Tucker continued. "There's a reason why everyone you went to pleadin' for help turned ya' down. Nobody wants to disgrace the walls of their theata' by announcin' that a Negro is gon' be the main act. They're afraid they'd be run outta business 'fore they could blink their eyes."

"Isn't that nice," William murmured, only half listening after turning his attention back to his letter.

"B-but that's where things are different with me, ya' see. I-I ain't got no fear 'a such a thing," Tucker continued.

"Yes, that's exactly what I assumed after that little line about shooting your eyes out," William sarcastically reminded Tucker, while continuing to write in the midst of his nonsensical babbling.

"Well, if you'd 'a just been a little more patient we could 'a worked this whole thang out."

"Is that so?" William asked, still continuing to pretend as if he cared.

"That's right! But despite y'ur impatience, I've come here today with an offa' to help y'all out."

"*An offer*?!" William scoffed and dropped his pen in frustration. Tucker's words had finally garnered his full attention again. "Come now, spill it from your tongue then! I can go on no more listening to your insults! I have work to do!"

"W-well, I know how hard it must be for this gal to have to perform out there in the heat, night after miserable night with the bugs eatin' her and everyone else alive. A girl like her needs a decent place to put on her show, and her audience deserves betta' too."

"And let me guess, you suddenly have just the place for her, right?" William hypothesized, trying his best not to laugh at Tucker's pathetic attempt at playing the role of a concerned and convincing businessman.

"Not only that, but that show 'a hers needs some work. She's in dire need of the propa' guidance. Any idiot could see all the technical problems there were."

"Proper guidance?! Technical problems?! What the hell are you talking about?!"

"Oh come on, William, admit it! Tryna do a show like that at an outdoor facility is foolish! You need to have that show in a place where ya' have more control ova' the stage and lightin'. Hell, in a place with plenty of seatin', where people ain't forced to sit on the grass for Christ sake. And you can't very well make that girl continue to suffa' in the heat, lettin' mosquitoes make a meal out of 'er every night. In a theata' like mine, she'd be right at home! I-I can use my ideas to promote her show, to make it more grand and spectacula', and finally turn a true profit for ya'. You'd be rich!"

"Don't you mean *you'd* be rich?! Money doesn't motivate me, Tucker! Not the way it's motivating you right now to mock Lily's show and play like you truly care about whether or not she's suffering in the heat or being eaten by bugs!"

"Now hold on a minute! You ain't gonna question my sincerity! I'm here to offa' ya' a chance for this Negro to grow in a place with some integrity and…"

"Integrity?!"

"Damn right!"

"I may be old, but I'm not senile, Tucker! Everyone in this town knows that raggedy, crumbling theater of yours has had more mice than people these last few years. So don't come to my home now acting like Lily's savior and pretending that integrity and making me rich are more important to you than your desperation to earn enough money to stop that God awful tavern of yours from being torn down!"

"Even if there's truth in what you say, what does it matter?! Nobody else will let that little nigga set foot on their stage! You should feel honored to be offa'd such a gesture from me given y'ur circumstances!"

Tucker suddenly found his raggedy old suit collar in the grip of two powerful hands. "What'd you just say?!"

"N-n-nothin'," Tucker stammered, with his eyes nearly bulging out of their sockets.

"I guess you didn't learn your lesson the last time you called Lily out of her name!" James growled. He had appeared out of nowhere again and yanked Tucker within inches of his face. "I'm only gonna say this one time, you worthless piece of shit, so I suggest you listen real fuckin' good," he snarled through gritted teeth. "I'd eat a pile of dog shit before I let Lily walk through your theata' doors! Is that a *firm* enough answa' for you?!" he asked as he gave Tucker another hard shake. James did not know the same manner of calmness as William when it came to scum, and he wanted to be sure that Tucker did not misunderstand that this time around.

Oddly, his moment of fury was yet another act that proved to William that James's drive to help Lily was about far more than just trying to improve her musical ability or help her find a way to take care of herself financially. Over the months they had lived in his home, William had picked up on James's body language and the way he lit up whenever Lily was in his presence. It was all too obvious that those were tell-tale signs that betrayed the secret of his emotions for her. But even more telling than that was the fact that this was the second time James had had an over-the-top outburst over someone disrespecting Lily. Those explosively protective moments were something William had experienced himself during his younger years after he had fallen in love with Emma. As noble as James's actions were, though, William's experience had made him wise enough to know that James could not afford to let his emotions get the better of him. So although he was delighted by the fact that James obviously cared deeply for Lily, William prompted him to let Tucker go. "Come now James, turn him loose and let him return to preparing shows for his mice. We'll wait for the real businessmen to show up."

James continued to stare Tucker down with squinted eyes and then shoved him as hard as he could before he let go of his shirt collar. "Get the hell outta here! If you come back here again, your next stop will be to a dentist."

"You'll be sorry you eva' put y'ur goddamn hands on me! You two nigga' lova's 'r gonna be beggin' for my help 'fore it's all ova' with! You wait and see!" Tucker exploded, in an attempt to walk out of the room with at least an ounce of his dignity.

James and William just glared at Tucker as Samuel marched in and happily escorted him off of the property with his pistol pressed firmly to the back of his head.

Tucker's begging session was proof that William's plan was beginning to work. He had hoped that the shows on his land would steer up enough controversial gossip to help catapult *The Dream Symphony* to success. He wanted to garner the attention of theater owners and managers, who were willing to work out substantial financial deals to have the show presented in their venues. William had no doubt that many of the same money hungry businessmen, who could not foresee Lily's worth before the success of her symphony, would be amongst the first ones to come after her like lions after a hearty meal. He knew that green would prove to be the only color that truly mattered to any smart businessman in the end. Wisely, William was now ready to use that level of greed to his advantage.

By the time the heart of winter rolled around, William wanted to have Lily in the warmth of a cozy theater, so long as it was under the right circumstances. In William's mind, the right circumstances included the assurance that the subsequent money that would eventually roll in would truly be equivalent to Lily's value. Just as important, he was only willing to accept offers by men who were genuinely respectful to Lily from the outset. He was not willing to beg anyone to treat her like a decent human being. He would halt the show altogether in winter before giving in to anything less. And it was apparent to William, after the way that James had so eloquently worded things to Tucker, that his feelings regarding the matter were indeed mutual. The only other thing that William felt needed to be a mutual agreement between them was the way they went about handling the sort of men who *slithered* in for their business meetings, rather than walked.

"Listen James," William began right after Tucker was escorted out. "I understand your desire to protect Lily, but we must handle things in a certain way. We're bound to encounter tyrants and blood-sucking leaches, but despite it, our reputation must remain impeccable if this show is to continue to be a success. So as difficult as it may be, I ask that you please find the strength to contain yourself ... For Lily's sake," he added, figuring that just the mention of her name alone would be a strong motivator and would also remind him of what was truly at stake if he continued his impulsive behavior.

"Understood," James quickly replied.

* * * *

Lily was completely unaware of what had just taken place on the other wing of the house in William's den in regards to Tucker. She was far too distracted to care about anything other than the little project she was currently working on. Despite the demand for more shows, she had gone to William in private and requested this particular Saturday off and expressed to him the reason why. He simply told her that she need not ask such things for *her* show. He made it very clear to her that she was *not* working for him, that the show was hers alone, and that *she* was the one who was to make any final decisions. As always, William's words comforted and uplifted Lily and made her decision for a day of freedom an easy one.

Lily's symphony had grown to mean so much to her, but her reason for wanting the day off held just as much meaning and was the driving force behind the meal she was preparing. As she worked to perfect her dish, she hummed with a smile on her face, thinking about how the joy she found in performing and sharing her music with everyone had surpassed her expectations. She was astounded to learn that something she had done as a child just to soothe herself was now giving her a feeling of purpose and a reason to breathe. When she lost James, Lily had abandoned the possibility of acceptance by anyone, except for in her fairytale fantasies. But now with the genuine warmth she had received from William and her audience, she cautiously began to open herself again to the idea that people could see beyond her status and accept her in the way that every human being should be. The positive outpouring from people who did not know her was overwhelming, but Lily remained humbled by it all, remembering at every moment the two people who had afforded her the luxury of escaping slavery for a while and providing her with the opportunity to bound freely within the confines of her dreams.

The consequent change *The Dream Symphony* had caused in Lily's spirit in the weeks prior was apparent to everyone, but especially to James, who now stood leaning against the kitchen door frame, gripping his suspenders, listening to Lily hum one of William's piano tunes as she cleaned the last of the mess from the meal she had just made. Lily's cheerfulness was infectious and instantly melted the anger James was feeling after having dealt with Tucker. James smiled as he watched her, knowing that he now had a moment to be near Lily with the weeks of intense labor and preparation gone for a spell. With the cloud of distractions finally settled, it allowed him to see with clarity how much he missed having her undivided attention and giving her his.

"Glad to see you in such a great mood."

Lily spun around with her heart racing. "You 'bout near scared the life outta me!"

"Sorry," James laughed. "Certainly don't wanna do that."

"How long you been standin' there?"

James walked toward her sniffing the air. "Long enough for my nose to recognize that aroma."

Lily smiled at the comment. "Auntie always used to say, 'ain't a man alive who can't smell his favorite meal cookin' a mile away.'"

"That Auntie was a wise woman."

"Anna Mae and Ben was fixin' liver tonight, so I figured I'd stick with tradition."

Tradition started many years ago on the nights that James's mother insisted on Lily fixing liver for the entire family. Just for James, Lily would always secretly make a small side dish of either biscuits and gravy or his absolute favorite: spicy Jambalaya and cornbread. James always made a fuss about how much he hated liver, so Lily had taught him the trick of pretending to wipe his mouth after taking a bite of it while at the dinner table, but then spitting it into his napkin. After dinner, James would lock the door to his bedroom and pull out the plate full of biscuits and gravy or Jambalaya that Lily always hid ahead of time underneath his bed to make up for the liver that had made its way into the trash can by then. Cold or hot, for breakfast or otherwise, James would nearly swallow Lily's biscuits whole or shovel the spicy rice into his little face like it was his last meal.

James had grown an affinity for southern food after spending so many Sundays in the slave quarters. It was the one day of the week Jesse provided his slaves with plenty to eat. James would often huddle around the fire with Lily and listen to all the slaves sing old Negro spirituals and tell stories while eating bits and pieces of their post-church meals. Everyone would laugh at his greasy little face or at the way his lips would pucker after biting into anything spicy. The slaves always tried to warn him not to fill himself too much before heading back to the big house to eat the dinner his mother prepared, but James could never help himself. After acquiring a taste for food made with lots of seasoning and flavor, his mother's Sunday dinners were equivalent to chewing paper to his little taste buds.

The current look on James's face after smelling Lily's specially prepared Jambalaya and cornbread told her that his preference for spicy southern food still prevailed. He followed his nose to Lily's pot, opened the lid, and proceeded to lift the ladle to take a bite, but Lily smacked his hand down before it reached his mouth. "Now I know Auntie and yo' mama done taught you betta' manners than that!"

"Manners? What are those?" James laughed, scratching his head.

"Auntie would 'a whooped you good for diggin' in her food! She taught me to keep you boys on the straight and narrow. Now, get your nose outta there and let me fix you a plate," Lily said playfully.

"Yes, ma'am," he teased in return, enjoying the momentary return of the sassy and bossy Lily that he remembered as a boy.

By the time Lily wandered over to the table with his plate, James was ready with his napkin in his lap and his eating utensil in hand. Lily sat it down and watched him dig in as soon as the plate left her fingers. "It won't be much of a compliment to me if you choke ya'self to death on my cookin'," she laughed, sliding him a glass of freshly made lemonade.

James gulped the drink down without stopping and then took a moment to catch his breath. "I can't help it. I don't know what you put in this stuff, but once I start chewin', I can't stop."

Lily laughed as she filled his glass again, happy to see that he still enjoyed her food so much.

"Mighty kind of ya' to go outta your way for me like this," James managed to say in between bites.

"Well, I'd say this is really small compared to all you've done for me, don't ya'?" Lily replied.

James stopped chewing for just a moment when he sensed the seriousness in Lily's tone, but his modesty would not allow him to respond. He simply looked at her and shrugged his shoulders before returning to his meal.

Lily looked down at her hands as they lay resting in her lap, a place her eyes always seemed to fall whenever a wave of emotions started to overcome her. She stood up and walked over to the window that faced the lake, staring out at it a few seconds while she collected her thoughts. "I rememba' the day you's in the kitchen talkin' to yo' daddy 'bout bringin' me here," she suddenly said, catching James completely off guard with the topic. He stopped his spoon just as it was near his mouth and slowly put it back in the bowl, wondering where the conversation was about to go. "When the words came outta your mouth, I rememba' hopin' for…" She paused, feeling a sudden sense of shame for what she was about to say. "F-for God to strike me down right where I stood. Given all the circumstances ova' the years, I ain't neva' have a reason to think you wasn't tellin' the truth. Figured by now some man I ain't neva' met before would've…" She shook her head. "Well, that I'd be carryin' some man's baby by now," she said, changing her initial statement, unable to bring herself to say the dreadful things she was imagining. However, for James it was too late. The words had triggered the thought of another man lying on top of her, which made the meal in his stomach start to churn. He pushed aside the bowl of food that he had yearned for just moments before, with the hope that it would help him to keep down what he had already eaten.

"All the way here, I's bracin' myself for what was about to come. I sat in the back of that wagon and cried and cried 'til it felt like my insides was 'bout near dried up," Lily hesitantly admitted. "I's emptyin' myself. Emptyin' my mind of all the disgustin' visions that was gnawin' away at me. Emptyin' myself of anga', and fear, emptyin' myself of the ability to feel. Everythang … just empty. By the time we got here, I's completely numb. Mentally, physically, emotionally, I couldn't feel no more than that there oven ova' yonda'," she said, motioning her head in its direction. "And 'til all this foolishness was ova' with, that's the way I wanted it … didn't wanna feel a damn thang.

"It wasn't 'til the day I walked this plantation end to end that I started to question everythang you had said to yo' daddy. But even though I started to have my doubts 'bout why I's really here that day, I still felt numb through and through. Even afta' Anna Mae and Ben told me that incredible story 'bout what William had done for their family all them years ago, I still just wouldn't allow myself to feel anythang … I just couldn't."

James still sat quietly staring into his half-eaten bowl of Jambalaya, silently accepting responsibility for Lily's feelings, unable to let go of the visual seeds that her words had planted in his mind: an endless stream of bodies invading hers, impregnating her with a child that was not his. His stomach and his thoughts justifiably punished him in unison.

Lily was silent for a moment before walking back over to sit down across from James. She waited for him to raise his head up from the table and look at her before she continued. "It wasn't 'til I sat outside on that porch while you's eatin' dinna' and told you all that I knew about William that I's finally able to accept the fact that you had gone and lied to yo' daddy to get me here." As Lily spoke, she kept her eyes trained on James. Her eyes were a spindle of rare colors he had yet to see in any other, a hypnotizing sight he always found hard to turn away from. "The awful visions, the numbness, the coldness, the emptiness … all it took was for me to look you in the eyes that day, and I knew right then and there that I could finally set it all free and allow my body and my mind to feel all ova' again.

"The way I felt that day is a moment I'll neva' forget in all my life." Lily's eyes drifted down to the table as if she could see it there replaying all over again. "First day in years I felt like maybe I's worth somethin' to somebody again. And Lord knows I needed to feel that. Needed it more than anybody could eva' realize," she said, remembering how she once desired to end her own life. "Just that gesture alone meant the world to me but now it's come to all of this," she said, shaking her head in disbelief with a faint smile on her face. "That stage," she said, turning for a moment to look out the window at it. "I swear I could live up there." She turned back toward James again and, without taking her eyes off of him, took his hand and ran her finger over the scar that she had stitched and nursed back to health. "Feels like a new home you done went through hell and back to build for me with your very own hands."

James closed his eyes in the brief moment that Lily touched him, welcoming it and wanting it to continue. In an instant, he felt his stomach settle and the ugly visions fade away after her words had infused exuberance into every part of his being. After failing Lily for so long, here now, he was hearing the wonderful results of his attempt to atone for all of his mistakes. For years, he had found it nearly impossible to forgive himself, but her gentle touch and her genuine words helped to bring that possibility within reach.

"So afta' all you've done for me, there ain't no way in the world I would eva' consida' fixin' you your favorite dish as goin' outta my way for you. Hell, cookin' is certainly the least I could eva' do for you," she laughed. "In all honesty, it don't matta' how many meals I make for you, it'll neva' be enough to repay you for all you've done to change my life to this magnitude."

"Lily, don't say…"

"No," she interrupted, "it's the truth. I owe you more than I'd eva' be able to accomplish in this lifetime. So at this point, all I feel I can really do is say, thank you, James," she said, squeezing his hand with both of hers. "'Cause Lord knows I do. I thank you from the bottom of my heart for doin' what you had to do to get me here and for believin' in me enough to take me on this journey with you," she smiled, with fresh tears starting to glisten in her eyes.

There was so much James was eager to say in return that it was all wanting to come out at once. He was taking the time to organize it all in his racing mind until the contents of his vivid night terrors rushed forward and trumped it all. He closed his eyes hard and gritted his teeth. Beads of sweat and a thumping heart followed, just as it always did whenever his recurring nightmare jarred him from his sleep. He could see the images clearly as he sat there across from Lily and it shut him down immediately. His desire to communicate the beautiful things that he wanted to share suddenly evaporated and left him with very little that he was willing to express to Lily from then on. "Well, I'm glad it's all helped to make a difference for you, Lily," was all he could muster the courage to say as he slowly removed his hand from hers.

Lily was appreciative of how receptive James was, but she felt a slight emotional sting when he took his hand out of hers. The simple maneuver seemed to say a lot. Not only that, but somehow she could feel that there was something on his mind that he refused to share with her. It bothered her that he had a quick and unexplained shift to a very cold and unwelcoming disposition, especially because it was not the first time she had noticed the random odd reaction. Lily slowly got up from the table feeling a little embarrassed. She turned her back to James, walked over, and rested her hands on the counter, giving herself a chance to settle what she felt was an irrational and ridiculous need to cry about the change in James's demeanor.

When Lily walked away, James could easily sense that he had embarrassed or upset her. He blew out a breath of frustration at himself for always giving in to the powerful images that plagued him. He was beginning to realize that the images from his night terrors would take a great deal longer to overcome than he ever expected. In this instance, they had won the battle, but he was still not willing to give up on the war he was forging against them.

On behalf of this special day, though, Lily was not about to allow herself to sulk for long over James's reluctance to talk. She comforted herself by the fact that she was finally able to share with him her appreciation for his troubles, which was something she felt was long overdue. So with that in mind, she was able to pull herself together rather quickly. For just a moment longer, she stood with her back to James, though. Before speaking again, she needed to clear her throat from the shakiness that would have accompanied her tears. She exhaled and finally turned back around. "Could you come with me a moment?" she asked James, completely changing the subject, wanting to lighten the mood.

James looked at her strangely at first, but then obliged and followed her into William's library. He remained puzzled by her request when the two of them arrived to a room filled with silence.

"I's hopin' I could play a song for you," Lily told him, as they stood face to face near the grand piano. "If you have the time, that is."

"If I didn't, I'd make the time … *always*," James

assured her, without blinking or turning away.

Lily found herself helplessly staring at James in return after hearing that the warmth had quickly returned to his voice. A pulse of heat ran through her during their silent exchange, making her even more eager to play the song she had prepared. She eventually seated herself while James continued to stand alongside the piano. He watched Lily's every movement, but not long after the melody began, the need to close his eyes became too strong for him to withstand. He quickly found his mind drifting into another world after Lily's notes began to wrap themselves around him.

Listening to the lightness of Lily's melody began to drum up all of the repressed daydreams that James had been obsessed with in his youth. In the months since he and Lily had been reunited, all of those old fantasies were slowly being unleashed. The song Lily currently played now had them all pelting the forefront of James's mind one after the other, beginning with the fantasy of the way in which he had once imagined proposing to Lily. His mind took him from there to the vision of the way she would have looked walking down the aisle toward him on their wedding day. He then felt his pulse quicken, thinking about what it would have been like having the honor of lying inside of his new wife in the hours after their beautiful ceremony. James continued flipping through the catalog of his old memories, next recalling the way he used to smile when thinking about the joyous tears he would have shed the day Lily gave birth to their first child. With Lily's music still tenderly whispering in his ears and those memories flooding his mind, James suddenly became overwhelmed with emotions, especially when considering that, despite all of his prayers, God had yet to forge a legal pathway to make all of those lifelong dreams come true.

James suddenly opened his eyes and stared at Lily, wondering how it could ever be punishable by law for him to show such a lovely woman how deeply he cared for her by giving her the beautiful life that he felt she well deserved. James had mentally exhausted himself over the years trying to make sense of it. Needing to get his mind off of such an impossible dilemma, he let the visions fade and instead became fixated on the innocent look on Lily's face as she sat playing in the perfectly sunlit library. James began examining the intricate lines of Lily's lips, the simple style of her tight curly hair, her even features, and the beauty of her flawless honey-brown skin. Everything about her made him suddenly want nothing more than to make love to her right then and there. He was ready to happily disregard the laws, feeling as though what he would gain emotionally, mentally, and physically from his experience with Lily would be worth the brutal punishment he would receive in a court of law.

The desire to touch Lily, to hold her, to caress and kiss her was nearly too intense for James to ignore with her sitting so close, especially with her scent pleasantly invading his nose. Suddenly, though, the room fell silent and he was jolted from his fixation.

I see us, Lily thought to herself. *And the sort of life I wish we could have together.* "I see you," escaped her lips instead after opening her eyes and staring at the piano keys. "In my mind," she continued. "Wheneva' I play that song, I see you just as clear as you standin' in front of me now."

After the brief experience James had just had while listening, he was easily convinced of the truth in Lily's words. Her admission, though, suddenly made him crave to know the intimate details of her visions.

"I've played this song on this day for the last ten years." Lily finally looked up at James. "But I wanted you to hear it this time." She reached down and retrieved a box that she had placed underneath the piano earlier and then laid it on top of the piano. "And I wanted to give you this," she said shyly. "Happy birthday to you, James."

James began to smile. "Lily…"

"I-I'm sorry I wasn't able to buy you anything fancy," she explained as a disclaimer before he could open his present or express his gratitude.

James sat his gift down, took Lily by the hand, and helped her up from the bench so that he could be closer to her before he spoke. "Listen to me. Don't you eva' be sorry about that, not eva', you hear? The dinna', everything you had to say to me in the kitchen a while ago, and this gift, it's all wonderful. It really means a lot to me," he reassured her. "And that song was beautiful … *Really* beautiful, Lily. It's worth far more to me than any expensive gifts, I promise ya' that." The sentimental value of Lily's gifts really began to rise when James realized that his birthday was the reason Lily had wanted the day off. He was deeply moved by the fact that she would even consider wanting to celebrate his birthday after all the things he had put her through in the past, especially in lieu of her beloved show. "So please don't make excuses or feel embarrassed about any of this, okay?" James continued.

"Okay," Lily smiled. She perked up immediately after feeling comforted by his words and sensing his sincerity. "I have one otha' thing for you." She guided him back into the kitchen where she picked up a round, silver covered platter and carried it over to the table.

"What is it?" James asked.

Lily lifted the lid and revealed a beautifully decorated cake. "Strawberry, right? It's still your favorite … I hope," she asked nervously.

"Yes. Yes, it still is," James answered with a smile.

"Good." Lily let out a sigh of relief. "Certainly ain't right to celebrate your birthday without the right cake."

"Nor without the right company," James said while smiling at her. "So, can I ask one otha' thing of you this evenin', Miss Lily?"

"On your birthday, I shall humbly provide you with all

that you ask for, sire," she said, copying William's British accent and taking a bow. She had become fascinated by the British way of life after all of the stories William had told her about his time in Great Britain as a boy.

James played along, turning himself into a British royal as well. He took Lily by the hand. "Excellent, m'lady. Then have a piece of cake with me, won't you?"

"Why certainly," Lily smiled, as she proceeded to sit down at the kitchen table.

"No. Not here." James stopped her, taking her gently by the arm before she could take her seat. "Follow me," he instructed. He picked up the cake, along with his gift and a few other items, and led her out of the back door. He then guided Lily toward the place he always found her in her spare time. Many days he had joined her there after long, grueling days of rehearsals, wanting to assure himself that the show was not too taxing for her. More than anything, though, James just wanted to be near Lily. He wanted to talk to her with the same level of depth and introspection they once had prior to the disastrous eight years that preceded their journey to William's home. However, their relationship had yet to reach that level of effortlessness. Whenever James was with Lily, he could always sense her reluctance to open up to him, but he had already accepted that it would probably be a long time before he earned her trust again. So he continued to be patient, wanting her to move at her own desired pace when it came to the matter of rebuilding their very damaged friendship and deciding if he should be forgiven.

Lily continued to follow quietly behind James, wondering why he preferred to eat outside, but when she stepped around the massive trunk of the old oak tree, the answer to that became very clear. "Today is a very special day indeed," James told her, after she looked down at the array of things that were lying beneath the shade, in the area she loved to sit and take in the view of the lake.

James's trip into town, earlier in the day when Tucker had seen him, was for this very moment. After returning, James had asked Anna Mae to keep Lily occupied while he quietly went outside to lay out a blanket, a bottle of wine, glasses, and a wicker basket filled with fruits, along with a neatly wrapped present next to it all. It all served one purpose in particular. After setting the cake down, James turned to Lily and held both of her hands. "Happy birthday to you too, Lily."

By sheer coincidence, James was not willing to let this unique day pass by unacknowledged either. It was a day they had begun celebrating together on his eleventh birthday…

James was out by the creek with Lily after his party was over with, letting her use the new fishing rod he had gotten as a gift. She was casting the line out into the water as he stood next to her tossing grapes into the air and catching them in his mouth.

"So when's your birthday?" James had asked nonchalantly in between tosses.

"Don't know," Lily replied just as calmly.

The grape James was tossing hit him in the head when he turned his attention to Lily after hearing her response. "What do ya' mean you don't know when your birthday is?"

"Just what I said. I don't know. My mama was neva' certain of the date. She say I's born on the hottest day she could eva' rememba' in the summa' of 1834, just like you, but ain't nobody eva' tell her exactly what day it was. Say it wasn't neva' no need for a field slave to keep up with the calenda' and all. 'Sides, she say she was awful sick for days not long afta' I's born, from an infection or somethin'. She say she couldn't hardly rememba' much of anything, so a lot of it was just a blur."

"I ain't neva' heard 'a nobody without a birthday."

"Well, ya' heard of someone now I s'ppose," Lily said, reeling in the fishing line and handing James back his pole.

"You mean you ain't neva' had no party, or presents, or nothin'?"

"Slaves ain't got no money to buy presents, and even if we did, it'd be kind 'a hard to celebrate when you don't even know what day to do it on."

James just sat there staring at his fishing rod, perplexed at how such an important thing could be overlooked. "Well, you would if I give you mine."

"Gimme your what?"

"My birthday."

"You can't just *give* your birthday away, James!" Lily told him in a condescending tone.

"Can so! It's mine! I can do whateva' I please with it! And I wanna give it to ya'!"

"Well, I ain't gonna letchya'!" Lily fired back, with her hands on her thin hips and her head cocked to the side.

"But I want to. Just don't seem right that you ain't neva' had a birthday. I done celebrated eleven 'a mine already, and I'm almost a man now," James explained, flexing his arm and squeezing his own muscle. "So I don't need no more birthdays anyway."

"James, that's awful nice 'a you 'n all, but I can't take your birthday away from you. It's too special. 'Sides, you ain't hardly no man yet. I don't see a speck 'a hair on your face and your arms are 'bout near skinny as that fishin' rod," Lily laughed.

James sat down on a log nearby and hung his head low, not finding any humor in Lily's comment at all. He was serious and not in the mood for her jokes.

Lily looked over at her friend and could tell he was genuinely hurt by the rejection of his offer, and she suddenly felt terrible about herself. She sat down and scooted close to James and put her arm around him. "I'm sorry, James. That's really kind of you."

"But you still won't take it, will ya'?" he asked, truly sounding miserable.

"No, but maybeee…"

"Maybe what?"

"Maybe we can *share*?"

"Heeey yeeeah! I like that even betta'!" James perked up and smiled.

"Me too!"

"Well then, happy birthday Lily!" James exclaimed, handing Lily his brand new fishing rod.

"What're you doin'?" she asked.

"Here take it. It's your first birthday gift."

"James, I-I can't take this. Your daddy'll kill you."

"But you gotta have a gift. I'll just tell him I dropped it in the deep part 'a the creek tryna reel in a big fish or somethin'. He'll get me anotha' one."

"Oh, thank you, James!" Lily's eyes lit up looking at the brand new pole in her lap. She leaned over and gave James a huge hug. "Thank you so much!"

"You're welcome," he coughed. "L-lily y-you're ch-chokin' me!"

"Sorry," she said, letting go of the firm bear hug she had him in.

"It's alright," he said, rubbing his neck while trying to catch his breath. "Come on! Let's do some fishin'!"

The whole conversation seemed logical in the innocence of their youthful little minds. Oddly, though, as they grew, James and Lily never challenged the validity of her adopting his birthday as her own. Instead, they just continued to celebrate in unison year after year, in their own quiet but grand way, as if their birthdays had genuinely fallen on the same date. During their celebrations, it had become tradition for James to read a story of Lily's choosing. Wilbur even joined the festivities as they ate strawberry cake and the many other picnic items that James would sneak out to their favorite tree by the creek. They celebrated that way up until their sixteenth birthdays, but on their seventeenth, their tradition came to an end.

The day of their seventeenth birthdays, James sat near his bedroom window holding Lily's favorite book, the one he had given to her after they had spent a long summer apart. Since receiving it, Lily had requested for James to read it on every birthday as a part of their celebratory ritual. With that on his mind, James sat with his head resting against his bedroom window pane, holding on tightly to Lily's treasured story, unable to sit it down. He was feeling immobilized by the sadness he was feeling, but then jumped to his feet when he was surprised to see Lily walking from the slave quarters toward their usual birthday meeting place near the creek. But despite how badly James wished to follow swiftly behind her, he just stood there unable to bring himself to move at all.

James was surprised to see Lily headed to the creek, because in the months prior to that moment, he had already sentenced himself to a life without her. Due to his father's overbearing demands, he had barely spoken to Lily in months. So after having forced himself to celebrate with his family, there James sat, all dressed up, with Lily's favorite book in hand, dealing with the pain of knowing that she would be at *their* old tree, celebrating *their* birthday *alone*. Two hours later, still sitting at the window, James watched Lily return with her head down. Her body language told him of her pain. He figured it was parallel to his own. "Goodbye, Lily," he whispered, touching the glass as a single teardrop pelted the leather cover of the book he desperately wanted to share with her that day.

When Lily had long since made it back to the slave quarters, James eventually gathered enough willpower to stand up and move from the spot he had sat for hours while mourning what felt like a death to him. He opened the trunk at the foot of his bed, placed Lily's favorite book inside, locked it away, and refused to ever read it again without her.

Despite the fact that their friendship began to crumble in the months before their seventeenth birthdays, Lily had gotten down on her knees and prayed the night before turning seventeen. She had asked God to bring her and James together again for just a few hours. She missed him terribly and prayed that, at the very least, they could continue their tradition of celebrating their birthdays with one another as they always had. So while James sat silently sulking by his window, Lily had waited and waited at the creek that evening hoping for him to join her, but after two hours with only Wilbur by her side, she had walked back to the slave quarters in tears. When her prayers went unanswered, she finally accepted that their friendship was truly over.

… So, ironically, on a day that signified the official ending of their friendship for Lily, James now stood before her wanting to officially cement their precious bond all over again. In front of William's sparkling lake on a tiny plot of land that he knew she cherished, James was ready to show Lily, in yet another thoughtful way, how truly sorry he was for all of his mistakes. He hoped to move forward and create a new beginning for the both of them, one that slowly erased any and all pain from the past. James was ready to wipe those ugly memories away and stamp each and every day of their future together as happy. He felt there was no better way to begin that mission than by honoring the day that Lily came into the world with a beautiful picnic, underneath a tree where she often daydreamed of a better life for herself, the sort of life that James was giving up his own dreams to help give to her.

Filled with hope, James took both of Lily's hands into his. "Lily, afta' everything I've put you through ova' the last several years, maybe I don't deserve this, but please say you'll celebrate this day with me again." He squeezed her hands a little tighter. "Please?" he begged.

Lily looked down again at the spread that James had gone through the efforts of placing there for her, and she knew she could never reject such a beautiful invitation. "I'd love to," she smiled.

James smiled in return, helped her to sit down on the blanket, poured her a glass of wine, and after an eight-year hiatus, they resumed the celebration of each other's lives with a toast. James was the first to make his dedication. "To your extraordinary musical accomplishments this year and to the many more that will surely follow." They touched glasses, and each took a sip of the finely aged red wine before Lily took her turn.

"And I'd like to dedicate this to my closest, most dearest friend. He is a friend who has always been there for me through all of the ups and downs of my life, a friend that I once used to hold dear to me, and who I have missed terribly." She raised her glass. "So to you, Wilbur! I shall collect many flies and crickets in honor of your absence here this evenin'," she joked.

"*Wilbur*?!" was the only word James could get out through his laughter.

"Well, of course. Who else could I possibly be talkin' about?" Lily asked sarcastically.

James pointed to himself. "I have no idea," he said just as sarcastically.

"Oh yeah." Lily waved her hand at him dismissively. "And you too," she said dryly.

Lily's sarcasm set the tone for the evening. It was lighthearted and playful the way it had been between them as teenagers. They began talking and reminiscing with one another about the memories of their previous birthday adventures while they sipped their wine and ate the grapes and strawberries that James had packed in his basket. After sharing their thoughts for a while, Lily placed a few candles on the strawberry cake she had made and lit them. She closed her eyes to make her silent wish, but James decided to forgo the opportunity and chose instead to admire the soft features of the woman who had been the subject of all of his past birthday wishes. When Lily opened her eyes, they blew out their candles together.

Although James attempted to put Lily at ease about the gift she had gotten him earlier in the library, she still began to feel a bit uneasy when he started to unwrap it. However, she refrained from saying anything until he had retrieved the two pair of pants that the box contained.

"I-I mended 'em and cleaned 'em up good for you," she explained, feeling her nerves striking again. "I seen where you tore both of 'em up at the knees while you's workin' on the stage. Figured it'd save you from havin' to buy new ones."

James turned the pants over and scrutinized every inch. "I do believe you's lyin' to me, Miss Lily," he responded in a very serious tone.

Lily scrunched her eyebrows and looked at him very confused.

"I saw them sewin' fairies sprinklin' that mendin' dust on these just the otha' night." He shook his head.

"Dang it!" She snapped her finger. "Ya' caught me!" she exclaimed through a sudden burst of genuine laughter.

"Shame on you tryna take all the credit!" James joked, smiling and relishing the sweet sound of Lily's infectious reaction.

"I guess I sho' deserved that one, didn't I?" she asked, wiping her laughter tears away.

"Yeeeah ya' kinda did."

"Well, I'll be sure to thank the fairies the next time I see 'em," she replied, with a brilliant smile of her own.

"You do that," he demanded playfully. He continued to stare at Lily, suddenly wanting even more now to make love to her under the shade of her favorite tree, near the peace and tranquility of the waters.

Lily stared at him in return and the smiles slowly faded away from their faces in unison. She could feel what James wanted, and she found that her wanting for him was mutual. At that very moment, she would have welcomed him inside of her without a second of hesitation.

"Thank you, Lily," James finally told her, attempting to force his desires from continuing to affect his body the way that they had. The way she was staring at him had made the throbbing in his southern region nearly impossible to bear.

"You're very welcome," she replied, still refusing to take her eyes off of him. She was mesmerized by the fact that the simple tone of James's voice could set her body on fire the way it just had.

To distract his mind, James turned away and handed Lily the gift he had gotten for her. The simple maneuver finally gave Lily a reason to pull her eyes away from him, something he needed her to do in order to ease the mounting tension in his body. To further cool himself down, James took a deep, silent breath as he watched Lily proceed to unwrap her present like an eager child at Christmas. After she had torn the wrapper away, however, she froze. She was completely fixated by what was in her hands. "James," she whispered, unable to say anything else. She immediately recognized that she was holding onto the original novel he had given to her many summers ago. It was the very same novel that she would always find herself craving to hear again for each of her last eight birthdays.

James had taken it from his trunk and packed it along with his belongings before they traveled to Ohio, knowing all along that he had every intention of giving it back to Lily on this very day. He watched her closely as she stared at it for a long while, flipping through it, and running her fingers down some of its pages. She was remembering the first time she had heard it and the unforgettable emotions she felt as she hung on every word within it. She was

266

desperate to feel those emotions all over again.

"I can't believe you still have it," she whispered.

"It's yours. I wouldn't have dreamed of gettin' rid of it."

"Thank you for this. I didn't think I'd eva' hear it again."

"You're welcome."

"Well." Lily handed the book to James. "Aren't you gonna read it?" she asked softly.

"No," he stated boldly. Lily turned to him with a puzzled look on her face after he handed the book back to her. "*You* are."

"But, James, I can't…"

"I've lost count of how many times I've kicked myself ova' the fact that I made a promise to you years ago," James interrupted. "A promise that I've yet to keep," he said, remembering how every letter he received from MJ while he was away at school would remind him of that. "But one thing that I'm proud to say about myself is that I'm a man of my word. And because of that fact, Miss Lily…" He pointed to her book. "By our next birthday, I'm gonna see to it that you're able to read this here story from end to end without a single word missed in between." James took his hand and gently turned Lily's face toward him. "You have my word."

Lily wanted to keep her emotions at bay during their birthday to ensure that it was nothing but a joyous celebration, but James's gesture touched her too deeply to maintain control. She momentarily fought to hold back, but after realizing that she would soon have the ability to read the pages of a book that held such a great deal of sentimental value to her, she broke down into tears. Her tears represented her appreciation of the fact that James was willing to empower her with such an extraordinary birthday gift, and were a silent thank you to God for finally answering the prayer she had made on the eve of *their* seventeenth birthdays.

As always for James, the need to comfort Lily was too overwhelming to resist. He felt no words were required this time, however. Without hesitation, he simply slid over and embraced her. His embrace grew stronger the longer he held her, and so too did his desire not to let her go. When her arms slowly gathered around him, and she rested her head comfortably on his shoulder, letting go of her suddenly felt like an impossibility.

"Thank you," Lily told him after she rested there a moment and his embrace helped to calm her.

James then pulled back to look at her. "You don't owe me any thanks, Lily. I don't deserve it anyway. If anything, I should be thankin' you for your patience and tellin' you how sorry I am that this has taken so long. It botha's me every day to know that you can't read this book, or any otha' book for that matta'. But I promise ya', I'm gonna do all I can to make it right."

"And for that alone, I just want you to know how grateful I am."

James nodded his head and silently accepted her kind words. "Now, c'mon ova' here," he said with a smile, patting the spot next to him.

Lily smiled in return, slid over, and within an instant her brilliant knowledge-hungry mind was ready and eager to absorb every word James had to say. They both huddled closely together up against the old oak tree on Lily's little piece of heaven on William's plantation, and James patiently began the first of many reading lessons. Proudly, he began giving Lily a gift that could never be taken away from her, a gift that would undoubtedly last her a lifetime.

Chapter Fifteen

MJ Spent a good portion of her Saturday afternoon dolling herself up for yet another business dinner meeting with her father on the Adams plantation. She rode sitting across from him in their fancy carriage with her posture perfect as always, her hair frozen in strawberry-red spiral curls, and make-up meticulously pasted to her face, waving a hand fan that matched her dress. The weather had warmed considerably since the last time she had seen James in town at Albert's General Store, so she waved her fan vigorously. She wanted to ensure that not one ounce of sweat had the chance to ruin her porcelain face or her hair before she was due to see James again. She wanted to present herself to him looking like a treasure, a prize that she was convinced he would just have to have.

Not only had Mary Jo calculated her attire, but she had even preplanned where she wanted to sit. She wanted to ensure that her perfume had better access to James's nose and that her best side was always in his line of view. She had conversation prepared in her mind as well. As she rode along, she went over the topics in her head, smiling to herself as she imagined the possibilities of James's responses. When she was not rehearsing her lines, she was imagining the look of surprise on James's face when he first sees her looking so perfectly put together.

After speaking with him at Albert's General Store months prior, Mary Jo had obsessively fantasized about James, the way she was now as she made her way to his plantation. For days on end, she had envisioned the things that she desperately wanted from him, some of which were considered unbecoming of a young and beautiful debutant like herself before being honored with marriage. But Mary Jo Parker did not care. When it came to James Adams, she was oblivious to all the rules. For him, she felt every law, rule, and regulation was worth breaking.

Being her wealthy father's only child, Joseph Parker viewed Mary Jo as his most prized possession. He never once had the willpower to stop himself from giving his daughter *everything* she ever wanted throughout her life. Consequently, MJ grew to expect and demand all other people to give in to her accordingly, or else she would resort to screaming, lying, scheming, and stealing to get what she wanted. If her wishes were not fulfilled, the tantrums she would throw were dramatic enough to turn the head of a two-year-old child in the midst of his own meltdown. But, in the case of James Adams, Mary Jo did not just *want* him; she *craved* him, she *yearned* for him, she *needed* him. And despite the fact that she was an adult now, MJ was still *proudly* willing to stoop to childish, distasteful levels to have him, levels that would make the devil himself blush. But before she resorted to such measures, though, Mary Jo simply tried turning herself into the most visually appealing woman possible whenever she knew she would be in James's presence.

In the years while James was away at school, a string of other men had fallen helplessly at Mary Jo's feet. Unfortunately, they were never enough of a challenge for her nor did they have the sort of physical features that appealed to her. MJ's desires for them usually waned not long after she accepted the gifts they bestowed upon her in an effort to win her affections. She happily took their meaningless trinkets and then toyed with their emotions, and sometimes even their bodies, knowing they would never be anything more to her than human playthings to fulfill moments of boredom while she waited, *impatiently,* for the one man she truly desired.

Mary Jo's thirst for James grew to a state of dehydration in his time away at school, especially when he did not respond to her letters. However, after running into him at Albert's General Store and seeing how he had developed into a man with a body and face worth sculpting, her simple thirst for him had turned into an undying hunger. With months having passed without another glimpse of him, MJ's body was now in a ravenous state of starvation. It was in that state of famine that she arrived onto the Adams plantation ready to see James again, ready to be fulfilled, ready to finally have her voracious cravings satisfied.

MJ's carriage stopped on the dirt path just in front of Jesse's rundown porch. Her father exited first, and then he helped his daughter down. Mary Jo emerged in her baby blue floor-length gown, holding onto her shawl, stepping down like a queen arriving at a ball in her honor. She walked with her arm locked around her father's as he guided her carefully up the steps toward Jesse, who waited near the front door.

It had been people like Jesse who had perpetuated MJ's arrogance over the years. Jesse never failed to give her and her rich father the royal treatment during their visits to his plantation. In preparation for their arrival, Jesse always demanded a few of his field slaves to scour themselves thoroughly. He then summoned them into the house and had them dress in fine attire to give the appearance that a crew of cooking and cleaning house slaves was the norm in his home. Even Jesse himself managed to scrub the dirt from beneath his fingernails. He would actually cut his hair, find his way to a bar of soap, and stuff himself into a clean suit, all while his temporary house slaves set out his deceased wife's finest china and prepared a five-course meal fit for a king and his princess at a Thanksgiving celebration. Keeping Joseph Parker's business was essential to the lining of Jesse's pockets and the survival of his tobacco and cotton farm. Therefore, contract negotiations and business dinner meetings with Joseph were always as calculated a main event as MJ's hair, clothing, and conversation topics during her visits. In Jesse's eyes, the Parkers were equivalent to, if not more

271

important than, a real royal family, and he wanted to see to it that they were always treated as such in his home, to maintain the long-standing business relationship with the pair.

With the utmost hospitality in mind, Jesse met the Parkers at the door with his two faux butlers standing on either side of him. The two field slaves stood tall with their hands covered in white gloves, clasped in front of them just below the waist. "Evenin'," Jesse greeted, shaking Joseph's hand. "Welcome, welcome."

"Evenin', Jesse. Good to see you again, ol' friend," Joseph responded.

"Mary Jo, y'ur lookin' just as darlin' as eva'," Jesse complimented. "Hard to believe you done growed up just before my eyes. It seems like not long ago you could fit right on y'ur daddy's lap." He then leaned over and kissed her on the side of the cheek.

Mary Jo rolled her eyes. Jesse had been saying the same thing to her ever since she was about sixteen, and she was sick of hearing it. Besides that, she never really much cared for Jesse anyway. She considered him beneath her. No matter how much he cleaned himself up, he was always too filthy and disgusting for MJ's taste. She simply could not understand how a man as sloppy looking as Jesse had anything to do with producing a man like James. The thought of it never failed to make her silently question if he was truly James's father. If it was not for the fine specimen of a man Jesse had *supposedly* created, Mary Jo would not even bother to be at this particular meeting. She only attended Jesse's dinners in her early years because she was too young to object to her father's demands. Since reaching adulthood, she only continued to attend out of a need to quench her thirst for James, which was certainly the case on this evening. It had been well over five months since speaking to James in town, and MJ was certain that by now he would have returned from his business travels. So when her father let her know that he was headed over to the Adams plantation, there was no way Mary Jo was going to miss the opportunity to see James again, no matter how much she detested Jesse's filthiness and his predictable compliments.

Mary Jo entered the house after Jesse's compliment at the front door and halted in the foyer. She noticed that aside from the clinking of plates and pots in the kitchen, the house was fairly silent. She was instantly annoyed when her ears were not satisfied by a particular voice she was dying to her. She then suddenly heard the stomping of footsteps and the closing of a door upstairs, which instantly put a smile on her face. Joseph and Jesse continued talking as they walked past her headed toward the dining room. Mary Jo did not follow them, though. Instead, she took the opportunity to use the mirror in the foyer to double check her appearance. She quickly smoothed out her dress and dabbed a dainty cloth napkin at spots in her make-up that she wanted to even out and then laid the tendrils of her hair just the way she wanted over her shoulders. MJ much preferred for James to catch a glimpse of her from head to toe, so she lingered there in the foyer a while, hoping to catch him as he descended the stairs. However, after a few minutes there alone, Joseph called after her to join him and Jesse in the dining room.

Mary Jo sat poised at the dinner table at first, trying her best not to seem too eager, but inside she was oozing with desperation. She did not care about the salad that a slave had placed in front of her or the wine that went along with it. For reasons of grooming his daughter to take over the family business, Joseph had always told Mary Jo to pay keen attention to his meeting conversations, but so long as James's chair went unoccupied, she lacked the ability to focus on anything her father was saying. Instead, MJ just sat there continuing to stare at the two other place settings at the table that had been set with china in front of empty seats. As she grew more and more impatient waiting for James to finally take his seat next to her, perspiration began to threaten her make-up. Just before the perspiration turned into beads of rolling sweat, though, Mary Jo finally heard the sound of two distinctive deep southern voices and footsteps stomping down the stairs. She quickly sat up tall in her chair, patted her hair, and a smile stretched across her face as her anticipation soared.

"Pa, this the document you's lookin' for?" J.R. asked Jesse, as he arrived in the dining room next to his younger brother, Jacob.

Jesse glanced at it. "Yup, that's it! Thank ya' boys," he said to his two oldest sons in appreciation for their efforts.

"Not a problem," Jacob replied.

"Well Heeello, Ms. MJ," J.R. said, in a lust-filled tone as he pulled out the chair next to her. "Nice to see you again, sweetheart."

Mary Jo cringed at J.R. and his term of endearment and slid her chair a few inches away from him. His looks and the sound of his voice were so identical to his father's that he just as equally made her sick to her stomach.

"Yeah, sho' is good to see ya'," Jacob agreed, staring at her with his mouth open before taking the seat across from her.

"Mr. Adams," MJ interrupted, as he spoke with her father. "Won't James be joinin' us this evenin'?"

"Sorry to say lil' darlin' but not t'night."

"Oh, I see. May I ask where he is?"

"Mary Jo!" her father yelled. "That ain't any of y'ur business."

"It's alright Joseph," Jesse interjected.

"Well, I don't mean to be nosy daddy, but it's just that I had a welcome home gift I's wantin' to give James and I can't quite seem to catch up with him these days, and I'd really like to get it to him."

"I see. That's mighty kind of ya'," Jesse replied. "Well,

he dropped our house slave off to a breeder a few hours north 'a here, then went just 'cross the borda' to stay with a friend from his old university while he does some medical research with a professor there at the school. Shouldn't be long 'fore he's back, though. Lily should be good and swollen by now," he laughed, flashing his unsightly yellow smile. It always pleased him that Mary Jo still had such an interest in his son. In Jesse's estimation, her desire for James was another bonus in keeping his business with Joseph thriving.

"Jesse Adams allowin' a slave off his property? World must be comin' to an end," Joseph joked.

"Well, I thought it was 'bout time I start passin' things on down. I ain't gettin' any younga'. It's what my boy thought was best, so I went on and let 'em carry her up yonda'. He'll be takin' ova' this place soon. Won't be too long 'fore he's the one sittin' here doin' all the negotiatin'.'"

Mary Jo mentally blocked out the conversation after that. She did not care to know about where James would be sitting in future circumstances. What mattered was that he was not sitting next to her now, huddled close enough to her to smell her perfume. He was not there to see the hair and the make-up that she had spent all day crafting, and the dress that she had selected, in what she *thought* was his favorite color. Suddenly not caring about her debutant poise and posture, Mary Jo slumped in her seat, picked up the wine she had ignored earlier and chugged it all without stopping to take a breath. She wanted to quickly numb herself over the fact that she had to survive another evening without James Adams there to satisfy her cravings for him … again.

Chapter Sixteen

A "Quasi-free" Slave:
A slave who is hired out by his master as free for the benefit of financial gain.

Slave Code
Article VI Section II
Every person whose grandfathers or grandmothers were Negro, although all other progenitors were white, are to be deemed as "Negro." Any person with one quarter or more Negro blood is to be deemed "Mulatto."

"What the hell is this?!" James yelled. He had nearly knocked the hinges off of the swinging doors of Buck's Tavern before walking up to Tucker McCormick and demanding answers for the article he had just read. He slammed the newspaper down on the counter where Tucker sat flooding his stomach with whiskey at the bar. James knew he would find him there. Drowning his sorrows at Buck's Tavern had been Tucker's daily pastime since the bank had finally seized his bar, McCormick's, a few weeks earlier.

"I don't know what the hell y'ur talkin' about, schoolboy," Tucker said calmly, still sipping his whiskey. It was barely noon and Tucker had already drank enough liquor to slow his reaction to being startled. However, the same could not be said for the few other patrons who had all suddenly ceased their conversations and turned in their direction. Oblivious to all of the eyes on him, Tucker picked up the newspaper, held it close and then far away, trying to get his intoxicated eyes to adjust.

ATHENS DAILY JOURNAL
Sunday Edition
June 5, 1859

WARNING TO POTENTIAL INVESTORS

James Adams, a slave owner from Virginia, recently discovered that his alleged former house slave is a self-taught pianist, who possesses the ability to play musical arrangements after hearing them only once. Since then, Mr. Adams has been using his house slave's abilities to his advantage by exploiting her acts at small taverns, galas, and side shows. Mr. Adams' hope is to earn the money necessary to pay off gambling debts and bills owed to the plantation that has been in his family for four generations. Currently, Mr. Adams is in the process of propositioning owners and managers of different theaters and orchestras to hire out his alleged former house slave, in an effort to turn his usually small profits into significant gains, under the pretense that the aforementioned slave has been legally manumitted. However, sources have yet to find proof as to the evidence of Mr. Adams' house slave's manumission and are, therefore, warning potential businessmen to steer clear of the Virginia slave owner and his counterpart, William Werthington. Mr. Werthington is a well-known composer, musician, and retired music teacher, who resides here in Athens. Mr. Werthington recently deceived an entire audience during a show held on his property on April sixteenth of this year, which was advertised to the public as "The Return of William Werthington." Many patrons were upset to find that Mr. Werthington had actually masked the truth about the true producer of the evening's ensemble: the alleged recently freed house slave of Mr. Adams. It is assumed that Mr. Adams and Mr. Werthington's deception was an effort to garner the attention of the public, attract potential investors, and eventually hire out the aforementioned slave. We hereby remind all citizens that the practice of hiring "Quasi-free Negroes" was outlawed in Slave Code Article XX Section I, enacted in 1793. All potential businessmen are hereby forewarned that the

277

penalty for breaking this law shall be carried out to the fullest extent allowed by law.

"Pppphh!" Tucker fluttered his numb lips with little droplets of his spit flying everywhere. "I ain't have nothin' to do with this shit." He tossed the newspaper aside and proceeded to try to take another drink until James grabbed his arm and slammed the glass back down.

"You're a goddamn liar! You make me and William out to be tyrants in this article!"

The whiskey gave Tucker the liquid courage to stumble off of his bar stool and stand toe-to-toe with James. "I told you, I ain't have nothin' to do with that shit!"

"Bullshit! I know you're behind this! Honestly, I don't give a damn what you or anybody else in this town thinks of me, but I won't let you get away with defamin' William! And you betta' hope to whateva' God you believe in that Lily neva' finds out about this slanderous garbage! For you to try to make her think any of this is true is low, even for a piece of outhouse shit like you!"

"No point in your fears then, schoolboy! Y'ur little monkey can't read anyway ... Music or otha'wise, I'm sure!"

Only the memory of William's lecture kept James from grabbing Tucker by the throat and squeezing until his lips turned blue and his beady eyes bulged from his head. James gritted his teeth and clenched his fists together, but then composed himself and headed toward the saloon exit without another word.

"That article is right, ya know!" Tucker yelled out as James walked away. "You might've deceived a few people into comin' to that shit you call a show, but it won't be long 'fore er'body gets sick 'a you and that lil' nigga'! She'll fade away like a fart in the wind!" Tucker nearly fell over laughing at himself. "Face it! She'll neva' be anythang more than the bottom-feedin' servant that she is!"

278

James was almost to the door before he turned back around and overturned the table that stood as the only barrier between him and Tucker. Shattered glasses and alcohol spilled everywhere on the floor.

"Oohhh, temper, temper," Tucker said, waving his finger at James. "Maybe I'm wrong. I notice you get awfully uppity ova' that lil' piano playin' bitch. Maybe you've already found out she's good for one otha' thing too," he said, with a smug look on his face. Do tell, schoolboy … Is y'ur little brown suga's pussy any good? I've often been tempted to get a taste 'a that sweet little ass 'a hers myself."

James's fist caught Tucker clean across the mouth, tearing a deep gash on the inside of his lower lip. Tucker saw black for a moment and then found himself on the floor lying in a pool of whiskey and broken glass. "Report that to the papers, you son of a bitch!"

Tucker licked the blood off of his lip and gave an arrogant laugh as James walked away. "Her pussy's that good, huh?"

James jumped on his horse and rode away from Buck's Tavern in a full gallop. He had a sudden desire to visit a few so-called friends at his old school after learning from another one of his frat brothers that a man, fitting Tucker's description, had been nosing around the University asking questions about him. It was true that James had once done some gambling and borrowed money on his father's behalf, but the story published in the *Athens Daily Journal* had been embellished far beyond the truth, and now James was eager to set the record straight with any and all who had been bold enough to betray him with their lies.

* * * *

"Might I have a word with you, James," William called out from his study, after hearing his footsteps in the hallway.

James blew out a breath of frustration, not wanting to

talk to anyone after the day he had had. He was ready to climb into his bed and sleep the rest of the evening away.

"Close the door," William instructed James, after he walked into his study with his hands on his suspenders and a scowl on his face. William sat at his desk with his hands clasped together, staring out of the window.

"Listen, William, I'm a little tired, and I's hopin' to…"

"I had plans to rehearse with Lily today," William interrupted. There was a coldness in his tone that James had not heard before. "Do you happen to know what has delayed my chance to do that?"

"No sa'."

"A knock at my front door."

"And?"

"And well, I was expecting the usual … You know, businessman, postman, old friend, things of that nature," he said, waving his hands in the air as he spoke. "But a sheriff!" William stopped and pointed one finger in the air. "No! Now, that I was *not* expecting. *That*! is most certainly *not* the usual, wouldn't you say?"

James dropped his head and exhaled. "Yeah, about that…"

"Do you even care?"

"About what, sa'?"

"About Lily? Or about any of the things I spoke to you about not long ago?"

"What things?"

"Don't pretend to be a fool in my presence, James."

"Yes, of course I do, but did you see what they wrote in…"

"I DON'T CARE!" William slammed his hand on his desk and stood up, scrunching his face up, and cutting his eyes hard at James. "When you go into a tavern making a damn fool of yourself or go to a school tormenting your old classmates, you're giving everyone in this town a reason to believe that the garbage they wrote in that paper is true!

We're already dealing with the most delicate of situations here with Lily, trying to navigate her through uncharted waters! And I swear it's like you *want* to tip her boat over with your very own hands! So tell me! What is it going to take for you to listen to me?!"

James just looked at the floor.

"Tell me!?" William insisted. "Sitting in jail, is that it?!"

Still, James did not respond.

"Or maybe, having the authorities drag Lily back to Virginia to your father while you're locked up?! Is that what you want?!" William continued. "Or worse! Giving someone reason to come here and hurt her?!"

James quickly looked up at him with fire in his eyes. The words were equivalent to a punch in the stomach.

"TALK DAMN IT! Tell me what the hell it's going to take for you to start giving a damn about your actions?!" William walked from behind his desk and approached James. "You're allowing a man as weak and stupid as Tucker McCormick to manipulate you like a puppet! He's tap dancing you right into his little web! It's pathetic and you're too damn caught up in your emotions for Lily to see it!"

"*Emotions*?!"

"Don't insult my intelligence! Don't you dare!" William said, pointing his finger at James. "Even a blind man can see how you feel about her!"

"Sa', I don't know what you're talkin'…"

"Shut up! Just shut up! No more of your nonsense! I've had enough for today! For someone so smart, you sometimes act so bloody stupid!"

William's level of hostility was more proof to James that he thought of Lily like a child born of his own blood, which pleased him, but at the same time, he was stunned that such a softhearted man was capable of becoming so angry. After William's tongue lashing, James felt reduced to the level of a scolded puppy but agreed that he rightfully deserved every bit of it. "You're right, William, I'm sorry. I'll do all I can to fix this."

William started to continue his tirade, but then caught himself and went silent. He turned instead and walked toward Emma's portrait. He needed the sight of her face to bring himself back to peace before he spoke again. "If you don't break things to begin with, James, then you won't have to crawl back, expending extraneous amounts of energy trying to *fix* them," he said with calmness finally having returned to his tone. "If you truly care for Lily, the way I know you do, you'll let go of your ego and *always* do what's in her best interest from the start ... *always*."

James continued to stand there silently, feeling like a soldier who was afraid to leave without being dismissed first. He simply watched as William stared at the woman in the picture who was a mystery to him. "What's her name?" James finally asked, after standing there a moment. "The woman in the portrait?"

"Emma. Her name is Emma."

"Who is she to you?"

The simple question instantly ignited William's nostalgia and gave him reason to tell a story that he felt might actually do James some good, especially considering the current circumstances. "Emma was the owner of a small country store that I frequented many moons ago. She was the type of woman who didn't know a stranger. She was hardworking, kind, patient, and always smiling. Her brilliant smile," William said while smiling himself. "It was that smile of hers that made my trip into town to her store worth it every day. I even found myself there purchasing things I didn't need, just to see that beautiful smile of hers," he admitted, chuckling at himself. "Some days I wouldn't even buy anything. I'd just wander in and help Emma restock her shelves while we talked upwards of an hour or more, if it was slow. I realized in that time, not only was she beautiful, but she was incredibly intelligent, and wildly funny! With every conversation, I found myself more and more intrigued by her and found it harder and harder to leave. When I finally would find the willpower to go, I'd count the hours until I could see her again," William whispered, remembering how the hours seemed to fly while he was with her, yet drag after he had left her for the day.

"Even though I was helplessly drawn to Emma, I'm embarrassed to admit that I was a bit intimidated by her. Oddly, I could talk to her about anything, but I could never quite get the nerve to ask her to have dinner with me … until one December. During one of our many conversations, she happened to mention that she had nobody to spend Christmas with, and I knew," William said, putting a finger in the air, "that this was finally my chance. I explained to her that my family was in another country, and that I also had nobody to spend Christmas with, so I suggested that perhaps she and I should spend the holiday together. It felt like an eternity to me before she said anything. My heart was in my throat the whole time while I stood there, frozen, waiting for her to answer." William smiled at the memory. "I'll never forget all of the fireworks that went off inside of me the moment she finally said that she'd love to join me. I swear I felt like dancing all the way home!"

James had walked over and was staring at Emma's portrait alongside William. Out of the side of his eye, James caught a glimpse of the smile on his face as he talked about that memorable moment. He could not help but feel infected by William's joy.

"I offered to cook for her for Christmas," William continued, "but Emma wouldn't hear of it. Instead, she came to my home and prepared the most wonderful meal for me. After we had eaten, we exchanged gifts. Knowing my love of reading and music, she had hand carved me two bookends in the shape of musical notes. To this day, it still remains one of my favorite gifts from her," William smiled.

"With all the time she had spent making those bookends, it made the necklace I gave her seem so unsentimental, but she loved it, especially because of the lily-shaped pendant I had custom-made to go with. That was her absolute favorite flower, and her favorite piece of jewelry, for that matter. She rarely ever took it off."

James glanced back up at Emma's portrait and indeed saw that very necklace displayed proudly around her neck.

"After exchanging presents, we sat at the fireplace together, near the tree we had just decorated," William continued. "With her resting in my arms, I found myself helplessly telling her things about myself that I had never shared with any other. There was just something about her that comforted me enough to set aside all of my fears and worries about her ever judging me or betraying my secrets. I rambled on and on, eager to share my life with her. But oddly, after I told her a rather happy story about my mother, that smile I had come to love about Emma was gone. Out of the blue, she suddenly began to cry. I feared I had said something wrong.

"'Why the tears?' I remember asking her.

"'I haven't seen my mother in years,' she replied. 'I'd give anything to see her again,' she admitted, with tears still cascading down her cheeks.

"It broke my heart to see her in that kind of pain, and I remember wanting right then and there to do whatever it would take to see Emma back into her mother's arms again. 'Tell me,' I begged of her. 'Tell me how I can fix this for you.'"

James looked over at William again and noticed the sudden change in his demeanor. It was as if he was reliving the actual moment.

"Emma got up and walked away from me and stood with her back to me," William continued. "She faced the fireplace and wouldn't look at me anymore, so I knew it was something serious.

"'Thank you, William,' she said to me, 'but there is no fixing this.'

"'Why not?' I asked. 'Has your mother passed?'

"'No, my mother made me promise never to see her again,' Emma replied.

"'Why ever would she do such a thing?' I wanted to know. I got up and stood closer to her, hoping that just my presence behind her would comfort her, but it did nothing. I felt helpless standing there, unable to do anything to soothe her, just waiting for her to find the courage to speak to me again.

"'My mother … Sh-she was a slave,' she finally whispered, after the longest silence in between the sniffling of her tears. 'I'm a Negro, William,' I remember her boldly confessing."

James looked at Emma's portrait again and squinted his eyes in disbelief. He initially saw nothing in her features that would have made him think twice about whether or not she was white. Her eyes were as blue as his, but after looking again, he finally noticed the fullness of her lips and the curl of her dark hair and the slight tint in her skin, things he would never have picked up on before.

"Emma turned around and looked at me, and I will never forget the shame in her eyes," William continued. "'I'm so sorry I didn't tell you sooner,' I remember her saying. I think she could feel that there was something incredible between us too, and she wanted to be honest with me before things went any further.

"After her confession, she began to gather her things to leave. Without hesitation, I walked up behind her and took away everything she had in her hands and put them down. I guess she was expecting that I would be upset over her secret, but her honesty and her vulnerability only drew me closer to her. I turned her around near the front door and just held her. I didn't whisper another word, I just held her for the longest time, feeling as though my words would never have been enough for me to express that I accepted her … *all* of her. I wanted to do whatever it took to let her know that her confession would never stop me from feeling what I felt for her … not ever. Emma was the first and only woman I'd ever had the sort of deep connection with and I didn't want to lose that, so there was no way I was willing to allow her just to walk out the door and possibly out of my life. Had she done that…" William shook his head. "There's no doubt in my mind that I would've been devastated … *absolutely* devastated.

"Fortunately, my embrace was all it took to settle her and convince her to stay. After that, she cozied herself next to me near the fireplace again and finished telling me the story of how her and her mother were both fathered by white slave owners, and that she was considered mulatto. She even said that since she was only one-quarter Negro, some people referred to her as a *quadroon* or some strange term of that nature. Anyhow, she went on to further explain that her mother had worked hard to save money while she was carrying her so that she could buy their freedom. Her mother wanted to ensure that her child never knew one minute of what it was like to be a slave nor have the savage cycle of abuse continue with her daughter. She wanted more for Emma, so much so that she had unselfishly let her go when she was eighteen and told her never to return to the city that was her home. Her mother believed that as long as Emma never again claimed herself to be a part of their Negro family that she would easily pass as a white woman. She felt that Emma should use the gift of her fair skin to her advantage and go on to create a better life for herself. And for all that her mother had endured and sacrificed for her, Emma did just that. She got a higher education, moved to a prominent town, and soon opened the little country store where she first caught my eye.

"With all that she had accomplished, it may have seemed like the fortune of her physical traits were a blessing, but for Emma, the secret of who she really was haunted her every day. She hated denying her family and her heritage. She hated not being able to return home and see her mother and other family members anymore. But she knew that's what her mother wanted. Some days, though, she told me that she wanted to give her fancy lifestyle away just to have the honor of announcing proudly to everyone who her beloved mother really was.

"I was entranced by Emma's story, her courage, and her strength as she spoke to me that Christmas night. In fact, we spoke until sunrise, each of us continuing to reveal the things about ourselves that we feared for any other to know. In that time, I learned that the woman I had gotten to know for months had actually been suffering in silence without her family. But despite it, she had never once let it stop her from always being so kind to everyone or from wearing the beautiful smile that drew me to her in the first place. I also learned that she had never once let her guard down and revealed her sorrows in front of anyone, until that night in front of the fireplace … with *me*. It was the utmost compliment that it was me she chose to be vulnerable enough to share her pain and her secrets with. That meant I was special to her and that I was worth the risk. I felt so honored to have her trust in that way. It was one of the many things that made me fall in love with her that Christmas night … *Madly* in love," William whispered, closing his eyes, willing himself not to let his tears fall.

William pulled himself together and continued. "In the months that followed that Christmas evening, Emma and I were inseparable. And it wasn't long before I knew beyond a shadow of a doubt that this was the woman I wanted to marry. But I also knew that if people ever discovered the truth about her identity, they would never see my love for her as right, that in their eyes it would be a sin, punishable by law even. I also knew that my music career and even my life would be at risk. Taking all of that into consideration, I asked myself something: Should I spend the rest of my life worrying about society's rules and take the risk, in years to come, of lying on my death bed utterly alone, regretting every moment I spent breathing? Or was I going to lie on my death bed recalling all of the beautiful memories I had created with the woman I wanted to spend the rest of my life with, while she sits at my bedside comforting me as I take my last breath?" William turned to look at James. "My heart did not make it to the next beat before I knew the answer to that.

"So, the woman in this portrait," William said, pointing at her, "who was she to me, you ask?" He turned his head back toward Emma. "She was a woman I was too stubborn to live my life without. She was a woman I was prepared to lose my career over, a woman I would not have hesitated to lose my very life over. She was my heart, my life, my soul, my inspiration, my true love … She was my beautiful wife and my very best friend," he said, as he touched her portrait. "She died in my arms some time ago, but not before giving me two incredible sons and forty glorious years of marriage. She was *everything* to me, James … *Absolutely* everything," he said, with his voice cracking. "That's who she was to me."

William exhaled deeply before he was able to continue. "I miss her so. Every breath I take now seems like such an insurmountable task without her." He walked over to his desk to grab his pipe and to clear his throat, trying not to let the memory of his wife completely break him down in front of another man.

"Funny thing love, though, isn't it?" A much lighter tone had finally returned to William's voice. "Seems you don't have much control over who you want to bestow it upon, do you?" he asked, as he lit a match. "Can make even the sanest man do the craziest things, I tell ya!" He put his pipe in his mouth, inhaled, and let out a puff of smoke. "I spat on society's rules, and I must admit, I've never regretted it for a goddamn minute, my boy … Not a single minute!" William laughed as he pat James once on the back. William then turned his head toward the door when he suddenly heard that the faint sound of Lily's music down the hall had stopped. He took out his pocket watch and realized that he was well over an hour late for a collaboration session with her. "Well now, if you'll excuse me," he said, patting James on the back again, "*Lily awaits*." He winked and gave James a telling glance to let him know that he wanted those words to hold far deeper meaning than just their face value.

As William and James both stepped out of the den and into the hallway, Ben approached. "William, y'all have anotha' visita' at the front door," he informed them.

"Who is it?"

"Anotha' unknown. Young lookin' fella'. Don't look or sound like he from 'round here eitha'. Got a funny little accent. He sho' is mighty strange. Most folks them bandits escort to the door with them pistols look like they 'bout to mess themselves right time I open the door, but this youngin' ain't hardly broke a sweat yet."

"Interesting," William replied. Ben's description intrigued him, so he decided to greet the unknown young man at the front door himself.

"Ahh, Mr. Werthington, please excuse the unannounced visit," the young man said after William arrived at the front door. He extended his hand to shake. "I'm Landon." He was smiling despite a pistol near his skull.

"Pleasure to meet you," William said, looking at him strangely as he took hold of his hand. The young man's German accent was easily recognizable to him. Even his name sounded somewhat familiar, but William could not quite place his face.

"It's an honor to see you again. I've attended quite a few of your performances as a boy," Landon explained.

"Is that so?" William nodded his head to his security bandit, Samuel, to let him know it was okay to remove the pistol he had pressed against the young man's head and return to his post at the front entrance. The subtle signal wiped the adrenaline-fueled smile off of his toothless, dirty face.

"Yes, I actually…"

"What can we do for you?" James rudely interjected. He was still not in the best of moods and not at all impressed by this stranger's familiarity with William.

Landon stared at James a moment, sensing the coldness in his voice, but despite it, he pressed on with poise and confidence. "Well, I know the two of you are probably very busy men, so I'll get on with the reason for my visit. I'm here because I was hoping to speak to the lady of the house."

"The lady of the house?" William questioned.

"Yes, the beautiful young lady from the show here on your plantation. Ms. Lily … Umm, I'm sorry, I wasn't told her last name."

"You don't need to know her last name!" James spat. "And what do you need to speak to her for?!" There was even more ice in his tone this time. William cut him a cold look, but James ignored it and continued to stare at Landon, but yet again, he was not rattled by James's attitude.

"Well, I was hoping to speak to her in regards to her show."

"You can speak to *us* about that," James answered.

"Oh, I see. But it was my understanding that it is *Lily's* show, correct?"

"Yes, that is true," William replied.

"Well then, with all due respect to the both of you, I would much prefer to have a word with *her* … in private. If she doesn't mind, of course."

James was about to speak again, but William placed a hand on his shoulder to calm him. Landon's desire to speak directly to Lily had piqued William's curiosity about him even more. Normally, he would approach with the same skepticism and fire in his tone as James, but no other man, who had come to his door to inquire about Lily, had ever bothered to consider that she was worthy of being a part of the conversation. That small detail alone was enough to make William feel as though the young man deserved a chance to plead his case. Not only that, but he was also eager to figure out why his name and face seemed so familiar.

"James, go and fetch Lily, please."

"But…"

"Have her meet us in my den."

Lily was already preoccupied in the library with another guest who had arrived just minutes before Landon. Her unexpected visitor was the reason she had abruptly suspended the work she was doing on her new melody. He had walked in quietly and surprised her.

"Hello, Lily!"

"Elijah! How nice to see you again!" Lily had said after he stepped around the corner.

"Good to see you too!" he expressed, approaching her with an extremely confident stride in his step. He had been eager to see Lily again since the fundraiser, especially since Isabel went on one of her nonstop, mindless talking sessions and mentioned to him that Lily thought he was attractive.

"Oh my! What's all this for?" Lily asked, after being presented with a single rose and an array of wrapped chocolates.

"Just my way of congratulatin' you on the success of your show."

"Thank you so much! That's really very kind of you!" She set her gifts aside and gave him a warm hug.

"I'm so sorry I haven't been able to attend," Elijah told her, holding her longer than she had anticipated.

"Oh, no need to apologize," she replied, finally able to free herself from his embrace. "Sounds like congratulations are in orda' for you too! Your sista' told me you's tryna start a new business and all. She say you been travelin' quite a bit."

"That sista' of mine can't hardly hold wata'."

"Oh, sorry. Was I not supposed to know that?"

"No, no, it's quite alright. It's no secret. Just wish she'd leave a little left for me to talk about with folks sometimes," he laughed.

"Well, I'm sure she means no harm. She's just awful proud 'a you."

"Sounds like the two of you talk pretty often."

"Yeah, she sort 'a feels like a sista' to me."

"Really? Well tell me then, what otha' little secrets has she whispered to you about me?" he asked, staring at Lily in a way that hinted at what was on his mind.

Lily stared back, knowing exactly what he meant, but she refused to betray Isabel. "Nothing. Nothing at all. We mostly talk about girly things. You know, stuff you men wouldn't have no interest in," she smiled.

"I see," he said, continuing to gaze at her. "I must say, Lily, you have a very beautiful smile."

"Th-thank you," she stumbled, after not expecting the compliment. She was not yet used to being in an environment where men could so brazenly approach her. She looked down at the floor to escape his eyes when the discomfort of the moment took over.

"So, how have you been?" Elijah asked after she was silent for too long.

"Umm, good … really good," Lily answered, happy he was attempting to change the subject. "Mostly real busy. We's constantly makin' small changes to the show and all. But I enjoy it."

"Glad to hear that," he said, as he walked around and fiddled with a few keys on the piano. "So, do you eva' take a little time to yourself away from this here piano? You know, to relax?"

"Every so often, but it's hard to find the time some days. I'm so absorbed in writin' music and workin' on the show. I ain't complainin', though, 'cause I love it so much."

"I'm sure you do, but it's good to step away sometimes, ya' know? Can't spend your whole life workin' hard and neva' takin' a moment to play."

"You're right. It is nice to have a break once and while … I s'ppose," she replied nervously, after suddenly sensing that there was an ulterior motive behind his questions.

"And afta' the sort 'a show I've heard you put on if anybody deserves to relax, it's definitely you." Elijah walked toward Lily again, staring at her in a way that intensified her nerves.

"Thank you. That's very kind of you to say," she replied with a shy smile.

"You know what?"

"What?"

"You should let me cook for you sometime. A quiet dinna', a little wine, some nice conversation, no betta' way to relax than that."

"You can cook?!"

"Wow, you mean that chatty sista' of mine didn't tell you?" Elijah laughed.

"Naw, she neva' said a word about it."

"Yeah, I love to cook. It's the reason I've been wantin' to open my own restaurant and bar. My motha' believed in raisin' me and Isabel to be well-rounded and independent, so she taught both of us to be really great cooks."

"I'm impressed! I'd've neva' guessed."

"So, what do ya' say? Would you like to have dinna' with me? When you have the time, of course."

"Hmm, well, I'll have to think about it."

"Okay, fair enough. I'll tell you what," he said, taking

a hold of one of her hands. "Now that I'm done travelin' for a while, I have all intention of bein' at your next show. So how about this? You take some time to think about my offa', and if you say yes, then maybe afta' the show I can put somethin' really nice togetha' for you. Believe me, there's nothin' like a home-cooked meal afta' a hard day's work, and I'd be honored to prepare you one just as soon as you set foot off of that stage."

"That's awful sweet of you, Elijah," Lily replied shyly. "I'll definitely think about it."

"Well, regardless of your answa', one thing is for sure, I can't wait to see you perform. I'll be front and center, and I swear I won't miss a minute. You can count on that!" He brushed Lily's cheek with the back of his hand.

"That'd be wonderful," she said, feeling a slight jolt from the warmth of his touch.

"Well, I gotta get goin'. Congratulations to you again, beautiful."

"Thank you!" Lily blushed.

"See you soon."

"Bye."

Elijah smiled and let his eyes linger on Lily a moment longer before leaving. He then exited the library and nearly ran into James, who had watched and listened to the tail end of their conversation from the hallway with his blood boiling.

Elijah halted just before crashing into James on his way out. "So sorry Mr. Adams. Please excuse me."

James just stared at him, refused to speak, and rudely refused to move. He forced Elijah to be the one to step aside to proceed out of the house. Simply because of Elijah's attraction to Lily, James already harbored a deep-seated hatred for the man, and he clearly had a hard time not showing it. James was trying his best to accept the fact that any man now had free reign to approach Lily, but after the uncontrollable way he had overreacted during the times that he had witnessed Elijah trying to court her, he realized that that was going to be a damn near impossible task.

Listening to the want in Elijah's voice during his interaction with Lily was the last thing James needed to see at the end of a brutal day. He tried to take a few deep breaths to calm himself over the matter before entering the library. "Lily," he called out in a very flat tone.

"Yes." She stopped and turned around just as she was about to sit down again at the piano. As soon as she looked at James, she could read all over his face that something was bothering him.

"You have a guest here to see you."

"To see *me*?"

"That's what he said."

"Okay. Well, where is he?"

"He's in William's den."

Lily stopped before she left the library and put her hand on James's shoulder. "You alright? I can tell somethin's botherin you. Do you wanna talk about it?"

"Don't worry about me, I'm fine. You have a guest waitin'," he replied very coldly. After what he witnessed, he simply could not force himself to pretend as though he was in a good mood ... not even for Lily's sake.

"You can't stop me from worryin', so whoever he is, he can wait. We can sit and talk for a minute if you need to," Lily insisted.

"I said I'm fine!" James snapped.

Lily scoffed, slowly took her hand off of his shoulder, furrowed her eyebrows, and looked at him like he was crazy. She knew she did not deserve the unnecessary outburst. She shook her head and walked away, not wanting to deal with his attitude.

James ran his hands through his hair, instantly feeling like a fool for taking his frustrations out on her. "Lily, I'm sorry!" he said to her back, but she never turned around to acknowledge him.

Lily arrived in William's den to the sight of a tall, skinny, brown-eyed man, with blonde hair, sitting in an arm chair, speaking with William as he sat at his desk. By his lavish clothing, she could tell that he was someone rather important.

"Hello," Lily said as she entered. "James says you're here to see me?"

Her guest immediately stood up when she made her presence known, and then made his way over to her. "Oh yes, hello." He extended his hand as he got closer. "My name is Landon."

"Hello, I'm…"

"Lily," he finished. "Ms. Lily … Umm, I'm sorry, but I don't know your last name."

"Adams," James interjected. Lily looked over at him standing in the doorway. He answered for her in an effort to spare her the embarrassment of explaining that she had no last name, at least that was how he attempted to justify it in his mind. It was the first time Lily was hearing of any such thing. She stared at James a moment after his statement and then simply went along with his lie.

"Ahh, Ms. Lily Adams. It's lovely to finally meet you. I'm pleased to make your acquaintance," Landon said, sounding truly delighted to officially know her. He then lifted the back of Lily's hand and kissed it gently, which caught her off guard.

"Thank you. Nice to meet you too," she replied, looking at him a bit strangely after his very formal greeting.

"It is truly an honor to be meeting with you this evening. I read the article about you in the paper this morning and…"

"*Article?*" she asked, looking at both William and James in confusion.

James felt his stomach clench and his anger flare up again. He knew he had no right to be mad at Landon for mentioning the newspaper story, so he bit his tongue and silently prayed that the day's influx of aggravations would eventually come to a halt. He then cowardly turned his head away, not wanting to acknowledge Lily or the article, not even with eye contact. Fortunately, Lily did not press further about the subject.

"Yes, I can't help but wonder, is it true?" Landon continued. "What they said about your ability to replay music? After hearing it only once, I mean?"

Lily looked over at James again to see if he would look at her, but when he just continued to stare out of the window, she let it go and turned her attention back to Landon. "Yessa', that's true."

"How do you accomplish this?"

"It's the way I first learned to play. I'd have to memorize everything I heard. Guess it's just somethin' that stuck afta' all these years."

"Simply astonishing," Landon replied in his thick German accent, looking at Lily a moment in disbelief. "That's certainly a feat I'd love to see."

"But I much prefer to create my own music," Lily explained. "I appreciate the gift that God gave me to memorize music, but there ain't no greata' feelin' than bringin' what I hear in my head to life."

Landon unknowingly continued to stare at Lily, making her feel a bit uncomfortable with the way he was looking at her. It's not that he was intentionally trying to be rude, he was just instantly taken aback by her answers, her poise, and by her raw beauty. "Well, listen," he finally said after a moment. "William tells me that I've caught you both just before your rehearsal together, so my apologies for the interruption, but I was hoping I could speak with you about your show, if you don't mind?"

She looked Landon up and down at first. She was impressed with how sophisticated he seemed for someone who looked so young, but she was curious about his foreign accent. It was not quite like William's, but she knew it was not American either. While she contemplated whether or not to speak with him, she turned to look at both James and William, who stood there silently. They did not want to give her any indication about how to proceed, wanting her to make her own decisions. She was not in the best of moods after the small incident with James in the hallway, but she decided to hear what Landon had to say despite it. However, since this was her first time meeting him, she did not feel comfortable being alone with him. "Sure, but only if they can stay," she finally answered.

"But of course," Landon agreed. He then took her hand and guided her to a sofa nearby, allowing her to sit first before joining her. "I guess I'll begin with just a little insight about myself, Ms. Adams, if I may."

The way he addressed her instantly made her feel important, which helped to relax her. She nodded her head for him to proceed.

"When I was just a small boy, back home in Germany, my father began taking me to symphonies quite regularly. He's dragged me to so many I've honestly lost count of how many I've seen over my lifetime. I used to enjoy them in the beginning, but now you'd be lucky to find me awake by the third or fourth song. By then my snoring is resonating in the theater along with the orchestra," he joked.

His comment finally got Lily to smile.

"Don't get me wrong, I have an appreciation for fine music, but for decades now, it seems there has been nothing but the same old dull, redundant style of music. Many people simply try to emulate such greats as Mozart or Beethoven, and even our dear William here. In all my years, in the countless symphonies I've attended, I have yet to hear anybody who isn't afraid to step outside of the molds they have created." Landon got up from the sofa and walked over to the window that faced the stage. "Until, by chance, I sat in the second row, just on the corner there in that amphitheater." He closed his eyes to revisit his memory of that night. "And heard you," he said, opening his eyes and turning back to look at Lily. "What my eyes and ears were witnessing was unlike anything I've ever seen or heard before. This, I can tell you after having been to dozens of symphonies all over the world. You, your music, the brilliance of those dancing shadows, made me feel as though I was dreaming the most unforgettable dream. Quite frankly, as a man, I would not usually dare to admit this, but for the first time in as long as I can remember, instead of being lulled to sleep by a show … I was nearly brought to tears."

Landon walked back over to the sofa and sat down next to Lily again. "Ms. Adams, I have had the great fortune to see a lot in my life, and I readily admit that it has caused me to be a man who is not easily impressed by anything anymore. I now only seem to be drawn to things that absolutely command my attention and respect. And trust me when I tell you that there are very few things that would motivate me to happily expend my money, and more importantly, my valuable time to attend. And so the fact that I have seen your show, not once, but twice now, I hope serves as a clear indication to you about whether or not I felt it was a spectacle worthy enough to be placed at the very top of my incredibly short list of things that have met these criteria. And if *that* is not a clear enough indication then let me further explain that, despite missing the comforts of my home in Europe, terribly I might add, I have chosen to forgo my chance to depart. I have made this choice *only* because I was so moved by what I had the opportunity to see just outside that window there. And so, instead of sitting on a cruise ship at this very moment and sailing the seas back home, you and your unforgettable symphony have motivated me to stay and sit here before you now, so that I may extend what I hope you will consider as a very valuable invitation."

"What sort of invitation?" Lily asked.

"An invitation to allow me to help you in a way that I have, selfishly, never bothered to help any other in my life."

"How so?"

"Well, my guess is that you have much more buried in that genius mind of yours. More you'd love to do with your show? Elements you'd love to add? And perhaps many other places and people you'd love to share your music with?"

"Yes, of course … so much more."

"I'm positive that I can help you then."

"Your words are so gracious; believe me they are. To know that my show could eva' touch somebody the way it's touched you, inspires me to wanna give even more of myself to my music, but…" Lily paused and looked over at William and James. "What could you possibly do for me that they haven't done already?"

Landon glanced over at both men as well and then turned his attention back to Lily. "Ms. Adams, I hope that you don't take what I'm about to say the wrong way. That amphitheater is certainly beautiful, but incredibly small in comparison to many of the grand theaters I've had the opportunity to attend, which I'm sure William can also attest to. The magnificent visual imagery that you've created should undoubtedly be presented on the sort of stages that will allow your ideas to flourish to their full capacity. Your show should also be able to expand inside of the sort of theaters that will be able to accommodate the massive audiences that will undoubtedly be drawn to see you. Not only that, but a show as remarkable as yours deserves to reach far beyond the gates of William's estate."

"So what're you sayin'?" Lily further questioned.

"I'm saying that I want nothing more than to take any and all limitations away from you, to tear down every obstacle in front of you, and allow you to let your dreams continue to grow in places you may have never imagined."

Lily was silent for a moment. She looked over at William and James again while she questioned Landon's sincerity. "With all due respect, sa', it sounds like you're eitha' sellin' me a dream, or wantin' to sell me out to make money," she replied once she finally turned back to look at Landon.

"I understand your skepticism."

"I don't need you to unda'stand it," Lily quickly bit back. "I just need you to give me a good reason why I shouldn't be skeptical about you or any of this."

Landon gave an arrogant laugh. "I see that your intelligence stretches far beyond just that of music," he smiled devilishly. "You will most certainly go far in this business with your mindset," he explained, thoroughly enjoying the fact that Lily was not so easily swayed by his usual charms. A woman with confidence, boldness, intelligence, blended with unique physical features, was a combination Landon was rarely graced with in his young life. It instantly deepened his intrigue and respect for Lily. After staring at her briefly, his voice suddenly took on a more serious tone. "Ms. Adams, I will be more than happy to explain to you in detail anything that you desire, and I will most certainly do all that I can to prove myself to be loyal and worthy of your trust. But for now, in hopes of putting the fire of your skepticism out, let's just say that I am a man who has the power and the *money* to make men part the seas for you if I wanted. It's a not a power that I use for anyone other than myself, unless I'm compelled, convinced, and captivated by someone … like I am by you. It's not *money* I need, so I would *never* waste my time *selling* dreams or *selling out* someone who has warmed a heart as ice cold as mine. Anyone who possesses the sort of ability to touch me in that way is a rare and precious gift in my eyes, and certainly the last person I would ever wish to bring any harm to. In fact, it's a rare and precious treasure that I would love to help share with the world." Landon let the room fall silent in hopes that his words had a chance to resonate with everyone.

"It's my best guess that because of your life circumstances it's rare that you've been able to truly trust anyone," Landon continued after a moment. "And I understand that these two gentlemen have stood by you after proving they were worthy of your trust and that your loyalties lie with them for all they've done. But just consider this one last thing…" Landon glanced in William's direction. "William's power lies in creating, teaching, and mentoring you in music, whereas my power lies in clearing the path in whatever treacherous forest you choose to travel in." He took hold of one of Lily's hands. "If you let me be a part of this journey with you, I assure you that you will quickly learn how truly loyal I can be to you as well. I will make certain that it is a decision you will never regret. William and James have certainly helped you to take off, but if you give me a chance, I swear I will move heaven and hell to help you soar to unbelievable heights."

* * * *

Lily sat on the porch swing with William, resting her head on his shoulder long after their intense meeting with Landon earlier in the day. They swayed slowly with the sweet smell of William's pipe enveloping the air, sipping lemonade from time to time as they talked. The little ritual had become their nightly tradition after dinner and long rehearsals. It was in these moments that William often dove into the lighthearted and funny, nostalgic stories that Lily loved so much about his life in Great Britain. After yet another tale in the saga of his life on this evening, though, William could sense that Lily's mind had quickly strayed to other things, which was evident by her sudden question.

"William, have you eva' been afraid of anything before?"

"Well, of course. Let's see, there was the time that my

brother and I were supposed to be part of a wedding when we were just five and six years old. Being the antsy little boys we were, we just had to do something to pass the time. So, we decided just before the ceremony to play hide and seek. I was always so good at that game. I'd sometimes have my brother searching for a half hour or more, sometimes until he was in tears fearing that he'd truly lost me," William laughed. "So of course, wedding ceremony or not, I had to maintain my reputation as the greatest 'hider' in all of Great Britain. Sooo, I got the wise idea to hide … in a chimney."

"William, you didn't!"

"With a *white* suit on."

"Dear Lord!" Lily began laughing hysterically.

"Oh, it gets worse. My brother, to his credit, had learned to look for me in the oddest of places by then. He slithered his way into the chimney too, confident that he'd find me there … in *his* white suit."

Lily dropped her head in her hands as she continued laughing at William's childhood stupidity.

"Just as you are now, my brother and I were laughing, having a jolly old time … until my mother found us just minutes before the ceremony, covered from head to toe in soot! The way she snatched us by our scrawny little necks, I was truly *afraid* it was going to be my last day on earth," William laughed.

"I sho' can't blame yo' mama. I'd'a tore both of ya' up good," Lily teased.

"Oh, trust me … she did!" William laughed. "But somehow I know you're not asking me if I was ever afraid of anything because you wanted to hear another one of my foolish boyhood tales."

"Your stories aren't foolish, William. I always look forward to hearin' 'em."

"Come now, tell me what's really eating away at your mind."

Lily let out a breath, stood up, and walked over to the porch railing. "It's just that … well, my whole life I ain't neva' had to make any real decisions 'bout my own welfare. I ain't been no different than a horse just doin' whateva' I's told. Now, 'fore I can blink my eyes, here I am," she said, staring out at her second home standing in the middle of the expansive plot of land, "havin' life alterin' decisions laid at my feet. And these decisions not only affect me but nearly everybody around me. And I'd be lyin' if I said that didn't make me a lil' afraid to decide what's best."

"Lily?"

She turned to face William and saw him patting the seat next to him. She hesitantly joined him again.

"In my whole life, I've never met another as intelligent and wise as you. And please do not think that I mean only within the boundaries of your color or your gender. I genuinely mean of *anyone* I have ever met. And I have known a great many people over my lifetime, mind you. I have realized in my short time knowing you that you possess a rare and precious instinctive wisdom, musically. Effortlessly, you always seem to know just what to do. I have seen you grow more and more confident day after day in your own ability to expand on the elements of your music, the dancing, the theatrics, and the show as a whole. It is awe-inspiring to watch from my old eyes. But even more precious than that, you carry that same instinct into your everyday life." William took hold of Lily's hand. "You just don't realize it yet. You don't see it the way that I have or in the way that James clearly has. You move people in a way that you aren't even aware. You seem to know, without even trying, how to make everyone feel a sense of importance in your presence. It is that rare instinctive nature that you were born with that allows you to touch so many people in that special way.

"So, Lily, I have every bit of confidence in you that

you will always know exactly what to do, be it with music, or when making decisions that could be life altering. Your ability to make the right move is there, but you've yet to grow the confidence to let it guide you without questioning it the way you have musically. Somehow, I know it speaks to you now ... Listen," William paused and patted Lily's hand. "Just listen. Soon the voices of fear will begin to fade into silence. Then, and *only* then, will you hear how loudly the voices of reason are speaking."

Soothed by William's words, Lily said nothing in response. Instead, she drew her legs up into the porch swing and laid her head back down on his shoulder. William usually would have continued to entertain her with his childhood tales, the way Lily always wanted, but on this evening he was silent. He put his pipe back in his mouth with one hand, put his other around Lily, and pushed back on the wooden planks beneath his feet to start a gentle swaying motion in the swing and said not another word, in hopes of allowing Lily the opportunity to "just listen."

The sound of crickets and croaking frogs in the distance soon increased in volume as the sky darkened and the stars illuminated the crystal-clear night. After Lily and William had swayed together for a while, he turned and soon found her fast asleep. He brushed her hair aside, and just as he would have with his own child, he innocently kissed her forehead, silently hoping that her dreams were just as beautiful to her as she was to him.

Chapter Seventeen

Slave Code
Article X Section VII

No contract between a white person and a Negro for labor or service for a longer period than two months shall be binding on such Negro without a license obtained in writing, signed by a white person before a court justice.

"Simply brilliant," Robert Branaugh told Landon after the curtains had closed onstage and Lily and the other performers had retreated to the wings of "Branaugh Theater." Robert was the owner and manager of the small venue in New Lexington, Ohio, two hours north of William's estate. Robert had just witnessed an entire practice run through of *The Dream Symphony*, sitting in the middle of the fifth row, alongside Landon, surrounded by an array of empty seats inside of the single-story complex. "Every moment of the show was just as magnificent as you said it would be," he further expressed to Landon.

Agreeing with the notion, Landon nodded his head, draped his arm over the seat next to him, leaned back, and let an arrogant smile creep onto his face. He was not surprised. He was already confident that Robert would undoubtedly appreciate the artistry of the show. Any human who did not, he felt would have to be blind and deaf, or perhaps just plain stupid.

"Until the Negro girl showed her face there at the very end," Robert continued, letting the words escape nonchalantly as if his comment was not the least bit offensive.

That part of Robert's comment, however, *did* take Landon by surprise. But Landon was never one to show outwardly that anyone had an effect on his calm and collected demeanor, no matter what the situation. "Pardon me?" he replied calmly in his German accent.

"She's not really going to show her face here is she?" Robert questioned. "I don't find it the least bit necessary, after such a lovely and artistic performance, to go and ruin it all by having some Negro meandering out in front of everyone like some princess being presented at a royal ceremony."

"She's a beautiful young lady."

"Beautiful or not, she's still a Negro. Can't you see that? Or are you color-blind?"

"You met her already. You knew that."

"Yes, you're right, I did. But I didn't ever expect to see her face. Not here! Not on *my* stage! When you described the show to me, you never said anything about her flaunting herself in this manner. I assumed that she'd always be portrayed as a shadow behind that curtain contraption … where she belongs," he added, with obvious disgust in his voice.

"Well, we all know what happens when you assume."

"Joke all you will, Mr. Von Brandt, but if you want to ensure that this little show gets to continue here, I will not, by any means, be seeing that Negro's face again on that stage. And nor will any person who pays to sit within these very seats expecting to see an elegant and respectable show."

"Then you're asking to be sued. You can't just breach our contract. You've already signed and agreed to have her show here."

"Oh, the show can go on. But certain things within that contract allow me to modify things to my discretion. And I will *not* have that girl set one foot out from behind that curtain and into that spotlight … *Ever!*"

Landon was silent for a moment before slowly standing up and turning around to let his eyes fall on every aspect of the exquisite interior of the theater. "Small details," he began, as he slid his hands into his pockets. "Ever since I was a child, I've always paid attention to details. No matter how small they were, they were never able to escape me. For instance, once my father took me to a symphony where the conductor wore a toupee. I could not help but notice the way it jumped slightly from his head every time he would swing his baton. Distracted me from the whole damn show. You'd think he could afford the proper glue for the dreadful old thing. Then here tonight, as I watched Lily play her last piece." He closed his eyes, envisioning it. "I watched her face and the way her eyes remained hidden behind her eyelids and the way her facial expressions gave away the secrets of what she sees behind them. Simply watching those small details of her beautiful face, I have no doubt it is the most heavenly place she has escaped to." Landon opened his eyes again. "Even now as I look at this lavish theater of yours, I can't help but notice the fine details." He turned to a particular place and motioned with his head. "The workmanship of the wainscoting." He turned his head in a different direction. "The dark and brooding eyes on all of the sculptures and the design of all the light fixtures." He turned in a complete circle. "And there is, of course, all of the *red* in this place. *Red* walls, *red* cloth, covered seats, *red* stage curtain. Yes, it could never escape my attention how undoubtedly '*in the red*' this place is." He turned to look at Robert. "I'd say it matches quite perfectly with its financial state, wouldn't you?"

"What?!" Robert replied, caught off guard by his question.

"Yes!" Landon pointed a finger at him. "There it is again! My keen sense of small details picking up on that slight quiver in your voice."

"I don't see the point in anything you're saying, Mr. Von Brandt!" Robert fired back at Landon.

"Details! I'm telling you, I don't miss a thing! But you don't have to have as keen an eye as I do to see that for almost five years now this place has run '*in the red*' and not a single profit thus far this year either. There it was, plain as day, at the bottom of the financial documents I sifted through. Nothing but numbers plummeted far, far beneath zero. I believe you Americans call that being '*in the red*' … isn't that right?" he asked rhetorically, while turning to look at the theater again. "Just like the dreadful color of these walls," he murmured under his breath.

"You have no access to my financial affairs, boy!"

Landon ignored Robert's comment and continued. "Honestly, I've never seen figures so low in all of my life. After the first year of opening any establishment, maybe yes, that's certainly quite the norm. But here we are, nearly five years after this place has been in operation and it seems you've been robbing Peter to pay Paul. Or should I say, robbing Peter to pay…" He turned from the walls he was staring at and looked down on Robert again. "*My father*."

Robert squinted his eyes at Landon as beads of sweat began to form on his brow. "Y-your *father*?" he asked. "Christoph?"

"Christoph! Yes!"

"*Von Brandt*," Robert murmured under his breath after realizing the connection with their last names.

"Christoph Von Brandt! That's him! That … is … *thee* … one!" Landon replied, in an intentionally gleeful, annoying tone, while pointing his finger at Robert with each of his words. "The same Christoph that you've recently gone to and asked to borrow money for … oh, what is it this time?" He scratched his head. "A *hotel!* That's right! Yes, he's also the same Christoph that I can't wait to go home and talk to about all of the fine details of this theater of yours. The lavish sculptures. The wainscoting." Landon looked up at the ceiling. "That fabulous chandelier and all of the artwork." He looked down at Robert again. "I certainly can't wait to bring up the way you treat the guests in your establishment, and of course … all of the *red* in this place. Should help you with convincing my father to fund that little hotel venture of yours, don't you think?" He paused for a moment, enjoying the sight of the sweat continuing to accumulate on Robert's brow. "Oh well, now, I guess that all depends on which *red* I decide to detail for him, doesn't it?"

Landon's sarcasm disappeared, and the look on his face suddenly became as expressionless as a dead man's. He took a step forward and loomed down on Robert, piercing him with his dark, unblinking eyes. "You need a show like this, Branaugh, and fifty more of the sort. You will *not* deny Lily from doing what she wants here! Not tonight, not tomorrow, nor during a single moment of her show when this place is packed to the ceiling … am I clear?" he asked smugly, slightly tilting his head to the side.

"You're asking me to disgrace this place! T-to defame it! To run it right into the ground!" Robert fired back.

"Seems you're doing a fine job of that already." After he let his eyes linger on Robert a moment, Landon's face suddenly lightened and the sarcasm returned to his voice. The quick flip in his personality was like that of a bipolar patient who had returned from the abyss of his depression and instantaneously into another high. "Landon Von Brandt Theater!" he suddenly exclaimed, waving his hand in front of him as if he were picturing the words on a towering marquee. "Has a nice ring to it, wouldn't you say?" he asked Robert with a smile as if there had been nothing but pleasantries exchanged between them in the moments just before. "Oh, the things I could do with this place! Let's see! First, I'd certainly get rid of *all* of the God-awful *red* around here." The smile suddenly left his face as his eyes drifted down to Robert again. "Right after I get rid of *you!*"

Chapter Eighteen

Slave Code
Article XIII Section XII

Any free Negro of African race, whose ancestors were brought to this country and sold as slaves are not "citizens" within the meaning of the Constitution of the United States. Therefore, the special rights and immunities guaranteed to citizens do not apply to slaves or free Negroes. A slave or free Negro has no civil rights, and therefore is not entitled to sue in a court of the United States nor shall be allowed to serve as a witness or to testify against any white person.

Friday Night
July 1, 1859

Lily stood at the forefront of Branaugh stage in front of a sea of onlookers that stretched from wall to wall of the meticulously decorated theater. Moved by the entire showing of *The Dream Symphony*, every audience member was on their feet, applauding for what seemed like an eternity. Much like the opening night on the outdoor amphitheater, many patrons were unaware that the entire ensemble had been composed and choreographed by a Negro woman until Lily revealed herself at the very end. Once again, though, that surprise did not stop an overwhelmingly warm reception from her appreciative audience. It was a moment that should have meant the world to Lily, a scene for her to embrace as yet another memorable highlight in her life. It should have been touching and full of joyous emotions. It should have conjured up an emotion of some sort, something … *anything*. But instead, it all felt cold, empty, and meaningless to her. Lily's mind was simply not in it. Her thoughts were elsewhere as she forced a smile to everyone

311

who had gathered to see *The Dream Symphony* for the very first time inside of a genuine theater.

At first, Lily stood alone at the front of the enormous stage, stiffly accepting the commendation of the crowd. But, in a spontaneous last minute decision that surprised her, the entire student orchestra all trickled out one by one from behind the curtains to stand proudly alongside her, revealing themselves to an audience for the very first time. The very same body of students who once felt a sense of shame and embarrassment simply accompanying Lily with background music, who once threatened to quit without the assurance of their anonymity, now all proudly stood beside her to celebrate and praise her for achieving yet another milestone in her life. The warmth that the group exuded as they surrounded Lily normally would have ignited her tears, but in this instance, the sadness that Lily was drowning in had disconnected her from her surroundings. It was that very sadness that had moved the students to join her onstage. Knowing that Lily was hurting inside, they suddenly found themselves unconcerned with hiding and secrets. Instead, they all felt the strong need to comfort a woman who, over the past few months, had slowly become a friend and mentor to them. They wanted to be there for her because James, a man who believed in Lily enough to set his ambitions aside to begin an incredible journey with her, a man who had built the first stage she had ever performed on, was nowhere to be found on her very first performance inside of the walls of a real theater. James had missed every minute of a precedent-setting night that Lily undoubtedly owed to him, William, and now to one Landon Von Brandt.

Landon, a man who had quickly proven himself as a force to be reckoned with, was the only son of Christoph Von Brandt. Christoph was a very rich and successful old German acquaintance of William's from the Old World that William had not seen or spoken to in nearly two decades. A few weeks before William made the choice to forgo any assistance from his old acquaintances, he had sent a letter to Christoph on Lily's behalf. William knew that Christoph had invested in a few theaters, hotels, and businesses in the United States and wondered if he might be of assistance to Lily somehow. Landon was the first to read William's letter when it arrived. Since the letter was so intriguing, he convinced his father that it would be best to respond to William in person. Landon elected to travel to the United States on Christoph's behalf by playing the role of a caring son who wished to ease the burdens of his father's hectic life. In all truthfulness, Landon's desire to travel was under selfish pretenses. He wished to escape his father's command for a spell and utilize the free time to drink, attend galas, and meet an array of women.

After many weeks of sailing, traipsing from state to state, enjoying fine wines, feasts, and plenty of women, Landon had reluctantly attended Lily's symphony only to fulfill his obligations. He actually had all intention of returning to his father with nothing but negative reviews and urging him not to waste his time, his good name, or his money on William's cause. Never did Landon expect to be genuinely taken aback by what he had seen the night he first saw *The Dream Symphony*. The show moved him to do one of the few unselfish things he had ever done in his life: help someone other than himself.

While attempting to accomplish his selfless endeavor, Landon could have very well divulged who his father was when he first approached William. Instead, Landon intentionally withheld his last name, hoping that William did not recall meeting him when he was just a small boy twenty years ago. Landon's choice to withhold that information, at first, was because he did not want William or Lily to feel as if he had been forced by his father to assist. He wanted it to be clear that his father had nothing to do with his desires and that his motives were not to profit off of Lily like she was some pawn in one of his father's business deals. Instead, he wanted Lily to know that he had genuinely been motivated by nothing other than the beautiful music and stories in her shadow-filled symphony. Most importantly, he wanted to convey that he had left Lily's concert with an unyielding desire to help her share her brilliance with the world.

Landon could hardly contain his excitement about the prospect of presenting Lily's show to millions of people. He felt like a child who was eager to show off his newest gift with everyone, wanting so badly for the masses to share in his enthusiasm and to have the same rush of emotions he had experienced following *The Dream Symphony*. But perhaps the most unsuspecting part of Landon's excitement was knowing the opportunity that Lily would now have to speak, through her music, to people who believed in a need for slavery. Landon was appalled by the institution. Despite his self-centered ways, he felt a great deal sympathy for those who were trapped in the pits of oppression.

Landon's distaste for slavery and disdain for slave owners was attributed to traveling the world with his father from a very young age for matters of business and fancy vacations. During his travels, he had had dealings with people from all backgrounds. His multicultural ventures had helped him to achieve a sort of colorblindness in dealing with all walks of life. In that time, Landon also developed a deep disgust for any person who attempted to justify slavery. He never preached to people about his beliefs, but his example always spoke for him. Although he was indeed arrogant and selfish at times, he was still somehow gentle, sincere, and genuine in his approach toward everyone. It showed in the way he spoke to people, in the way he looked at them, and in the way that he had the ability to make every person he came across feel as if they were on his level. William, James, and Lily had all felt that sincerity the day he had arrived at William's estate wishing to meet with them. It was one of the defining elements that made all the difference in the decision that Lily would ultimately make about whether or not he was worthy of becoming their ally.

Lily, however, was not as easily convinced by Landon at first. She had sat with him for hours, asking an onslaught of critical questions. She was strong in her approach, determined not to be taken advantage of. The way she handled herself made even William feel like a beginner in handling arrangements of that sort. Most importantly, her poise and confidence served to increase Landon's level of respect for her. With such an appreciation for her tenacity, he was ready to work like a steam engine on Lily's behalf when she finally made the decision to welcome him aboard.

Lily's decision to bring Landon aboard was a wise one. He quickly proved himself to be the much-needed missing piece to *The Dream Symphony* puzzle. Landon was intelligent and business savvy, having truly paid attention to his father's teachings throughout the years as he negotiated and manipulated business deals. Ironically, though, it was his selfishness that proved to be the greatest asset in ensuring that Lily would never receive a penny less than she was worth for presenting her one-of-a-kind musical artwork. Landon's arrogance simply would not allow him to back down or be defeated by anyone he dealt with on Lily's behalf. He was ready to strike quickly and slyly with his venomous tongue while seeing her toward the riches he felt she deserved.

To further help the show along, Landon had also come to the table with objective ideas and viewpoints. He explained that he felt William's first fatal mistake had been telling everyone in advance about Lily's color. For advertising purposes and for finalizing financial negotiations in the future, Landon was adamant that they continue to use the famous Werthington name as the key selling point, exciting theater managers with the fact that William had discovered a supremely talented young pianist whose abilities superseded his own. He felt it would be wise to omit anything about Lily's status or race and instead focus on painting a mental image of the brilliance of her show. The blatant reality that the show's true producer was a Negro was something Landon felt his fellow businessmen could witness with their own eyes when she showed up for stage rehearsals. By then, Landon figured the impending venue would be sold out, making it highly unlikely that anyone would complain about Lily being brown after their pockets had already been lined with green.

For William, having Landon eased the burdens of having to deal with things that were never his area of expertise. He had to admit to himself that he could not hold a candle to the young man and his talent for selling the show to prospective theater managers. William had never been required to book venues or make negotiations of any kind. Those were petty things handled by his entourage during the time in his life when he was touring. He had always been allowed the luxury to concentrate on his beloved music, show up where he was told, and simply perform. So, handing the reins over to Landon now freed William to focus solely on assisting the woman he had quickly adopted in his heart as his very own child.

While William worked tirelessly with Lily expounding on her show, adjusting lighting and visuals, and adding new songs and dances, Landon had worked feverishly, manipulating and negotiating in the shadows with perspective clients. Within three weeks, he had already booked the symphony for three different theaters, on a mini-tour of sorts. After a considerable amount of research and sifting through the files of different theaters that his father was affiliated with financially, Landon had learned of how poorly mismanaged Branaugh Theater was. He knew right then and there that it would provide the perfect loophole to force his way in and attempt to set a precedent for *The Dream Symphony*. His undermining methods quickly proved how ruthless he could be on Lily's behalf.

Landon's ruthlessness had ultimately helped lead to this very moment: Lily onstage, being figuratively embraced by the student orchestra in front of a wave of onlookers inside the beauty of her first real theater. Unfortunately, as Lily stood there, though, she was unable to fully appreciate the joy of her grand finale because of the absence of James. Her current state of numbness had been compounded by the fact that Landon had incessantly expressed the importance of perfection for opening night. He constantly reminded everyone that it would set the tone for shows to come and that the reviews would be crucial to giving strength to the legs that would carry it forward. This notion weighed heavily on everyone and began to make the pressure nearly unbearable for Lily. That pressure had already been preceded by unforeseen challenges that had arisen while transporting supplies and props on their way to dress rehearsals in New Lexington. To further add to the madness of their tumultuous travels, even more salt was added to that wound when Lily was told she would not be allowed to stay in the hotel that had been reserved for everyone. Not a single other hotel in its vicinity welcomed her either, forcing her to use the dressing room in the theater as a makeshift bedroom for the entire week. With every challenge, though, Lily did not allow herself to be broken. She pushed through her stresses with her spirits high and a positive outlook, until just hours before the opening number of the show. It was not until then that Lily allowed the dark cloud drifting over her to cast a shadow of doubt on the confidence everyone had in the fact that they would have a successful opening night.

In the hours before showtime, Lily was not enthusiastic and energetic and full of life the way she was at all of her previous shows. Normally, she was commanding professionalism from everyone, taking charge, and ensuring that everyone was prepped and ready. Even in the previous days, after having slept on a cot in a theater dressing room, she had remained stoic … but not on this night. When the opening number was approaching, and eager patrons were already filing into their seats, Lily was still not herself. It was as if nobody was home behind her eyes. She lacked focus and sat in her dressing room hardly saying a word to anyone as her mind swirled with genuine concern over what could have happened to James. With him nowhere to be found, Lily began to realize how much strength and courage she gathered simply from his presence. After days of not seeing him, the hours until she was due onstage seemed to fly by as she waited for him to show. In that time, she found herself in a downward mental spiral. The change in Lily's demeanor had been so drastic that everyone in her entourage began to fear that the show would be a disaster if she remained in her despondent state of mind. Her anxiety was so obviously crippling that the most unlikely person felt a need to step forward and say something to her.

As Lily sat alone in her dressing room waiting to be called to the stage, she had been briefly shaken from her trance after hearing a light knock at the door. "Come in," she responded quickly, turning to see if it was James. The murmurs of the crowd rolling in to take their seats suddenly enveloped her room as the door slowly opened. "Oh, hey, Austin," she responded, with obvious disappointment in her tone. She then turned back around to continue emptily staring into the mirror.

"Hi, Lily," Austin said, closing the door behind him, drowning out the sound of the low rumble of voices in the background. "Could I have a word with you?"

"Sure," Lily replied, more out of obligation than a desire to hear what he had to say.

Austin did not venture far from the door, feeling a little more at ease with talking so long as he was not facing Lily. "Look, I-I know I ain't so good with words, 'specially the nice ones … as you've probably already noticed," he said, attempting to make a joke. He then nervously put his hands in his pockets when Lily did not laugh. "Ya' know, a few weeks ago William gave us all the option of endin' our agreement to perform with you any longa'. He said somethin' 'bout some house orchestra that could take our place from here on out if that's what we preferred."

Again, Lily did not respond to the surprise of that news.

"A few months ago, I'll admit that hearin' that would've been music to my ears, but now…" Austin paused when he felt his nerves getting the best of him. He took a deep breath before he continued. "The moment William said it, I rememba' feelin' this … this pain in my chest," he admitted, grabbing his shirt in the place he remembered feeling it. "See, it's just that my whole life I ain't eva' know what direction to go in the world. I always felt so lost until these last few months. For the first time in my entire twenty-three years, I feel like I finally have a future for myself, like I got some purpose, ya' know?" Lily finally looked at Austin in the mirror as a way of communicating her understanding of his sentiments. Austin held her gaze for a moment, finally feeling a sense of comfort by the sight of her eyes. "So, when William told us we could escape all this, all I knew was that I didn't wanna feel lost again. And besides…" Austin paused and walked closer to Lily. She finally turned around in her chair to find him towering over her. "Playin' with you has been one of the greatest joys of my life, and I just couldn't bring myself to walk away … None of us could, Lily. We're *all* proud to play behind ya', and we're all here for *you,* no matta' what happens tonight and beyond, we'll always be here for ya'. I-I just wanted you to know that."

Lily was stunned to say the least. She would have assumed it was some sort of hoax had Austin not looked and sounded so incredibly sincere. Not only was she stunned by his words, but also by his transformation. Austin had shaved the peach fuzz off of his youthful face and had cut his stringy, long brown hair. He was even wearing a brand new tailored suit. As he stood in front of Lily on display, it was the first time she had ever even noticed the color of his eyes. They were a deep dark brown, which stared at her now in the most innocent and gentle of ways. "Thank you, Austin," Lily replied, sounding equally as sincere. "There ain't enough words for me to express how much that means to me."

Austin nodded his head and turned to walk away, but stopped just as he put his hand on the doorknob. "I'm sorry," he said quietly, still facing the door.

"What?"

He took a deep breath, found some courage, and turned around to face Lily again. "You ain't been nothin' but kind to me afta' all the cruel things I said to ya'. And well, I honestly ain't neva' felt more guilty for the way I've treated somebody than you. And I'm awful sorry, Lily. I really am."

"It's okay, Austin, I…"

"Naw, it ain't okay," he interrupted, not wanting her to make light of the situation or make excuses to let him off the hook so easily. He walked halfway across the room again and put his hands back into the pockets of his fancy tailored pants. "Ya' know, you's the first person to hug me when you found out my mama passed away?" He shook his head and looked up at the ceiling as if tilting his head back would somehow help him to hold in any potential tears. "Not my daddy, not my brotha's, not even my sista's … *You*," he said, lowering his head to look at Lily. "You were the only person who eva' botha'd."

Lily remembered that moment very clearly but was

unaware that not a single person had yet to comfort him until that day…

During rehearsals that particular evening back on William's estate, Austin had been out of sorts, lagging behind while playing, unable to focus, and failing to keep up with the rest of the orchestra, far worse than usual. William kept stopping everyone because of how much of a disruption it was to the fluidity of the number they were all learning. After about the fifth scolding, Austin threw his mallets across the room in frustration and stormed out of rehearsal session. Everyone looked around at each other, sitting silently in discomfort after he slammed the library door behind him on his way out.

"What's goin' on?" Lily leaned over and asked one of the violinists. "This ain't like him at all."

"I heard his mama just passed away," the young lady whispered back, "I guess he just needs a little time."

"Take a break everyone," Lily stood and announced. She then headed out of the kitchen door to look for Austin. Ironically, she found him in *her* comfort zone near the oak tree by the lake. He was picking up rocks and chucking them into the water. Lily walked up slowly behind him, watching him angrily throw rocks one after the other as if he was firing his ammunition at whatever he blamed for taking his mother away from him. Austin's mother was the only person in his life who had ever shown him the slightest bit of love, but she was gone, and Austin was aching badly over the matter and had no idea how to cope.

Lily saw Austin glance over at her as he searched for more rocks to throw, but he did not say a word or break stride in collecting his ammo. Cautiously, she continued to close in on him. He had thrown a few more before she reached him, but by the time he went to throw the last one, Lily gently took hold of his wrist and removed the rock from his hand without a struggle. Austin could feel her looking at him. It took the last little bit of his bravery to glance up from his hand at her, though. Slowly, he raised his head and returned Lily's gaze. Reading the empathy in her eyes, Austin's tears were instant, but so too was Lily's embrace. She dropped the rock and held him tightly as he wept. She felt him getting weaker and more limp as she held him as if the strength in his body was slowly draining away with each minute that passed. Austin did not attempt to pull away, but rather put his arms around her too. He allowed himself to be vulnerable and let go of his pain in the arms of somebody who finally dared to show that they cared about his plight. After a few minutes, he finally pulled away, walked over to the tree, and sat down. He lacked the strength to stand any longer. Lily followed suit, sitting just inches away from him.

"This my favorite spot here on this plantation," Lily said, her voice adding to the sound of the wind rustling through the leaves that surrounded them. She was not expecting Austin to reply, but she hoped that maybe he was willing to listen for the time being while his heart and mind were wide open and struggling to heal from their wounds. "I come out here almost every day to think, sometimes 'bout music, or sometimes just to daydream, and sometimes just to reflect … especially when I'm hurtin'."

Still, Austin sat there silently absorbing Lily's words, wiping his face while he waited for his strength to return.

"I's ten years old the last time I saw my mama," Lily continued. "My daddy took me and sold me away from her," she said bluntly. It took those words to finally garner a reaction from Austin. He turned his head to look at her for a moment with disbelief in his bloodshot eyes. His relationship with his own father was abysmal, but after hearing what Lily's father had done, he considered that maybe he did not have much to complain about.

"Far as I know my motha's still alive and all, but with the pain I used to feel afta' not seein' her for so long, it sho' felt like she died. I used to hurt somethin' awful. Used to lie in my bed at night and cry for hours, sometimes 'til I made myself sick to my stomach. Didn't even wanna eat some days, no different than if I's truly in a state of mournin'. But then one night afta' cryin' myself to sleep, I dreamt of her. Dreamt of this silly little song she taught me, ya' know, to one of those childhood hand clappin' games," Lily said, smiling at the memory. "I woke up from that dream for the first time in weeks with a smile on my face afta' rememberin' how hard me and my motha' used to laugh wheneva' we messed up the rhythm while clappin' our hands togetha' and had to start all ova' again singin' that silly little song," she recalled with a hint of laughter in her voice. "It was such a small thing at the time, but now, to this very day, wheneva' I'm hurtin' ova' missin' my mama, that's what I do … I rememba' her. I rememba' her and me togetha', laughin' and singin' and how happy we were at that moment. Or sometimes I think about this old telescope she'd somehow gotten her hands on and had hidden away in her room. It was her most prized possession. She loved that old thang! One day, when I's about five years old, she pulled it out and showed it to me and made me swear not to tell a soul on the plantation about it. My eyes were as wide as quarta's when I first saw it. It was the most amazin' contraption I'd eva' seen! From then on, wheneva' the sky was clear late at night, we'd sneak out into the woods, lie on our backs, and look out into the heavens togetha' and give names to the biggest and brightest stars we could find. And to this very day, I still rememba' the names of every last one of 'em," Lily smiled. "Those were some of my mostfondest moments of me and my motha' togetha'. And so now, wheneva' I reminisce about any of it, I swear it neva' fails to numb the pain, to take all the hurt away, and put a smile on my face." Lily paused briefly and let silence take over while the memories invaded her mind. "Even been times right here unda' this very tree, I've sat here and remembered those moments," she finally continued, after the vivid images faded away. Lily turned and looked at Austin's profile as he stared out at the lake. He would not return the gaze, but she could tell he was still listening.

"Close your eyes," Lily asked Austin, after staring at him for a moment. He did not move and kept his eyes transfixed on the water, unwilling to do as she had asked at first. "Go on," she prompted him again. "It's alright." Austin looked down at the ground before slowly honoring her request. "Rememba' her," Lily said softly, once Austin's eyes were completely closed. "Rememba' you and your mama togetha'. Rememba' somethin' that only you and her found special or somethin' that she always did to let her know how special you were to her … somethin' that brought both of ya' the utmost joy." At first, Austin's eyes were squinted hard while he reached deep inside of his catalog of memories to find one that meant more to him than all the others. As the minutes passed, though, Lily watched as his facial features started to relax and the twitching in his eyelids began to cease. When tears escaped from the corners of his eyes, she knew at that moment that he had finally found it. There was no smile on Austin's face, but Lily could feel the joy that he emanated. She was moved enough by it to put her arm around him while he continued to close his eyes and just *remember her*.

… Austin had been touched by the whole experience with Lily that day, and now, as he stood with her in her dressing room, he wanted desperately to help her in return. After his apology, he dug deep for the right thing to say. "Lily, I know you ain't been feelin' so good 'bout that James fella' not bein' here and all tonight, and I know good 'n well that it ain't a single one of us can replace him, so I's thinkin' that you could, you know…" He shrugged his shoulders. "M-maybe rememba' somethin' about 'em that makes ya' happy."

324

"Thanks, Austin, but this is a little bit of a different situation, don't ya' think?"

"Well, yeah, I know he ain't passed away or nothin', but you ain't been yourself lately, and I know it has to do with him not bein' here for ya'. You'd be lyin' to me if you said that wasn't true. And you said yourself that your mama might still be alive and that's what you do when you's feelin' down about her. So, I just figured maybe it couldn't hurt if you did the same with James. Maybe it'll stop ya' from worryin', and put you in a betta' mood." Austin stopped a minute and remembered that day sitting with Lily at that lake. "Sho' did work for me," he said with his voice trailing off.

Lily fought hard to create an excuse to get out of it. She was intentionally defiant, hoping Austin would give up and let her go back to being alone before the show. "But I..."

"Go on, just give it a try, can't hurt," Austin interrupted. He simply would not be deterred, fighting just as hard to help her as she had him. It paid off. With his persistence, Lily finally gave in and silently agreed that he was right. She took a deep breath and let her eyes drift to the floor, but she was hesitant to close them at first, just like he had been that day by William's lake. "Come on," Austin insisted, approaching her again. "Close your eyes," he said softly. Lily first looked into his dark brown eyes and, for the first time since meeting him, saw behind them a man who actually possessed compassion. Most importantly, he was exuding that compassion at a time that she desperately needed it. After being warmed by his sentimentality, Lily finally gave in to Austin's request and suddenly found herself engulfed in darkness. "Rememba' somethin' great about him," she heard Austin say just before the darkness was suddenly flooded with vivid images. Lily could have chosen from a thousand things from her past, but in this instance, her mind selected the most recent of her happy memories with her childhood best friend…

As promised, James had spent every evening with Lily after rehearsals down by her favorite spot on William's lake underneath the oak tree, continuing with her reading lessons. When he learned that William planned to teach Lily to read and write music, James secretly requested of him not to teach her any more letters or words than was necessary to accomplish his goal. William happily obliged after hearing about the beautiful promise that James wanted to fulfill on Lily's birthday. During Lily's lessons, James was as meticulous as any schoolhouse teacher. He was prepared with a small erasable writing board, pens, papers, flash cards, and instructional materials. He even gave Lily homework to help improve her writing, spelling, and punctuation, as well as a list of daily vocabulary words to look up in a dictionary. But Lily went far beyond the short list of words that he gave to her and began reading multiple pages from a dictionary every night. With her insatiable appetite for learning and her potent memory, Lily was soaking up words and definitions at an astonishing rate. She absorbed all the knowledge James gave her as effortlessly as she had learned to read, write, and play music. In fact, within just two weeks, she had slowly read to James every word of the book that she had treasured for years. *Remembering James* had started there. The fond memory of sitting side by side with him near the lake was fresh in Lily's mind all over again as she sat with her eyes closed in her dressing room with Austin watching on. Once again, she could see the mist in James's eyes after she finally read the very last words of her beloved story aloud to him.

Remembering him continued in that dark world behind Lily's eyes as she drifted through the hours that followed the completion of her favorite book, and how she had sat for nearly two hours writing and rewriting a letter to James.

She was determined to perfect her penmanship and the words she wanted to say to him. When Lily was finished, she then folded the letter neatly and placed it on his pillow for him to find:

Dear James,

Reading has been the most incredible escape for me, nearly as much as music. I find myself now picking through all of the books on William's shelf here in my room and reading all of the summaries on the back of each and every one. I had hoped to find at least one book to read before I fall asleep at night, but instead of finding one, I've found twelve! I guess I better get busy! I found one called *Oliver Twist* by a man named Charles Dickens. It's about an orphan boy. I think I'll start with that one. They all seem like they will be so wonderful, but I'm certain there will never be one that I'll cherish more than the one you gave to me so many years ago, and that you have now so graciously taught me to read. I'm overjoyed that I can write now too, but I don't think there are enough words I can use in this letter to express how grateful I am to you for giving me the ability to abandon the tribulations of life for a while by escaping into the beautiful world of fantasy. Now that my lessons are over, I'll miss our evening reading sessions by the lake, but I'll always cherish the memories of the precious gift that you have bestowed upon me.

Thank you kindly,

Sincerely,

Lily

That very next morning Lily found a letter from James folded neatly, lying next to her when she awoke. She opened it with the excitement of a child unwrapping a Christmas gift. Lily smiled the entire time she read it, excited at how the words were no longer foreign to her, but more so at their sentiment:

Dear Lily,

No need to search your soul for any words to say thank you. Just to know that the words of the letter that I found here on my pillow were crafted by your hand means more to me than you'll ever know, and so too was hearing you speak the final words of your favorite story tonight. It honestly moved me just as much as the grand finale of your symphony. I too admit that I will greatly miss our lessons by the lake. So to remedy that, how about you, me, and that Oliver Twist fella meet down at the lake tomorrow *evening after rehearsals? There's nothing I'd love more than to hear you share each and every one of the stories you've chosen to escape with.*

Hope to see you then,
Sincerely,
James

Those two short letters began yet another tradition to add to James and Lily's list from over the years. From that evening on, they exchanged letters with one another on a nightly basis. They wrote about random things, from funny memories to the day's events, or elements of the stories they read together every evening from then on. After a while, it started to become less about the stories in each letter and more about the anticipation of receiving one, as well as the feelings that they felt when they read them. Every morning that followed a letter, the after effects of each other's words had the pair exchanging funny glances and inside jokes that only they found hysterical. Their quirky behavior and odd outbursts of laughter were infectious and seemed to keep everyone around them in a wonderful mood throughout the long work days. Most importantly, the simple letter-writing ritual proved to be a strong force that was quickly beginning to pull the once distant pair back together.

… A slow smile crept across Lily's face as she sat in her dressing room remembering the feelings that she had when she would awaken each morning to find another one of James's letters. In a matter of a few minutes, Austin had set his pride and ego aside and helped to pull Lily out of the dark place she had been lost in just before her show. Just the way he predicted, remembering something about James indeed had her temporarily drowning in a happy place, content not to come up for air. In fact, Lily was so lost in her joyous memories that she forgot Austin was even in the room with her. The moment was awkward when she opened her eyes and returned to the reality of her surroundings to find him still standing over her. But outside of the awkwardness, Lily emerged from her memories refocused and ready to join the student orchestra. She honestly felt like herself again and was more than prepared to be there for them, the way they had all professed they would be for her.

After sensing a positive shift in Lily's demeanor, Austin offered a hand to help her stand. As soon as she took hold of it, though, there was a knock at her dressing room door that startled both of them. Before Lily could respond, the knocking turned into a hard, impatient thumping, mangled with the sound of a commotion and loud voices intermixing in the hallway.

"Lily Adams!" a deep voice called out from the other side, as the pounding continued.

Lily looked at Austin before walking toward the door. He shrugged his shoulders, looking just as perplexed as she did. By the elevated voices and the repeated beating on the door, they both knew that whatever lie on the other side was not something they would be happy to deal with. Lily reached for the doorknob, but Austin pulled her away and stepped in front of her, wanting to be a protective barrier for her before he opened it.

"Yes, can I help you?" Lily answered as Austin continued to stand like a wall in front of her. Her first thoughts were of James when she finally saw the two large deputies standing there. Her stomach turned to knots, and her mind raced with the possibilities of what they might have to say. Whatever it was, Lily was not emotionally prepared for any of it, especially if it had anything to do with James.

"We need to have a word with you," one of the deputies told her.

"Is there a problem?"

"What's going on here?" William asked, after suddenly showing up with Elijah by his side.

"This little show 'a hers is ova', that's what's goin' on here," the deputy announced. "We got word that this here nigga's a runaway."

"Watch your mouth!" Elijah protested, bucking up in Lily's defense.

"Who the hell you think y'ur talkin' to, boy!" the other deputy bit off, taking a step toward Elijah.

Elijah lowered his eyes and never flinched.

"The question is, who the hell's been talkin' to *you*?" Austin interjected, ending the stare down between Elijah and the officer. "Who fed you that load of horse shit about Lily bein' a runaway?!"

The officer motioned his head toward one of the back wings of the stage. Tucker stood there chewing sunflower seeds, moving his mouth as gracefully as a cow. He was disrespectfully spitting the shells on the theater floor with a smirk on his face while letting his eyes gloss up and down Lily's body.

"Sho' do look purty tonight, pumpkin. Gon' be the finest thang I eva' saw in handcuffs," Tucker told Lily before spitting out another mouth full of sunflower seeds.

"What's he talkin' about?" Lily asked. "I didn't do anything wrong."

"They say y'ur the one what created this here lil' show," one of the deputies began. "So, I assume y'ur smart enough to know that, despite this here bein' a free state, the law states that any slaves roamin' around within it will still be treated as such and any runaways will be jailed until they're able to be returned to their owna's. You do know that, right sweetheart?" he asked in a condescending tone while staring Lily up and down.

"But she's no runaway!" William interjected.

"Well, unless you can show us some paperwork as to the proof of that, we'll have to consida' her as such. If you ain't got no paperwork, you can forget about her settin' one foot on that stage, 'cause she'll be on her merry little way down to the jailhouse 'til we can straighten this whole matta' out." The sheriff took out a pair of handcuffs and began walking toward Lily.

Elijah stepped in front of the deputy. "You can't arrest her without probable cause!"

"His word *is* probable cause, boy!" the deputy replied, pointing at Tucker. "And without her carryin' documented proof, in the eyes of the law, I'm gonna have to consida' her a runaway! Now take y'ur ass outta my way 'fore I arrest you for obstruction!" He stepped around Elijah and proceeded toward Lily.

"Now hold on a minute! You ain't arrestin' nobody!" Austin shouted, continuing to block the deputy's path to Lily. "We got a show to put on!"

"I don't give an outhouse shit 'bout no goddamn show! I'm here to uphold the law!"

"No worries. Everyone calm down," Landon interrupted, walking up in his usual calm and collected manner. "Nobody's going anywhere."

"Who the hell're you?" the other deputy asked.

"I'm La…" Landon cleared his throat and suddenly replaced his German accent with a horribly replicated southern one. "Larry … Larry Adams. I'm James Adams' brotha'. He's the owna' of this beautiful young lady." He touched Lily on the shoulder and smiled and then extended his hand to the officer for him to shake. "Please, pardon the confusion here tonight. See, my brotha, James, is away on business and he's left me as her ova'seer. But no worries! He's left all the appropriate documentation in my care."

"He's a goddamn liar!" Tucker shouted.

"Gentlemen," Landon continued, taking both deputies

by the shoulder, completely ignoring the conniption fit that Tucker was having. "If you'll step with me out to my carriage, I'll show you both exactly what you need to clear up this little misunderstanding." Both sheriffs followed Landon out, and everyone else left in the hallway turned in unison to look at Tucker, who suddenly cowered in the corner.

While everyone waited for Landon, Elijah walked over to speak to Lily. Earlier in the week, he had offered to ride back to Athens to find out why James had yet to join everyone in New Lexington for stage rehearsals. He could tell that Lily was on the verge of tears when he returned with no news of James's whereabouts. Since then, he had done all he could to lift Lily's spirits and comfort her. "Are you okay?" Elijah asked her, opening his arms and inviting Lily into his embrace.

Lily hesitantly stepped forward into his arms. "As well as I can be unda' the circumstances, I s'ppose."

Elijah pulled Lily back from his embrace and touched her on the cheek. "I know this whole week has had one storm afta' anotha', but I'll do all I can to help see you through this mess, okay?"

"Thank you, Elijah. I really appreciate it."

"You! Come with us!" everyone suddenly heard one of the deputies snarl. Lily turned around to see both officers headed toward her. Her heartbeat instantly became erratic, but, to her surprise, they breezed right past her and grabbed Tucker by the elbow. "Get y'ur ass outta here 'fore we take ya' in for makin' false reports." The largest deputy gave Tucker a good hard shove in the back and marched behind him to be sure he found his way to an exit.

"What?! Y'all got it all wrong! That man ain't his goddamn brotha'!" Tucker objected, pointing at Landon. "That nigga's a runaway! I'm tellin' ya'! They're all goddamn liars!"

"Hey Larry," Lily teased, nudging Landon on his

shoulder. "How on earth did you handle that?"

"Well, let's just say that I showed those deputies the only sort of *papers* that anyone really ever cares to see." Landon had not the slightest clue what sort of paperwork the sheriffs needed, but figured that paper colored in green always sufficed, especially those with three-digit numbers beautifully embossed on the outer edges. Lily laughed at Landon's devilish deceit and then turned and continued watching Tucker being hauled away, still loudly protesting every step of the way. In all truthfulness, though, Tucker had every reason to be upset, because if anyone knew for a fact that James was not away on a business trip, it was definitely him...

Just a week before, it was Tucker who once again found himself at the entrance of William's estate, stirring up a commotion with the bandits. This time around, however, he was given far less of a problem gaining access to the grounds because of the two gentlemen who accompanied him: two uniformed deputies. They were joined by Buck Harley, the owner of Buck's Tavern: the place that Tucker frequented daily since the demise of his establishment. The security bandits gave as much resistance to their entry as they could, but were forced to step aside and let them enter after the deputies had their say.

As Tucker and the deputies trotted onto the grounds, they saw a multitude of people milling about in the yard loading up wagons and carriages, preparing for travel. James was securing the last bit of show equipment and instruments into his wagon until his attention drifted to the sight of horses riding onto the plantation. He and everyone else suddenly stopped what they were doing. By the time Tucker and his entourage made it to the front of the house, almost everyone from the orchestra had gathered near the porch, staring fiercely at the unwanted intruders.

"Can we help you?" William called out.

A rather unkempt deputy dismounted his horse. After whispering to Tucker, he turned in the direction of the man he was there to see. "You James Adams?" he asked, as he spat and wiped his mouth.

"I am," James admitted without hesitation.

The deputy held up a piece of paper. "I got a warrant here for your arrest."

In his peripheral vision, James saw William mouth a curse word and shake his head. James stepped down off of the porch and snatched the paper out of the deputy's hand. He quickly read the list of allegations that were listed: simple battery, disturbing the peace, destruction of property, disorderly conduct. Each allegation stemmed from his scuffle with Tucker at Buck's Tavern after confronting him about the slanderous newspaper article. Immediately incensed over the mediocre matter, James crumpled the warrant and dropped it on the ground. "I'll deal with this petty shit when I get back." He then proceeded to walk past the deputy to finish loading his wagon.

"You ain't goin' nowhere, boy!" the deputy said, grabbing hold of James's arm before he could take another step.

James looked down at the deputy's hand around his arm, then glared up at him and threatened him with his eyes. James suddenly calmed himself a bit after looking over at William, whose face spoke volumes. He then turned his attention back to the deputy and snatched his arm free. "Look, can't I just pay a few fines and be done with this bullshit? I got somewhere to be," James asked with an attitude.

"That ain't up to me, boy. You'll have to talk to the judge about that." The deputy spat near James's foot and wiped his mouth. "I'm here to take ya' in," he answered, slapping a pair of handcuffs on one of James's wrists before he had a chance to move.

"You're arrestin' me, now?!"

"You learn fast, boy!" The deputy wrestled James's other arm behind his back, cuffed the other wrist, and began to move him toward his wagon.

"Can you give me just a minute?!" James asked. The officer kept on walking, holding tight to his arm. "Just one goddamn minute!" he said, snatching his arm away.

"You got one minute, boy! If y'ur ass ain't in that wagon by then, I'm gonna add resistin' arrest to y'ur charges!"

James listened to his threats with his back to the deputy as he stalked off and walked up the porch steps. Lily had her arms folded and was staring out into the field, refusing to look at him. "Lily? Lily, can you look at me, please?" She took a deep breath before turning to face him. "You trust William, don't ya'?"

"Of course I do," she replied, in a way that she hoped made him feel foolish for even asking.

"Good. Y'all carry on as planned. Austin, Max, and Douglas have all helped me set up equipment and lighting before." James looked over at the three boys, and they all shook their heads in agreement. "They'll know what to do so you can get started with rehearsals. Afta' I talk to the judge and clear all this up, I'll meet y'all at the theater and make any adjustments if need be. This mess shouldn't take long at all. I'll be up in New Lexington lata' today or tomorrow at the latest. I promise, ya' hear?"

Lily nodded her head in response. It was not equipment setups she was worried about. She simply wanted the comforts of James being there. Despite being happy to be away from Jesse's farm, it was scary for Lily to be in such an unfamiliar environment at first. Having James with her at all times had helped her fears to subside. But now, venturing out into the world outside of the comforts of William's home without him had her instantly riddled with anxiety.

"You okay?" James asked her.

"I'll be fine," Lily quickly replied, not wanting him to be privy to any of her reservations. She truly believed that, as always, her strength and resilience would settle her nerves when the time called for it. She wanted James and everyone else to believe that too.

"Good," James said, suddenly looking around at all of the frustrated faces that stared back at him.

"We have to get going," William announced, refusing to look in James's direction. He was eager to get out of his presence and allow his blood pressure to settle back to normal levels. Everyone began filing off of the porch and out to the convoy of awaiting wagons and horses.

"Minute's up, boy!" the deputy called out after spitting into the dirt again.

Lily and James were the last two remaining on the porch. "Guess you best get goin'," Lily said with her arms still folded up. "Don't need no mo' trouble for ya'self."

James read Lily's body language and silently cursed himself for the moment he had given in at Buck's Tavern and laid Tucker to the floor. A simple moment of indiscretion had ruined his opportunity to be there for yet another important transition in Lily's life. He was already sick over the fact that he would miss the once-in-a-lifetime chance to see her face as she walked into a real theater for the very first time. For that alone, he instantly hated himself. James had come to love taking care of all of the details behind the scenes of *The Dream Symphony*. Even more, he loved being by Lily's side to see the delight in her eyes and feel the happiness she emitted as she continued to grow during her musical expedition. Watching and sharing in every aspect of her incredible journey had come to mean everything to James, and he could tell by Lily's body language that him being by her side meant just as much to her, even if she was not willing to admit it.

With his hands cuffed, James could not touch Lily or

hug her the way he was dying to do at that moment. He wanted so badly to help settle the disappointment he felt emanating from her. The sting of not being able to do so was made worse when Lily breezed by him and down the porch steps without another word. She did not offer a goodbye or even attempt to comfort him with a hug, despite her hands being completely free. All James could do was turn and watch her climb into the lead carriage with William and Landon and join the convoy as they trotted off and carried on to New Lexington without him, while he, in turn, was carried off to his awaiting jail cell. The further and further Lily trailed away from his sight, the harder and harder the consequences of James's mistakes started to hit him.

James's state of mind only became worse in the days to come when it became clear that trying to clear up the issue for his minor misconduct was going to be a major problem. Day after day, he begged the deputies and the sheriff for his opportunity to speak to the judge and post his bond or pay any necessary fines to be released from jail. But, time and time again, he was ignored or fed a multitude of excuses about the delays in his case, everything from problems with processing his paperwork, to the judge just being too busy to see him. James could, therefore, do nothing more than wait *impatiently*, pace *incessantly*, complain *very loudly*, and try to calm himself enough to sleep from time to time.

In the few times that James was able to doze off, his mind was invaded by the nightmares of the conversation between Elijah and Lily that he had overheard while standing outside of the library doors. The recurring dream of the two of them would immediately awaken him and refresh the memory of the lust in Elijah's voice as he made his dinner proposition to Lily that day. The entire scenario played over and over again in James's mind while he sat idly in jail with nothing but silence and the images of the pair together reeking havoc on him. His obsessive thoughts over the matter, however, proved not to be unwarranted.

While James stood wrapping his hands around the bars of his jail cell in protest, Elijah had seized that time to wrap his around Lily. James's absence gave Elijah plenty of space and time to show Lily the type of man he could be for her in times of adversity. He now had the opportunity to prove that he could offer an extreme amount of comfort to a woman, especially the sort of comforts only a man could bring. Elijah was there for Lily day in and day out, attempting to fill the void that James's unwanted hiatus had created.

Since Lily was denied access to a hotel, William had initially been staying with her in the theater so that she would not be alone. When Elijah arrived in New Lexington, however, he decided to take William's place and stay with Lily instead. After being rejected from the hotel as well, Elijah could have very well ventured back home, but he much preferred to seize the opportunity to be with Lily. Lily, however, was not made aware of the impromptu switch the pair had made. The evening of the sudden change, William had gone out to retrieve dinner for himself and Lily at a restaurant across the way from the theater and had run into Elijah there. While waiting on her food, Lily was lying in her cot in a dressing room, reading one of the many books she had brought along with her. She closed her book, though, when she suddenly heard the faint sound of piano music coming from the stage. Assuming William had returned with their meals, she got up to join him but was surprised to see that it was actually Elijah playing the elegant ballad. Lily walked around to the front of the piano and Elijah smiled at her as she continued to watch him play.

"William's a wonderful teacha', isn't he?" Lily asked when he completed the simple piece.

"The best!" Elijah agreed.

"I think it's so wonderful that he taught you and Isabel to play."

"Yeah, I'm a little rusty, though. It's been a while."

"I sure couldn't tell."

"I'm certainly nowhere near your level of skill, though."

"Well, I enjoyed it nonetheless."

"Thank you," he smiled.

The simple gesture sent a rush of warmth running through Lily that she was not expecting. She suddenly turned away to escape Elijah's gaze. She then walked toward the edge of the stage to look out at the interior of the theater.

"Beautiful place, isn't it?" Elijah asked, walking up behind her. He stood next to her and stared at all of the features of the interior along with her.

"Sure is."

"Amazin' what a pair of hands can craft."

"So true. I said that to myself when William's amphitheater was finished. It came out to be so beautiful, but this place … this is the grandest thing I've eva' seen in my life. Didn't know they could even build such things. Can't hardly believe I'm blessed enough to be standin' here in the middle of all of it, let alone the fact that I'll be playin' in this very spot in front of an audience full of folks."

"Is that what's troublin' you?" Elijah's booming voice echoed through the empty theater. "I appreciate that you're tryna put on a happy face, but you seem a little tense to me." He stepped behind Lily and began rubbing her shoulders lightly.

"Naw, it's not that. I've ova'come my fear about playin' in front of folks. It's just…"

"Just what?"

Lily looked at Elijah's hands as they caressed her shoulders. The massage felt good to her. She then turned to look up at him. "Well…"

"I tell you what." Elijah turned her around to face him.

"How about you tell me ova' dinna'?"

"Dinna'?"

"Yeah, I bought us some food from the restaurant across the way. I wanted to cook somethin' for you, but it's a little tough without an oven here," he laughed.

"Yeah, I guess that would pose a problem," Lily laughed nervously in return.

"So, will you join me?"

"I would, but William's s'pposed to be back with some food in a little while."

"I know. I ran into him at the restaurant. When he told me you were stuck staying here, I told him he could go on and get a room at the hotel and that I'd keep you company. A man his age don't need to be sleepin' on a cot."

"Oh, I see. I guess that's true," she replied, suddenly feeling a little uneasy about being there alone with him.

"Any more excuses you care to use?"

Lily smiled sheepishly.

"Come on," Elijah said, taking her by the hand and leading her into his dressing room. Inside, he had set up a makeshift table and laid out the dinner like they were at a fine restaurant, complete with champagne glasses, candles, and cloth napkins.

Lily was impressed by the setup and smiled when she saw it after realizing his efforts. "Smells really good," she said, as he pulled out her chair.

"I hope it tastes even betta'. I've heard their food is great, but I'm sure it's not nearly as great as mine," he boasted.

"Well, you ain't the least bit arrogant, are you?" Lily laughed.

"It's called confidence when it's the truth," Elijah smiled. "Go on, try a bite."

Lily cut into a small piece of the steak and let it melt in her mouth. She closed her eyes. "Mmm," she could not help but let out as she chewed.

"Mine would be far betta', but I guess this will have to suffice … For now."

"Somehow, I just can't imagine you bein' this great at cookin'," she teased.

"Trust me, I'm great at a lot of things," Elijah replied while staring at Lily with a different sort of hunger in his eyes.

"I'm quite sure you are," she responded, returning his gaze with a sudden curiosity about him running through her mind that she had not experienced before. Feeling the sudden strength of the sentiment in his words, she dropped her eyes and returned to her steak and forced the thoughts from her mind.

Elijah sensed the shift in her demeanor and sought to change the subject as he cut into his steak. "So, I was askin' earlier, what was troublin' you? You're pretty good at hidin' your emotions most of the time, but I can see right through that little shield you have up."

Lily put her fork down and stopped eating when his question prompted her true worries to return.

"Did I say somethin' wrong?" he asked, after feeling her emotionally drifting away.

"No, of course not."

"Well then what is it? You ain't eatin' all of a sudden. You alright?" He put his fork down as well. "Lily, you can talk to me about anything. Whateva' you say will stay between you and me."

"Thanks. I appreciate that, but I don't wanna bombard you with my troubles, especially afta' you done went through so much trouble for me tonight."

"You wouldn't be bombardin' me. Lily, I wanna help. Is somethin' goin' wrong with the show?"

"Naw, rehearsals are goin' just fine. It's just … I'm worried."

"Worried about what?"

"About…"

342

"Your *masta*"? William told me he's yet to make it up here."

Lily scoffed at his terminology. "He's not my masta', Elijah."

"Is that what he's tellin' you these days?"

"No, it's just not that way between us. He's … He's a *friend*."

Elijah laughed, wiped his mouth, and tossed his napkin on the table.

"What's so funny about that?" Lily asked.

"He's a *friend*?"

"Of course he is."

"A man whose father paid for you at an auction is a *friend*? A man who dragged you up here without you havin' so much as a say in it, is your *friend*?" he asked as if that possibility was ludicrous.

"I know what it seems to everyone else but…"

"Yeah, I had a *friend* once too," Elijah rudely interrupted. "I knew him damn near my whole life. A white boy named Nicholas … Nicholas Wellington. He lived up the road from William. Me, him, and William's boys used to climb trees and fish togetha' on weekends and nearly every day in the summa's. Truth be told, we were so close for so long, Nicholas felt more like a brotha' to me than anything else.

"Nick was talented. He was good at everything. He was the only boy in town who could give me a run for my money at foot racin' and fishin'. But I couldn't hold a candle to him when it came to drawin' … Nobody could. That boy was one hell of an artist. Could draw and paint anything with the utmost precision. People, animals, landscapes, you name it. He planned to go off to school for it, so he could improve and make a livin' at it. But before he went off to college, we saved up enough money and bought ourselves some tickets to ride a steam train togetha'. We were both fascinated by trains, and we'd been dreamin' about ridin' one for years. We planned to travel from one end of the state to the otha'. It's all we eva' talked about sometimes, all the adventures we'd have while we were seein' everything Ohio had to offa'. And afta' years of savin' up, that's exactly what we did. So there I was, with my best friend, our first time on a train togetha', ready to make our dream a reality. While we rode, Nicholas sat next to me starin' out the window at the landscape, capturin' everything he saw on a drawin' pad. You'd think I'd have my eyes pasted on the landscape whippin' by us too, but that's not what caught my attention at all. Instead, I couldn't take my eyes off of this poor old Negro man I saw shovelin' coal into some sort of compartment in the engine. I realized he was shovelin' the fuel to keep the train movin'. He was hunched ova', covered from head to toe in soot and sweat. Hell, he was covered so thick, he could 'a been a white man unda' there and I'd'a neva' known the difference. For some reason, I thought about that poor old filthy man breakin' his back for days afterward, thinkin' to myself that there had to be an easier way to keep that train movin' than to force some old man to slave away and suffa' the way he was.

"Oddly, not long afta' that day, I had a dream … a dream about how I could improve that train. I dreamt about a holdin' compartment for all that coal that could be placed high up above the engine, so that the coal could be funneled *downward* into the engine by simply pullin' on a lever. So instead of shovelin', all a man would eva' have to do is open that storage compartment and release as much coal as he needed before closin' it off again. No more shovelin', no more sweatin', no more soot, no more watchin' an old man damn near break his back to keep a train rollin'.

"When I woke up from that dream, I was hell-bent on makin' it a reality. I wanted to get a patent for the idea and sell it to every train manufacturer in the United States. I wrote up a summary about it and tried to draw a figure to go along with it. The problem was, I couldn't draw no betta' than a five-year-old, but Nicholas Wellington—*my friend*—he could draw anything. So, I took my basic sketch to him, showed him the write-up on my idea, explained a few things, and asked if he'd do a professional version of the artist's renderin' for me. Nicholas was more than happy to do it. He shared in my enthusiasm because he was just as convinced as I was that this idea would be a change that no train manufacturer would eva' turn down. He had no doubt in his mind that somethin' so simple would make me rich, and my *best friend* wanted to do all he could to help. He told me to give him forty-eight hours so that he could be sure the drawing was done to scale. He said he'd have it complete by then for sure. Two days lata', I returned to retrieve it, just to find out that my very *best* friend, a friend who was like a brotha' to me, had gotten on a train and road south with my idea tucked away in his pocket. His first stop … E.M. Baldwin Train Corporation.

"So, if you eva' have the chance to get on a steam train, just know that it'll be my coal funnelin' system helpin' to propel it forward, but more importantly, that my *friend,* Nicholas Wellington, will neva' have to work again a single day in his life because of it. And worse yet, there ain't a damn thing I can do about it because there ain't a court in the land that'll believe some dumb Negro actually thought of an idea like that.

"That was my ticket, Lily! My ticket to a betta' life, a life of not havin' to work like a dog to make ends meet, to supportin' a family when I have one, a ticket to givin' somethin' meaningful to my folks afta' everything they been through for me and my sista'. My so-called *friend,* he took that ticket from me, signed his name on it, and took my seat on a train with a destination to an easier life. So long as I live, I'll neva' forgive that bastard for it!

"'I'm your *friend!*'" Elijah pointed his finger down hard on the table with a scowl on his face. "White folks!

345

That's what they'll tell ya', Lily! They'll smile at ya'! Hug ya'! Or do whateva' they have to do to get close enough to ya', just to be sure it's easier to take what they want from you wheneva' it comes a time that they need it!"

Lily stared at him feeling uneasy with how upset he had become. "I'm sorry for what happened to you, Elijah, I really am, but how could you say that afta' everything that William's done for you?"

"William's an anomaly!"

"And how do you know that James isn't!?"

"Oh come on, Lily, don't be so blind! He hasn't even tried to hide it! It was all ova' the newspapa's, how he's usin' you to make money to pay his daddy's debts!"

"That ain't true!"

"If it ain't, then answa' one question for me … Of all the money you've made since performin' on William's estate and out of all the advances they've given for this show, how much of it has *your masta'* laid in your hands, huh?"

Lily leaned back in her chair and stared at her plate, embarrassed to answer truthfully.

Elijah scoffed. "A *friend*, huh?" he smiled arrogantly. "Betta' start rethinkin' your definition of what that really is. You should be happy your masta' got locked up, 'steada sittin' here sulkin' ova' him the way you are. He deserves to be sittin' in that jail cell dealin' with the consequences of his actions, not to mention for the way he's *stealin'* your money."

"Stop talkin' about him that way! You don't know James the way I do!" Lily scooted her chair back quickly, got up, and stormed out of the dressing room.

Elijah immediately jumped up and caught her in the hallway. "Lily wait! Please!" He gently turned her around to face him. "You're right. I'm sorry. I had no right. I'm really sorry. I didn't mean to get upset at you. I didn't realize how bitta' I still was about what happened to me.

The whole scenario makes me so mad because I just don't want the same thing to happen to you. I know I may not have expressed myself right, but I just want to protect you from what I went through. But, you're right … I don't know this James guy at all, so I shouldn't have said those things about him."

"You're damn right you shouldn't have!"

"I know, I know, but can you at least try to unda'stand where I'm coming from?"

Lily just stared at him with a scowl on her face and refused to utter another word.

"Can you give me anotha' chance? I was outta line, and I probably don't deserve it, but I'm askin' for your forgiveness anyway?"

Again, she was cold and refused to respond.

"Please?" he begged. "I know I've made a complete mess out of dinna' tonight, but to make it up to you and show you that I'm not such a bad guy, how 'bout I ride back to Athens tomorrow to see if I can find out what's goin' on with James?"

"I-I'd appreciate that."

"Then that's what I'll do."

"Thank you."

"So now what do you say we forget about the last ten minutes and start ova'?" Elijah extended his hand for Lily to shake. "Hi, I'm Elijah … And you are?"

She finally could not help but smile at his sarcasm. "Lily," she said, reluctantly placing her hand in his.

"Wow! You have a smile that lights up this entire room."

"Well, thank you … Umm, what did you say your name was again?" she responded, playing along with a silly sarcasm in her tone as well.

"Elijah," he laughed.

"Well, Elijah, that's very sweet of you. You have a very nice smile too."

347

He took hold of Lily's hand and guided her back to his makeshift dinner table. They sat back down together and finished off the meal in better spirits with plenty of wine, dessert, and lighter conversation. They later tinkered on the piano together and then sat next to one another in the theater seats laughing at funny stories about each other's lives. They carried on with the fun of their impromptu date until Lily grew tired and departed back to her dressing room well after midnight.

From her few interactions with Elijah, Lily had learned that he was more than just a flawlessly handsome man who possessed the ability to simply look at a woman in a way that would melt her insides. He was witty, intelligent, ambitious, very attentive, and had a confidence about him that was unparalleled to any other Negro man she had ever known. He was the sort of man that any Negro woman would love to marry, have children with, and have an all-encompassing, ideal life with. By the end of her night with him, Lily was surprised that she was still thinking about Elijah, wondering if maybe she just might be the right fit for a man of his caliber. In fact, as she lay in her tiny cot that evening, it dawned on her that while she was with Elijah, she did not once think about James. Simply Elijah's presence had temporarily freed her from her anxieties about James's whereabouts, something that even her music had failed to do while he was missing.

It was the mere thought of potential moments of that nature that tortured James as he sat idly in jail. Those thoughts were exacerbated by the fact that he was yearning to be there for Lily behind the scenes, just as he had been from the very beginning. As time grew closer to opening night, he could feel the pressure within him beginning to mount whenever he dwelled on the fact that he might miss Lily's very first show inside of a theater, and, worse yet, miss the feeling of the warm embrace that she always gave him after every show. Simply the possibility that he would not be there to experience the joy of the succession of those significantly meaningful events had James ready to explode.

On top of missing Lily terribly, the lack of food, water, and sleep added fuel to James's obsessive thoughts about Elijah making advances toward her. It cast him into a temporary insanity of sorts and was at the root of the reason he continued to obsess over the fact that Elijah would be the sort of man to capitalize on Lily's emotions during such an opportunistic moment. As he lay in his filthy little jailhouse cot staring at the ceiling, he was tormented by the look he had seen in Elijah's eyes that telegraphed his unrelenting internal desire to have Lily. Logically, James understood that he had no right to be upset at Lily for accepting Elijah's advances if that's what she wanted, but logic was a foreign concept when it came to the matter of his feelings for her. Logic also had no power to stop the graphic visions of Lily and Elijah that continued to erupt in James's jealous mind, visions far worse than any simple dinners or casual hugs. Those erotic visions suddenly caused James to hop out of his tiny cot, wrap his hands around his cell bars, and begin yelling at the deputies in the front office. His begging and pleading echoed down the hallways of the jailhouse and fell on deaf, unsympathetic ears as usual. After nearly going hoarse, James stood with his head resting against the bars of his cell with the mounting vile images of Elijah and Lily continuing to add to his madness. The visions ceased, though, when a familiar voice suddenly began to berate him.

"You mean they ain't let you outta here yet, schoolboy?" Tucker teased from outside the small barred window near the ceiling of James's basement cell. James tore himself away from the cell bars and turned around briefly to look up at the person he was convinced had played a role in ensuring his extended jailhouse stay. After he saw Tucker's face, he turned back around and rested his head back on the bars. Despite James trying to ignore him, Tucker continued to torment him. "Now don't you worry y'ur pretty little head if you don't get out on time, ya' hear? I'm sure somebody'll volunteer to keep y'ur honey warm t'night afta' her show. Just might be that nigga' William done raised up all them years. I saw the way he was lookin' at 'er durin' that fundraisa'. He seemed awful sweet on y'ur lil' monkey," Tucker teased. He squatted down and cocked his head to the side to be sure he had a good view of James's reaction. "Or maybe William's ol' dried up ass still got enough juice in 'em to get it up and give y'ur little honey-brown bitch a pickle tickle," he laughed. "Or hell, come to think of it … just might be *me*." He licked his dried-up lips. "I swear, I ain't been able to get 'er sweet little ass off my mind since the day you laid me out at Buck's. I been dyin' for her to give me the kind 'a lovin' that'll make me wanna knock a man smooth on his ass!" It took every bit of effort for Tucker's lungs to force his laugh through the cigar-tarred congestion in his throat. "I'm jealous of ya', schoolboy! I ain't neva' had me no ass good as that … *yet*. I'm'a fix that t'night, though," he smiled, showing his tobacco-stained teeth. "Well, I best get goin' if I wanna make it to the show on time. I got quite a long ride ahead 'a me. You sleep well now, ya' hear?" Tucker looked up at the sky. "You be sure 'n cova' up good, schoolboy. Gonna be awful cold layin' in that cot t'night all by y'ur lonesome," he said, letting out another phlegm-filled laugh.

James refused to give Tucker the reaction he was looking for, despite the intense visions he suddenly had of grabbing him by the neck. He was itching to watch the blood drain from Tucker's face as his eyes turned bloodshot red and his lips a deep purple. He wanted to squeeze him until his chest ceased movement and then let out a sigh of great relief when Tucker's limp body slumped to the ground. In order to refrain from giving in to his desires, James simply kept his back turned, tightened his grip on the cell bars, and waited for the annoying town outcast to leave. After he rode off, though, James actually felt a twinge of envy knowing that Tucker was headed to the place that he desperately wanted to be. When he was long gone, James walked up to the small window above his cell and saw nothing but the dust Tucker's horse left behind. When the dust settled, his attention drifted to two filthy boys playing together nearby who both looked to be eleven or twelve years old, wearing tattered clothes and no shoes.

"Heeey fellas!" James called out to them in a husky tone, trying to keep his voice from reaching the ears of the deputies down the hall. He looked over his shoulder to see if anyone was coming before calling out to them again. On his second attempt, both boys looked around, wondering where the voice was coming from. James stuck his arm through the cell bars and waved them over. "Ova' here!"

The two boys looked at each other before wandering over to see what James wanted. "What is it, mista'?" the scrawniest of the two asked.

"You boys wanna make some money?" James held up two five-dollar bills that had been tucked away in his back pocket.

Both boys' eyes widened at the possibility of having that amount of money. "Sure!" they said in unison.

"Then listen, I need both of you to go and find a fella named Harrison Mitchell. He's a good friend of mine. He lives on Post Road, not far from the big fishin' creek. You know where that is?"

"Sure! We fish there all the time."

"Good, well Harrison's got the only big white house on that road, 'bout a quarta' mile from there. Tell 'em that James Adams is down at the county jail and that I need his help. Tell him that it's real urgent and that I need him to come right away, okay? Can you rememba' all that?"

"Yessa'!" both boys said in unison.

"If you get him down here quick then this ten dollars is

all yours, okay?"

"Yessa'!" they both replied again, sounding as giddy as two boys could be.

"I'll give ya' five dollars now, and you can get the rest when ya' get back, ya' hear?" he promised, as he handed one of the bills over to them. "Go on, now. Go as fast as your little legs'll carry ya'." Both boys bolted down the road, kicking up as much dust as Tucker's horse did on his way out of town. When they were out of sight, James sat on his bed and waited with his stomach in knots, hoping that giving up ten dollars would be worth it in the end.

James had been trying to summon the deputies to contact his old roommate and frat brother for nearly a week. Harrison had never failed to be there for James while they were in school. He had always invited him to stay with his family during school breaks, since he knew that James had no desire to return to Virginia. Despite the fact that they were close, James had never confided in Harrison about the details of the reason why he refused to go home. Harrison never pressured him about it either, sensing that it was a very sensitive subject. Instead of pushing James to get past whatever issues he was running away from at home, Harrison simply welcomed him to stay at his. Having been there for him faithfully in the past, James was confident that Harrison would most certainly be there for him again, so long as those two little boys were successful in finding him.

Just over an hour later, James heard footsteps outside his cell window, followed by the sound of two young voices. The two little boys had gone to the big white house near the fishing creek, but Harrison's wife informed them that he was still at the courthouse. Eager to fulfill their mission for the remainder of their money, both boys found Harrison there just as he was wrapping up a minor court case. They then quickly ushered him across the street to James's basement cell window. "He's ova' here, mista'!"

the scrawny one pointed out to Harrison.

James stood on his bed again and handed over the remainder of the money that he had promised his tiny heroes. "Thank you, boys."

"Thanks, mista'!" they exclaimed, before running off to spend their earnings.

Harrison squatted down to see James better. "Well, well, well. What the hell kind 'a mess you done got ya'self into these days, Adams?"

James was not in the mood for sarcasm. "Listen, I don't have much time. You gotta get me the hell outta here. I've been here for almost a week ova' some bullshit charges."

"Just what kind 'a *bullshit* charges are we talkin' about?"

"I got in a fight with some asshole at Buck's Tavern a few weeks back. A deputy came out to the house a couple 'a weeks lata' with a warrant for my arrest. That was a week ago, and I've been sittin' in here eva' since."

"I need to know more than that. Give me specifics. What exactly was on the warrant?"

"Simple battery, destruction of property … Umm, disturbin' the peace, and disorderly conduct, I think."

"You've been stuck here a week for that?!"

"Yeah."

"You haven't seen a judge yet?"

"No, nothin'! I'm tellin' ya', I haven't left this goddamn cell! Somehow, I think the little shit who put me in here has everything to do with the reason I'm still sittin' here, but that's anotha' matta' for anotha' time. All I know is that you gotta get me the hell outta here!"

"What little shit're you talkin' about?"

"Guy named Tucker."

"McCormick?"

"Yeah, that's the one."

Harrison laughed. "Damn! Yeah, you certainly chose

the wrong piece of shit to tango with. He and Sheriff Tolliva' been friends since they were boys."

"That explains a lot. Lucky me."

"Have you asked for an attorney?"

"I've lost count of how many times I've asked them to get a hold of you! I'm tellin' you, they don't give a shit! I just kept gettin' fed all these goddamn excuses, and now they're just ignorin' me!"

Harrison realized that the line of questioning was only agitating James more. "Well, unfortunately, the courts have just closed for the day, but I can draw up some papers t'night and then first thing Monday mornin'…"

"I don't fuckin' have 'til Monday!" James erupted. "I need to get the hell outta here! *Now*!"

"Whoa man, hold your voice down," he said looking over James's shoulder to see if he had gotten the attention of any deputies.

"Don't worry, they're good at ignorin' me by now," James replied, briefly looking over his shoulder too. "Look, I'm sorry, bro. It's just … you gotta help me. Please," he begged, "You gotta get me outta here. I got somewhere I need to be tonight. It's important to me. *Really* important," he sighed.

Harrison let his thoughts consume him for a moment while he tried to think of a quicker solution. "Alright, I think I got somethin'. I'll be back. Just hold tight."

"What the hell else am I gonna do?" James mumbled after he walked off.

"Sheriff Tolliva', how do you do?" Harrison asked, after walking into the front lobby of the county jail that had been James's home for the last week.

"Well, well, well, Harrison Mitchell," the sheriff replied, standing and taking hold of his hand to shake. "Ned," he said, speaking to a young, goofy-looking, rookie deputy at a desk nearby. "This fella here is one of the finest damn attorneys I've eva' laid my eyes on." He turned to look at Harrison again. "Neva' did get to thank you for what you did for ma' sista'."

"No thanks necessary, Sheriff. Afta' I saw what her husband did to her face, there's no way I was gonna let that son of a bitch get away with it."

"It may seem like no big deal to you, but I can't count how many otha' jackass attorneys failed 'er. Eitha' they were too damn timid, or they were easily swayed by her ex-husband's money. Bunch 'a damn crooks," he snarled. "But you! You were like a goddamn rabid dog attackin' her ex-husband while he was up there on that stand!" He gave a hearty laugh. "In all my years, I ain't neva' seen nothin' like it!"

"Well thank you," Harrison smiled. "I knew your sista' needed a strong voice on 'er side and I didn't wanna let 'er down."

"And you didn't. That's somethin' she'll neva' forget you for eitha'."

"Trust me, I'll neva' forget her eitha', nor those tears she cried durin' the verdict when it was all ova'. Tears of Justice, that's what those were to me. I's just a rookie attorney then, and it affected me pretty deep knowin' I had the powa' to help give 'er that sort of justice. That's what I live for now. It's what I fight for. I crave it. I yearn for it. I dream of it. I want every one of my clients to know the feelin' of justice. No matta' how big or how small the offense, I wanna feel that euphoric victory vicariously through them. I ain't lost a case yet because of it, and I owe that to your sista' given me a chance to fight on her behalf. She lit a fire unda' my ass, that's for damn sure."

"Seems you've both gained a lot from each otha' then. I tell you what, son, any man should be proud to have you as his attorney knowin' how hard y'ur willin' to fight for y'ur clients."

"You're too kind."

Sheriff Tolliver nodded his head and sat back down.

"Well now, what can I do ya' for today?"

Harrison walked over nonchalantly and looked at a few of the sheriff's plaques hanging on the walls. "It's an election year, ain't it?"

"Sure is."

"You runnin' again?"

"Sure am."

"Must be important to ya', then … to portray yourself to the vota's as a man who upholds and abides by every aspect of the law."

"Of course," Tolliver responded, leaning back in his chair, starting to look at Harrison a bit oddly about his choice of conversation.

"Ya' know, I've been in that courtroom a whole hell of a lot in the last two years since helpin' ya' sista'," Harrison continued, as he strolled from plaque to plaque. "And it neva' escapes my attention how many people pack into the pews durin' those public hearin's on a daily basis. I see all kinds of different people driftin' in there. Everything from little old ladies who like to be nosy, to bored retired old men. Hell, some folks're just lookin' to get outta the heat or the cold. All different kind 'a people, all there for their own different reasons. But one thing 'bout all of 'em is the same … they're *voters*. Every last one of 'em. Each and every one of 'em gets to cast their ballot come election time. All those folks want to be sure they cast their vote for the sort of politicians that are honest, for judges who are fair and just, and for a *sheriff*…" Harrison finally turned around to look at Sheriff Tolliver. "For a sheriff who upholds and abides strictly by the laws. The people want a sheriff that ain't swayed by money or politicians or … oh, I don't know, old friends who ask unlawful favors. A diligent, law abidin' sheriff who believes wholeheartedly in *every* citizen's right to *swift* due process, that's what the people want! Ain't that right, Ned?" Harrison asked, while still staring at Sheriff Tolliver.

"See Ned, the people of this town don't wanna think that a sheriff they voted for is the kind 'a man who would lock a man up for minor offenses like *simple* battery, causin' *minor* property damages, or somethin' as silly as disturbin' the peace, and then neva' botha' to let 'em see a judge and post his bond or pay his fines within a *reasonable* amount of time the way the law states. The good people of this town would be outraged to learn that a sheriff they elected was the sort 'a man to deny a petty criminal an attorney afta' he begs for one for a whole week! Hell Ned! I've seen murderers who were granted lawya's and a chance to see a judge in less time than that! No! The good votin' people of this county, who pack those pews to the gills in the courthouse every day, wouldn't wanna know such a thing about their elected official, now would they, Ned?" Harrison walked over, placed both of his hands on Tolliver's desk, and leaned toward him. "And I highly doubt that's the sort 'a thing that a sheriff would like to explain to a judge in front of all 'a those vote-castin' citizens loiterin' in the courtroom every day when there's a *rabid dog* questionin' him while he's up there on that stand!"

Tolliver jumped to his feet and fearlessly leaned across his desk toward Harrison. "You must be outta y'ur goddamn mind, boy! I don't believe you'd really be dumb enough to put y'ur career on the line for that nigga' lovin' piece 'a shit!" he growled, staring Harrison down with blood-red eyes.

"If you think that's the only thing I know about how corrupt you are, then you're the one who's outta his goddamn mind. I got enough dirt on you to fill the fishin' creek near my house two times ova'. I'll snuff it dry with all y'ur dirty little secrets if that's the chance you wanna take," Harrison threatened, bluffing with rumors he had heard about Sheriff Tolliver, but had no real evidence to back up.

Tolliver didn't blink, hoping to refrain from showing the slightest hint of fear. "Get the keys to the cell, Ned," he demanded, without turning his eyes away from Harrison.

"You do that, Ned. Quick, fast and in a hurry." Harrison finally stepped back and smirked at Tolliver when he heard the cell keys rattling. "You tell Buck that my client agrees to pay for all 'a the damages done to his property within thirty days of receiving a written estimate, not a penny more or less," he told the sheriff once James was out of his cell and standing beside him. Harrison was about to walk away after that but then stopped and turned back toward Tolliver. "Oh, and uh, bein' the *law abidin'* sheriff that you are, somehow I think you'll find it in y'ur heart to make all those otha' charges magically disappear." Tolliver crumpled James's warrant and dropped it into the trash. "Now, that's magic if I eva' seen it. You're damn sure worthy of my vote!" he joked.

"Get y'ur asses outta my jailhouse!"

"Good luck with that re-election." Harrison tipped his hat. "Have a fine day gentlemen."

"Don't know what kind 'a strings you just pulled in there," James said, squinting after the sunlight hit his eyes for the first time in days, "but I can't thank you enough."

"Don't mention it. Neva' could stand ol' Tolliva's fat ass anyway. Felt good," Harrison replied, as they walked toward his carriage across the road. "So, I hear there's a big symphony t'night up in New Lexington. My guess is that's where you're so eaga' to go."

James didn't say a word, but the look on his face said it all.

Harrison grabbed James's shirt sleeve. "Well, I hope you're not goin' there lookin' like this." He leaned in and sniffed him. "Or smellin' like that eitha'," he laughed. He slapped James on the shoulder. "Come on, Adams, let me help my ol' frat brotha' out."

"Thanks. I owe you big time for this, Mitchell," James

said, as he climbed into his carriage.

"No. Seems you owe it to a certain someone else to get y'ur ass to that symphony on time," he replied. He then snapped the reins to prompt his horses into a gallop toward his house, where he planned to loan James some clothes, a razor, a toothbrush, and some much-needed soap.

Just as with all of his other issues in the past, Harrison did not question James any further about why he nearly fell apart emotionally over the fact that he might miss Lily's performance in New Lexington. He was now fairly confident of what the answer to that would be anyway. A few weeks prior, James had invited Harrison and his wife to come and watch Lily perform at William's estate. While there, Harrison quickly noticed that there was something unique and special about the relationship that James had with Lily. Harrison had stayed and attended the after party as well and noticed how proud James was to introduce him to Lily. Harrison continued watching the pair throughout the night and noted the way that James lit up at the mere sight of Lily. In Harrison's estimation, James was like a dramatically different person while in Lily's presence. So long as Lily was nearby, Harrison could feel *genuine* happiness emanating from his friend for the first time since knowing him. It left Harrison thoroughly convinced that Lily was the answer to all of the questions surrounding James and his odd behaviors while in school: why he fought the desire to return home for holidays and school breaks, why he seemed to constantly drink his sorrows away, and why he used women as toys and never bothered to involve himself emotionally with any of them. If his suspicions were accurate, Harrison did not blame James for what he felt for Lily. He, too, had been taken aback by how intelligent, funny, warm, and stunningly beautiful Lily was. He instantly became sympathetic to the uniqueness of their circumstances and fully understood how Lily could easily make a man like James feel torn and end up resorting to bizarre behaviors.

Harrison was also certain that Lily was undoubtedly the reason why James had just rushed through shaving and bathing, and why he was currently watching his longtime friend ride off of his property with the speed of a midwestern twister, under the legs of his strongest horse, dressed in the finest attire from his very own closet. The sight of it further proved that Harrison's assumptions about James's feelings for Lily were right. But, as usual, just as with all of the other intimate details of his buddy's life: "Your secrets are safe with me," Harrison whispered, as he watched James gallop out of sight. "Ride like the wind, my friend."

* * * *

While Lily had spent two hours pushing to focus mentally and deliver another stellar performance, James had spent nearly that same amount of time pushing Harrison's horse to near death in order to be there for another once-in-a-lifetime moment in Lily's life … but it was far too late. Lily had already taken a final bow to her grateful audience, only for her eyes to hone in on the empty seat next to Landon that had been reserved for James. With all of the orchestra members surrounding her, Lily finally exited the stage, feeling just as emotionally drained as the horse that James was currently dismounting. James quickly wrapped the horse's reins around a post near a troth of water and began fighting his way through a sea of people exiting Branaugh Theater. Hearing no music playing within the building, his heart sank into his stomach. He was already struggling to come to terms with the fact that he had missed it all and that there was no way of going back in time to relive yet another precedent-setting evening in Lily's life.

"James!" Landon called out from behind him, putting his hand on James's shoulder. Landon found him panting in the wings, looking as lost as a puppy. "A successful night, wouldn't you say?! Did you hear that crowd!" With the culmination of missing Lily's show and his week-long nightmare in jail, the excitement in Landon's voice was equivalent to screeching nails on a chalkboard in James's ears. James simply could not instantly bring himself to that level of happiness. He was angry, tired, frustrated, irritated, and therefore, thoroughly annoyed by Landon's joy. Besides that, Landon was certainly the last person that James wished to see or whose voice he wished to hear.

In the midst of all the bodies backstage, Lily had yet to see that James had finally arrived. She had walked off stage toward William, Anna Mae, Ben, Isabel, and Elijah standing in the wings, who all welcomed her with delight on their faces. Anna Mae let go of tears of joy the moment Lily hugged her. "I'm so proud 'a you, baby!" she boasted.

"Thank you, Ms. Anna Mae."

While Lily and her friends celebrated on one side of the stage, Landon was holding James up on the other side, rambling on and on about the show. Not far into the conversation, though, James became *completely* incoherent to Landon's words while he searched for the woman he needed to settle his agitation. He was looking over Landon's shoulder, his eyes bolting from face to face, trying to find Lily in the clutter of orchestra bodies and dancers lining the hallways. Since Landon had helped to afford Lily the opportunity to play at Branaugh, James wanted to escape his meaningless chatter without being disrespectful, but suddenly, his desire to be respectful went out of the window. The only woman who possessed the power to remedy everything that currently plagued him, James finally spotted … in the arms of another man.

After presenting Lily with a massive, beautiful flower arrangement, Elijah stood in the corner embracing the one woman that James had been dying to hold for nearly a week. James abruptly bolted past Landon without a word, leaving him standing there alone, looking confused by the sudden change in his demeanor. The blood in James's veins had instantaneously reached its boiling point after seeing how closely and tightly Elijah held Lily. As he flew in a beeline toward the pair, James's face was stone cold, his body language emitted his agitation, and his ears had become deaf to the laughter and praise coming from all of the smiling faces surrounding him. All James could hear in his head were the array of compliments Elijah had showered Lily with in the past, as well his offer to cook dinner for her. The playback of those moments was intertwined with the sight of how receptive Lily currently was as Elijah smiled at her now. The combination made the innocence of their current embrace seem far more intimate to James. Hunger, exhaustion, frustration, and anger had taken its toll on his ability to effectively rationalize what was happening in front of him. It left James in an unstable state of mind as he approached a man that he loathed, who just so happened to be stealing a celebratory moment that had usually been *his* after every last one of Lily's shows.

"LILY!" James called out.

Lily turned her head toward the sound of a voice she had been longing to hear. "JAMES!" Her eyes lit up and she smiled when she saw his face through the sea of people. "You're here!" She quickly let go of Elijah; after seeing James, he was immediately of no concern to her. She felt a strong gravitational pull to hug James after feeling the instant relief of his presence. That fact instantly angered Elijah as he stood there and watched Lily happily walking toward another man, a man that he considered as nothing more than her manipulative, money-hungry *master*.

"Get into the carriage!" James told Lily coldly, as he approached with an evil expression on his face and rigid body language. He even sidestepped her offer for an embrace and stared directly at the man who had him beyond irate.

"But why?" Lily asked as James breezed by her.

"We're leaving!"

"But James, I's…"

"I SAID WE'RE LEAVING!" he yelled, in a pitch that stopped the celebration cold and silenced all the chatter in the hallway.

"James I…"

"NOW!" he screamed again, startling everyone. James tried, but his jealousy and anger would not allow him to turn his eyes away from Elijah, who stared back with just as much ice in his eyes. Not much had been said, but James's sudden unexplained appearance and his explosive attitude had instantaneously killed the joyous mood of the celebration. All of the orchestra members stared curiously at him, perplexed by his bizarre behavior. Of all the people there, they expected that James would be, by far, the happiest of everyone after such a successful night.

Unable to bring herself to move after feeling the immediate aftershock of James's attitude, Lily just stood there with her mouth partially agape. She held onto her bouquet, wearing yet another one of Anna Mae's fancy designer gowns, but at that moment, she did not feel so beautiful in it. She was feeling extraordinarily embarrassed by the way James had just treated her. She was highly confused about why he was just now arriving and about what had just triggered him to humiliate her in front of all of her friends.

When James was finally able to tear his eyes away from Elijah, he looked over at Lily's face and knew immediately that his jealous tantrum had just ruined her night. Feeling the embarrassment of the moment full force, Lily had dropped her head low, reminding James of her reaction during the many occasions that his father was nasty to her. James mentally kicked himself after realizing that he was solely responsible for the way that the joy had just drained from her face. And just as with all of his actions that had erupted from his uncontrollable anger in

363

the past, he instantly regretted it.

Already emotionally weakened from a turbulent week, it took very little to drain the rest of the life from Lily's spirit, and she simply conceded to James's demands. "Yessa'," she finally replied. She had quickly reverted back to her slave mentality and acknowledged him accordingly. As she walked away with her head hanging in shame, the clicking of her fancy shoes against the concrete floor sounded more like cannons going off in the midst of the awkward silence that lingered in the hallway. James briefly watched her retreat to the carriage and then turned to stare at Elijah once more with a look in his eyes that he hoped was conveying his thoughts about him touching Lily. Without another word, James then turned to head toward the carriage along with Lily, leaving everyone else behind to speculate in confusion about what had just happened.

"ADAMS!"

James stopped and turned around to find Elijah walking up behind him.

"Can I have a word with you?" Elijah asked.

"Go on to the carriage, Lily," James told her without taking his cold eyes off of Elijah. "What the hell do you want?!" James snapped with irritation obvious on his face.

Elijah gave an arrogant smile. "Same thing as you it seems," he replied boldly, walking calmly toward James. "I see the way you look at Lily. And you're a damn fool if you think I haven't noticed the way you look at me wheneva' I talk to her. I've seen it from day one."

"Get to your fuckin' point! I don't have time for this shit!"

"Come on, Adams. It's just you and me here alone now." Elijah stepped even closer, walking with an overly arrogant swagger. "I know your little conniption fit here tonight had nothin' to do with Lily, so why take it out on her?"

"You don't know a damn thing!"

"I *know* I was here for her tonight! I *know* I was a comfort to her while you were nowhere to be found! I *know* that she didn't deserve to be treated the way you just treated her! I *know* that a *real* man would've taken his anga' out on *me* ... not her!"

James took a step closer to him with an evil intensity in his eyes. "I'd be careful what you ask for," he said through gritted teeth.

Elijah fearlessly took another step closer to him too. "You betta' be careful too. You don't know who you're fuckin' with eitha', greedy white boy!" he snapped. "But I can assure you that I'm a man who knows good 'n damn well that you can't possibly offa' Lily the sort 'a life that I can, and you're a goddamn lunatic if you think otha'wise." He scoffed and shook his head. "Lemme guess, you dragged Lily up here to a free state thinkin' things will be different or easy somehow, didn't ya'? Well, I can promise you that, outside of William's mansion, nobody will give a damn about Lily bein' free or not free anywhere else in these racist United States, trust me on that," he said while recalling his lingering bitterness over what his friend had done to him years ago. "Outside of William's gates, without those filthy guards he hired, Lily's fair game. She'll have a target on her back the size of New York for hatred, ridicule ... hell, even death, if anybody catches wind about the little love affair you're hopin' for. So, I suggest you let go of any twisted fairytale fantasy ideals you have about her. Or betta' yet ... why don't you just let *her* go?!"

"And I suggest you stay y'ur ass the hell away from her or the only thing left in that smart ass mouth 'a yours will be your tongue!"

Elijah gave an arrogant laugh and stood there unscathed by his threat. "You're so hell-bent on tryna pretend like Lily's free, so don't you think she oughta be the one to make the decision about who she wants?" he smirked. "Go on and ask her, *Masa' James* ... 'cause I'm certain that afta' the week I just spent with her, she'll be beggin' for more of *me*."

Although James sensed the lies in Eiljah's implications, every ounce of him wanted to swing for even having the audacity to suggest such a thing. But he knew that's what Elijah wanted: more proof that Lily need not be with a man who possessed such a volatile temper. It would have been another reason to drive her away and perhaps into Elijah's arms, and James was definitely unwilling to give him that satisfaction. Instead, James stepped to within an inch of Elijah's face. "Seems I'm not the only one with a twisted fairytale fantasy," he finally replied.

They stood there with each other eye to eye in silence afterward, both looking like two animals ready to square off. After a few seconds, James finally found the strength to turn and walk away in an attempt to diffuse his fury.

"If you really gave a damn about her, you'd let her have the sort 'a life she deserves!" Elijah yelled to James down the hall.

His words rang through James's ears loud and clear, but his temper had caused him enough turmoil for the night. Remembering that fact left him content to let Elijah have the last word and gave him the strength to continue marching away from a potentially bloody battle scene.

Chapter Nineteen

Master:
A man who owns servants or slaves
OR
A skilled practitioner of a particular art, technique, or activity.

The carriage ride back to William's estate seemed longer than usual to both Lily and James. It was nightfall, but James did not need light to know that Lily was crying. Her body language spoke volumes to him, as did her silence. She sat next to the bouquet that Elijah had given her with her body turned slightly toward the window, looking out into the darkness, sniffling lightly every few minutes. James wanted to find words of comfort, but William was along for the ride as well, and he did not want to embarrass himself or Lily any further in his presence.

When they arrived, Lily was out of the carriage and up into her room before James and William even reached the porch steps. Immediately afterward, William turned to James and scolded him with his eyes while pointing his finger toward where Lily had just gone. "That beautiful young lady up there, she was a complete and utter wreck before the show tonight, pacing and worrying herself sick, wondering what had happened to you! Then! After all the heartache and trouble you caused, you had the audacity to walk in there and treat her that way! You-you imbecile! Did you not see the instant look of relief on her face the moment she saw you?! She was herself again for the briefest of moments until you ripped it all away from her again! And to know that your little tantrum had everything to do with..." William stopped and snickered and began pointing his finger repeatedly at James. "Yes, jealousy is undoubtedly a very natural emotion James, but only an immature weakling would allow it to unravel him. And *you*

… you bloody fool!" he scolded, "are hanging by the thinnest of threads … a very, very frayed thread at that!"

"I don't wanna hear any of your wisdom-filled riddles right now, William!" James replied, putting a hand up.

William shook his head. "I'm too disgusted to waste any more of my oxygen speaking to you anyway." He walked upstairs and slammed his bedroom door.

Once he was out of sight, James immediately ascended the stairs, two steps at a time, and entered Lily's room without bothering to knock. Lily still had her dress on and was standing by the fire she had just started, trying to warm herself and calm her severed nerves.

"Lily," James said, quietly closing the door behind him.

"Yessa'?" she replied with her back to him.

"You still cryin'?"

"No sa', I wasn't cryin'," she lied, trying to hide her face by continuing to gaze at the fire.

"You're not a very good liar." He approached her from behind. "Can you look at me, please?"

Lily refused to turn around, hoping to continue hiding any evidence of her lie.

James stood patiently behind her. "Please, tell me your troubles."

"I'm fine," she insisted. "Just a lil' tired is all."

James didn't want to hear that. He preferred for her to punish him with her words for ruining her evening. "No need for lies. Tell me what's wrong."

"I ain't got nothin' to say, *masta'*."

"I know you, Lily, and I ain't neva' seen you cry for nothin'."

"I'm fine," she lied again.

James finally initiated the conversation after realizing that Lily would be too stubborn to speak first. "Look, I figured you wouldn't feel like talkin' to me 'cause you're angry with me, and I don't blame ya'. But I came up here anyway because I at least wanted to tell you how sorry I am."

"For which part, huh?" she asked in a sarcastic tone. Her arms were folded across her chest, and she still refused to turn around and look at him. "For beatin' up that moron? Landin' yo'self in jail? Missin' the show? Or for remindin' me in front of everybody in that hallway t'night that you own me? Which one is it … *masta'*?"

"Stop callin' me that!" he shouted in frustration.

"For what!?" Lily bit off, finally turning around to face him. "You own me, don't ya'?! You's my masta', ain't ya'?!" Her voice echoed with just as much fire as his. There was finally no denying her anger as she began punishing him with her words the way he had silently begged her to do. "You demand what you want of me, and I'm always to oblige with a respectful answa'! Ain't that the way it is now?!"

"I don't *own* you, Lily!"

"Six in one hand, half a dozen in the otha'!"

"What the hell's that s'pposed to mean?!"

"It's all the same! You may not have paid for me, but I still ain't nothin' but the subservient little toy yo' daddy bought for you to play with all them years ago!"

"My *subservient toy*?! You know goddamn good 'n well I ain't neva' thought 'a you like that!"

"Could 'a fooled me! 'Cause you always been awful good at *playin'* with me," she said smugly, putting her hands on her hips. "Hell, sometimes I think if I wasn't able to play piano you'd've neva' botha'd to say anotha' kind word to me eva' again!"

"You don't believe that!"

"Well, what else am I s'pposed to believe, huh?! It seems awful strange that afta' all these years, you find out I can play, and suddenly you treatin' me nice and talkin' nice to me. Then tonight, afta' you and William make all that money, you go right back to snappin' at me the way you used to!"

"You think this is about usin' you to make money?!" James asked, truly in shock that she would say such a thing.

"Elijah told me 'bout that article … The one 'bout you usin' me to make money!"

That fact seared James's insides and added another layer to his hatred for the man. "You can't possibly believe those ridiculous lies!"

"What I can't believe is how foolish I've been all this time! It all makes so much sense now!"

"Lily, I *asked* you if this was what *you* wanted! I neva' *forced* you to do any of this!"

"More than one way to get what you want!"

"None of this was eva' about *me* or about what *I* want!"

"Please just stop!" She threw a hand up. "I swear I don't know what to believe outta you anymore!"

"Come on, Lily! You know me!"

"Do I?!" she fired back. "'Cause the James I thought I knew was kind and gentle! He didn't go 'round beatin' folks up! A-and tellin' lies! Or-or gettin' arrested!" she scoffed. "So, it sure as hell feels like I don't know who the hell you are anymore!" She gave him a look that conveyed how serious she was and then abruptly turned back around toward the fireplace when she felt her tears stirring.

"Yes, you do!" James said, taking her by the arm and spinning her back around to look at him.

"NO! I DON'T!" she screamed. "The James I knew was the only person who eva' made me feel like I's free wheneva' we's togetha'!" She yanked her arm from his grip. "THE JAMES I KNEW WAS MY *BEST FRIEND*!" she cried out, suddenly breaking down into heavy sobs. "H-he was my *only* friend," she whispered, through a sea of now falling tears. "He was all I had … Y-you were all I had, James," she admitted. "But before you left all them years ago, you treated me like I's nothin'!" She wept while penetrating his eyes with hers so that he truly understood the depth of the misery he had caused her. "And then you just … you just abandoned me like I ain't eva' mean a damn thing to you!"

James realized right then and there that what had happened at the theater that night was only the tip of the iceberg. It was clear that Lily was tired of holding on to anger that had raged in the pit of her stomach for far too long. In her sudden verbal assault, she was unleashing years of deeply buried, repressed emotions that had been dug up after a week of extreme anxieties surrounding the show, days of worrying about what had happened to him, and fears that perhaps he had left her again. All of that compounded with his outburst in the back halls of Branaugh was enough to trigger the explosive tirade he was now witnessing. Despite feeling he deserved it, Lily's volatile verbal attack cut James deep, so deep that his eyes began to well with tears. He fought hard to hold them back, but the more she spoke, the more they threatened to fall, and the stronger his urge grew to silence her. He was not yet ready to see years of tears pouring from her eyes, nor hear the words of what his betrayal had done to her, words filled with so much anger, disappointment, and pain that he struggled to understand her as she spoke. James always knew at some point that he would have to address the things about their past, but had hoped that it would be on his terms, when he had emotionally prepared himself. This was certainly not that time, and his response to her outpouring undoubtedly reflected that fact. "What was I supposed to do, huh!?" he fired back. "I had nothin'! I had no money! No job! *Nothin*'! Whateva' could I have done for you?!" He gave a sarcastic laugh, running his hands through his loose locks. "As ironic and as twisted as it may sound, my fatha' could offa' you a betta' life than I could at the time," he laughed sarcastically again at that notion. "If anything, I left home to go and make somethin' of myself, to come back with two strong legs and two strong arms to carry you outta' that *prison* my fatha' had you in! So despite what it seems Lily, I didn't *abandon* you!"

"I ain't mean abandon in the physical sense," she replied in a much softer tone as she wiped the remaining tears from her face. "Emotionally, though, that's sho' what it felt like to me."

"I'm sorry I made you feel that way and for the way I left everything. And Lord knows, I could neva' be more sorry for the way I treated you all those years. If I could take it all back, I swear I would, but please trust that I neva' behaved that way to hurt you. As difficult as it may be to believe, the things I did were for a good reason."

"*Good reason*?!" Lily scoffed. "Talkin' mean to me, lookin' at me like I disgusted you, makin' me feel that you hated me was for a *good reason*?" she asked, looking at him as if he had lost his mind.

"I was tryna to protect you! In the best way I knew how!"

"I didn't want no damn protection! I wanted my friend!"

"Trust me! You needed it!"

"Needed it for what, huh?! 'Cause the only person I felt like I suddenly needed protectin' from at the time was *you*!"

James glossed over Lily's question, not ever willing to give her the ugly reality of that answer. But the true reasons instantly made him recall the horrific memories and graphic nightmares they had created since then. "You have no idea the things I was goin' through back then, Lily! I was young and foolish, and I admit that I didn't know how to handle it. I know I could've done things betta', but…"

"Whateva' it was, we could 'a figured things out *togetha*', the way we *always* did," she interrupted, "We were a team. You know you could've trusted me enough to tell me what was goin' on."

"No! Not this!"

"But we used to tell each otha' everything."

"You mean like the way you told me about the fact you played piano?"

"That ain't fair!" she yelled, with fire returning to her voice. "You can't possibly compare the two!"

"Maybe not, but the point is that I'm not the only guilty party here! We both had our secrets, for whateva' our own good reasons. And as for me, I can certainly say that none of those reasons had anything to do with me intentionally tryna abandon you emotionally, or in any otha' way for that matta'. Nor was I tryna make you feel small!"

"You really s'pect me to believe that afta' you's so hell-bent on remindin' everybody in that hallway tonight what I am to you!"

"And just what is that?!"

"Nothin' but your damn property!"

"GODDAMN IT LILY, YOU'RE EVERYTHING TO ME!" The ferocity in his voice immediately shot her verbal assault down. She stood there frozen. The crackling of the fireplace was the only sound in the room for a moment. "Absolutely *everything*," he added softly. "Can't you see that?" he asked with conviction in his tone.

Despite the plea in his voice, Lily struggled to find the words to respond.

"Lily, I swear to you, it wasn't my intent to make you feel that way in front of everybody in that hallway tonight, it's just that I couldn't handle it anymore!"

"Handle *what*?!" she asked, looking confused.

"ELIJAH!" he erupted again.

"*Elijah*?!" Lily repeated, once again looking thoroughly perplexed. "What in the hell does he have to do with anything?!"

"*Everything*! I swear, seein' you in that man's arms tonight 'bout near drove me mad!" James fired back quickly through gritted teeth. "Watchin' him with his arms all ova' you!" A look of disgust overcame his expressions as if the image of it was affecting him all over again. "I hated it! Makes me sick on the inside! The way he looks at you! Way he touches you! Way he talks to you! Way he smiles at you! I don't like *any* of it!" He balled his fists up, wishing now that he had hit him when he had the opportunity. "He's been cravin' you since he laid eyes on you, and I'm tellin' you, I just couldn't handle it anymore!"

Lily's mouth fell open. She furrowed her eyebrows and scolded James with her eyes. She tilted her head and looked at him like he was an immature little boy who was in the midst of a tantrum. "So all this is about you bein' *jealous*?!" she asked with disbelief in her tone.

"NO! *THIS*!" he said, pointing his finger toward the ground, "is about the fact that, no matta' how fast I try to run, or how many damn excuses I make, or-or where I try to hide, and no matta' how many lies I've told myself, I can't get this-this feelin' to go away!" He pointed to his chest. "I just … I can't make it quit," he admitted, sounding frustrated by the notion. "*This* is about admittin' to myself that I don't want you in no otha' man's arms … goddamn it, I want you in *mine*! 'Cause no matta' what I do, Lily, I swear to God, I can't get myself to quit lovin' you!"

The wounding words Lily had locked and loaded suddenly faded away, along with the angry expression on her face. She took a moment to search her racing mind to express the truth about how his words initially made her feel, but her thoughts simply spiraled out of control. "Y-you don't mean that," she finally brought herself to say, taking a step backward as if she wanted to get away from his words. "You don't mean it," she insisted again, truly not wanting to accept him or anything he had to say.

"You just don't wanna believe that I mean it. You wanna deny it. I know all too well about that. It'll get ya' nowhere … Trust me," he said, as he began to walk toward her, never once taking his eyes off of her.

"No! You're a liar! Th-this is just some damn illusion you tryna create to get me to keep doin' what you want," she said, thinking of Elijah's story and the contents of the newspaper article. She continued her retreat while staring James up and down like he was some strange man she had never met before.

"Lily," James said softly. "I would neva' lie to you about somethin' like this," he tried to assure her. He continued to stalk toward her like she was his prey and nothing, not her words, nor her objection to his presence would stop him. He preyed on her until he had backed her into a corner. "But go on," he said calmly, standing so close to her now that she could see every detail of his face and feel the heat of his breath against her skin. "Go on and unleash whateva' you have to. Don't shut down and shut me out anymore. Yell at me, hit me, let it out. All your anga', all your frustrations … just let it all go, right here, right now. I know I deserve it. Go on and finish openin' up all the old wounds I caused you, and then give me the chance to heal 'em right this time."

Lily refused to respond and drew her arms up to her chest as if that would somehow stop him from his current attempt at painstakingly removing the bricks from her imaginary protective emotional wall.

Her defensive movement did nothing to stop James, however. He took her arms and gently moved them back down. "Do what you need to, to flush it all outta your soul and make room for me to be close to you. Let me in again, Lily … *Please*," he begged of her.

Lily's continued silence and her attempt at defending her barrier was futile. James pressed on with verbally tearing it down. He refused to be derailed in any way, praying silently that this time around, instead of a wall, his words would encourage her to want to rebuild the once unbreakable bond between them.

"I know you feel like I don't deserve it anymore, but I

375

swear I'll do anything to be worthy of bein' called your best friend again. 'Cause, even afta' everything that's happened, I ain't neva' once stop considerin' you as mine," James confessed.

Not able to handle the intensity of his proximity or his words, Lily began to tremble and simply had to look away after no longer being able to face the sea of blue that was trained on her. But yet again, despite her continued emotional retreat, James was undeterred in using his words to draw her in, feeling as though it was now his turn to be the one releasing what he had held onto for years.

"You're the only reason I eva' set foot back on my fatha's farm again," he confessed. "I hate that place. I hate everything it stands for. But *you* … I've *always* loved you. Loved you from the very first day I eva' met you. Since then, you've always been the center of my world, Lily. Everything I say, everything I do, my thoughts, my every decision revolves around you. And I swear, I would 'a died first before I let you live out the rest of your days in that hell there with my fatha'."

Lily still lacked the willpower to return James's gaze. Her eyes remained fixed on the floor as she blinked away the few tears that emerged after his bold confession. "I wish you would 'a told me these things back then," she finally said, with not an ounce of fight left in her voice. "It would 'a left me with so much hope … instead 'a so much pain. You hurt me, James. You crushed my world, and I hated you for it," she admitted, as another tear trickled down the side of her face.

"I know," James continued, after the sting of her words subsided. "But I swear to you…" He gently lifted her face toward him. "It wasn't a day that went by all them years that every part of me didn't hurt without you too, Lily." The sudden rush of emotions caused his voice to crack. "Felt like I was dyin' on the inside without you," he admitted, slowly running the back of his fingers down the side of

Lily's face.

Although James had yet to shed a tear, Lily could hear weeping in the sound of his voice and in the strength of his words. With the blend of such sentiment, not only did her mind finally comprehend his sincerity but her body did as well. James's genuine outpouring and the intensity with which he still continued to look at Lily suddenly ignited a feeling of warmth all over her as butterflies began to dance in her stomach.

"Tell me that you've neva' felt it…" James continued, with his lips so close to Lily that they grazed her skin. "How much I loved you back then…" he whispered, unable to resist the intense desire to gently kiss her forehead. "How much I *still* love you."

"Don't … Please, don't," Lily instinctively replied in an effort to protect herself again. At the same time, though, she could not find the power to pull herself away or deny how good the way his touch made her feel.

"Tell me that you've *neva'* felt anything for me." James placed his hands on either side of Lily's face to be sure she would not turn away. "Go on," he dared her, while their eyes were locked on each other. "Lie to me." He could feel her trembling and hear that her breathing had deepened, but she refused to acknowledge him. "Go on," he prompted her again, running the back of his hand down the side of her face again to calm her, then tracing his finger along the outside of her lips. "Lie to me … tell me that you don't love me." He paused and waited, but once again Lily remained silent. "Tell me," he demanded again, continuing to gently trace the outline of her lips. "Tell me right here and right now, and I'll walk away and neva' look back," he promised, caressing her face and watching her carefully as he waited patiently for her response.

"I … I'm scared," was all Lily could bring herself to say while she searched for comfort in the sea of blue that were gazing so lovingly at her, a gaze that exponentially drove the warmth she felt inside to a level she had never felt before in times past.

"I know," James acknowledged, still holding lightly to the sides of her face. "But I wanna take all of that away and make you feel whole again. I wanna heal you, heal *us* … I wanna make you feel free with me again," he whispered.

Those last words instantly ignited another sea of intense tears, which meant more to James than Lily's words ever could. To see such a response trailing from her eyes drove his desire to comfort and console her to another level, to a place that would certainly no longer leave the lines between them blurred. With no reservations or hesitation, James moved slowly down, and after years of wanting, finally tasted the sweetness of Lily's lips as she continued to weep. Lily did not attempt to pull away from his grasp nor beg him to stop this time. She offered no resistance at all, only acceptance, and the parting of her lips to allow James further inside. He moaned after she granted him access to delve deeper, caressing her tongue gently and slowly with his, taking his time to savor a simple moment that he had envisioned for over a decade.

After reveling the sweet taste of Lily's mouth, James reluctantly pulled back, feeling the need to study her facial expressions for any signs of fear, or hurt, or disapproval of his actions. He wanted to be sure that the mutuality of the moment was not just his imagination running away with him or that he was taking more than Lily wanted him to. He would take his own life before violating her in such a way. James then wiped away Lily's remaining tears. Much to his delight, he found that her river of sadness had finally stopped its flow and that his worries were unwarranted. He saw nothing but pure satisfaction written on Lily's face and finally sensed that calmness had overtaken her body.

James had certainly read Lily well. The outpouring of his decade-old secrets, his patience, and even his jealousy, had affected her deeply. But ultimately, it was the combination of the undeniable love she felt in the passion of his kiss and the way he now looked at her with such warmth and adoration that immediately ceased Lily's tears and laid her fears to rest. Sharing his genuine emotions had finally broken through her wall and left her completely vulnerable. Realizing her vulnerability, James pledged silently to himself to never take advantage of how Lily had graciously opened herself up to him or ever to take for granted the honor of being close to her again.

"There you are," James smiled, after looking at Lily and seeing that the veil of fear and doubt that shrouded her had finally been lifted, revealing the look of innocence in her features that he adored so much. "Beautiful Lily," he whispered, running his hand slowly down the length of her thick, dark hair, suddenly remembering how her beauty had shocked him into speechlessness just moments before her very first performance.

Lily closed her eyes and reveled in James's touch, the sound of his voice, and the sentiment of his words, which led her desires to begin guiding her actions. She leaned toward him, seeking that connection with him again, that feeling of contentment when his lips were pressed against hers. She was like an instant addict, searching for the instantaneous high she had felt the first time he touched her in that way, expressing his feelings for her so loud and clear, yet, in such a silent and pleasurable manner.

Lily's actions were the finality that James had been patiently awaiting. The simple motion of her lips closing in on his was reassurance that they indeed possessed a mutual wanting for one another. It all allowed James to relax completely and turn his attention back to the sweetness of lips he had waited years to taste. He now felt free to proceed with expressing his feelings for Lily without words, without guilt, and without the potential of regret.

It was Lily this time who moaned when James invaded her mouth. This time, their kiss was drawn out, with not a single moment of stopping or hesitating at first. It was slow and deep, filled with passion, warmth, and the indisputable love that Lily had felt there the time before. After a while, James then pulled back from time to time to suck on Lily's swollen lips, taking each gently into his mouth one-by-one before diving deep to dance yet again with her tongue. The long overdue passionate exchange that had only lived in Lily's daydreams until that moment, sent every vision, every craving, and every fantasy she ever had about James crashing to the forefront of her mind, inflaming her body with desire. The dark abyss between her thighs began pulsating with want, aching to be filled, and preparing for an already much-needed eruption.

James's mind and body were unanimously in sync with Lily's. Only seconds in and the heat of Lily's breath, the feel of her soft skin, her touch, her embrace, the way her lips moved, the look of lust on her face, every outward expression of her want and desire for him, left a certain part of his body aching in desperate need of explosive satisfaction.

As difficult as it was for him, James stopped kissing Lily, took her by the hand, and guided her back across the room near the warmth of the fireplace. The light enhanced the flawlessness of her features, making James just want to smile at her for a moment. He then placed both hands on either side of her face and kissed her forehead again, trailing his lips downward from there toward her ear and then tenderly guiding them down the side of her neck. His gentle touch was causing her breath to catch and goose bumps to rise from the pleasurable sensation each kiss brought to her highly stimulated body. While James continued to delight Lily's skin, he reached behind her and began unbuttoning her dress, but felt her body tense when the buttons were all undone. He stopped altogether after sensing the change in Lily's disposition. He pulled back to look at her, wanting to be sure that he was not forcing her to go any further than she felt comfortable going. "You okay?" he asked, looking at her with an expression of great concern.

Lily's breathing quickened. She held her loosened dress in place and looked away without a word.

"Lily?"

Still, she did not speak nor would she look at James.

He then took her face gently and turned her toward him. "What is it?"

"I-I ain't neva' did this before," she hesitantly admitted as her heart began to race from the sudden feeling of embarrassment.

James was already as hard as steel but had he not been, Lily's words would have just done the job. Hearing that no other man had ever been inside of her was like the beautiful melodies of her symphonies to his ears. He did not take her confession lightly. He felt honored to know that she would allow him to be the first, and if he had it his way, the *only* man to ever have access to her hidden treasures. Being her first, James now wanted to be sure that he treated Lily as delicately as the flower that her name represented, yet ensure that her first time was even more unforgettable than all of the other firsts they had experienced in their lives together. With that as his goal, he placed his forehead against Lily's and caressed her face again with his hands. "I'll be gentle ... I promise," he whispered, in an effort to soothe her.

Lily nodded her head. "I-I trust you," she replied, her lips quivering from the sudden onset of nervousness.

Again, James took great honor in hearing those words and wanted to do everything in his power to maintain the trust that Lily had just bestowed up on him. He, therefore, slowed the pace, feeling that perhaps disrobing her in front of the firelight in the middle of an open space would be too much, far too soon. Instead, he picked her up and carried her in his arms over to the bed, taking his time on the way there, never once breaking eye contact with her as he gently laid her down. Seeing Lily lying there prepared to give herself to him completely, James's heart began to beat like a wild stampede against his chest as he grew even more anxious to be inside of her. He sat down next to her and ran his hand slowly down the length of her arm, examining what he felt was a beautiful contrast in their skin tones. He then intertwined his fingers with hers and raised the back of her hand to his lips to kiss it. "I'll take my time," he promised.

Lily nodded her head. "I know," she replied, still feeling nervous despite the fact that she truly did trust him.

James stared at the lusciousness of Lily's full lips as the words escaped and then descended down on them, needing to taste them again after already feeling the withdrawals of not having them against his. Wanting to allow her to relax again, he left her clothes alone for the time being and resumed relishing with his mouth the areas of her body that were visible. He returned first to her neck, softly tickling her delicate skin with his tongue. With such gentleness in the tender touch of his lips, it did not take long for James to feel the tension leaving Lily's body again. When it did, he began to trail his way down to the bare skin of her cleavage, letting his hands and lips linger there for a while. As James basked there, enjoying the suppleness of her womanhood, he reached up and gingerly slid the strap of Lily's dress down onto her arm. He moved up and kissed the shoulder he had just uncovered and, at the same time, slid the strap even further down, revealing the fullness of her breast. He glided his lips and his tongue across her skin, from her shoulder all the way to her dark, hardened nipple, encircling it again and again, before fully devouring it in his mouth, invoking an audible sound of delight from Lily immediately thereafter. The other strap of Lily's clothing followed suit, soon leaving both of her breasts exposed and free for the luxury of James's eyes and for his tongue to enjoy. He consumed each one like a much-needed appetizer before his main course, sending shock waves of heat to Lily's southern region, setting ablaze the pool of moisture between her thighs.

After savoring Lily's breasts thoroughly for a time and enjoying the sweet sound of her soft moans, James moved further on in his descent, nipping at her midsection through the silk fibers of her dress, slowly pulling it off of her as he descended, revealing inch by inch the artistic lines of her body. Like he was unveiling a priceless gem, he took his time along the way, gently kissing each section of her skin that he uncovered as his way of welcoming it to the wonderment of his eyes. Once Lily's abdomen was fully exposed, James then feathered light kisses across it, hoping to distract her mind with constant pleasure as he continued to unleash the hidden parts of her body. And just as he had hoped, with each soft brush of his lips against her skin, Lily continued to react physically and verbally in a way that let him know that she was thoroughly enjoying his efforts. Feeling and hearing that his attempts to soothe her were working, James carried on in that fashion and soon uncovered enough of Lily to find himself at the outline of her right hip. He could not help but tickle it with his tongue, gliding it the entire way across her curvacious line, evoking a slight bit of sensual laughter from her, at which he smiled before christening it with a kiss like every other part of her skin. For such a lovely part of her anatomy, however, he moved in a very lax manner, wanting his lips and tongue to have the pleasure of memorizing the curvature of Lily's womanly design.

While his tongue roamed from hip to hip across Lily's tightly toned abdomen, James had worked her dress far below her waistline. He stopped, however, when his hands came in contact with the inside of her thighs. The feeling of the elevated heat radiating from between them caused him to ache with a sudden and intense need to bury himself deep inside of her. In an instant, he pulled the rest of her dress away and dropped it to the floor. He struggled hard at that moment to maintain his composure, fighting the urge to unleash himself and slide immediately between her folds until every bit of his hardness was immersed within her.

James's composure quickly returned, however, when he looked up from the floor where Lily's dress was lying, and his eyes fell onto the landscape of the exquisitely sculptured masterpiece in front of him. He sat on his knees between her legs, frozen in place, mesmerized, as his eyes glided over every detail of the voluptuous curves of Lily's nude body in awe. Touching her as delicately as a rare and precious treasure, James ran his hands slowly up the outside of her thighs all the way to her hips, across her stomach, along the side of her waist, and then traced his fingers across her breasts before leaning down and pressing his lips lightly to her abdomen. Lily closed her eyes and moaned as he then pressed them to each of her breasts. James rose up thereafter and moved his mouth to her neck and then, at last, tasted her lips again before pulling back to gaze at the unique artistry of her alluring figure once more. "You. Are. *Perfection*," he whispered, the truth of his words evident by the way his eyes continued to glide appreciatively over the elegance of Lily's heavenly physique.

As James sat there hypnotized, continuing to imprint the images of Lily's naked body into his mind, his hands began gliding back down her sensuous frame. With a need to feel the heat that lingered there again, he eagerly slid them down to the fragile skin on the inside of Lily's thighs. Wanting desperately for his lips to be seared by the fire emanating from between them, James began to make a slow descent down below. It was hard to tear his eyes away from such a magnificent view, but he found that the exchange was well worth it after he felt the heat of Lily's skin singeing his lips. He felt rewarded even further after

384

planting his very first warm and inviting kiss on the inside of her thigh and feeling her legs shudder from the pleasure.

James was still in no rush as he began trailing kisses from one of Lily's legs to the other on his way north, wanting to be sure that no parts of her delicate skin were neglected. As he approached Lily's dark abyss, though, delicate kisses turned into wet and hungry suckling of her skin. He stopped just shy of tasting her opening, closed his eyes, and inhaled her intoxicating scent. His voracious appetite came alive the moment it enveloped his nose. With great urgency, his mouth quickly engulfed her hidden jewel, suckling it from its hiding spot and nestling it in between his lips. The shocking gasp, followed by the raspy purr that escaped Lily immediately thereafter, made James drool with delectable contentment and milked drops of impatiently waiting semen from within him.

Lily's fingers had been the only thing to penetrate her warmth until the moment James moved down from her pearl and began a slow invasion into her opening with his tongue, moaning in satisfaction as he tasted the sweetness of her insides for the very first time. Lily was completely ignorant to such things but quickly found his actions provocative and extraordinarily satisfying. As the pleasure began to invade every nerve in her body, she completely relaxed, and her legs fell further apart. She instinctively arched her back, thrust herself toward James's mouth, and amassed her hands in his hair to ensure that he did not stop the sudden wave of pleasure that was rolling through her too soon.

James was pleasing her in a way that he had refused to please other women in his past, wanting to wait and share that level of intimacy with only Lily. He wanted to fine-tune his taste buds for her and taste the sweetness of her insides on his tongue long after the experience had ended. For years, James was yearning to permanently implant the scent and flavor of the only woman he had ever loved in his memory forever. And he certainly continued to devour Lily in a way that told the truth of those desires.

As the sounds of Lily's panting began to rise, James submerged his tongue deep within her, ravenously lapping her internal walls, eating her like a decadent, fulfilling dessert. He suddenly withdrew his tongue and licked her from her opening to her highly sensitive, engorged, protruding nub and then back down again, immersing his tongue deep inside of her all over again. He was heightening Lily's pleasure, then pulling it back, teasing her until she was dripping with silky wetness. Knowing that her body was now more than ready, James then glided a single finger deep inside of her. He slid it gently in and out, guiding it upward to Lily's sensitive hot spot, tickling it while his lips remained suctioned tightly around her pearl. When Lily suddenly began thrusting her hips in rhythm with his movements, James went from one finger to two. The added pleasure quickly ignited Lily's nether region. Within mere seconds, her lips and legs began to quiver, her stomach clenched, and her back arched high off of the bed. She then suddenly gripped her hands tighter in James's hair and cried out his name in a heated tone while unleashing a stream of orgasmic juices flowing hard and fast down into his mouth. James did not pull back, but instead drank mercilessly from her like a man in a state of severe dehydration, sucking her until every drop spilled from within her, even after he felt her body relax and her moaning begin to subside. Still lost in the exuberance of the explosive ending, Lily lay there with her eyes closed, stroking James's hair gently, silently thanking him for an unbelievably erotic eruption, unlike anything she had ever felt. Even her fingers had never taken her there.

After James had gotten his fill and he was certain that Lily was completely satisfied by the first wave of pleasure, he retracted his fingers from within her and lifted his head to look at her. "You taste so sweet," he confessed, sucking her warm internal creams from each finger in plain view of her eyes. Lily's mouth fell open at the sight of it. She was mystified and turned on by his actions, loving the way that he indulged exotically in the contents of her body.

James sat up when he was finished and took off his shirt. Lily's eyes widened again as she marveled at the definition in his chiseled chest and at every muscle in his abdomen that protruded from underneath his skin. She reached up and guided her hands across his torso, having always wanted to know how every ripple in his body would feel, especially after seeing him working shirtless on the stage out in the fields. She, too, found herself closing her eyes and memorizing every curve, cut, and hard aspect of James's manly build. While storing the blueprint of his rock-solid chest and arms away in her mind, Lily's body began to ache and moisten for James all over again.

James looked down at Lily as she stroked his skin, feeling pleased at how quickly she had relaxed. He loved that she did not seem the least bit shy about touching his body or about the fact that she was now nude. He would have been proud to learn that the sudden absence of Lily's timidness was the result of his lips gently touching every aspect of her unexplored skin. His patience, the look of awe on his face when he gazed at her, his genuine words, and ultimately the explosive release his lips had just given her had completely dispelled how awkward Lily felt at first. The combination of it all had freed her of the self-consciousness that initially plagued her, helping her to quickly let go of the meek and shy girl who was trembling with nervousness near the fireplace over the mere thought of removing her clothing. In a handful of significantly meaningful minutes, James simply had Lily's mind and body floating in a tranquil place, ready for yet another round of ecstasy.

Lily finally opened her eyes and let them absorb the sight of James's perfectly carved frame up close again.

While she gazed at him, her hands wandered all the way up his chest, onto the sides of the shadowy whiskers on his face, and through his hair. She then glided her finger across his moist, reddened lips, wanting to feel the very things that had just elevated her body into the clouds. The lingering memory and the aftershocks of her eruption left her with an insatiable desire to live out years of graphic dreams that she had had about this magical man. That undying desire from her dreams to make James soar came roaring to life and suddenly took full control of her actions. She wrapped her arms around his neck, pulled him down to her, and entangled her tongue hungrily with his, wanting to taste herself on his lips. From there, she ran her tongue down the side of his neck, up to his ear, and began suckling on his lobe. Lily was just eager to have her lips on any part of James, needing to touch and taste more of the man who had just indulged in her in the most exotic of ways. But more than anything, she was ready to reward him with the heat of her tight, wet flesh constricted, unrelentingly, around every inch of his manhood. "I wanna feel you inside of me," she whispered seductively in his ear.

Lily's words induced a deep barbaric moan from James. He let out yet another carnivorous growl when she then pushed him up, glided her hands back down his abdomen, and unbuckled his belt. Her outward, fearless craving for him had his member pulsating in desperate need of climactic deliverance. After his buckle was undone, James immediately descended again and began planting succulent kisses along Lily's inner thighs while hastily loosening his pants, feeling as though he could not free himself quick enough. He then ascended back up, continuing to kiss Lily along the way while crawling from his trousers until he was completely out of them. As his lips made their way up her body this time around, though, the knowledge of Lily's starvation for him had turned the heat up inside of James. He had morphed into a greedy madman as he navigated north around the curves of Lily's body, sucking and kissing savagely on every part of her skin that his lips encountered. James's cannibalistic appetite and the feel of his naked hardness gliding along the inside of her thighs sent even more blood and heated moisture rushing down to Lily's nether region, preparing her for an erection that her body was now begging to feel. Her eyes, her heavy panting, her words all spoke loudly of that desire and hungrily welcomed James. After making his way back up to her face, James could easily see that hunger in Lily's eyes. He sensed no resistance and no objection from Lily whatsoever, but still, he wanted to be absolutely certain. "If you need me to stop, I will ... I promise," he whispered while tenderly caressing her face.

"I won't want you to," Lily assured him, her words escaping more like the sound of her light and airy moans.

The confidence in Lily's words sent heated shockwaves through James's body, causing semen to now drip in steady spurts from his flooded, hardened flesh. His aching manhood now pulsed and waited in unforgiving agony just a hairsbreadth away from Lily's uncharted abyss. Despite the throbbing pain, James wanted to enter her for the first time with loving patience, wanting to take great care of the precious gift that the woman he loved was about to give him. Passionately, he covered Lily's mouth with another hungry kiss as he took his hand and centered himself, preparing to glide himself inside of her. Cautiously, James thrust his hips forward. The tip of his manhood was then set aflame with an intense, piercing pleasure as it slowly and carefully parted Lily's tight, silky virgin skin. But as the feeling consumed him, Lily broke their kiss and let out a gasp of pain, blended with the sweet sound of a pleasure-filled moan. Not yet fully inside of her, James paused and looked at Lily with great concern. "You okay?" he asked, caring more about not hurting her than with his own pleasure.

"Please, don't stop," she begged in a raspy, lust-driven tone. Lily was determined to push through any painful sensations, especially after James had already given her a glimpse of the exhilaration that was soon to come.

Satisfied by the conviction in Lily's tone, James continued on. He kissed her tenderly again to distract her from any more pain before gently sliding himself further inside of her. His eyes closed and his mouth parted instinctively when the tightness of Lily's insides fully enveloped him. Finally feeling James submerged deep within the warmth of her velvety folds, a pleasurable tsunami flooded Lily's body, and she let out a deep groan of passionate contentment. "Myyy God," James moaned in unison with her, after his body nearly shot straight to the pinnacle of pleasure.

For longer than he could remember, James had fantasized about this very moment, this opportunity to please Lily and satisfy her in every way that he knew how. Just like in those vivid daydreams, here he was, finally lying inside of the only woman he had ever loved, but fearing now that he would erupt inside of her before he even had the chance to move. How James felt within Lily, just lying there between the warmth and wetness of her thighs, he could not put into words. The euphoria was unlike any other pleasure that had ever coursed through his body. The feel of her eclipsed his dreams, his fantasies, and all that he thought was possible in reality. Having been intoxicated by her scent, her warmth, the taste of her, and the sound of her breathy cries had overwhelmed his senses in a way that he was unprepared for, in a way that he had never experienced before with any others from his past. With the culmination of it all, James knew that maintaining his control and preventing a quick, explosive eruption of climactic pleasure within the silky heat and wetness of his beloved woman was truly going to take an act of God. And so while within her, stroking slowly and tenderly, James began praying, begging God not to let his body prematurely betray him as he attempted to express his love for Lily without words.

James prayed hard, but it was simply the look on Lily's face that finally settled him. It was a look that thanked him for the hedonic tidal waves that were beginning to roll blissfully through her body. At that moment, James realized that all he ever truly needed to do was focus on her lovely features while he was inside of her. It was that beautiful, intense look on her face and in her eyes that he wanted to keep there. It motivated him to keep her riding on her wave, rising, and climbing until every nerve within her was ignited in the same immense pleasure that had caused him to break down and pray, that damn near had him on the verge of tears.

James moved delicately inside of Lily, at first, covering her mouth in deep, slow, and fiery kisses throughout every stroke. Lily fell under the spell of his profound affections and, suddenly, any and all pain was overshadowed by the euphoria she felt while he rode passionately through the tight cavern of her body. "Jaaames," she sang in a velvety tone after his soft stroking began pushing her body faster up its blissful ascent.

The sound of his name escaping Lily's lips fueled James's desire to make this moment last for her, to ensure that she did not ever regret allowing him to be the first man inside of her. He found even more strength when he saw Lily's eyes roll back and her eyelids darken her world. He marveled at the sight of her slightly parted lips and the overall look of gratification on her face, like she had just been welcomed into a heavenly realm. James felt proud to have taken her to that world, a world in which he prayed that Lily was feeling completely free in.

In response to his slow and loving patience, Lily spread her legs even wider to welcome even more of James into her. At that moment, the pair began reading and feeding off of each other, one understanding what the other needed as if they had made love in another life, merging physically just as naturally as their souls had as children. They moved in sync as their sweat-slicked bodies glided erotically across one another in perfect rhythm and harmony, all of which was illuminated beautifully by the flickering firelight nearby.

Manifested within every stroke into her body, was an emotion or feeling that James wished to silently communicate with Lily. His efforts proved not to be in vain. In every kiss, in every gentle touch, in every soft glide between Lily's folds, she could feel the sincerity of James's apologies and the confession of his love for her radiating through every inch of her body. Over and over again, Lily was absorbing and relishing in every anguished emotion that James had attempted to convey to her that night and throughout the years. It was because of those silent, sincere, impassioned confessions that Lily's tears began to fall and her angelic moans began to rise. Hearing her reaction, James gently buried himself even further within her, hastening his strokes and turning Lily's breathy moans into guttural cries of elation. The heat he created within her began to rage, and she buried her nails into James's back. Her body began begging for mercy and yet more of him at the same time. Pumping her hips up toward James, meeting him thrust for thrust, Lily arched her back, her insides tightened, clenched, and erupted violently, covering the length of him in her juices. She then cried out his name again like a sultry song as the elation of pure pleasure rippled throughout her entire body.

The look on Lily's face was a luxurious treat for James's eyes and the sound of his name erupting from her in that lascivious tone brought joy to his ears. The beautiful combination ultimately gave him the freedom to finally let go too. His body rewarded him with a long, intense, soul-piercing climax that tensed every muscle within him and reverberated into every inch of his being. He let out a guttural groan of overwhelming gratification as he ejaculated hard into Lily, pumping his seed deep within her womb before collapsing weakened and limp on top of her.

The pleasurable sensations were pleasantly drawn out for both of them, taking its sweet time to secede from the tips of their nerves. They breathed heavily in sync as they made their long descent from the heavens together, their chests rising and falling in perfect rhythm. While lying there waiting to catch his breath, James began kissing Lily's forehead lightly and caressing her face. "Are you alright?" he asked her when he was finally able.

Lily did not reply. Instead, James felt a tear trickle onto his hand.

"Are you cryin'?" he asked, suddenly fearing that he had hurt her in some way. He shifted to move his weight off of her, but she stopped him.

"Please, don't move," Lily begged, holding on to James even tighter. "Stay here inside 'a me. Just a little while longa' … Please?"

"I'm here," James assured her, continuing to caress her face and run his hands through her hair. "Let me in, Lily … Please," he whispered, wanting to know the secrets of her thoughts at that very moment. "Tell me what you're feelin'?"

"Free," she said through her tears. "I feel free when you're inside 'a me."

James closed his eyes tight, trying desperately to fight back the sudden rush of emotions that threatened to surge forward through them. He kissed Lily softly in response and let his lips linger on hers for a moment while he lay there content to be inside of her for as long as she needed him to be.

"I ain't neva' felt nothin' like this before in my life," Lily said after they had lain there for a while and James's comforts had helped her tears to subside.

James kissed her again before slowly rolling off of her. From behind, he pulled Lily toward him, molded his body next to hers, and wrapped his arms tightly around her. "That's what it feels like to be loved," he whispered in her ear, caressing her gently, hoping to still convey his feelings for her through his touch.

Soothed and relaxed by the feel of James molded against her, Lily fell into a slumber not long after that. As she lay there, James continued his nightly tradition of watching her sleep, but this time with the honor of holding her close and kissing her soft, bare skin lightly from time to time. He then fell into a sound and peaceful sleep of his own unlike any other his body had ever allowed him in his adult life—one that was completely free from the nightmares that usually plagued him. It was a feat that only proved possible with Lily nestled lovingly in the protection of his arms: the place where James finally had the courage to admit that he had wanted Lily for years.

Chapter Twenty

THE NEW YORK TIMES
SUNDAY NOVEMBER 13, 1859

The Dream Symphony

The Critically Acclaimed
Visual and Musical Showpiece
Playing
One Night Only
at
Winter Garden Theater
Christmas, 6 pm.
Tickets now on sale

December 1859

A stunning photo of Lily seated at a grand piano with the image of a floating, shadowed angel in the background accompanied that short *New York Times* front page listing. Within twenty-four hours of hitting newsstands, at three times the normal ticket price, *The Dream Symphony* had completely sold out at Winter Garden, the most prestigious theater in the United States.

In the beginning, Landon Von Brandt had helped clear the path for the journey that had led the show to this point, using his clever, relentless strategies. On this occasion, however, he did not have to haggle with the coordinators of the theater, using passive-aggressive verbal exchanges, or dig into incriminating documents in hopes of having Lily perform there. Instead, it was the powers that be at Winter Garden who extended an invitation to Lily after her show quickly proved itself to be the powerhouse that it was. They simply could not pass up on the opportunity to welcome

395

Lily with open arms after so many newspapers in the North began writing feverishly about her journey to success. A multitude of articles had deemed Lily as *The Prodigy Slave*: a supremely talented pianist and composer, who had earned her freedom by bringing her dreams to life as dancing shadows, infused with a style of music ahead of its time, in a mystical, ingenious, "must-see" phenomenal show.

As the demand for tickets to see *The Dream Symphony* continued to grow, Landon had made the tough decision, along with Lily, to let the lie about her freedom continue to further enhance the fascination about her theatrical masterpiece. Most wonderfully, though, not only did the curiosity about her show continue to grow but so too did the respect from those who welcomed Lily and her entourage to their cities. Gone rather quickly were the days when journalists were eager to tell lies to abort Lily's musical ambitions. Gone with it was the humiliation of being rejected from hotels, sleeping in the back rooms of theaters, and of owners demanding demeaning changes to her show. With the blend of controversy and overwhelming praise from critics, Lily's color began to have little relevance. In a matter of just six short months, she was now being embraced with the dignity she well deserved, in every place her journey was taking her.

While Landon was *proudly* handling the dirty work behind the scenes on *The Dream Symphony* journey, William had been loyally by Lily's side, passing on his life wisdom and helping to make her transition into the world of music as seamless as possible. Through his dedication to her, Lily had learned to conduct herself as a true professional, and garnered mass amounts of attention from the public. Day by day, she continued to grow exponentially as a musical success, all while her symphony traveled slowly west on a tour through the southern cities in Ohio, Indiana, and Illinois, and then back eastward through the northern portion of those same states before playing in a multitude of cities in Pennsylvania. Lily's stint in Pennsylvania had long since ended, and she was now in the midst of yet another sold-out showing at a popular venue in Jamestown, New York, playing the final show of a five-night stretch. After the completion of her show there, she would soon be pressing further east for her highly anticipated Christmas performance at Winter Garden. The state-of-the-art, well-known theater was located in Manhattan on an up and coming street that was starting to become synonymous for its artistry, eclectic entertainment, and unique performers … a street known as *Broadway*.

To say that Lily's life had evolved tremendously while on her journey to a prestigious theater on a famed stretch of road would be a monumental understatement. *Everything* that Lily had experienced within the last several months of her life had a profound effect on her. But despite coming from a life where she had absolutely nothing, it was not the fancy hotels, the one-of-a-kind tailor-made dresses and shoes, the fine dining at fancy restaurants, performing in elaborate theaters, seeing the country, or the money that now poured in like a heavy summer rain that had the greatest impact on Lily. She indeed appreciated those things, but what impacted her more than anything were simply *people*. All of the perfect strangers who gathered at her concerts and the looks on their faces as they stood and applauded while she bowed at the end of every performance brought Lily an immense amount of joy. The people who approached her at post-show events to confess how moved they were by the two-hour experience of her dream show had mutually moved Lily as well. Lily's massive mental collection of those accepting, appreciative Negro *and* Caucasian faces never once left her psyche. Each and every one of them had infused themselves into her soul, empowering her to write the sort of music that erupted from the warmth they bestowed upon her. Her beloved fans were always one of the many reasons why she broke down into tears as she prayed every night, thanking God for allowing her the honor of finally knowing what it was like to feel human.

But far above any other person, Lily's mother reigned supreme and remained at the root of the emotion in her music. Her mother was also the reason that Lily never forgot her tumultuous beginnings, nor took for granted the life she felt God was now granting her. Always remembering that her mother and other slaves had never been afforded such luxuries helped Lily to remain humble. She absorbed every new experience, no matter how big or small, with profound appreciation, and accepted the help she received from everyone with the sincerest gratitude, no matter how significant their contribution to her cause.

Along with her mother and her fans, there were three other people that Lily held dear to her during her time on the road. They were three brave men who had put their lives on the line and used every bit of power they had to catapult her from the filth of a cotton field into the spotlight of a highly regarded stage on Broadway. They were three men who stood steadfast by her side throughout every step of her journey, watching in complete awe at the way she handled the transformation of her life with such grace and humility. They were three men who, while helping Lily's life change, consequently had theirs change for the better as well. *William Werthington* often thanked God for sending Lily into his life and giving him a reason to climb out of the dark hole he was living in after losing Emma. *Landon Von Brandt*, the imperial narcissist, had set his selfishness aside because of Lily and finally found a greater purpose in his life outside of himself. But none was more affected by Lily than the only man of the three who had embraced her years before he ever knew about her musical gift. Long before newspaper articles were written about her, years before there was an overwhelming demand to see her sold-out show in a multitude of cities, and talks of performing on

Broadway, Lily had changed *James Adams*. It did not take something as epic as the wondrous musical adventure they were now on in order to transform his life. Lily's presence, her being, simply the fact that she existed in his world, had altered James's life from the very first moment she became a part of it.

Weeks earlier, during Lily's photo session for the *New York Times*, James had stood in a corner absorbing the beautiful sight of her smiling while experiencing yet another first: a photographer creating visual proof of her existence. As he proudly watched her, James began to wonder what his life would be like without Lily, but then realized that he already knew the answer to that question. Without ever taking his eyes off of her as she posed for the camera, he began recounting how miserable he had been during the years they had spent apart. He remembered how denying his feelings and living his life so far away from her had caused him to morph quickly into a man that he was ashamed of. He recalled how angry he then became at himself for not having the resources or the courage to stand up to his father and take Lily with him when he left home. He thought back to how he was in serious denial about the fact that mistreating Lily and leaving her behind was at the root of his rage, drinking, and promiscuity. But with the way his life had changed since he walked through the doors of his boyhood home back in January, James now knew that he could never again question that Lily was undeniably the problem *and* the remedy to all that troubled him while he was away. Simply being in her presence had instantaneously halted everything that had been ailing him through the years, no different than the day they first met. The truth in that, however, was something that James had only summoned the courage to *completely* give in to six months prior after her concert at Branaugh. That night, it was Lily's willingness to forgive James and express it through her words, her emotions, and the sharing of her body, that had the power to permanently seal off that chasm in his soul, the way a thousand women, gallons of whiskey, and dozens of bar fights would have failed to do. With Lily considering him once again as her confidant, best friend, and now her lover, James finally felt like the sort of man he could be proud of again, and most importantly, one that Lily could be proud of.

Consequently, letting go and giving in to what he felt for Lily not only healed James, but also gave him the strength and motivation to help her begin to heal too. He charismatically began sealing her wounds with the passion, patience, understanding, and love that he swore to give her this time around. As a result, he quickly witnessed Lily's confidence explode and saw a more intimidating, courageous woman begin to emerge. James was extraordinarily proud to see how her transformation showed in the way Lily commanded the stage, in the way that she now walked with her head held high, and in the way she now looked people in the eye whenever she spoke to them. But of course, what he enjoyed more than anything was the change in her sensual side when it finally began to flourish.

James had been slow with Lily intimately, at first giving her the opportunity to explore and ask anything of him that she desired while she went about discovering a side of herself that was a mystery. He had catered so well to Lily emotionally and physically that being one with him and trying new things had quickly become an addiction for her, nearly as strong as her drive to create music. With her newfound obsession, all of the awkwardness that Lily once felt when James would simply look at her with want in his eyes had completely vanished. In place of that timid girl, a fearless lioness was born with sexual desires that proved to be unrelenting and parallel to her man's. Her desires were so strong that *Lily* soon became the aggressor on their conquests, taking the lead on their spontaneous escapades, gazing at *James* in crowded rooms during large gatherings with lust-filled eyes that seductively eluded to what she wanted. And James *certainly* obliged in every way possible, never once daring to deny her.

Before her tour began, Lily had continued her ritual of leaving letters for James on his pillow, but this time containing graphic verbiage or instructions that sometimes led him out to her favorite tree on William's estate at late night hours. James would eagerly make his way there only to find Lily's clothing left behind on the shore of the lake as she swam nearby, enticing him with the knowledge of her nudity. Seeing Lily there, dying to touch her, to hold her, James would nearly tear his clothes off before diving in and chasing her down as she playfully tried to escape. All the while, both would be laughing as carefree as children at their silly antics. It was never long, though, before James caught his woman and their laughter was replaced by the sounds of soft moaning as he tasted every visible part of her soft skin and devoured her full lips. In those moments, the cool water did nothing to stop the heat within Lily from rising. Thoroughly aroused by James's affections, she would wrap her legs firmly around his waist, begging him to penetrate her without a single word. Responding immediately to what Lily wanted, James would quickly bury himself deep within her and passionately make love to her under the soft glow of the moonlight, letting the echo of their pleasure-filled sighs mix harmoniously with the sounds of the nocturnal creatures of the night. Afterward, they would sneak back into the house and lie together near the fireplace where James would then slowly kiss and massage every inch of Lily's body with Anna Mae's specially made lotion the way Lily had once fantasized. Once his woman was warmed and relaxed, James would pull her in close to him, arranging her in such a way that as much of her bare skin was pressed to him as humanly possible. The simple pleasure of having Lily wrapped tightly in his arms, keeping her safe and warm, continued to give James the peace of mind to sleep soundly and completely free from his nightmares throughout every night.

After setting out on tour, Lily grew even bolder, initiating numerous playful trysts with James in their enclosed carriage on their rides to hotels or in dressing rooms after her shows. She would tease and arouse him with her lips in the most erotic of ways, tempting him in places she knew she should not, turning on his carnivorous craving to ensure that he would be ready to greet the warmth between her thighs when their hotel room door shut behind them. It was on one of those incredible nights that James realized Lily truly had defined for him the true meaning of passion and lovemaking, just as his dreams had predicted. The power and intensity of what they shared had further cemented their bond and added yet another layer to James's plethora of reasons to love Lily. Their newly rebuilt bond was the reason why James had stood in the corner watching the *New York Times* photographer capture images of Lily, realizing that there was no looking back, that the torture of his life without her now would easily eclipse any and all pain he had ever felt in his life.

During their past few months together, James could feel from Lily how much their newly reformed bond and their intimacy meant to her as well. After causing her so many years of trauma, it was gratifying for him to finally bring so much pleasure into her life. It was the reason why he reveled in the jubilance she emitted after making love to her in the late-night hours after her shows. Seeing her smile, hearing the sound of happiness in her voice, and listening to her laughter was a bright and sunny side of her that he wanted to ensure he never stripped away from her again. Knowing that Lily was happy was all James needed to feel completely settled at the end of their long days.

Lily's happiness had become so intertwined with his

own that James was bothered by the fact that she was so silent as they lay together following her final performance in Jamestown. Lily's hunger for him had been present and strong and the passion was explosive just as he had come to love, but afterward she emitted no emotion whatsoever. James was stroking her hair and kissing the back of her neck and shoulders, waiting for her to relax, melt into his arms, and let his favorite side of her emerge as they recounted the ups and downs of the day or laughed over silly things into the early morning as usual. But instead, he could feel the tension in Lily's body as she lay there unusually stiff, staring across the room at nothing in particular, having yet to say a word.

"*Lily*? What is it? Somethin's botherin' you."

"Nothin'," she lied, trying not to bring a dark cloud to their sunshine.

"No need for lies. Tell me what's ailin' you." James shifted his body upwards to get a better look at the profile of her face. "I can feel in your body somethin' ain't right."

Lily blew out a frustrated breath knowing she could not hide anything from him. He read her too well. "I just can't seem to get 'er off 'a my mind today."

"Who?"

"My motha'."

James slowly rolled her over to face him and was greeted by the distant look in her eyes. "What about your happy memories? Ya' know, the one of you and her and that hand clappin' song? Or layin' out at night with the telescope and namin' the stars togetha'? I rememba' you told me years ago that thinkin' about those times always helped."

"I know ... But not today. All day I done tried, but it ain't a thang I can do to stop myself from missin' her. Can't nothin' seem to stop the pain this time ... Nothin'."

James wiped away an escaping tear from Lily's eye as he listened intently to her every word. "Maybe a new memory'll help. I'm sure there must be a dozen or more knowin' all the things you told me about her. Let's see, how 'bout the time when y'all were tryna take the clothes off 'a the line before it started rainin' too hard, but the both of ya' just ended up slippin' and slidin' in the mud, droppin' clothes everywhere … or how 'bout that time when you both…"

"Thank you James, but memories ain't what I need," Lily replied, cutting him off, despite being impressed by how he had remembered those stories from so long ago. "Somehow, I just know in my heart the only thing gon' stop the pain this time is seein' my mama's face again. Until then, somehow I feel like I deserve the pain I'm feelin' this time," she said, rolling over angrily.

"Why would you deserve it?"

"'Cause! All this damn money we got, and here I am layin' in this fancy hotel while she's layin' God knows where! She should be here … with *me*! Not workin' in no filthy cotton field or layin' in some damn rundown shack!"

"Lily." James rolled her over to face him again, wanting to ensure that she did not begin to shut him out. He instantly adopted her sorrow as his own and wanted to do all that he could to take it away from her. "We can find her. You're right. We've got the money. I'd do whateva' I had to to bring the two of ya' back togetha' again. It should be easy. I can look through my fatha's records and find out the plantation you were bought from and…"

"I swear, I'd give up every dolla' I have to see my motha' sittin' front row at my show all dressed up, lookin' just as beautiful as I rememba' her. That's what I want, James, trust me I do, but as crazy as it may sound I'm … I'm afraid."

"*Afraid?* Afraid of what?"

"Afraid of the truth," Lily whispered.

"I don't unda'stand."

"Last time I saw my motha', she was in the middle of a

dirt field, layin' face down, *unconscious,* afta' gettin' beat like nobody's business. She was fightin'! Fightin' hard on the count 'a me ... Fightin' to keep me with 'er. To this day, I don't know if she eva' woke up afta' the way my half-brotha' beat her senseless. And now, I'm afraid to know whetha' she lived or not. Right now in my daydreams, she can be whateva' or whereva' I want her to be. In my mind, she's alive and well and thinkin' of me just as much as I think about her. In my mind, she got up outta that dirt field stronga' than eva', determined not to let what happened to us tear her apart. In my mind, she's happy ... she's *alive.* And I don't think I could handle it if I eva' found out that she lost her life that day ... 'cause 'a *me.* I just couldn't handle it."

"Trust me, I know how the sight of somethin' so gruesome can scar you for life," James replied, after recalling the source of his recurring nightmare. "But I'd put money on the fact that your motha's alive and well because of how strong you told me she was ... mentally *and* physically. Knowin' all that, I bet there's a great chance that she's somewhere thinkin' about you every day, maybe even at this very moment. So, don't you think it'd be worth it to at least *try* to find her?" He turned Lily's head back toward him when she looked away. "Lily, I'd be here to see you through it all, no matta' what the outcome. You wouldn't be alone in this."

"You're right, my mama was strong. Every bit of me wants to believe she's alive too. But as foolish as it sounds, I still can't help but be so scared, James. 'Cause I know I'd neva' be the same again if I found out she wasn't ... 'specially not if it was on account 'a me."

"Well, just know that if you say the word, I'll do everything in my powa' to find your motha' for you, okay? I swear to it." James cupped Lily's cheek with his hand and caressed her face slowly with his thumb. "Just a word and it'll be done."

Lily slid her hand over his and held it. "Thank you," she said, kissing him lightly on the lips. "But I s'ppose it doesn't really matta' at this point anyway, does it?" she asked, sounding slightly more relaxed after his words and his touch had genuinely settled her.

"Why not?"

"This is all bound to end, anyway."

"*End?* What's bound to end?"

"All *this*." She waved her hand in the air. "This fairytale we livin' in."

"*Fairytale?*" James sat up, now the one suddenly feeling perturbed. "Lily, this *ain't* no fairytale. It's *real*. You, me, the show … all of it."

"I know that. I just meant that yo' daddy s'pects I'll be home soon. It's been nearly a year. Ain't no way we can carry on like this for much longa'."

The thought had crossed James's mind many times, but he was not ready to face it. "Listen to me. I don't want you worryin' about such things. You let me carry that burden. I'm gonna do everything I have to, and say anything I have to to keep you away from that damn plantation!" he said with conviction, after the thought of Lily returning there began to anger him.

"Hell, you'd have to tell yo' daddy I's dead 'fore he'd allow me to stay away from there one minute more than necessary. Even then, I think he'd drag my dead body back to the farm just to see to it that he has the honor of burnin' it."

James took Lily by the arm and helped her to sit up. "Lily, I swear on Auntie's soul, you'll neva' see that farm again." She looked down at the sheets to avoid his eyes, but he quickly slid his hand underneath her chin and forced her to look at him. "So long as I can help it, you'll neva' set one foot on that land again. I promise you that, ya' hear?"

She nodded her head. "I believe you," she said, with some semblance of life finally returning to her eyes.

"We got a little while before I need to address anything with my fatha' anyway. 'Til then, I want you to think about nothin' but preparin' for Winter Garden and decidin' what pretty dress you're gonna wear to that gala tomorrow night," James said, kissing Lily tenderly on the lips. "And about how much I love you." He placed both hands on the sides of her face and began kissing her again, but this time with the sort of passion that instantly brought Lily's optimism and hope back to life and removed every bit of the tension from her body that James had felt in her just moments before.

Lily lay back down and pulled James on top of her without breaking the kiss that had just followed words that set her body ablaze with want and desire. Needing nothing more of foreplay, she maneuvered her hips to align herself with what she suddenly wanted to feel inside of her. "Show me how much," she said seductively, reaching down and gliding James into her wetness. The feeling of him submerged deep inside of her reached all points of her body at once. She arched her back and let out a groan of pure bliss. James inhaled sharply when the erotic tone escaped her. Nothing fulfilled him more than the sound of her satisfaction. With long powerful strokes, he began melting away all of her anxieties and evaporating her inhibitions, hell-bent on sending her soaring, once again, into the heavenly clouds of freedom, gladly showing her along the way just how much he truly did love her.

Chapter Twenty-One

Slave Code
Article VI Section XI

Any free person convicted of enticing or persuading a slave to run away shall forfeit and pay the full value of such slave to its master or owner.

As Lily and her entourage trotted through the snow-lined streets of Manhattan on the way to a fundraising gala in the warm comforts of her new fancy, black enclosed carriage, she gazed with pure fascination at all of the towering buildings surrounding her. Manhattan was definitely unlike any other city she had seen, and she found it hard to pull her eyes away from the uniqueness of it all.

Before departing from their hotel, William had instructed the lead driver of the convoy to take a particular route on the way to their destination. When what he wanted to see came into view, William called out to the driver to stop. "Lily, come along. I'd like you to see something," William told her once the carriage halted. He stepped out of the carriage first and a cold breeze swept his scarf into the air as he helped Lily down. "Look there," William said, pointing in the air. Lily's eyes followed his finger to the words on a towering marquee: ***The Dream Symphony, Christmas night, 6 pm.***

"Winter Garden," Lily said with a slow smile creeping onto her face.

"Winter Garden," William repeated, gazing at the prestigious building along with her. "Before we carry on to the gala, I believe a brief tour is in order."

After reluctantly tearing her eyes away from the marquee that boasted the name of her show, Lily walked into Winter Garden holding onto James. She excitedly squeezed his arm tight, and her face lit up with a brilliant smile as she took in the sight of a theater that was three times the size of any she had yet to play in. She released James's arm and slowly turned around, looking up at the three stories of balcony seats that lined the walls. Her eyes then panned up to a ceiling that was meticulously painted like a crystal-clear, star-filled night sky. The beautiful art instantly transported Lily back to her very first performance underneath the night sky on the incredible outdoor amphitheater that James had built her, a place where her dreams had literally started to come to life and set the wheels in motion that had led her to this moment.

They had been to many theaters over their six-month travels, but William never once tired of seeing the expression on Lily's face whenever she walked through the doors of a new theater. His heart melted a little more as he watched her closely and noted her bright smile, the way her eyes widened, and the innocence she exuded. In William's estimation, it was all so pure and genuine, like the awestruck look of a child seeing the moon and the stars for the very first time. The innocence and excitement that showed on Lily's face always brought him back to the youthful part of his life. He had become desensitized to the enchantment of seeing the world since then but watching the way Lily lit up over every new thing reminded him of how grand that sort of life really was and how fortunate he had been.

William had never made a special stop or personally given Lily a tour at any theater before they were due to rehearse there like he was doing now. He always much preferred standing at a distance, following Lily with his eyes, allowing her to absorb her surroundings in solace as she stood on the edge of the stage or walked the aisles admiring the décor. But Winter Garden held a special meaning for William on so many levels. So, on this occasion, he felt a personal tour was warranted. After he had guided Lily and James through a tour of the view from the balcony and of all of the backstage amenities, the three of them stood alone in the middle of the massive stage. "Believe it or not, this theater seats 6,000 people … 6,400 to be exact," William informed. The number shocked James and Lily since it was more than double the capacity of all of the previous theaters, yet had sold out the quickest. After sharing that bit of information, William put his hands in his pockets, turned, and marched forward a few steps to look out into the spread of seats. "The very last time I performed here, though … 6,397 of these seats were empty," he continued.

Lily looked at William curiously. She was in disbelief that only three people would show up to one of his concerts.

"It happened the second time I ever played here," William further explained. "I'd played here once before in my career, about fifteen years before that night. On that first occasion, this place was completely sold out, and the show went off without a hitch. It was flawless. Every moment of it. But what made my first time playing here so special was that my Emma was there, like she was at so many of my shows. She had seen me play at countless venues before that, and many more after that, but that night when I first performed here was unforgettable to her." He paused a moment. "When she fell ill many years later, everything in her memory was slowly slipping away from her: details of our wedding, birthdays, the little country store she used to own … my name." William hesitated and regained composure over his emotions before speaking again. "The names of our sons … even her own. Such vital memories all faded away. But that night she saw me perform here at Winter Garden, on this very stage in front of that packed audience, was the one performance she never ever forgot. It was as if her experience watching me play here was the *only* lingering memory that God had allowed her to keep. Even after she was suffering through the worst parts of her illness, for some reason … Winter

Garden was literally *unforgettable* to her.

"'You were so brilliant last night at Winter Garden! I can't wait to see you play there again!' That's what my Emma would say to me at some point *everyday* when she was ill. And I do mean *every. Single. Day.* There was always a soft enthusiasm in her voice and a lovely smile on her face as she looked at me with life shining briefly in her beautiful eyes whenever she said it. In a matter of a heartbeat after that, though, her mind would quickly slip away into darkness again, taking my hope for her to get well along with it.

"'I can't wait to see you play there again,' was the very last sentence my wife ever uttered to me ... and that seat over there," William said, pointing to the place he spoke of, "was the place she sat when I brought her back here for a second time to fulfill that wish. I rented this entire venue, and my sons and I traveled with her here. They sat huddled next to their mother as my old orchestra and I replayed every single song from that night she remembered from so many years ago. As sick as Emma was, as lost as she was in the depths of her mind, as disconnected from the world as she always seemed to be, I swear to you, for the ninety minutes I played here, she never once took her eyes off of me." William glanced over to where his wife had once sat. "Nor was I ever once able to take mine off of her. I just couldn't. For those ninety minutes, m-my Emma w-was back." His lip began to quiver as he spoke. "Th-that brief flash of a smile, that I looked so forward to seeing when she uttered those words to me every day, was there on her face the entire time my fingers were dancing across that piano. H-her eyes were so full of life again," he said as his voice cracked. "And mine were full of tears," he admitted, patting his handkerchief at the ones that now fell. "To this very day, I still believe it was what she hung on so long for, to relive the one and only memory she had left ... just one last time." William dried his tears and collected himself.

"Less than twenty-four hours after we brought her back home … my Emma slipped away."

Lily struggled to control her emotions as she took hold of William's hand. Despite feeling the warmth of her soft hand around his, William still could not take his eyes off of the seat where Emma once sat. "I'm sure you already know that your Emma will be sittin' right there again in spirit watchin' you on Christmas night."

William simply nodded his head.

"And I promise you, I'll do my best to honor her memory," Lily sniffled. "And do my best to make you proud."

William finally turned his eyes away from Emma's old seat and let them fall on Lily. "I'm afraid it's much too late for that, my dear." He reached up and caressed her face. "You've done that many moons ago."

Lily embraced William after his kind words. The heartfelt affection finally helped to subdue their emotions. When they had calmed one another, they turned to gaze out into the empty seats of Winter Garden, both quietly staring at the area that would soon be filled by the fortunate patrons who were able to secure a ticket to watch an indentured woman emotionally free herself for two hours in the most enchanting way.

After appreciating the view for a moment, everyone returned to the carriage and carried on another fifteen minutes to their final destination. The time passed like seconds to Lily as she sat in her seat with her eyes closed, still enamored with William's story about Emma, the exquisiteness of Winter Garden, and the sentiment behind how much it was going to mean to play with William there. Before she truly had a chance to let it all wash over her, the carriage came to a halt in front of another pristine building with tall columns leading from the top of stone steps up to the crest of the roof. The design of the elegant establishment could have easily blended in with the beauty of unique Roman architecture.

A convoy of carriages soon halted behind Lily's as well. Anna Mae, Ben, their children, and the student orchestra all began filing out, every one of them dressed in their finest. Out of the lead carriage, Landon and James assisted Lily as she exited in another of Anna Mae's carefully crafted gowns, but it was covered in the warmth of a stylish full-length winter coat with a matching shawl and gloves. After Lily stepped down, James immediately extended his elbow for her to grasp onto to help guide her up the stone steps. The crisp, cold winter air instinctively made her huddle closer to him. Their breath was easily visible as they climbed the stone stairway together. At the top awaiting them near the massive double door entrance stood two men, both dressed as exquisitely as everyone else who had just arrived. As Lily approached and got a better look something about their demeanor, their dark brown hair, their glasses, and their green eyes seemed familiar to her. The man to her right spoke first after she made her way to the top and was only a few feet away. "The brilliant Lily Adams, I presume," he complimented, gingerly taking her by the hand and kissing it.

Lily nodded with a smile.

"I'm Wilson," he then told her with a slight bow.

"Pleased to meet you," Lily replied.

"And I'm Emerson," the man standing next to him announced, also taking her by the hand and greeting her similarly. "By all my father has written to us about you, I'd swear you were not a stranger…"

"But rather our long-lost sister," Wilson finished, in a very proper dialect similar to that of Emerson's.

With their comments and the mention of their names, the familiarity of their identical faces finally made sense to Lily. "Well now, I couldn't forget those names if I tried. I've heard so much about the both of you! You must be William's twins!" she smiled. "I should've known! You both look shockingly similar," she said, looking from one to the other like her eyes were playing tricks on her. "And just like your fatha' for that matta'."

"Except we're a younger more attractive version," Wilson replied sarcastically, pulling at the lapels on his suit.

"Less wrinkled, stronger, better hair," Emerson added, lifting his hat and a single eyebrow, with a wink that followed.

"And more of it!" Wilson laughed.

"Yeah, yeah, yeah, you buffoons! She gets it!" William interjected after finally making the long ascent up the steps. "Laugh while you can," he continued while pointing to himself. "This thinning gray hair and this face of mine are what you both have to look forward to in thirty years."

Lily laughed, already loving the playful banter between the three of them.

"How are you, Father?" Wilson finally asked, stepping forward and embracing William in that special way that fathers and sons did when they truly missed each other but were too manly to verbally admit, however, could never hide in their actions. Emerson followed suit and hugged his father as well. The twins were just as happy to see and embrace the other people they considered as family: Anna Mae, Isabel, Ben, and Elijah. They introduced themselves to Landon and James afterward with the typical manly firm handshake, each man grasping the other's hand tight, silently sizing the other up for no other reason than natural testosterone-driven instinct.

After the formalities, Wilson and Emerson extended their elbows toward Lily. "May we steal her from you for a while?" Emerson asked James, who simply nodded in reply.

Lily looked at the twins closely again. "I ask your forgiveness in advance if I confuse the two of you. It's gonna take an act of God for me to tell you both apart," she admitted, as she left the crook of James's elbow and grasped on to Wilson and Emerson.

"No worries, soon your eyes will adjust, and you'll realize that I'm the slightly younger, but *much* better looking one of the two of us," Emerson joked with Lily, as he and his brother escorted her into the building. She laughed at his remark as they entered and then immediately paused for a moment after her eyes fell onto the interior of the building. She turned her head slowly from side to side to appreciate all of the fine pieces of art that clung to the walls and the sculptures placed strategically about the floor.

"Beautiful place, isn't it?" Wilson asked.

"Utterly breathtakin'. I've neva' seen anything like this," Lily said. The awe in her voice and the look on her face immediately made William smile.

"Well, you've yet to see the best. Come along, we'll personally give you a tour before the festivities begin in The Grand Hall," Emerson said, using words in which Lily finally heard a hint of the British accent that he had naturally adopted from his father.

"Thank you. I'd like that."

"As you can see, Lily, my boys never took after my love of music. They could care less. They took after their mother with their love of art instead," William complained, after they had walked along for several minutes, and he had listened to his sons explain every intricate detail of the pieces they had shown her.

"Oh, father's always one to exaggerate," Wilson replied to Lily. "He's always felt that we loved our mother more than him and cherished *all* the things she loved more than the things he does."

"He's a delusional, nutty old man, I'm tellin' ya'," Emerson joked, pretending to whisper in her ear, but actually speaking loud enough for his father to hear.

Emerson and Wilson's lighthearted comedy put Lily in the most cheerful mood. She was thoroughly enjoying the way they strolled along with her on their arms, rambling on about the pieces they were passing and infusing bits and pieces of knowledge about their childhood and their parents. Their interaction with her made Lily feel instantly accepted—like family.

"So, if I rememba' correctly, William tells me the both of you are professors, right?" Lily asked when she finally had a chance to speak.

"I see that memory of yours is just as grand as my father has eluded to. You are correct!"

"Well, maybe my memory is startin' to fail 'cause I can't seem to rememba' which one of you teaches philosophy and which one teaches English."

"The great and wise English professor would be *me*," Emerson boasted, continuing his comical arrogant facade, making Lily smile again.

"Leaving me as the *much* greater and *much* wiser *head* of the philosophy department," Wilson said, smirking at his brother.

"But you're here to raise money for the *arts* department?" Lily asked, looking confused by that notion.

"Yes, well, you see, our mother always loved raising money to give to the charities and causes most dear to her. Our mother loved art, but she was a selfless woman and spent a good deal of her time raising money for the Ohio University music department for my father. So much time, in fact, that she rarely had the time to help the organizations that really meant so much to her. So now, in honor of her, my brother and I help to raise money every year for the arts department at our school and to help keep this place up and running," Emerson explained.

"Yes, she loved this place," Wilson added. "She'd spend hours here with my brother and me, fawning over every detail of the paintings and sculptures."

"Sounds to me like your motha's selflessness rubbed off on the two of you, right along with her love of art," Lily replied, truly empathizing with the power a mother's love could often have.

"Such a lovely compliment," Emerson replied, kissing the back of Lily's hand again.

"Yes," Wilson interrupted, stealing her hand from his brother. "From a very lovely lady," he added, determined not to be outdone by his slightly younger brother.

"Watch it you two! She's taken!" William warned playfully. "This one here is bound to turn into a rabid dog over her," he said, motioning his head toward James.

The twins and James laughed, all knowing that no harm was meant in their silly charms, but Elijah stood behind them with his blood simmering over the memory of once facing the rabid dog that had now "taken" Lily. Elijah did not appreciate William's reminder of their relationship. Over the last few months, he had already been nauseated enough by the sight of James and Lily together on a regular basis. And now, witnessing such an insignificant scene had significantly ruined Elijah's evening, yet again. Fortunately, the curator of the museum approached, finally giving cause for Elijah to stop trying to murder James with his eyes.

"William! Good to see you again old friend!" the curator said, taking hold of William's hand and shaking it. He then turned toward Lily. "And you must be Ms. Adams." He extended his hand, taking hers in a gentle shake as well.

"I am."

"I'm Preston Mills, curator of the museum."

"Pleased to meet you," Lily replied with a smile.

"It's certainly an honor to have you here this evening. I was one of the fortunate few who was able to secure a pair of tickets for your show. My wife and I are very much looking forward to it, as is the rest of this city, it seems. Everyone is buzzing about it!"

"Thank you, Mr. Mills. You're too kind."

"Please, by all means, call me Preston."

"Well then Preston, I must say, your facility is

incredibly beautiful. I can't seem to pull my eyes away from all of the fine artwork. I see why William's wife used to spend hours here."

"Oh, well now, *you* are too kind."

As they spoke, another man approached. He had intentionally messy hair and was dressed in flamboyant, brightly colored, tight, red attire with white ruffles protruding from the collar and wrist areas of his clothing. Lily's eyes were instantly drawn to him.

"William, you remember Piers LeRoux, I'm sure?" Preston said, referring to the colorfully dressed man who now stood by his side.

"Of course. How could I forget?" William replied, grasping onto Piers's hand. "He's done most of the art in my home, including the magnificent portrait of my wife. He's one hell of an artist."

"Thank you, Mr. Werthington," Piers replied.

"Yes, I certainly agree," Preston said. "And fortunately for us, your sons have convinced him to display some of his most precious pieces for the auction tonight."

"Well, when they told me how fond your wife was of my work and this facility, there was no way I was going to turn down an opportunity to honor her in such a way," Piers responded, in a French accent so thick that he was difficult to understand.

Piers's uncommon attire had certainly caught Lily's attention, but his accent intrigued her even more. She had become fascinated with the different intonations in voices that came from different parts of the world. It was much like music to her, each country being a different instrument with its own unique sound. It lent itself to her desire to travel the world.

"You are too gracious, Piers. I can assure you that this would have meant the world to my wife," William said appreciatively.

Piers then turned and honed in on Lily. Unaware at that

point that she was "taken," a devilish smile emerged on his face as his eyes glided up and down her body, absorbing what he felt were extraordinarily incredible features. One would have guessed by his flamboyant attire that he enjoyed the company of his own gender, but the way Piers looked at Lily, like she was an exotic dish that he was dying to taste, proved otherwise. "Ms. Adams," Piers announced, taking her by the hand and bowing slightly. "Pleasure to finally meet you." His eyes still roamed her body.

"So wonderful to meet you too, Mr. LeRoux," Lily replied, a little surprised that he already knew who she was. "I can't wait to see your pieces this evenin'."

Piers raised an eyebrow at her. "Yes … I certainly hope to *please* you," he said, in a way that left no secret about the fact that he was alluding to much more than art.

"Well, Ms. Adams, fortunately, you won't have to wait too long then, the festivities are set to begin in The Grand Hall momentarily," Preston interrupted. "So sorry to cut your tour short."

"It's quite alright. Lead the way."

* * * *

After the bidding had gone better than expected in The Grand Hall, an orchestra played elegantly in the background while drinks and hors d'oeuvres were served, and an array of people glided about the dance floor to their classical melodies. The atmosphere was happy and light, but judging by Elijah's face one would never have guessed that. He stood next to a table of drinks, holding on to a glass of liquor with a scowl on his face, guzzling it from time to time and ignoring the burn that erupted in his chest afterward. Isabel pranced over to him with a joyous grin on her face, thoroughly enjoying the festive spirit, completely oblivious to her brother's foul mood, as she typically was to all things. "Dance with me, brotha'," she smiled, taking him by the hand and trying to pull him toward the dance floor.

"Not now, Isabel!" Elijah fired back, snatching his hand away, finally making his rotten attitude blatantly obvious, even to her.

Isabel followed her brother's eyes, looked over her shoulder, and saw what had darkened his evening: Lily smiling and laughing, arm in arm with James as they waltzed happily around the dance floor.

"Sore losa'," Isabel teased, after turning back and seeing the nasty expression still plastered on her brother's face. "Everybody in they right mind knows those two belong togetha'. And I think they make a beautiful couple."

Elijah furrowed his eyebrows and tightened his lips. "I've neva' struck a woman before." He lifted a finger from his glass of liquor and pointed it at his sister. "Anotha' word and I promise you'll be the first."

"You wouldn't dare," Isabel replied confidently, sticking her tongue out at Elijah like they were kids all over again. "You know I'm Daddy's favorite. He'd beat you senseless!" She threw her hands on her hips. "Hmph, I didn't really wanna dance with you anyway! I just felt sorry for you, standin' ova' here lookin' like a lonely lost puppy that nobody wants! But now I'd ratha' dance with one of the twins, instead of a *sore losa'*. They's always betta' dancers than you were anyway," she scoffed, sticking her tongue out at him again. "Sore losa', sore losa', sore losa'!" she chanted as she pranced off again and danced her way into Emerson's arms and out onto the dance floor. Elijah watched her float away and then went back to trying to kill James with his eyes while drowning his jealousy with whiskey.

"Ladies and Gentlemen, may I have your attention, please?" Preston announced, after taking to the stage again. The music silenced, and everyone turned in his direction. "I hope you are all enjoying yourselves this evening. We will get back to the music and festivities momentarily, but if

you would please find your seats once again." He waited
for everyone to do so before continuing. "First and
foremost, I would like to say thank you to Mr. Piers
LeRoux for the lovely pieces he has provided here tonight."
He motioned his arm toward Piers who stood just to the
right of him with his posture perfect and his hands clasped
behind his back. "His work is simply extraordinary,
wouldn't you agree?" Everyone applauded in unison and
Piers bowed slightly to acknowledge their warm reception.
"That is why it gives me great delight to let you all know
that there is one final piece that he has yet to show this
evening."

Preston stepped away and let Piers have the floor. He
stepped forward with his unique mannerisms and pierced
the brief silence with his thick French accent. "This piece
was inspired by something I saw not long ago, something
that was so poetically picturesque, it awakened every one
of my senses. The imagery stayed with me for so long that I
dreamt of it several times afterward. Every vivid detail was
engrained into my memory so vibrantly that I wanted to
savor it in my mind for a lifetime. Before it had a chance to
fade away from my mind, I etched it in permanence so that
I may revisit the precious memory whenever I so desire. It
is a memory so inspirational and precious to me that I wish
to revisit it here with you all tonight." Piers then turned and
dropped a black satin cover from the expansive canvas
behind him to unveil his painting. When it was revealed,
Lily inhaled sharply and leaned forward in her seat.
William followed suit, pushing his spectacles up higher on
his nose to see with more clarity the picture that neither he
nor Lily were ever made privy to.

At the very top of the portrait, the apparition of an
angel with expansive wings was stretched across it. It was
floating high above shadowed figures dancing in unison
amidst a dragon, an oak tree, and a sword-yielding knight,
all of which depicted various scenes that had been infused

into the sheer tapestry during *The Dream Symphony*. In front of the shadows, an array of musicians with various instruments were scattered about the stage, all being directed by William Werthington, who stood in front of them with his baton high in the air and his signature split coattails trailing behind him. Every aspect of the portrait was in black and white except for the image in the very center. In the midst of all of the orchestra bodies, sitting perched at an extravagant grand piano with her eyes closed and her fingers delicately tickling the keys, Lily Adams was painted in vivid colors, dressed in a satin gown that flowed glamorously behind her. Her illustrious spiral curled hair, her multicolor eyes, the red in her gown, her matching make-up, her piano, and even the tinted hue of her skin, were all meticulously detailed with such painstaking accuracy and colors so vivacious that every bidder in the room threw up their paddles in hopes of becoming the artwork's owner.

"I had the privilege of speaking with the creator of this unbelievable show, Ms. Lily Adams, who has joined us here tonight," Piers said, motioning his hand toward her. "And after such a lovely and revealing conversation with her, I'd now like to call this portrait *Musical Dreams* … after learning that Ms. Adams' dreams have most certainly come true."

"Ah-ah-ah-ah," Preston said, stepping forward and waving a finger, after seeing that dozens of eager bidders had their bidding paddles high in the air. "I hate to disappoint you all, but this portrait is not up for bids." An audible groan from all the patrons grumbled through the room as people put their paddles down. "Piers has offered this priceless piece to be added to this gallery. It will now serve as the centerpiece of our music-themed exhibit and will remain so until the day these walls come tumbling down."

Lily glanced over at the twins, who both gave her a

telling smile about their knowledge of the surprise. Both were happy to see such delight on her and their father's face after hearing that the piece they were featured in would become a part of their mother's favorite museum.

"As most of you may already know, the inspiration for this work of artwork, The Dream Symphony, will be playing Christmas night at Winter Garden Theater here in Manhattan," Preston continued. "However, it is my understanding that the show is already completely sold out." Another groan erupted from the audience. "But! For a lucky few of you, I have *just* the remedy for that! You see, in place of his priceless portrait, Mr. LeRoux has provided yet another way to share the experience that inspired this piece. So although he remains adamant about not letting anyone bid on this particular piece of work, he is more than happy to let you all bid on these!" Preston raised a handful of tickets in the air. "Four center balcony seats to The Dream Symphony for Christmas night! Shall we start the bidding at, let's saaay … ten dollars!"

Lily heard Preston's announcement, but she simply could not pull her eyes away from what was Piers's interpretation of her show. After being entranced by it for a moment, she slowly looked around the room as the battle for tickets to her show began. She thought that perhaps it would be yet another scene where every minute detail would become embedded in her mind and added to her collection of fond memories. However, as the bidding prices rose higher, the room suddenly fell silent in Lily's world after the entire scene triggered the memory of the very first time bids were ever placed on her behalf. She was ten years old, barefoot, in a filthy dress, shivering, scared, and feeling hopelessly alone. Lily was an innocent child back then, recently stolen from her mother by her own father. Her father's callousness had left her to believe that she was nothing more than a meaningless animal to him after he so easily sold her away to serve a tyrant, a man who took pride in demolishing her spirit.

But now, after her turbulent journey, Lily had finally ended that once depressing chapter of her life where she was frozen in time as that broken young lady who once stood alone on an auction block in a tear-stained, tattered dress. She was now beginning a whole new story as a dignified grown woman, adorned in handmade silk gowns, fancy matching shoes, and fur coats. In this new chapter of her life, instead of being looked at on an auction block, Lily was being looked at on a grand stage by a variety of people with tear-filled eyes that reflected how much they appreciated her. Now, a slew of perfect strangers, both black and white, spoke to her with the sort of kindness that her father never did. They told her "thank you" after opening their arms to embrace her in a way that Jesse never had, despite all she had done for him. She was finally living the sort of life where the people that now surrounded her, while she stood on display, never once viewed her as a piece of property. In their eyes, Lily Adams was now an awe-inspiring, gifted, brilliant, and beautiful woman, who was currently sitting at an auction in the midst of a crowd full of people who were bidding not to *own* her, but instead, to *honor* her by paying to be a part of her mystical, musical dreams.

Lily sat through what she was witnessing inside of a *grand* ballroom, feeling swaddled in the *grand* warmth and love of those who surrounded her at the table—a complete contrast from the last time bidders had fought for her. That contrast suddenly struck a chord in her. Lily once believed that the dreadful day she was bid on as a child was the beginning of the destruction of her life. But now, in the midst of the current bidding mayhem and the love that she felt at her table, she realized that perhaps that day was the beginning of God's plan, that it was a means to a fifteen-year journey to free herself from oppression, but more importantly … to free her mother.

As that epiphany dawned on Lily, James took hold of her hand and kissed it, after innately sensing that she needed to feel his touch. The simple affection suddenly brought her sense of awareness back to reality. The sights and sounds of the crowd in the ballroom returned as Lily turned and stared at the strapping man who was now holding her hand, and she suddenly remembered one of the first things he had ever said to her when they first met by the creek as children: *I've been prayin' real hard that you'll see your motha' again.* Lily then thought of yet another of James's wonderful gestures from just the night before: *Just know that if you say the word, I'll do everything in my powa' to find your motha' for you. I swear to it. Just a word and it'll be done.* As James continued to caress Lily's hand at their table, she realized that with a few simple words she would be handing him the power to answer his very own prayer, an incredibly selfless prayer that he had placed to God on her behalf nearly fifteen years ago that still resonated with her to this very day.

As the prices for *The Dream Symphony* tickets continued to rise, Lily's sudden epiphany was helping her to see God's plan with great clarity. She now felt that it could not have been a coincidence that she was sold to a home where she was able to uncover her God-given gift, to a place where the young boy who lived there, not only fell in love with her but believed in her gift enough to make such a huge sacrifice in order to nurture it. With that revelation so clear, Lily was finally able to let go of her fear of searching for her mother, especially knowing that the man who sat beside her, currently caressing her hand, would be there by her side through it all. Lily then looked one by one at all of the other faces that were gathered at the table with her: Landon, the comical twins, William, Austin, Anna Mae, Benjamin, and Isabel. Lily felt that each and every one of them were her new family, and she had no doubt that they would all be there for her as well. She was positive that they would help her deal with the heartache of knowing that her mother was no longer living, or they would prepare a magnificent celebration to help welcome and embrace her mother into their family like she had always been a part of it. But with the confidence that Lily now had in what she believed was God's plan, she was thoroughly convinced that her pseudo-family would indeed be doing the latter.

As the long drawn out bidding battle finally came to an end, James placed yet another soft kiss to the back of Lily's hand. Her eyes fell on him, and she began to glow as her face lit up with a smile that brightened his evening. Lily knew at that very moment, beyond a shadow of a doubt, what the topic of their conversation would be after James made love to her and she lay melting into the loving embrace of his strong arms during the late-night hours.

After the winning bidder had retrieved his tickets, Landon walked up to the podium to make an announcement. "Good evening," he greeted. "First, I'd like to say to the gentleman who just purchased those tickets … I can assure you that your money has been *very* well spent. By the time The Dream Symphony comes to a close, I swear, you will feel like you can fly."

The winner simply nodded his head with a smile as he took his seat.

"Anyhow," he continued, "for those of you here tonight who don't know me, my name is Landon … Landon Von Brandt. And while you are all in your seats, I have one more thing I'd like to share this evening. At first, I thought maybe I would share this as a private matter, but while Ms. Adams is displayed so beautifully in this magnificent portrait, I suddenly feel compelled to share my news with all of you now." He paused a moment and turned to take in the sight of the artwork. "Behind the scenes of this magnificent show, I have watched the young lady in this picture work tirelessly without complaint. There is such enthusiasm and joy in her spirit as she goes about orchestrating and perfecting every minute detail of her ensemble in her attempt to bring this artistic symphony to life. To watch Ms. Adams work is truly a thing of beauty. After a short time in her presence, the happiness she exudes, and her passion for what she does, will start to infuse itself into your soul. You become drunk with it and quite frankly … it makes you want to become a better man. At the very least, you will want to make an *attempt* to achieve greatness in the way that she strives to do. In my case … I find that I now strive for *both*. I want to be a better man. I also want to perfect my craft the way Ms. Adams has … Although." He thought for a moment and put a finger to his temple. "I have yet to discover a craft," he said sarcastically, infusing a bit of humor into his speech and invoking a bit of laughter from the audience. "But!" Landon put a finger in the air. "I can assure you that I'm working hard to find one." He looked at Lily. "And I undoubtedly owe that to you, Ms. Adams."

His words made Lily smile. James caressed her arm, gazing at her in a way that expressed how much he understood the sentiment of Landon's words.

"I presume that most of you are very familiar with William Werthington," Landon continued, motioning in William's direction. The crowd applauded in affirmation of his statement. "Well, several months ago, my father received a lengthy heartfelt letter from Mr. Werthington. It is actually that letter that has afforded me the opportunity to be inspired by the young woman who is now the subject of this fine piece of artwork here." He motioned his hand toward it again. "You see, the letter Mr. Werthington wrote was regarding a certain matter with Ms. Adams. After reading such touching words, my father became extraordinarily curious and was willing to travel here himself to the United States to learn more about this fascinating young lady. But my father works very closely with the royal court in the United Kingdom, and needless to say, he is an extremely busy man under those circumstances. So, I suggested that I make the journey here for him. At first, he was not so keen on the idea because, unfortunately, he knows that I'm not easily impressed by anything, which is a fact I cannot argue. In fact, I was certain that I would return to my father after my adventure here to America and explain to him what a disappointment the journey was and to be glad that he never bothered to waste his time." Landon inhaled sharply and looked down at Lily. "Well, I cannot tell you how very wrong I was.

"I must admit, I've stolen many a heart thus far in my life," he joked, letting his narcissism shine briefly. "But after watching this beautiful young lady here, this was the first time that a woman had ever stolen mine … But not in the *usual* manner. After seeing Ms. Adams' show, I confessed to her that what I saw captivated me like nothing else in my life. I immediately understood the passion and motivation with which Mr. Werthington had scripted his letter to my father. Because, much like Mr. LeRoux was moved to create a masterpiece after the experience of watching Ms. Adams' symphony, I too was moved to dedicate every resource in my power to Ms. Adams' cause.

"And now the very same show that I was so hell-bent on giving my father negative reviews about, is one that I can't seem to stop myself from bragging on and on about to him. Letter after letter, it seems there is just more and more I find to tell him about this brilliant young woman and her incredible show. And now, after receiving dozens of my letters, my father has finally written back…" he said, raising an envelope in the air, "expressing that he has grown tired of me talking about her." Landon paused when everyone looked at him curiously. "My father now wants to *see* with his very own eyes, this phenomenon that has captivated his only son, a son that he knows full well is usually so cynical about *everything*. He just has to meet the woman and see the show that has transformed me: a feat that he feels he has hopelessly failed at," he joked. "He wants, at the very least, to say thank you to Ms. Adams for accomplishing what he was unable to do for the last twenty-seven years." The crowd laughed again. "But! My father hopes that he will get to meet her for far more than that." With that, Landon turned to Lily again. "Ms. Adams, would you be so kind as to join me here on stage for a moment?"

Not expecting to be in the center of attention at all for that evening, Lily looked at James curiously. He shrugged his shoulders, but then helped her to stand, escorted her up the stairs to the stage, and went back to take his seat.

"Unfortunately, with my father residing an ocean away, it would be impossible for him to journey here in enough time for your final performance at Winter Garden," Landon explained to Lily once she was standing next to him at the podium. "However, he thought that perhaps there might be a solution for that. You see, when my father wants something, he will do *everything* in his power to acquire it. That, coupled with the fact that he knows I am rarely excited about anything, makes my father trust that you are more than worthy of this," he said, handing Lily the envelope he was holding. Lily looked down at the folded letter that Landon had placed in her hand, which had an official red wax seal with the emblem of a winged horse holding its folds together. She then glanced back up at Landon with a perplexed look on her face.

"Go ahead, open it up and read it," Landon insisted.

Lily loosened the seal, unfolded it, and took a moment to read it silently. She looked back up at Landon again when she was finished. "Is this real?" she asked with tears starting to well in her eyes.

"Every word of it," he assured her.

Lily then turned to look out into the crowd. "William?" she questioned, seeking reassurance from him as well while staring at him with hope glistening in her eyes.

The artwork was a secret that William's sons had kept quiet from him. He was genuinely unaware of that surprise. For two days, however, he had remained tight-lipped about the contents of the letter that Lily now held as she questioned him with her innocent doe-like eyes. In response, William simply nodded with pride stamped into his features, afraid to utter a word for fear that he might let loose the waterfall of emotions that had built in his chest after sensing how emotional Lily had suddenly become.

"Well, don't leave everyone in suspense," Landon chimed in, breaking Lily's fixation on William. "Tell everyone what it says."

Lily cleared her throat, but was still unable to keep her emotions from shining through in nearly every word as she began to read:

Ms. Lily Adams,

It is our pleasure to extend an invitation for you to present The Dream Symphony in the United Kingdom, here at Buckingham Palace. Upon affirmation of this invitation, you will be furnished with any and all necessary equipment and items required to complete your show. All measures will also be immediately put into place for you and your entire cast to journey here. Further details of this arrangement can be discussed in future correspondence after receipt of your response, which we very much look forward to, with the hope that The Dream Symphony will soon be here to witness.

Sincerely,
Queen Victoria

Lily's eyes met William's again. "The very same Buckingham Palace you've told me stories about playing in?" she asked him softly.

"Thee *one* and *only*," William replied.

"I've been dreamin' about playin' there eva' since you told me about your experience there."

"Now here the chance lies before you," William replied, still fighting hard to swallow the swell of emotions in his chest. "Took me half a lifetime to get an invitation there, but you … only half a year!" he smiled. "What's your secret?" he asked, infusing humor into the atmosphere to settle the rising dam threatening the overflow through his eyes. It worked momentarily, bringing lighthearted laughter to everyone in the room. But for Lily, it was no laughing matter.

"Havin' one hell of a mentor to help guide me there," she replied, with nothing but deep and appreciative sincerity in her tone. With those words, and the sight of joyous tears streaming down her cheeks, the dam that held William's tidal wave of emotions back finally crumbled, allowing his tears to come surging forward and rush from his innocent green eyes. He removed his spectacles and lowered his head, attempting to hide the moisture accumulating on his face as both of his sons placed a hand on his back. It was the second time Lily had seen him cry that night. His passionate response to her words, the sight of the show of love from his twins, and suddenly imagining that Emma was there with the three of them, added to the sentimental river flowing down her own cheeks.

"Well, one word from you, Ms. Adams," Landon interjected, placing his hand gently on her shoulder as she patted away her tears with the handkerchief he had given to her, "and I have no doubt that you are capable of infusing that part of your dreams into your extraordinary symphony. *One word*, and I'll prepare a letter to my father *and* the Queen this very eve, giving them the much-anticipated

431

word that you have graciously accepted their request …
just one simple word."

The room was silent for a moment while Lily pondered
something she thought would be so easy for her. She
looked down at the invitation written by the Queen herself
and then looked over at William, who finally held his head
up and put his spectacles back on. She then glanced to
William's left and met the eyes of the man who had
initiated this journey with her in a beat-up wooden wagon
as she sat in the back, barefoot, in a dress nearly as old as
she was. James had sat at those reins driving his horses
forward with nothing but hope and a deep belief that Lily's
talent would lead her to a better life. His belief and faith in
her were evident when he began the journey with her, even
without a single guarantee of the outcome. And it was
certainly evident on this evening in his body language and
in the way his eyes lingered on Lily with pride and
admiration dancing in them as he nodded his head at her to
let her know he was behind her, no matter what.

"Say yes!" Lily suddenly heard Austin scream,
breaking the eye contact she had with James.

An array of scattered "say yeses" then began to erupt
from various members of the orchestra until it began to
build into a slow chant with rhythmic applause to support
it. "SAY YES! SAY YES! SAY YES! SAY YES!" they all
continued to chant.

Lily scanned the room of happy faces, chanting in
support of her and a smile overtook her face as she finally
nodded her head.

"Yes?" Landon asked her, after seeing the slight
movement that he was certain nobody had noticed.

"Yes," Lily replied softly, but barely audible over the
sound of the crowd.

"You're certain?" Landon asked.

Lily looked back down at her letter written by the
Queen. "YEEESSS!" she erupted, no longer able to contain

her enthusiasm after seeing the words *Buckingham Palace* there in front of her again. "YEEESSS!" she yelled again, holding her letter in the air this time, bringing the entire student orchestra to their feet. They all suddenly disregarded the formal nature of the ceremony by applauding loudly, whistling, dancing, and hugging one another in a youthful energetic fashion. They could not help but to share in the excitement of Lily's good fortune and to celebrate the fact that they would soon be performing for a queen and an entire royal court, in a place they thought they would only ever visit in their dreams.

Even the older crowd who were there to bid on art could not help but be entranced by the celebratory spirit engulfing the room. They all stood as well and applauded Lily's decision. "Bravo!" echoed throughout the room, blending in with the sound of the giddy students.

Landon took his assistant by the shoulder and leaned in toward him so that he could better hear amongst the noise. "Prepare a letter to my father immediately." He then turned to look at Lily. "Send him word that The Dream Symphony will soon be on the steps of Buckingham Palace."

"As you wish," his assistant replied, before trotting off to do as Landon had requested. The assistant breezed right by James, who had finally made his way over to Lily and lifted her from her feet in a warm, long, and loving embrace.

* * * *

William stood on the stage alone after thanking Piers LeRoux, unable to turn away from the portrait that eternally depicted him and Lily. He was wishing that he could see his wife's reaction to hearing that a piece of art he was featured in would soon be hanging in a gallery she cherished. He closed his eyes attempting to visualize the joy on her face, but he knew that his imagination could never do Emma's true emotions justice. "I wish you were here, Em," William whispered after opening his eyes, needing to stop the visions of her before he cried for a third time that evening. He collected himself and turned when he heard footsteps approaching.

"Mr. LeRoux certainly outdid himself," James said, standing off to the right of William, staring in awe at Piers's creation. "Feels like I'm sittin' front row at the show."

"It's incredible. No doubt about it," William replied. Both men then stared in appreciation for a moment before William completely changed the subject. "I've been hard on you, James." William turned toward him. "When it comes to Lily's welfare, I know."

James nodded and slid his hands into his pockets. "Ain't nothin' been said that I didn't need to hear. I deserved every tongue lashin' you've given me thus far."

"And I don't apologize for any of it. However, it seems that I always forget about how extraordinarily unique the circumstances really are for you and Lily. I now admit that it was a mistake on my behalf not to take your frustrations about that into consideration."

"Jesus! That's somethin' I sure wish everybody else in this world would forget about as easily as you do!"

"Trust me, I know. Even though it was much easier for Emma and me to hide our secret, I still very much empathize with how much you wish the differences in you and Lily didn't matter so much to everyone. With your differences being so obvious, I know it must be far more taxing on the both of you than it ever was for me and my wife."

"I'd be lyin' if I said it was easy."

"I know. And that's why I must say, it's truly commendable the way you've come to handle it all. Despite the weight of the situation, though, I still couldn't help but be hard on you before. But, I want you to know that that's only because I truly love Lily. I love her as if she were my own child, and I truly want nothing but the best for her." William put a hand on James's shoulder. "And as of late, that's all you've given her, James … nothing but the best of you. I see now how much you truly love that young woman. I see that you're now being the sort of man that she needs by her side. I think I was always so angry at you before because I was convinced that that was the sort of man you could be for Lily from the very beginning, and I wanted so badly for you to just let him emerge."

"I think it just took a while before I could convince myself that that's who I could be for Lily too. Just had some growin' up to do, I guess. Needed to learn my lessons the hard way."

"Ha! Don't we all?! We're all just a bunch of stupid men after all!" William waved his hand dismissively. "We're all guilty of losing our wits over a woman from time to time," he laughed. "I guess I was just trying to do what I could to keep you from making the mistakes that we all fall victim to at one time or another. But hell, maybe it's best just to let every man fall flat on his face and pick himself back up. After all of the scars and broken bones, he'll be a stronger, wiser man."

"I couldn't agree with you more."

"Well, anyhow, I'm just glad that you've come around, and I just wanted you to know that I'm proud to see that you make Lily so happy." William put a hand on James's shoulder. "Because that's all I ever truly wanted for her."

"You and me both, William … You and me both."

"What are my two favorite men in the world ova' here plottin' and plannin'?" Lily asked, approaching the two of them with a smile.

"I," James began, greeting her with a smile and gentle kiss on the lips, "was just plottin' and plannin' to go and take advantage of some more free alcohol," he joked.

"Can't blame you for that," Lily teased in return. James kissed her again before heading to the bar and leaving her alone with William.

Lily then walked over to the portrait that she was

featured in and gently touched it while absorbing all of its fine details. "Emma would be so proud," she said with a smile, as she admired the painting along with William.

"Just as I am of you." He turned to Lily. "Have I ever told you that?"

The sound of those words brought instant warmth to Lily again. "Trust me, I don't think I'll eva' forget that moment tonight when you did," she admitted, recalling exactly where they stood at Winter Garden when he said it.

"Please, forgive my repetitiveness, but I am, Lily … So very proud of you," William confessed again.

"No need to ask forgiveness. I don't think I could eva' tire of hearin' that."

"If not for that then, perhaps I'll require your forgiveness for keeping the secret about Buckingham Palace. I'm so sorry I had to withhold it from you. I wanted so badly to be the one to tell you, but Landon swore me to secrecy. He was insistent that he be the one to deliver the news."

"I could neva' be upset with you for that eitha'."

"Good because, no matter which of us told you, all that really mattered to me is that you'd soon be able to make yet another of your dreams come true … an incredible dream that I absolutely believe you deserve to live out."

"Thank you, William," Lily said, touching him gently on the arm. "I can't even tell you how thrilled I am to be travelin' there! But what makes me happier than anything, is knowin' that you'll be there to experience it all with me."

"Trust me … Nothing would give me greater joy," William replied, thinking about how much he loved to live vicariously through her. "It will certainly be unforgettable. Most often people say that the anticipation of an event always far outweighs reality, but in this instance, I can assure you that the reality of performing in Buckingham Palace will far supersede the way you have dreamed it up in your mind. *That*! I can truly promise!"

"Oh, I believe you!" Lily smiled. "And I can hardly wait! I swear I'm ready to get on that ship tonight!"

William laughed at the child in her emerging once again. "If you left tonight, there would be 6,400 people who will be awfully disappointed come Christmas night!"

"Lord, I'm so excited, I 'bout near forgot!"

They both gave a light laugh and turned to continue appreciating the portrait together in silence for a brief moment.

"Ya' know, William, I guess I should take this opportunity to apologize to you too."

"Why is that?"

"This gon' sound horrible, but I have to confess that I hated you before I eva' even met you."

"Oh!" he replied, shocked by her candidness. "Is that so?"

"Unfortunately, yes, that's the truth," she said sheepishly, "but let me explain … Ya' see, James neva' told me the truth about why he was takin' me to meet you. In fact, he neva' directly said anything to me at all about where we were goin'. I just so happened to ova'hear him tellin' his fatha' that he was takin' me to a slave breeda'."

"To a w*hat*!?"

"Yeah! That's exactly what I said in my mind … along with a few otha' *choice* words," she laughed.

"Well, James admitted to me that he was going to get you away from his father by any means necessary … I guess he certainly wasn't lying. But after using such extreme measures, I certainly can't blame you for the way you felt about me. My God! Under those circumstances, I would've hated me too. No wonder you seemed scared to death the first day I met you."

"Oh, I's terrified! No! *Petrified,* more like it. Actually, I don't think there's really a word to describe how I truly felt when James first rolled me through your gates."

"I'm so sorry he tortured you in that way."

"It's alright. I think we both know by now that James isn't perfect."

"*Really*? I never noticed," William joked.

Lily laughed. "As always, he was just doin' what he thought was best … in his own *odd* little way. Now, in hindsight, though, I can say that I appreciate what he did. It shows me just how desperate he was to get me here. But I admit, it sho' would've been nice if he'd explained everything before I had the chance to meet you. Hell, I don't think he said more than five words to me the whole two-day trip to your estate!"

"With the way you two carry on now, that's certainly hard to believe," William laughed.

Lily smiled. "Yeah, things have certainly changed since then. But at that time, that's the way it was between James and me, and he just wasn't willin' to say a thing to me about who you really were. He let me walk through your mansion doors believin' that you was nothin' more than a slave breedin' monsta'."

"The thought of such a vile, so-called *profession* makes me sick to my stomach. Makes me even sicker to know that you had to suffer, even for a second, believing that I was about to destroy your life in such a cold and heartless manner."

Lily turned to William. "That's exactly why I feel the need to apologize to you. Because believin' that awful lie left me hatin' you before I eva' laid eyes on you. Even afta' we met, I had horrible nightmares about you, because James had still yet to say a word to me about who you were. For days, I didn't want no parts of bein' near you, talkin' to you, or even lookin' at you. Didn't wanna eat your food or sleep in the bed you's kind enough to let me use. I didn't want a single thing you's offerin' me … not even your incredible piano. Because, despite how nice you's bein, deep down I figured you's nothin' but a monsta' in sheep's clothin' tryna lure me in." Lily turned to admire the huge canvas in front of her again. "And now I look at this portrait and think about all the things you've done for me since we've met, and I can't believe I eva' thought anything of the sort about you. All of the beautiful things I see here on this paintin'…" She turned back to look at William, "there's no way in the worl' I could've accomplished any of it without you. You've been so much more than a mentor to me, William," she said, taking hold of his hand. "You've felt more like a fatha' to me … a fatha' who's used all of his heart and his valuable time to help build my confidence and my self-esteem. Then you protected me enough to let the real woman that's been hidin' inside 'a me step outta the darkness and into the sunlight. And I can't even begin to tell you how good it feels to finally stand in its warmth with you.

"It's for all of those reasons that I stand before you now confessin' the sin of my evil thoughts about you. I wanna let you know that I regret every single one that's eva' crossed my mind. Because with everything that's transpired in this last year, I've grown to learn that you're, honest to God, the kindest, most generous, and gentle soul I've eva' met in my life … and I wanna thank you from the bottom of my heart for all you've eva' done for me."

"Lily…" William whispered, as his kind eyes began to well, yet again, with tears.

"If only your heart beat in the chest of every man alive, this world would be like heaven on earth," Lily added.

"Your words touch me very deeply. But in my estimation, it is *you* who has given so much to *me* for all these months. It is *I* who has not the words to express how much working with you has been one of the greatest joys of my life."

"Mine too," Lily smiled, touching his arm again. She then looked over at the twins after she heard them laughing together while talking to two ladies. "I hope your sons know how lucky they are to have a fatha' like you," she commented, after watching them for a moment and realizing that they always seemed to be so happy. "William I know you've done so much for me already, but…"

"But what m'lady?" he asked, turning his attention from his sons back to her.

"W-will you dance with me?" she asked shyly. "The way a fatha' would with his daughta'? I-I've just always wanted to know what it would feel like."

"Lily." William took both of her hands into his. "You have no idea how truly honored I'd be," he replied, with the slightest crack in his voice as he continued to fight his tears.

James was still near the bar drinking a glass of whiskey when he turned and saw William and Lily step out onto the dance floor together. On his way to get a drink, James had walked by Elijah, whose evil expression was powerless to take away the joy he was feeling that evening, especially as he watched Lily being waltzed about the dance floor by William with a smile on her face. James did not know what Lily and William had talked about after he left them alone, but he could tell by the way they danced that there was something special about the moment, something that made him even more impenetrable to Elijah's nasty attitude.

"She is your lady, no?" Piers suddenly asked James, motioning his head toward Lily. Seeming to have appeared out of nowhere, he stepped up alongside James and watched Lily drift across the dance floor as well. Piers had finally come to realize that James and Lily were probably a couple after watching the pair closely during the night's festivities. But despite it, he still boldly questioned James, with a sliver of optimism that maybe Lily was still fair game.

James looked over at Piers. "She is my *lady,* my *queen,* my *best friend.* She's…" He turned for a moment to watch Lily smiling as she danced with William. "My *everything.*

I'd give up my own life for her."

Piers stared at James's profile as he watched Lily. By the expression on his face when he looked at his woman and by the tone of his voice when he spoke of her, Piers was left with no doubt that James meant every word that he had just uttered. "A beautiful answer such as that makes you even more worthy of this." Piers handed James a drawing that he had crafted on a piece of paper earlier in the evening. It was a picture of James and Lily dancing very closely together. Lily's head rested on James's chest and James rested his head on top of Lily's. Both of them had their eyes closed, completely lost in the essence of one another. Piers had captured with perfection a moment that screamed *love*, and he did it with splendid accuracy. "A man with a woman, who has been blessed with such lovely features, should have her beauty to admire whenever he so desires … Cherish it."

"Trust me, I will," James replied, truly appreciating the way he had captured Lily's beauty. "Thank you for this Mr. LeRoux."

"You are quite welcome. It was most certainly my pleasure," Piers said, with thoughts of Lily's illustrious body dancing close to his instead.

James had become aroused by simply looking at the image of himself so close to Lily. At that moment, ironically, he glanced up from the picture to find Lily staring at him with a hunger in her eyes that he was pleasantly familiar with. It was a hunger that James was always willing and able to satisfy at a moment's notice, whenever, wherever, and however Lily wanted. And with the way he was feeling after staring at her picture, James knew he would certainly have no problem fulfilling whatever erotic desires that were invading her mind. His eyes spoke back to Lily, letting her know that his body was ready to meet her demands. Lily read his mutual longing and bit her bottom lip in anticipation of yet another fantasy that was on the verge of coming to fruition. James then quickly tucked the drawing away neatly into his inner jacket pocket. "Will you excuse me a moment?" he asked of Piers.

"But of course," he replied.

After watching the enticing exchange between them, Piers understood full well the nature of the sudden urgency. He actually felt a twinge of irrational jealousy as he watched James and Lily disappear down a dark corridor. However, Piers was not the only jealous person who was privy to the lust-filled exchange between them. Hovering close by the bar nearly the whole evening, Elijah had rarely taken his eyes off of Lily either. Therefore, the look in her eyes when she gazed at James, the way she had just bitten her bottom lip, and the desire present on her face was impossible for him to miss.

After the time he had spent with her alone at Branaugh Theater, Elijah simply could not purge himself of *anything* about Lily Adams. Even five months later, his feelings for her had yet to fade. In fact, they had gotten stronger. During the entire time that James was in jail, Elijah had continued to enjoy dinners and long talks with Lily while sitting next to her in the middle of all of the empty theater seats or sometimes while sitting on the edge of the stage with their feet lazily hanging off of the edge. In that time, there was lots of laughter and intimate stories shared between the pair. Elijah was happy for the time he had alone to connect and learn more about the incredible woman that Lily was. It deepened his attraction for her far past her physical beauty and talent. Lily's humor, the way she laughed, her intelligence, charisma, strength, and her willingness to openly share her life story had completely enchanted him. After their short but intense time together there, Elijah genuinely thought there was a spark that ignited the beginning of something special between him and Lily. He was convinced that the deep feelings that had roared to life were mutual. It, therefore, angered him how quickly all of that had evaporated when James returned, as if their week in close quarters and the chemistry Elijah felt suddenly meant nothing to Lily.

Since that debacle, Elijah had graciously offered to step in and take the place of a percussionist in the show, who was suddenly unable to travel with the other orchestra members. As a new member of the cast, Elijah had taken advantage of the opportunity to work closely with Lily on music-related issues. He was always more than happy to offer his opinions for changes to the show, ask Lily to lunch, or do anything else that would allow him a little more intimate time with her, but he could feel the emotional distance that she had placed between them. Suddenly, the ease with which they once spoke to one another was gone. Elijah even noticed that she rarely laughed or smiled anymore when she was alone with him. In fact, all of the things that had drawn him toward her were suddenly completely absent in his presence. Elijah was convinced that James was the reason behind Lily's sudden changes and that absolutely infuriated him.

Despite the fact that Elijah's intricate dealings with Lily were music-related, James did not care for his proximity to her either. But he trusted that Lily would always do right by him and never once felt it was necessary to voice his opinion on the matter. But unbeknownst to James, it had become a challenge for Elijah to take Lily away from him. Time and time again, though, Lily proved how worthy she was of James's trust by always politely declining Elijah's constant onslaught of advances. However, Lily kept quiet about his disrespectful behaviors, feeling the need to keep the peace for the sake of the show, but most importantly, to keep James from viciously beating Elijah's face in and ending up back in jail.

With no knowledge of his disrespectful behaviors in his absence, James had quietly breezed right by Elijah at the bar in The Grand Ballroom, like he did not even exist. In his haste to satisfy his woman, James had not even noticed the way Elijah watched him walk past with a grimace of pure hatred settled into his features. Elijah's look of disdain was the result of the mere prospect of what James was on his way to do with a woman that he had developed serious feelings for, a woman that he *still* felt had no earthly business submitting herself to a man who technically owned her. The notion of it all disgusted him on an immeasurable level. In this ironic mirrored twist of fate, Elijah was now the one feeling jealous and sick to his stomach after digesting the sight of James and Lily enjoying themselves together, in the same way that James felt watching Lily with him. And, yet again, much like James, the alcohol in Elijah's veins made it far easier for his vile thoughts to seep through his mental filter of rationale. It left him with no inhibitions about putting a quick end to any impure acts the pair had planned at that moment.

Hazily turning and stumbling in his inebriated state, Elijah began to quietly pursue James, who was eagerly pursuing Lily. Elijah was hell-bent on doing *anything* he had to do to shake Lily from her foolish fairytale. He wanted to force her to realize the massive mistake she was making by submitting herself to a slave-owning white man, rather than opening her eyes to the potential they had together.

Unaware that she was being pursued by both men, Lily was walking briskly, well ahead of James, down a dimly lit hallway. She was sashaying with an intentional provocative sway to her hips, initiating a chase of sorts, which James was more than happy to partake in. James, however, got halfway down the corridor and lost sight of her in the darkness and no longer heard the sound of her shoes clicking against the stone floor. A few minutes passed, and Lily did not hear a thing either. She peered from behind the stone column she had playfully hidden behind to find the hallway empty. She began to walk back, wondering what had happened to James, when a hand reached from an empty office room, pulled her inside, slammed the door shut, and locked it. Her lips were instantly devoured as strong hands held her pinned against the wall of the moonlit room.

Just as Elijah had watched Lily, Piers had watched Elijah curiously from time to time throughout that evening as well. He was uncomfortable with how rude Elijah seemed to be toward everyone. Piers noticed that he was the only one not joining happily in the festivities along with everyone else and that he seemed very detached from the excitement of the festivities, even after Lily's epic news. Elijah's distant behavior disturbed Piers to the point that he could not help but keep a watchful eye over him. He then became even more bothered by the way in which Elijah's eyes seemed to follow James and Lily throughout the night. It was then that Piers easily sensed that Elijah's bizarre behavior had everything to do with his displeasure of the couple. Ironically, they were a couple that Piers was enamored with as well. So much so that he could not help but capture them together on paper in a loving embrace. And so as Piers had enviously watched James and Lily make their escape for a passionate rendezvous, Elijah caught his attention, yet again, as he crept curiously down the hallway moments after James. Something in the pit of his stomach told Piers that there would undoubtedly be trouble erupting from the darkness of that corridor without a quick intervention.

"Another drink, my friend?" Piers asked, holding tight to Elijah's arm. Piers had slipped with cat-like precision through the dancing crowd to catch Elijah midway down the corridor.

"What the hell!" Elijah objected in his drunken stupor. "Get your fuckin' hands off 'a me!" He tried to escape

Piers's grip, but the alcohol had made him too weak to snatch his arm away.

"Perhaps you've had a little too much to drink this evening. Come. Sit with me," Piers insisted calmly, pulling Elijah along. "A cup of coffee might suit you better." Within seconds, Piers had put a quick end to Elijah's pursuit. He wanted to ensure that the beautiful young lady, whose show had invaded his dreams, would have her fantasies thoroughly fulfilled by her lover—a man he truly envied—without any interruption from the likes of a drunken imbecile. Piers turned back momentarily to look down the hallway with an envious curiosity sweeping through him and smiled at the visions of his fantasies as he hauled Elijah away.

Piers's brazen interception left Lily happily in the arms of the man who had playfully abducted her. "Makin' me chase what I want, huh?" James asked, barely able to find the willpower to pull his mouth away from Lily's for the two seconds it took to ask her that question. "You want me here?" he asked in a hot and heavy tone. He then covered Lily's mouth again with his.

"I don't *want* you," Lily replied, suddenly tearing herself away from James and walking in a tantalizing stroll to the other side of the room. With the full moonlight casting through a nearby window, James had no problem seeing the sensual look on Lily's face when she turned around. She began slowly unlacing the strings of her dress and let it glide down her body afterward, revealing her silky form-fitting lingerie and the length of her long, toned legs. "I *need* you," she corrected, calling him with her eyes to come to her.

Watching the aggressor emerge in Lily made the bulge in James's crotch threaten to tear a hole in his trousers. He began licking the taste of her off of his lips as he made his way over to her, never once removing his eyes from hers. In record speed, he threw his suit jacket aside. He had broken into an immediate sweat from the swell of heat coursing through his veins, ignited from Lily's seductive show and her impassioned verbal confession of her *need* for him. As much as James loved the look of the sheer two-piece ensemble hugging the curves of his woman's body, he was beyond ready to tear it off of her by the time she was within his reach. He was dying to have access to what was hidden underneath, wanting nothing more than to try to satisfy her insatiable appetite. With the way James ached to plunge deep inside of Lily, it took every bit of his willpower to maintain some semblance of control just to leave her lingerie all in one piece. Instead, he turned her around and impatiently slid her top up and off of her body and dropped it to the floor. With his hands now free, he traced the curves of Lily's thighs, back up through her hips, around her waist, and up to her supple breasts, all the while suctioning soft wet kisses along the nape of her neck, drawing soothing purrs from her with every touch of his lips. Lily gasped at the tingling sensations of his fingers tickling and tugging gently at her nipples, then tilted her head back, and caught his mouth in another fiery kiss. As their tongues still danced together, Lily guided James's hand down her stomach into her panties, through her light thread of hair, then forced his fingers into the moisture of her searing insides. James broke their kiss and let out a long moan the moment her heat and wetness covered his finger. Lily began to go limp and let loose a guttural moan of her own when James then began repeatedly dipping his fingers into the tightness of her folds.

Lily's hands were wrapped around James's neck, and her mouth was parted as the sensations began rolling through her from the blissful feeling of her man's fingers. "Taste me," she demanded of him in a breathy tone, as he happily continued to slide in and out of her. Upon her demands, James withdrew from her. Lily then turned to watch him carefully. The heated liquid between her thighs began to pool again after her arousal was heightened by the sight of James relishing the taste of her. The enjoyment of her flavor showed in James's actions and in the look on his face as he indulged, slowly suckling the moisture of Lily's hot creamy insides from each of his fingers. Suddenly, though, Lily grabbed his wrist and guided his fingers from his mouth into her own while looking seductively into his eyes. James moaned at the sight and feel of her soft tongue delicately sucking his fingers one by one, sending a surge of blood rushing to his groin that caused his manhood to begin mercilessly throbbing.

Hungry to taste more of her, James ushered Lily over to a sofa in the corner, laid her back, tore her panties off, spread her legs wide, and immediately began suckling on the sensitive skin of her inner thighs, heading quickly northward to get to the prize he was yearning for. In a swift motion, he then slid his tongue inside of Lily's pulsating cavity, causing her to sing out his name in a long, titillating tone. For minutes on end, James continued lapping her insides like a starving beast until he had completely satisfied his addictive craving for the taste of his woman's sweet nectar. He then withdrew his tongue, replaced it with his fingers, and began milking the sensitive tissues of her velvety insides. Wanting to enhance Lily's pleasure, he then greedily engulfed her swollen bud with his mouth, sucking madly on it as he guided his fingers upwards, in and out of her, over and over again. Lily's cries of elation immediately peaked. Her legs quivered violently, and she nearly tore James's hair out after losing control from the overwhelming euphoric rush that suddenly released spasm after spasm of her juices raining down into his mouth. James's name, once again, sensually escaped Lily's lips during her powerful release, causing his blood-red hardened shaft to pulsate and drip with envy in anticipation of its own deliverance.

Lily had been spoiled by James enough, though, to know that this first wave of pleasure was only her appetizer. She knew that he would soon serve her body the main course, something that she was desperately craving at the moment as she breathlessly unbuttoned his shirt, pushed him down onto the couch, and descended down on his reddened lips. Her forceful ways were further proof that the meek and timid woman she was during their first encounter no longer existed. That fact evoked another growl from James. After Lily had pushed him down, he lay still and let her have her way with him, feeling extraordinarily turned on by the sight of her tearing at his belt buckle and pants like a madwoman trying feverishly to unleash what she needed to finish satisfying her ravenous cravings. Lily's aggressive nature, her impatience, her unabashed, outward, dire wanting for James, stroked his ego in a way that her words never could. Her actions left him already on the verge of climax as she mounted him and slid him deep inside of her in one smooth motion. "Yeeesss," she cried out, as her eyes closed and her head fell backward. James inhaled through gritted teeth as her insides melted around him. He then released another blissful moan after seeing and hearing the euphoric affect his hardness had on his woman while rippling through every portion of her existence.

The moment they were one, despite an entire room full of people a short distance away, James and Lily were immediately oblivious to everything. Much like drifting in their tiny fishing boat as children, they were now in a world where only the two of them existed, in a world where they were hugged by happiness, love, and the pleasures of their bodies intertwined. It was a phenomenon that never failed to occur whenever they were joined in this way. While they were suspended in their desolate fantasy world together, James pulled Lily in, held her close, and ran his hands up her back and down her waist, loving the look and feel of her soft honey-brown skin contrasting against his. As he caressed and absorbed her, his eyes coasted over the landscape of her curves. However, he could not help but pause and marvel at the sight of the entire length of him buried deep inside the thickness of Lily's tightly constricted folds. Simply the essence of Lily had pleasantly overloaded every single one of James's senses, already leaving him on the verge of bursting inside of her with one simple thrust of her hips.

Fighting to hold back, James exhaled sharply after Lily pushed his hands down onto her buttocks, forcing him to grab on tight to her backside. She then placed one hand tight behind his neck and the other on his tensed muscular thigh to steady herself. After settling in for the ride, she began maneuvering her hips, rocking back and forth in a slow motion, at first, then picking up pace, riding him swiftly, bucking up and down, mimicking a rider at full gallop on her horse. The intensity of the pleasure left neither of them able to hold back the erotic sighs that accompanied the blissful sensations cascading through their bodies as Lily continued her alluring, rhythmic ride.

Usually, it was Lily's release that ignited James's eruption, but after sensing he was near, she began to ride him harder, coming down with forceful strokes, choking his hardened rod in a death grip, building the volcanic pressures within him quickly. As James watched Lily swallowing the entire length of him inside of her dark abyss over and over again, it became far too much for him to take, and he lost all of his resolve to hold back. In an instant, he unleashed with cataclysmic force inside of her, belting out virile groans of gratification from the pit of his stomach in deep pleasure-filled tones that penetrated Lily's ears with ferocity, pushing her over the edge, bringing her to yet another explosive ending along with him.

They lay limp afterward, still connected in a mound on the couch, tired after another unforgettable climb together. Both were breathing like two horses that had just run in a derby, their chests heaving as one as they silently allowed the high to linger for a while longer.

"That ... was ... heavenly," Lily purred breathlessly.

"You ain't lyin'," James replied, sounding just as out of breath. "I swear I just saw the stars up-close."

Lily giggled at his comment and then rested her head back on James's shoulder. James then began stroking her back slowly as she lay nestled next to him. When he caught his breath, he gently pulled Lily up after suddenly feeling compelled just to gaze at her. He was greeted with her smile when he looked at her. He smiled back, and then ran the back of his hand gently down the side of her face, quietly taking a moment to absorb the exquisiteness of her features. James's sudden need to gaze at Lily was owed to gratitude. After everything they had been through, he was grateful that his best friend—a beautiful, strong, intelligent woman—was truly *his,* in every way imaginable. He drew Lily in and kissed her tenderly as his way of silently thanking her for that fact.

"I'm sorry I couldn't wait 'til we got back to the hotel," Lily joked, after pulling back from their kiss and tracing the lines of his muscular chest with her finger. "I couldn't help myself."

"Trust me." He lifted her hand. "I-am-not-complaining," he said, kissing it between each word. Lily laughed lightly, and James pulled her in closer to hold her tighter, stroking her again, not daring to get up and break their connection, knowing she loved to remain one with him for as long as she could after they made love. "Lily," he began, after he lay there thinking quietly to himself for a few minutes. "We don't eva' have to come back here, ya' know?" he said, continuing to glide his hands lovingly up and down her back and along her arms.

"Why wouldn't I want to? It's a beautiful museum, and I haven't had the chance to see the rest of it yet."

"No, I'm not just talkin' about this museum. I mean *all* of this ... These *entire* United States. We could leave and neva' come back to this place."

Lily sat up and looked at James with questioning eyes, wondering if he was being serious.

"I mean it," he replied after reading her mind. "This has become a country that I don't want no parts of anymore, and I certainly don't want you bein' a part of all the ugliness here." He sat up taller, leaning closer to Lily as she sat still straddled in his lap. "Lily, I really think this is our chance. We're goin' to the United Kingdom soon, and who says we eva' have to come back here?"

"James, what are you sayin'?"

"I'm sayin' we can start a new life ova' in Europe, in the Old World as they call it. We can escape this place. As soon as you read that letter from the Queen, I knew this was the answa' I've been prayin' for. This is our chance to start ova' in a place where you'd be a world away from my fatha's reach, and most importantly … in a place where slavery doesn't exist anymore. I'm certain William and Landon would be more than willin' to help us settle in and make a life there," he explained, still caressing Lily's arms, hoping and waiting for a smile or a reaction of excitement about the prospect of his idea. But instead, she was expressionless and silent while the possibility of it rolled through her head. Then suddenly *Lily*, for a change, broke their connection. Without a word, she then got up to retrieve her dress.

"Lily, are you alright?" James questioned, with immediate concern coursing through him. He expected a joyous response from her, especially after knowing how obsessed she had become with British culture.

"But what about your family, James?" she finally asked while trying to get her dress into place. "You'd just leave 'em all behind?"

James stood, buckled his pants, and then went over to help Lily with her dress. "*Family*?" he scoffed. "My fatha' gave me life, yes, but outside 'a the blood we share, I feel

452

not one ounce of a connection to that man. My motha's dead and my brotha's have hated me since the day I's born … and trust me, the feelin's mutual." He turned Lily around to face him. "They ain't no family to me, Lily." He placed his hands gently on her face. "*You are* … you and the beautiful children I pray you'll give me someday. You'll all be my family."

"B-but your home is here," Lily replied, sounding as if she had not heard a word he said.

"*Home* is whereva' you and our children are, no matta' where we are in this world."

"James that's a serious move. Don't you think you might regret makin' such a drastic change in your life just for *me*?" she asked, her puzzled eyes staring straight into his.

"Maybe you haven't been listenin' to me these past few months when I tell you every day how much I love you. Or maybe you just don't believe me. I know afta' everything I've put you through in the past, maybe I don't deserve to be fully trusted by you yet, but Lily…" James made her look at him after her eyes drifted to the ground. "You are my world. I'd *do* anything for you, and I'd most certainly *go* anywhere for you. If I haven't proven that to you already, then I don't know what else I could possibly do to make you believe me." He threw his hands up. "Hell, except for lettin' you watch me get on that ship and sail away from here without hesitation or one single reservation about it. And so for *us* … would I have any regrets about makin' such a drastic change in my life? Hell no! I'd leave this place with you in a heartbeat and neva' give it a second thought!"

"I believe you," Lily replied, but there was still no excitement in her eyes. She was distant and cold, and James felt it, but he could not understand why she remained that way.

"Lily, what is it?"

She removed his hands from her face and turned away from him.

"Lily, tell me that you want this too, so we can sail away from this place and neva' look back. Tell me that you wanna start ova' a world away from here and take nothin' but all 'a the wonderful memories you and I have created with us. When we get there, we can create a lifetime full of new unforgettable memories ... and a beautiful family of our own."

Lily was still silent. Her mind already seemed to have drifted a world away.

"Lily?" James persisted. "You'd want that, wouldn't you?"

"You really are serious about all this, aren't you?" she asked, still staring across the room at nothing.

James walked around to the front of her and turned her face toward him. "I've neva' been more serious about anything in my whole life. I want you an ocean away from my fatha' and my brotha's ... in a world where I can finally feel secure that he has no way of gettin' access to you. Where I know you and our children will be safe."

"I can't do it, James," Lily finally replied, catching him off guard by her refusal.

"*What*? Lily, w-why not?" he stammered.

"Not without my motha'," she continued, instantly helping James to understand her sorrow and the reason for her reservations. "I don't wanna go ... not unless I can take her with me. I can't leave her here."

"If that's what you want, then I'll find her. I swore that to you, and I will. As soon as we're settled there, and I know you're outta harm's way, I'll come back and find her for you. But..."

"But what? You made a promise to me," Lily reminded him with a very serious look on her face.

"I know, and I swear I'll stand by that. It's just that I know your reservations about wantin' to find her, and I don't want you to feel rushed into this because of what I'm askin' here. So I'll do it, but *only* … only if you're *truly* ready for me to do it."

Lily stepped past him and walked over to glance out of the moon-filled window at the troubled world that her mother was still trapped in. It was a troubled world that Lily had the power to help free her mother from with just two simple words. Ready to exercise that power, Lily closed her eyes and let out a cleansing breath. "I'm ready," she announced.

Feeling great relief after hearing the sincerity of Lily's words, James came up behind her and slid his arms around her waist, and they gazed out of the window together.

"I know I can do this, so long as you're with me to give me the strength to get through it," Lily added.

"So long as I'm alive, I'll always be here for you … through *everything*."

"Then I'm *truly* ready…" Lily finally relaxed in the arms of the man who continued to prove that he truly loved her. "Ready to start our new life … *togetha'*."

"*Togetha'*," James repeated, letting a soft kiss linger on the side of her face for a moment afterward. "In the Old World," he continued, as he rested his head against Lily's and swayed gently with her in his embrace.

"The Old World will be our *new* world," she whispered.

* * * *

What Lily was currently feeling was a familiar anxiety that began to manifest in her the very first time she saw James slowly roll out of sight in a wagon to go stay with his aunt and uncle for a few weeks during the summer. That childhood anxiety grew worse every time she watched him leave. It finally planted deep roots in Lily's soul the day she watched James pack up his wagon for college and ride out of her life for six long years without so much as a goodbye. That same sick feeling in her stomach struck her again when Sheriff Tolliver had come to haul James off to jail. James's unknown whereabouts in the days that followed gave even more grounds for the roots of Lily's anxieties to stay firmly planted in every fiber of her being. Now here Lily was, sitting snuggled next to James in her carriage, headed to the train station with that all too familiar sickness brewing in the pit of her stomach again.

In the few days before the art museum fundraiser in Manhattan, Anna Mae had struggled to rid herself of a cough that rattled her whole body, brought pain to her chest, and hoarseness to her voice. She had fought it for as long as she could, but it had gotten progressively worse. Amidst the art museum festivities, the bug that had invaded her body caused her to collapse. James had returned to The Grand Ballroom after his intimate rendezvous with Lily to find guests circled around Anna Mae as she lay on the floor. He immediately jumped in and put his medical training to good use. He found that Anna Mae's symptoms pointed to dehydration, brought on by her inability to hold much of anything down. James had forced her to drink as much as she could, and by the time they had gotten her back to the hotel, she was doing a little better. Once there, William insisted on finding a doctor in town who had the sort of equipment and medication that James lacked, but Anna Mae refused. She accepted whatever help James could offer her, but was fearful of what some other white doctor may do to a helpless Negro woman. Instead, Anna Mae insisted on being treated by the doctor she had trusted for years back in Ohio. Everybody tried to convince her that traveling while she was so ill would not be wise, but she remained stubborn. After months on the road, she was longing for trusted medical treatment in the comforts of her bed in the warmth of her own home.

With no other choice but to give in to her request, James decided that it would be the most practical for him to escort her and Ben back home, since he would be the most suitable person to handle any emergencies. Not only that, but he explained to Lily that it would give him the chance to collect all of their belongings before they sailed to Europe. In between a fit of body shaking, painful coughs, Anna Mae graciously thanked James for his willingness to help. He explained that he felt it was the least that he could do in light of everything she had done for Lily.

Before departing the hotel, Anna Mae's children and everyone else said their goodbyes to her and Ben. And now, as James helped Anna Mae to her seat, Lily boarded the train to bid them farewell too. She held Anna Mae tight and kissed her on the cheek. "I feel guilty, like I'm the one that done worked you clear to the bone tryna keep up with all the madness for the show. Don't seem like you eva' get a minute 'a rest."

"Don't you feel a lick 'a guilt, baby," Anna Mae replied, coughing into a handkerchief. "I'm the one been foolish enough to push myself too hard. I neva' trusted that absentminded daughta' of mine to make the costumes and yo' dresses by herself." She tried to laugh but began to cough again. "Guess I ain't got no choice now," she wheezed.

"I've seen Isabel's work. It's just as beautiful as yours. You taught her well. You should be proud."

"I am proud ... proud 'a the both of ya'."

"Thank you, Ms. Anna Mae," Lily said, taking her by the hand. "I'm gonna miss you. I don't know how to adequately thank you for all you've done for me."

"Seein' the joy on your face every time you put on one of my dresses been all the thanks I eva' needed, baby," she answered, breaking into another coughing fit.

"No mo' talkin'. You go on and rest now," Lily said, patting her free hand and turning toward Anna Mae's husband. "Ben, I know you'll take good care of her."

"Always have, always will," he replied, as he covered his wife with a blanket. "Don't you worry about her. All I want you to do is go and put on a show that Queen ain't neva' gonna forget, ya' hear?"

"Yessa', I promise I will." Lily embraced him. "For all the hard work that you put into the stage along with James, I wanna thank you too."

"It was my pleasure, sweetheart. I finally got to put these old muscles to work for a change. Had all them young'uns out there lookin' like a bunch 'a little girls compared to me," he joked.

"I sure am gonna miss you and that sense 'a humor of yours," Lily laughed.

"I'll miss you too. Take care, sweetheart."

After Ben kissed her on the cheek, Lily exited the train and walked up to Griff, the leader of the misfit security bandits. There were already two bandits back on William's estate guarding the grounds, but William still felt it was best to send Griff back with Anna Mae and Ben for added protection, since death threats still trickled in from time to time. Griff was the closest to Lily of all the bandits, and she suddenly found it hard to say goodbye to him as she approached him. As always, Griff had his thick, dark mustache perfectly twisted and turned down at the sides. He was wearing his typical jet black clothes and boots, his black Stetson hat, and had his two pistols hanging crooked in his holster from his hips. Lily had never once seen him without "the punishers" dangling from his waist, as Griff jokingly called them. She swore that he probably slept with them. By all accounts, Griff looked mean and hard as nails, but with the way he would always talk to Lily about the fondest memories of his three grown daughters with such tenderness in his tone, she was convinced that they had melted his cold heart. Lily found Griff's combination of soft and tough endearing.

Griff never said it, but Lily could tell that he never stopped missing his girls since the day the last of them had gotten married and moved away. So anytime they were back at William's estate, she would walk out to Griff at the front gates in the morning and serve him fresh brewed coffee, strong and black the way he liked it, along with a towering stack of her homemade pancakes. The pancake on the very top was always made into the shape of a heart the way Griff said his daughters used to do for him when they were younger. It was not only Lily's way of thanking him for risking his life to protect hers, but of trying to make Griff feel like his girls were there with him again, at least for a little while.

"I sho' am gon' miss them famous flapjacks 'a y'urs," Griff confessed to Lily when she stopped in front of him at the train station. "But *you* more than anything, Little Flowa'," he said, referring to her by the nickname that he had given her. Strangely, his term of endearment would always remind Lily of something that once happened to her while she was standing near an apple tree on her father's plantation when she was just three years old. Yet again, standing there hearing Griff call her that now, caused the memory to float into her mind the way it always did. She began to wonder if the event she was recalling was real or perhaps just a dream. Once her mother joined her in Europe, it was one of the many things she wished to ask her about.

"I'm gonna miss you too, Griff," Lily admitted, and then threw her arms around him. Griff wanted to keep up his hard reputation, but with his Little Flower hugging him, he easily lost his willpower and gently returned her embrace.

When Lily let him go, Griff returned to his intimidating demeanor, walked over to one of the other bandits, and slapped him on the shoulder. "Take good care 'a my Little Flowa', Samuel … Or I'll blow y'ur goddamn head off y'ur shoulda's and mount it on my wall," he threatened. Samuel swallowed hard, flashed a nervous toothless smile, and touched his forehead after imagining the wound. Griff then breezed by him to get on the train in his usual calm strut.

After her goodbyes to everyone else, Lily had to turn and face the inevitable: a goodbye that had already begun to sicken her. She felt guilty that she could not overcome her irrational anxiety since she knew that James was only leaving for a few days, and for a very noble cause at that. When she finally approached James, he ushered her to a dark corner outside of the station and had Samuel stand just in front of them for added protection from prying eyes.

"I wish you didn't have to leave t'night," Lily admitted.

"Me neitha', but I wanna be sure Anna Mae's well taken care of on the way back. Besides, once I can get 'er to her doctor, it'll give me time to tie up some loose ends, take the money outta our account, and gatha' up all of our things while I'm there, just like we talked about. The soona' we can leave this place afta' you perform, the betta'."

Lily nodded her head, knowing that he was right.

"Speakin' of your performance … I just looked at that train schedule, and it looks like I'll be runnin' a little behind gettin' back here in time for the start of the show Christmas night," James said with the cold air making clouds out of his breath. As with all things in regards to Lily, he noticed the quick change in her disposition after he mentioned when he would be returning. "Lily, it's alright. I'll be back for the show. I may be a little late, but I'll be there."

"I know. It's just that…"

"Just what?"

"Nothin'," she said, determined to ignore her anxieties. "But will you do me a favor?"

"Of course. Anything."

"All of our letters … I keep 'em in the chest at the end of my bed, would you gatha' 'em up and bring 'em too?"

she asked of him, thinking of everything she could to keep from having to say goodbye until she absolutely had to.

"I'd be happy to."

"I know it might seem like such a petty thing, but they mean so much to me."

"It's not petty at all. They mean a lot to me too. Anything else you can think of?"

"My book … *Our* book. I'd be sick if I left it behind."

"I already had it on my mental checklist," he said, pointing to his temple with a smile. "Anything else, m'lady?" he asked, playfully mimicking a British accent, attempting to cheer Lily up.

Lily wanted to laugh, but she felt a lump starting to form in her throat. "*You*." She closed up his large overcoat and pulled his scarf a little tighter, trying to distract herself from the tears she felt brewing. "And don't you dare be gone away from me long this time."

James brushed back a lock of her hair after the wind had swept it into her face. "I swear, I won't be gone from you a minute longa' than I need to be, Miss Lily."

"Not a minute longa', ya' hear?" she warned again.

"Not a minute longa'," he promised, remembering how his last unexpected stint away from her had affected her and not ever wanting her to suffer a similar fate. "Not one single minute," he said again as he caressed her face.

"AAALL ABOOOARD!"

James looked back at the conductor and watched the last few people funneling toward the train entrance.

"Well, you best get goin'," Lily said, dropping her head, still refusing to say goodbye first.

"I'll see you real soon, beautiful," James said, raising her head and kissing her quickly on the lips before turning to walk away.

"You were right all those months ago, ya' know," Lily called out to James before he had gotten too far.

He stopped just feet away from her and turned around.

"I've always felt it," she continued.

James looked at her a bit confused. "Felt what?"

Lily approached him and ran her hand down the front of his overcoat. "How much you've always loved me," she answered. "And I hope you've always felt it too." Her eyes were suddenly fixated on his. "How much I've always loved you."

James froze for a moment and let his eyes drift across the softness in Lily's face after she had spoken the words. "*Always*," he finally assured her, in a faint whisper.

"Good. 'Cause I do," she admitted, blinking away the tears she could no longer hold back. "I really do love you, James Adams. Through *everything* all these years … I *always* have."

James's eyes suddenly closed as an uncontrollable swell of tears surged forward and threatened to fall from the warmth and sincerity of her confession. In the six months since he had admitted his love for her, Lily had been willing to share her worries, her joy, her concerns, her happiness, her fears, her laughter, and even her body with him, but never had she shared those words … until this very moment. After his egregious errors of the past, James knew that such words did not come lightly and without great meaning from Lily. Speaking those invaluable words not only reflected how she felt about him, but was a symbol of her willingness to trust him. It meant that the healing was complete, that all had truly been forgiven, and that James was finally worthy of having *all* of her. She was now willing to be totally and completely vulnerable with him, without so much as a grain of the wall she had once erected around herself standing in between them.

As the train whistled in the background, with tears still welling in his eyes, James descended down on Lily's lips and kissed her with the sensitivity and finesse that he hoped would convey how much he understood the magnitude of her admission. Lily's confession and her lips against his suddenly made James feel impervious to the freezing temperatures and to everything else for that matter. He closed his eyes again while he kissed her and let the sentiment of Lily's deceleration seep into his heart, his soul, and his spirit as he mentally recorded the time, the place, the look on Lily's face, the tears in her eyes, the tears in his own, the sound of the train engine, the direction her hair was blowing, and the slight break in her voice as Lily professed her love to him for the very first time. He *needed* to be sure that everything about that moment implanted itself deep in the recesses of his memory for the rest of his natural life.

As the conductor called out for the last time, with great reluctance, James pulled himself away and let Lily go. Lily stood on the platform huddled next to Samuel and watched him board as the very last passenger and take his seat near Anna Mae, Ben, and Griff. As the train began to roll, James looked out the window and kept his eyes firmly planted on the woman who loved him until she was no longer in his sight.

* * * *

Lily was taken back to the hotel in her carriage with Samuel at the reins, and with James's passionate kiss having freed her from that sickening feeling in her stomach for the first time in her life after one of his departures. She quickly realized that it was all she had ever needed from James to feel settled whenever he left. Lily would have much preferred to be wrapped up in his strong arms on such a cold night, but she was comforted by the warmth that his lips had left her with, and by knowing that they would soon have the rest of their lives to spend curled up together across the sea.

"Good night, Samuel," Lily told her security bandit before walking into her hotel room.

"Night, Ms. Lily," he responded as he closed her door and then took his post right outside of it.

Lily wearily entered her room after a long day, removing her shoes as she walked in the dark toward her oil lamp. "Do you love him?" she suddenly heard a deep voice asking her from the corner of the room. She nearly jumped out of her skin after turning and vaguely making out a dark figure sitting in a chair near the window.

"How the hell'd you get in here?!" she screamed.

Samuel quickly opened the door. "Ms. Lily!"

"It's alright Samuel … It's only Elijah," she said after her eyes adjusted in the darkness and she realized who he was. Samuel grimaced at him, not feeling easy about the situation despite knowing who he was, especially after hearing Lily's reaction. He then looked at Lily once again to be certain. "It's alright, I'll let ya' know if I need ya'."

Samuel then hesitantly closed the door, and Elijah immediately continued with his line of questioning. "Do you?"

"Do I *what*, Elijah?" Lily asked, sounding annoyed. She finally lit her oil lamp and turned to get a good look at how unkempt and pathetic Elijah looked, sitting there leaned over in the chair with his elbows on his knees and his suit jacket and shirt loose.

"Love yo' *masta*'?"

"His name is James, and I don't see how that's any of your concern."

Elijah suddenly pounced to his feet, startling Lily again. "It *is* my concern because I don't wanna see you hurt! And that's exactly what'll happen if you keep bein' foolish enough to let yourself believe there can eva' be anything honest and pure between you and *your masta*'," he emphasized again.

"He's *not* my masta'!" she yelled, aggravated with his blatant disrespect. "And I don't know if you've noticed, but I'm a pretty big girl, and I don't need *you* or anybody else to tell me how to conduct my affairs!"

"*Affairs!* You couldn't have used a more fitting word!"

"And just what the hell is that supposed to mean?!" Lily asked with her hands perched on her hips.

"It means, that's all you'll eva' end up bein' to *yo' masta'* in the long run! An *affair*! Open your eyes Lily! He can't legally marry you! And even if he could, I'm sure he'd neva' want to! Afta' he marries a woman he'd actually wanna be seen with in public, you'll end up bein' nothin' but his secret little *affair* in backrooms and alleys unda' the pitch black night sky, where he can hide his shameful activities from pryin' eyes!"

"James shows me love and affection openly all the time!"

"Yes! And have you noticed it's *only* in front of all of us! Around people who care about you, where he knows he won't be puttin' himself in harm's way, or embarrassin' himself, or shamin' his family by bein' seen with a Negro! But in the real world there's no way in hell he'd display you proudly on his arm!"

Lily thought briefly about how James had ushered her to a dark area of the train station to say his goodbyes, but then quickly shook it from her head, not wanting to fall victim to Elijah's mind games. "He'd be tryin' to keep *me* outta harm's way!"

"Is that the lie he's been tellin' you, or worse yet, is that the lie you're tellin' *yourself* now?" Elijah approached Lily and touched her shoulder, but she shrugged him off and stepped away. "Lily, you're brilliant ... a damn prodigal genius, for that matta'. That's why it anga's me to see you bein' so stupid and naïve about this. I just wish you'd stop bein' blinded by what you *think* is love."

"It's not just what I *think*! It's what I *see*, it's what I *sense*, and what I *feel* runnin' through me like wildfire!"

Elijah backed up and looked her up and down. "So you *do* love him?"

"You're damn right I do!"

"Then why'd you lead me to believe there was

somethin' between us?"

"What?!" Lily erupted with an appalled look on her face. "Are you still drunk?!" She put her finger in his face. "How dare you have the audacity to accuse me of such a thing! I neva' *led* you to believe *anything*!"

"You'd be lyin' to me if you stood here and said there wasn't somethin' between us back at Branaugh, and that in all this time we've worked togetha', you haven't continued to feel it! You can't tell me that it was just my mind playin' tricks on me!"

"Yes! I *can* tell you that!" Lily erupted again, after having had enough of Elijah's intrusion, not only into her room but into her personal life. "You dismiss my feelings for James like I'm some kind 'a imbecile who needs your permission to know how I should feel! Then you have the nerve to disrespect me, him, *and* our relationship the minute he turns his back by pawin' all ova' me and smotherin' me 'til I feel like I can't breathe … and I'm sick of it! So right here and right now, I'm *demandin'* for you to tell me just how many times I have to turn you down for you to accept that there ain't a *damn thing* between us?!" She continued to stare at Elijah with her chest heaving after her verbal blows, waiting to see if he would actually answer her insulting question. When he cowered like a puppy and remained silent, she continued her tirade with just as much ferocity in her voice. "Tell me, dammit, so I'll be sure to meet my quota!" When Elijah refused to respond again, Lily finally took a bit of the steam out of her voice. "There has *neva'* been anything between us, Elijah … and there neva' will be. All along, this ain't neva' been nothin' but your damn imagination, and your undyin' hope that your twisted fantasies will come to life! Now it's time for you to get ova' it!"

Without warning, Elijah covered Lily's mouth with his while holding tight to her face. The taste of whiskey instantly seared her lips as she pushed hard on him to get away from his unwanted invasion. He held her so tight, though, that she was forced to pry his mouth off of her with all of her might. She gave him a hard shove and slapped him with as much power as she could muster after she finally got him off of her.

"Don't tell me that meant nothin'!" Elijah had the audacity to demand afterward.

"GET OUT!" Lily screamed, wiping hard at the residue he left lingering on her lips.

"YOU CAN'T TELL ME THAT MEANT NOTHIN'!" he still insisted.

"GET YOUR DRUNK ASS OUTTA HERE!"

"I'M IN LOVE WITH YOU!"

"I SAID GET OUT!"

"LILY, I'M SORRY!"

"GEEET! OOOUT!"

Lily's door flew open, and Samuel grabbed Elijah by the throat. "I done heard enough from you t'night," Samuel said as he wrestled Elijah into submission. "Get y'ur fuckin' sorry ass outta here!" Knowing that Elijah was part of the family and that he was inebriated, Samuel spared him the feel of cold steel against his temple and simply dragged him out of Lily's room after their brief tussle. Elijah conceded quickly after the contents in his stomach began to churn. He stumbled down the hallway, out of the hotel, and wandered off into the cold night air to clear his head, along with the alcohol that finally erupted violently from his stomach.

"You alright, Ms. Lily," Samuel came in and asked her after he was certain Elijah was no longer a threat.

"I'm fine," she replied, sitting on the bed in disbelief while wiping her mouth with a wet cloth, trying to get the repulsive taste of whiskey and Elijah off of her lips. While she sat there, Samuel walked around the room and checked the windows, the closet, and even under her bed, just to be sure all was clear before bidding Lily goodnight and walking out to stand guard outside of her door again.

After Samuel had left, Lily undressed and lay down, feeling beyond angry that she had been violated in such a disgusting way. After giving it much thought, though, she decided, once again, that it was best *not* to tell James about what Elijah had done. She feared that after hearing of such a heinous offense, James would literally be on trial for murder. After crossing the line the way Elijah had, Lily wanted him immediately tossed from the show. But she also decided to let his participation at Winter Garden stand so that nobody would question her reason for firing him so close to the Christmas performance. After tolerating him through the end of the show, though, she looked forward to telling Elijah that he would not be setting one foot on the ship bound for Buckingham Palace, a place that she suddenly began to sail to in her subconscious to help escape the memory of Elijah's liquor-covered lips violating hers. With thoughts of that distant land finally overtaking her mind, Lily's horrid encounter with Elijah faded away altogether. Instead, her mind began to replay the vivid visions of her erotic encounter at the museum with a man she currently wished was making love to her again. After making the euphoric climb together, she wanted so badly for James to swaddle her nude body against his while caressing her softly and lulling her to sleep by his gentle touch as she fantasized about what the future held for the both of them in the Old World.

Chapter Twenty-Two

Love:
A profound, tender, passionate affection, or feeling of warm personal attachment, deep passion or sexual desire for another person.

Christmas Night 1859
Winter Garden Theater
On Broadway

Now Playing:
THE DREAM SYMPHONY

LOVE: With a sea of shadowed hearts drifting around it, that was the one word written into the sheer tapestry halfway through *The Dream Symphony*, Christmas night at Winter Garden. In front of a packed house, two grand pianos sat facing each other in the middle of the massive stage with William Werthington seated at one and Lily Adams seated at the other. It was just the two of them, no strings, no percussion, no horns to add to the mix. There was just the sound of two masterfully played pianos, mixing harmoniously together, projecting a simple yet elegant ballad that Lily had written just a few days prior for this special night: a ballad inspired by the power of … **LOVE.**

In quiet moments, be it near her favorite tree, in her hotel room, or riding in her carriage from city to city, James sometimes peered at Lily in admiration as she scribbled music notes down onto sheets of blank paper. She would write feverishly, whenever, and wherever her creative juices began to flow while swaying softly from side to side, closing her eyes from time to time, and dancing to the symphonic sounds in her head. James noted how Lily seemed not to be in the same world as he was when she wrote. He could see in her face and in her body language that she had tuned out everything around her and was completely lost in the musical wonderland of her mind, the place where her memories and experiences were giving birth to all of the wonderful elements that made her shadowed show so unique and extraordinary. To James, she seemed so lost in that glorious world that he often wondered if Lily even noticed any of the moments he was stealing glances at her in utter fascination while pondering to himself where it all came from, why, and how music erupted so easily from within her the way it did. Although those answers eluded him, one thing was accurate: music came with ease for Lily. The melodies and harmonies flowed effortlessly into her creative mind, so fast that her hand sometimes could not keep up with the speed with which they came. The array of musical sounds in her head would fill dozens of blank papers in a matter of an hour or less. And for as many times as James had witnessed the phenomenon, it never ceased to amaze him.

In the midst of watching her script lines and dots that he could barely comprehend, little did James know that he had actually watched Lily transcribe a song that his love had inspired. Lily wanted to perform it for him for the very first time during this one-night-only Christmas event. But, on an impromptu move, after being deeply affected by the story of the last time William had played for his wife at Winter Garden, Lily decided to blend her ballad for James with a song that William had written for Emma years ago. And so now, the beautiful melody that Lily sat playing side by side with the only father figure she had ever known, was one that she hoped would honor the undying love that he had for his wife. At the same time, Lily hoped that it would adequately thank William for having the courage, the heart, and the strength not only to return to Winter Garden, but to return to the piano at all after the pain of losing the love of his life, because she so greatly appreciated that William had returned *solely* for the sake of helping her pursue her musical dreams.

The sentimental ballad surprise brought tears to William's eyes when Lily presented it to him on the piano, and he heard Emma's song infused within it. After hearing the blending of such melodic perfection, William insisted that it did not require the company of an elaborate show of shadow dancers telling a story on the sheer tapestry behind it, only two grand pianos and two people playing them for the people that they loved. He felt that the passion with which they played would be more than enough to ignite vibrant memories of every personal love story embedded in the minds of all who listened.

Hoping to convey those emotions to the crowd on this cold Christmas night, William played with the sort of immense passion that easily warmed everyone. He was fighting to hold back tears after looking out into the audience before he began and, to his surprise, saw his beloved sons in the front row, sitting on either side of a seat that housed not a person, but rather a beautiful, extravagant bouquet of white lilies: Emma's favorite flower. The elegant arrangement sat on display in the very same seat that their mother was seated on the day her loving husband had brought her back to Winter Garden to let her relive the very last remaining memory she had left in the fading last hours of her life.

Much like everyone in the crowd while the ballad was played, William's mind drifted to the memories of his love. Those flowers in her old seat faded away and he imagined Emma was there nestled between their boys again. He closed his eyes and the memories of when he first met Emma came crashing back to him: the way he walked into the little country store she owned and stumbled when he first caught sight of her, the way she wore her hair that day, the way he felt warmth flow through his body when she turned and smiled at him, how he struggled to pull his eyes away from the beauty of hers, and how he suddenly forgot how to speak when she said hello. He even still remembered her sweet scent as she approached, and how he could not figure out how to move after she touched him on the shoulder while asking if she could help him with anything. As William played the blended ballad Lily had written during his third stint in Winter Garden, he recounted every detail of the moment he had gladly made a complete fool of himself in front of a woman he had instantly fallen in love with.

The passion with which Lily played was obvious to the audience as well. Samuel had gone to retrieve James from the train station just before the opening of her show and, although she had yet to see him, she felt James's presence there while she played across from her mentor. As she played for the man she loved, Lily was suddenly happy that there were no dancers present to tell the secrets of her mind when that melody was born. She realized that the only person who needed to see the story had already lived it along with her. He had shared the laughter, the heartache, the birthday celebrations, great sorrow, the pain of distance and separation, the books they had read together, the tears, the losses, and the lovemaking. Through every peak and every valley, James was there. And as she sat at the grand piano expressing her love for him through her music, in Lily's mind, she was there with him all over again too.

Just like William, Lily sat playing with her eyes closed, lost in the memories of her love story with the passion of it all showing in her face, in her body, and in her movements. It showed as she swayed while remembering the wind whipping by her as she jumped down from an old oak tree, and raced with James along a creek, seeking out the turtle they had named together. It showed in her smile while remembering how a jumping fish once had James dancing like he was in the midst of a seizure until he fell from their tiny boat into the water. It showed in the anguish in her face, thinking of the years they had spent apart. And it showed, yet again, in the delight on her face when she thought about the moment he had returned. The passion Lily felt even displayed itself in all the tiny goose bumps that covered her body as she remembered the feel of the very first time James pressed his lips against hers, and in the tears that cascaded down her cheeks when she recalled the first time he ever made love to her. Every moment, every memory, sent warmth rushing through her with each musical bar she played that represented the times over the last fifteen years of her life that she felt showered in the love of James Adams.

There were so many of those glorious moments to recount that Lily could have done an entire two-hour show with that song alone. But with the ending of the five-minute melody, William stood and walked to the front of the stage, waiting for Lily to join him and take a bow just as they had rehearsed. To William's surprise, however, his sons emerged from the wings on either side of him and began walking toward him, holding onto the bouquet that had sat in their mother's seat. Overwhelmed by the surprise that his twins and Lily had planned, William's emotions began to swell in his chest, and so, too, did the lump in his throat when Lily began to play the original melody that he had written for Emma. On cue, Lily crescendoed into the piece at the exact moment the twins reached William and handed him their mother's flowers. Emerson and Wilson then put their arms around their father and turned him to face the sheer tapestry, where William found it already brilliantly illuminated with the figure of a shadowed angel. The angel's wings were spread far and wide, floating above the image of three shadowed men, two of whom had synchronized and mimicked the movements of Emerson and Wilson as they entered the stage and stood next to their father. While Lily continued to play Emma's song, the shadows that represented William and his sons stood together holding the beautiful flower arrangement, still mimicking the stance of William and the twins as they watched the silhouette story play out in front of them. The tears that William fought so gallantly to hold back while he had played suddenly began cascading in streams down his face the very moment the shadowed figure of his angelic wife slowly floated down, took hold of her flowers, and wrapped her wings around the shadowed version of her family in a loving embrace, in perfect timing with the last few notes Lily played just as the light slowly faded away.

Once the long standing ovation and the tears had ceased after the honoring of William's wife, the dancing shadows returned again for the rest of the show. Their elegant movements in front of elaborate lighting gracefully glided across the sheer tapestry, telling stories through dance, driven by the rhythm of Lily's brilliantly written classical pieces. For two nonstop hours, every stagehand, every dancer, every student orchestra member, William Werthington, and Lily had come together to complete another spellbinding show that riveted a sea of people, finally ending Lily's musical journey in the United States.

After delivering the gift of her music on Christmas night, well over six-thousand pairs of hands continuously applauded for the genius woman. The delighted audience was on their feet, cheering on and on for a prodigal woman, who, by law, was only considered three-fifths of a human being, who had no right to vote, no right to own land, no rights to education, no right to learn to read or write, nor any of the other basic freedoms they all had when they walked beyond the doors of the theater they were in. In the eyes of the law, the creator of *The Dream Symphony* was a woman who was *still* figuratively bound by chains, *but*, despite those ugly truths, as she took her final bow at Winter Garden, Lily Adams felt as free as a bird in a summer sky.

After absorbing the unbelievable ovation of the crowd,

the curtain finally closed, truly symbolizing the end of Lily's unbelievable journey to Winter Garden. But, ironically, instead of it feeling like the end, it felt more like a new beginning to her, something she was eager to celebrate with a particular man that she had not seen in days. Lily turned with a smile and watched the stagehands lowering the sheer tapestry behind her while all of her close friends mingled around it in different modes of celebration. While she searched for who she really wanted to see, Lily was greeted with huge bear hugs and innocent kisses on the cheek from many of the orchestra members as she made her way through the chaotic scene. Her happiness and adrenaline were fueled after listening to the sounds of everyone's cheers and champagne bottles popping around her as they celebrated not only another flawless night, but their excitement over soon drifting off to the Old World.

After being hugged and congratulated by nearly everyone in the crew, Lily had yet to spot James. While she had the chance, she retreated to her dressing room to retrieve a Christmas gift that she had wrapped for him. Before she could grab it, though, Landon caught her there. "Lily, do you have a moment?" he asked, peeking his head inside of her door after knocking.

"Sure."

"I have a few people here who have requested to meet you, if you don't mind."

Always having a true appreciation for those who attended her shows, Lily never once turned down an opportunity to meet anyone who wished to speak to her afterward. "Absolutely! They're more than welcome!" she exclaimed.

After giving her permission, Landon brought in a tall slinky man with a rugged beard and a top hat that made him seem even taller than he already was. Tagging along with him was a much shorter woman with a round plump face, dark hair, and two young boys that held tight to her hands.

"This is Abraham Lincoln, his wife Mary, and their two sons. Mr. Lincoln was once a member of the House of Representatives in Illinois, and he happened to see your show in Chicago. He's currently campaigning for the presidency here in New York and has brought his family along to experience the show with him this time," Landon explained.

Hearing that Abraham was such an important person suddenly made Lily a little nervous, but, as always, she quickly pulled herself together.

"Ms. Adams," Abraham began, extending his large hand toward her. "Mr. Von Brandt is correct. I had the pleasure of seeing you perform in Chicago not long ago. I told my wife and children about it, and they've been eager to see your show ever since. I thought it would make a wonderful Christmas present for all of them."

"Thank you. That's very kind of you to say," Lily replied, gently shaking his hand.

"And I must say, it truly *is* one of the best gifts he's eva' given me," his wife smiled, walking up and giving Lily's hand a dainty shake as well.

"Yeah!" their two sons agreed in unison.

"How do you make all those shadows dance?" the youngest of the two excitedly asked, speaking with a very difficult to understand speech impediment that Lily was somehow able to decipher.

The curious little boy looked to be no more than five years old, so Lily knelt down to his level before answering. "It's magic!" she said, waving her hand in front of him. "You believe in magic, don't you?"

He nodded his head, not blinking while looking at her with his eyes wide.

"What's your name?" Lily asked with a warm smile on her face.

"Thomas … but everyone calls me Tad," he explained through his impediment.

"Well Tad, magic starts right up here." She pointed to his tiny little head. "Whateva' you dream, if you put all of your heart and your soul into it, and you work real hard, you can bring it all to life."

Tad nodded his head again, still staring at Lily like he was mesmerized. He even had a huge smile on his face, which was something that his parents rarely saw him do, since his older brother always poked fun at the deformity of his teeth: a side effect of being born with a cleft pallet.

"Always rememba' that, okay Tad?" Lily continued.

"I will," he replied, suddenly wrapping his little arms around her neck.

Lily brushed her finger against his nose before standing up and being greeted with the warm, appreciative smiles of his parents.

"I read that you were once a slave, but that you've since earned your freedom by playin' the piano," Mary said to Lily. "Afta' seein' you play, I unda'stand now why your owna' felt you deserved to be freed. Somebody with your level of skill should neva' be forced into slavery," she smiled, attempting to compliment her.

"Well, in my mind, yes, I feel free. But on paper, I ain't no more free than any slave workin' in a cotton field at this very moment. Truth be told, whetha' any of us can play piano or not, I think we all deserve to be freed."

"I'm so sorry, I didn't mean to offend," Mary replied, feeling a bit embarrassed after realizing her mistake.

"Quite alright, ma'am. None taken. Forgive me, I was just expressin' my opinion."

"Daddy, how come only brown people are slaves?" Tad suddenly wanted to know after paying close attention to the conversation. He glared up at his father with curious, big brown eyes, waiting for a reply. His father looked from him up to Lily, and they held each other's gaze as the wheels turned in his head. He did not want to answer the question in front of Lily but then realized that even if she was not in his presence he still would not have had a logical explanation to give to his inquisitive son.

Lily scrambled to ease the tension of the situation when she saw the look of extreme embarrassment on Abraham's face. "Do you boys like chocolate?" she finally thought to ask.

"Yeah!" they both agreed in unison.

"Mrs. Lincoln, would you mind if they had a piece?"

"No, of course not. Only *one* piece, though, okay boys?"

"Yes, Ma'am," they promised as Lily handed them a bowl of candy to sift through.

Once the boys were occupied, Abraham turned his attention back to Lily. After learning that the newspapers had embellished the truth about her freedom, he was suddenly curious to hear the truth about her life. He wanted to hear in her own words how she had come to play piano in such an elaborate show. In response to that initial question and many more that followed, Lily began to satisfy Abraham's curiosity with the details of her long, turbulent life journey to Winter Garden. She was very open about the fact that her father had sold her, her unique friendship with James, and how she had secretly taught herself to play piano. She went on to explain how James believed in her talent so much that he had taken her to meet William and that he had even built her an amphitheater. She talked about Landon paving the way for her tour, the ups and downs of her journey along the way, the ridicule and rejection in the beginning, and finally being embraced and accepted in the end. Lily was not shy at all about sharing the vivid details of the events that eventually led to the rise of her musical success as well as emphasizing the fact that she was *still* nothing more than a slave.

Abraham had hung on Lily's every word as she spoke. He was absolutely intrigued by the entire phenomenon, as was his wife. However, Mary had become fixated on a particular part of Lily's story. Being a woman, she could easily sense Lily's emotions and hear the sentiment in her voice when she spoke of James, and she suddenly could not help but want to know more about him. "The piano piece that you played ... the one about love. Is James the one you played it for?" she asked with a gentleness in her voice that made Lily feel as though she could trust her with the answer.

Whether she could trust Mary or not, Lily suddenly did not care if the Lincolns, or any other person, was appalled by the fact that she loved a white man. She was not ashamed of her relationship with James and wanted to feel free in expressing how she felt about him. She knew they would be sailing away to Europe soon and felt confident that no harm would come to her between now and then anyway. Lily stared at Mary for a moment before answering. She felt a mutual understanding being exchanged between them in their eyes, expressing that her words would remain between the three of them. "Yes ma'am, he is," Lily finally answered.

A smile drifted onto Mary's face, and she encircled her arm around her husband's and snuggled closer to him. "That song was beautiful," she replied. "Simply beautiful."

"Thank you, ma'am."

"I'd sure love to meet this James you speak of ... and Mr. Werthington too. I've been to several of his symphonies when I was just a girl."

"Well, come right this way!" Lily gestured with her hand toward the door. "I can certainly arrange that," she smiled. She was eager to see James too anyway and was more than ready to go.

"Come on, boys," Abraham beckoned to his sons, who both had disobeyed their mother and were indulging on their fifth piece of chocolate while she wasn't paying attention.

"Yes, sir!" they said in a muffled tone as they chewed

on the last piece they had shoved into their mouths.

Before exiting, Lily picked up the Christmas gift she had meticulously wrapped for James, wanting to share it with him there at Winter Garden while everyone still celebrated in the back halls. She wanted to give him more than that, though. After not seeing him for so long, she was beyond ready to give him the pleasures of her body and release from within her what days without him had built up inside of her. The thought of it brought a mischievous smile to her face as she secured his gift in her hand and escorted her guests out into the hallway.

Lily walked down the hallway with the Lincolns, answering their questions about the production of the show while she went in search of William. The conversation, however, came to an abrupt halt when Lily stepped around the corner and gazed down the corridor. She immediately froze where she stood. There, straight in front of her, stood the man whose gift she held, a man she had just admitted to loving just a few days before, a man who had gone above and beyond the clouds to prove that he loved her, and was responsible for helping her to seize this rare moment at Winter Garden. Lily's eyes widened, and she became weak all over, but her reaction had nothing to do with him, and everything to do with the person standing shoulder to shoulder beside him, a person whose presence immediately brought flashes of her childhood back to her and memories that still affected her in many ways, a person Lily thought she would never again see in her lifetime. She stared in silence and utter disbelief as tears began to well in her eyes.

"Why the long face, girl?! You mean you ain't happy to see me?" Jesse said, glaring at her while standing with two deputies.

Lily ignored the question. With the hatred and fury she had harbored for Jesse her whole life immediately brewing to boiling levels, she simply stared at the man she believed was the devil himself.

After Lily had failed to reply, Jesse left the side of his son and the two deputies that had accompanied him and began to approach her with his face twisted in anger. "I'd'a snatched y'ur ass clean off 'a that stage had I not stopped and realized I's finally gettin' a return on my investment," he told her while standing a hairsbreadth away from her face, holding up a briefcase full of her hard-earned money. "'Cause Lord knows y'ur cookin' and cleanin' ain't been worth a goddamn penny all these years!" he snarled.

Lily's high faded away and the blood in her veins began to go cold as Jesse loomed over her, letting his eyes and his body language continue to speak for him. The reality of him so close to her, the sound of his voice, his vulgar stench, the memories of his hand across her face many times as a child, in combination with his cruel words, all held enough weight to crush her in a matter of seconds. Suddenly, the woman that Lily had blossomed into over the last few months, with confidence, strength, and the ability to look a man in the eyes, all shriveled and died at that moment. She quickly reverted back to her submissive ways, into the shell of the woman that Jesse expected her to be. She immediately dropped her head after not being able to withstand the menacing look on his face that she had seen in times past, a look that was often followed by grave pain. As Lily looked down, her eyes drifted to the briefcase filled with her money that Jesse had declared as his own. She then glanced over to the ownership papers in his hand claiming her as his, and Lily knew that it was all truly over.

Landon, Wilson, Emerson and William all suddenly approached and stood in a circle around Jesse, Lily, James and the deputies as if in a stand off. Their eyes were all darting from one to the other, each waiting for someone to speak. Easily sensing that something was horribly wrong, Austin, the other students, Elijah, Isabel, and the Lincolns, all slowly gathered on the outskirts and watched on, wondering who this strange man was berating Lily with his words and his devilish presence. They watched and waited, somehow knowing by the look on everyone's faces that a war was likely to erupt if someone did not intervene, but fearful to do so because of the presence of the deputies.

After staring at the ownership papers in Jesse's hands, Lily finally looked up at James through a haze of tears that had yet to fall. He just stared back at her with no expression on his face at all. He had yet to move, or say a word in her defense, or attempt to stop his father from making any claims over her. After Lily had held his gaze for a moment, in a swift movement, Jesse snatched her by the arm, twisting her skin tight, immediately snapping her from the hypnotic glare she had on James. She inhaled sharply, cried out in pain, and dropped James's Christmas gift to the floor, shattering the contents inside of it. "Come on here!" Jesse yelled as he grabbed her, his fire-red eyes piercing through her. Without another word, he yanked Lily along and began to walk with her down the corridor, still holding her arm in a death grip.

"Sir, if you please, I beg of you to let her go!" William interjected, his heart racing after watching Jesse handle Lily like a meaningless object. The realization of what was happening was setting in hard for William as Jesse dragged her further and further away; he immediately began to fight to regain control over the situation since it seemed that nobody else cared to bother, not Elijah, not Austin, not either one of the Lincolns, who stood horrified by what they were witnessing … not even James. William was the only one who proved that he was not deterred by the deputies or by the evil aura of Jesse's presence.

"Who the hell're you?!" Jesse demanded to know after stopping for a moment to look at William.

"Please, sir, I just beg of you to turn her loose!" William demanded again, ignoring his question, his hands visibly shaking in the air.

Jesse responded by tightening his grip on Lily and

yanking her toward him. Again, she cried out in pain.

"Please! You're hurting her!" William pleaded.

"Shut the hell up!" Jesse shouted at Lily, his face turning a darker shade of red. He began to stomp away again when William refused to answer his question.

The thought of Jesse taking Lily away sent William's mind racing to find a solution. "Sir! It's my understanding that you've appointed your son to take care of matters involving your slaves, correct?!"

Jesse stopped. "I ain't gonna ask you again, Brit! Who the fuck're you?!"

"Just someone who wishes to help resolve this matter…"

"I got my resolution," Jesse replied, holding up the briefcase full of money and shaking Lily hard with the other. He then proceeded down the hallway, but yet again, William jumped in front of him to cut him off.

"There must be a better way than this!" William continued to plea with great urgency and concern in his voice. "Can you please speak with your son?! Please?!" he begged, pointing to James, who had done nothing except stand there silently staring at Lily as she begged for his help with her eyes. "Please allow James to work things out with you! I beg of you not to do this!"

"My son," Jesse replied, turning around to look at James. "*My son?*" he repeated slowly, saying it in a way that sounded as if he questioned whether or not he truly was his own flesh and blood. Jesse suddenly walked toward him. Despite the things that James had already told his father about the situation, he suddenly did feel the need to know where his youngest boy's loyalties truly lay. Jesse wanted to test his son in front of the mass of people that surrounded him. "Maybe this ol' fucker is right. I gave you control ova' Lily," Jesse said, approaching James with his face still crippled by his menacing glare. "So, tell me, *son* … what do you think is best, huh?" He stood face to face with James. "You decide." He dropped the briefcase full of cash in between them. "Do we take *my* property home where she belongs?" He shoved Lily toward William. "Or do we hand 'er ova' to this ol' fucker, huh? If you wanna hand 'er ova'." He held up Lily's ownership documents in his hands. "I'll sign 'er papers right now and set 'er free right where she stands ... The choice is y'urs, boy."

James read the look in his father's eyes as they stared each other down in cold silence while everyone else watched on in suspense in the background. It had never been a secret to anyone in the show how James felt about Lily, so many of them suspected that his choice would be an easy one. Feeling the heat of their glares, James turned to face Lily's entourage and saw hope radiating from every set of eyes that stared back at him as they eagerly waited for him to speak. He then peered over at Lily and caught a pair of innocent multicolored eyes that sparkled with unshed tears, glancing back at him. James knew that the waiting tears in her eyes had nothing to do with the pain in her arm after being manhandled, but instead, had everything to do with the thought of being taken away from a man who treated her like she was his own beloved child and being returned to a man who treated her like an animal. As James continued to stare at Lily, he realized that his words had the power to decide the definition of her waiting tears. The answer that he uttered would be the difference between tears of great sorrow and misery *or* tears of great relief and joy. Even through her brimming tears, James could see the hope in Lily's eyes as to what his answer would be. He could see the trust that she had bestowed upon him and the confidence that she had in him to prevent her from being cast back into a torturous life. Even through the swell of tears in Lily's anguished eyes, James could see that she still even managed to look at him with an infinite amount of deep, impenetrable love and tenderness. The way she looked at him was so intense that it caused him to quickly snatch his gaze away without a word, leaving the definition of Lily's tears to await his decision for a moment longer.

"Speak, goddamn it!" Jesse barked at his son with great impatience.

After quickly pulling his eyes away from Lily's, James finally turned his attention back to his father. "Well, it's like I already told you earlier, Pa. I played the role … with *everyone* here," he emphasized, turning to look back at Lily again. "I said what I had to say, did what I had to do to orchestrate all 'a this. We needed to earn money for the farm, didn't we?" He bent over and picked up the briefcase full of money. "I'd say this little scheme was far more profitable than any baby breedin'," he said, pulling out a stack of one hundred-dollar bills and flashing it. "Wouldn't you agree?" He then thrust the briefcase back toward his father with a sinister smirk on his face.

Jesse snatched the briefcase filled with every dollar that Lily had earned. "*My* boy," he said proudly. He then turned to glare at William. "I do believe *this* belongs to me," he told him, snatching Lily away from his embrace.

As Jesse grabbed hold of Lily's arm again, she stared briefly into James's eyes and saw that ice had returned to them. Then, suddenly, the silence in the hallway was pierced by her heart-stopping shrill. It was an agonizing, stomach-wrenching shrill of a woman who had, *yet again*, been emotionally shattered and betrayed in the most evil of ways by a man that she thought loved her. James had finally defined Lily's waiting tears, and he was now forced to watch as sorrowful tears of misery began to rain down like a sudden flash flood from her eyes. The way Lily cried was unlike anything in that hallway had ever seen. Her body convulsed as the sobs of pain continued to erupt. Her chest heaved hard up and down, to the point that she nearly hyperventilated. It was like watching a woman cry who was dying an incredibly slow and excruciating death.

Realizing her fate, Lily's fears caused her to reflexively try to pull away from Jesse's grip. When she momentarily escaped, Jesse backhanded her brutally across the face. The move was swift and powerful, and the results of the force he exerted were instantaneous. Lily found herself on the ground after a moment of seeing black, her eye pulsating and swelling fast. The heads of all of her friends turned away quickly in horror after the heartbreaking brutal scene was too much for them to handle.

"Dear God!" William cried, rushing immediately to be by Lily's side, crouching down near her and helping her to sit up. "Have you no soul?!" he screamed, looking up at Jesse, who hovered over the both of them.

Elijah looked down at Lily lying on the floor, and his actions were quick, sudden, and unexpected. He lunged at Jesse, but before he could grab him, one of the deputies caught him with a fist to the jaw that staggered him.

"Know y'ur goddamn place, you uppity nigga!" Jesse spat, after turning around and realizing who had just tried to attack him.

Elijah held his jaw after being briefly shaken, but he quickly composed himself, looked down at Lily, and met her eyes as she lay there. Even through the swelling and blurred vision, Lily could read the contents of Elijah's thoughts easily. The look on his face caused her to replay the heated warnings that he had given her in the past in regards to James. Elijah then turned from Lily and looked at James in the most menacing of ways before storming out of the building.

Abraham and his wife had retreated just before Elijah. Appalled by the horrific scene they were witnessing, they had covered their sons' eyes and ushered them out in the opposite direction. Everyone else who remained did not dare to intervene, fearing that they would be met with the same force as Elijah.

Once all was settled, Jesse pried William off of Lily who was still trying to comfort her. He then picked Lily up off of the ground in one quick motion.

"Please let her go!" William continued to beg, rushing to jump in front of Jesse as he began escorting Lily out.

"Move aside, damn it!" Jesse demanded.

"Please!" William continued to shout, but Jesse did not bother to stop. "I'll purchase her from you! Please!" William begged, walking briskly to keep up with them.

"She ain't for sale!"

"Name your price!"

Jesse stopped and turned toward William. "I *said* … She! Ain't! For! Sale!" He had leaned in so close that his tobacco-coated spit particles were pelting William in the face as he spoke.

Still undeterred, William suddenly reached deep into his pocket and pulled out a wad full of folded one hundred-dollar bills. "How much do you want for her?!" William suddenly threw a bill at Jesse. "A hundred dollars!" he shouted, then threw several more. "Five hundred?!" He then took every bill in his hand and tossed them in the air. "TEN THOUSAND?! YOU SICK SON OF A BITCH!" he erupted as a rain shower of money floated to the ground. "Tell me how much money it will take to make you realize that Lily is not an animal?! SHE'S A HUMAN BEING!" William's hands were out in front of him shaking with rage. "And by far one of the finest I know," he said, with the utmost softness in his voice when referring to Lily. But the fire in his voice immediately returned upon continuing his onslaught of angry words toward Jesse. "And *you*! Are by far the most *despicable*!" William's lips were curled, and his eyes were squinted in the most hateful expression anyone who knew him had ever seen. Even his twins were shocked by what they were witnessing.

"Get outta my goddamn way, you old fucker, before I snap you in half!" Jesse growled, grabbing William by the neck and shoving him back hard.

"At least give me a moment to say goodbye to her!" William managed to choke out, holding onto his throat. "Please!" he begged. He reached his hand toward Lily, but Jesse snatched her away from his reach and quickly fled from the building with her. William fell to his knees and began sobbing uncontrollably into his hands, feeling no differently than if his own life had been stripped away from him. His sons both immediately knelt to embrace him.

As his father marched off with Lily in tow, James looked around at the swarm of people left standing in the hallway. Every last one of them had grown to care very deeply for Lily, and he could feel the heat of their angry eyes burning holes into his flesh. He gave a quick, sweeping glare to everyone before he boldly walked off to catch up with his father, without so much as an attempt to explain the irreparable damage he had just caused not only to Lily, but to William as well. On his way out, he glanced down at the heap that William had been reduced to and did not even bother to assist him in getting to his feet. He just kept on walking callously through the minefield of money on the ground, kicking some of it up in the air in the light trail of wind he left behind from his swift departure.

Hundreds of miles away from Winter Garden, by sheer coincidence, the very moment that William's knees had hit the floor, a bullet had ripped through the shoulder of Griff Buchanan, Lily's favorite security bandit. While sitting in the very place that he always sat enjoying Lily's homemade heart-shaped pancakes, Griff was now bleeding profusely.

After seeing smoke billowing in the air from the fireplace, a group of men riding on horseback with torches blazing all assumed that William was home along with all the Negroes that he housed there. It was the signal they had eagerly waited for in the hours before flooding onto Werthington Estate and instantly turning the cherished land into a battlefield. Adorned with ghostly white robes and sheathed faces, a crew of over twenty deep ambushed the property, waging a virtual war against William and every Negro who lived there. They intentionally attacked on Christmas night, feeling as if they were delivering the gift of justice to a white man who they felt lived with corrupt morals, and who openly defied the unwritten rules that white society had set forth. In the minds of the ghostly looking riders, housing a family full of Negroes was one thing, but helping with the uprising of one of them was another matter altogether. Knowing that William was assisting the sort of woman who had the power to use her success as a platform to speak on giving Negroes rights—rights that they never wanted to see come to fruition—was a major infraction that the night-riding terrorists planned to deal with in the most permanent of ways after they galloped with ferocity onto William Werthington's land.

Back at Winter Garden, where William was still crouched on the floor in tears, another gunshot rang out outside of the theater. It crackled through the air just minutes after James had walked out of the building, penetrating the ears of everyone left in the back hallway, instantaneously commanding their attention. Wilson, Emerson, William and all of the students immediately turned in unison toward the piercing sound that lingered in the air like the rumblings of a distant thunder. Soon, they would all learn that the thunderous blast ultimately proved fatal for the victim, whose skull contents were slowly seeping into the dirt below it. Screams from the crowd outside, the whinnying of reacting horses, and carriage wheels being swiftly dragged away were the only sounds everyone heard next. Still, everyone in the hallway stood there frozen, shocked into silence, fearfully speculating about what scene their eyes had to prepare for lying on the anterior walls of Winter Garden, in the aftermath of the storm-like force of Jesse Adams's wrath … a devastating storm that had just completely ripped everyone's world apart.

Slave Code
Article I Section I

Be it enacted that if any slave resists his or her master while being corrected, or for refusing to surrender him or herself contrary to law, and shall happen to be slain in such correction, the master shall be indemnified from any prosecution for such incident,
<u>as if such killing never happened</u>.

TO BE CONTINUED IN:
The Prodigy Slave
Book Two
The Old World

About the Author

Londyn Skye is a comical, 39-year-old mother of two, ex-all-American collegiate athlete, million-mile lady trucker phenom, and a romance novel junkie! She readily admits that her desire to become an author was for a very silly reason: FRUSTRATION! After years of reading romance, she was frustrated by the rarity of intense plots, memorable side characters, emotional depth, and interesting couples.

When she was a child, Londyn began creating stories in the fantasy world of her mind as a way to escape life's troubles. As an adult, her frustrations with the genre of romance led her to turn her comforting fantasies into a novel that had all of the elements that, in her opinion, were missing from many other books. That challenge led her to write *The Prodigy Slave* trilogy. Wanting the utmost quality for her readers, she has diligently worked to balance the saga with humor, drama, romance, unpredictable plots, and devious, neurotic characters that are equally as captivating as the erotic love scenes between the fascinating heroes and heroines.

She has painstakingly painted her fantasies with words that she hopes will help readers to see the images just as beautifully as her unique mind does. Most importantly, she hopes that everyone will feel just as emotionally moved and inspired by the heroes and heroines in her love story.

Connect with Londyn at:
www.facebook.com/AuthorLondynSkye